*Everyone talks about the weather
but no one does anything about the weather.*

Mark Twain 1897

ROBERT L RUSSELL

THOR'S
APPRENTICE

BOHANNON HALL PRESS

Library of Congress Control Number: 2023901749

Publisher's Cataloging-in-Publication Data

Russell, Robert L, 1963-
    Thor's Apprentice / by Robert L Russell ; illustrated by Emelia Ann Designs.
    Niceville, FL: Bohannon Hall Press, 2023.
    350 p.: 16 illustrations ; 23 cm.
    First edition.

1. Science Fiction, American. 2. Weather Control—Fiction 3. Meteorologist—
Fiction. I. Title. II. Russell, Emelia Ann, 1977- III. Mcleod, Bob (fictitious character)
PS3618.U77T46 2023   2023901749

ISBN 979-8-9850298-5-7 (softcover)

Published by Bohannon Hall Press

This book is not possible without my wife of thirty-five years, Cindy, and our daughters Kate, Emelia and Liz. They inspire, challenge, and encourage me to "be my best me." They are each wonderful humans who make me beam with pride and joy.

Acknowledgements

A special shout out to all those who serve our Nation in the Armed Forces, law enforcement, as well as, federal, state, and local government service. These are hard jobs. It requires personal sacrifice to do these jobs well, and we all benefit when those who choose a life of service succeed in their assigned work.

Thank you to all those with whom I have had the privilege of serving with in my 27 years of military service. To my brothers and sisters in arms, you inspired me to write this book, and shaped in my mind many of the characters and situations in this story.

Finally, a tip of the hat to my publisher and friend, Rip Coleman, and the folks at Bohannon Hall Press, without whom this book would still be a stack of papers on my desk and a few files on my computer.

TABLE OF CONTENTS

CHAPTER ONE

DISCOVERY

The morning was a typical one for Dr. Jim Auster, no patients to see just his lab to ready for the day's experiments and tests in atmospheric dynamics. Dr. Auster, a research scientist at a modest Midwest University, managed to secure a small but stable 5-year state government research grant to determine the deposition rates and environmental impact of various chemical combinations released into the atmosphere from local charcoal production plants. These plants release various combinations of exhaust and pollutants in each phase of production, and the Doctor's task was to measure the amounts of these pollutants and determine where, and in what quantity, they fell from the sky.

The study was funded to settle a dispute between the state and the charcoal companies over the downwind effects of the airborne contaminants. The state claims the pollutants are harmful to the hardwood forests and timberland covering the southern regions, while the charcoal companies maintain the chemicals actually benefit the forested areas by providing a nitrogen-based fertilizer which can be absorbed harmlessly through both the leaf and root systems of the hardwood trees. It all sounded rather tedious, even insignificant to Bob Mcleod, who himself was a meteorologist working on his Doctorate degree at the University, and making a small—very small—stipend as Dr. Auster's one and only assistant.

The day was like most days on this project, predictable, stable, uneventful, it was just boring. Bob was making the drive down to the first of a series of measuring and recording stations...what he affectionately referred to as running the trapline. Bob's task was to download the measurements to his laptop computer and check the equipment to ensure it was operating correctly. There were 27 traps in all, and it took him all week to run the line and process and analyze the data, which he then provided to Dr. Auster. The only real time they spent together was a few hours to go over the data and discuss any trends, issues, or concerns about the operation of the sensors, or anomalies in the data. Bob thought the Doctor's tutelage was lacking at best, and believed he held little more than indentured servant status in Auster's eyes, but didn't complain much because frankly he needed the Doc to finish his work so he himself could defend his own dissertation. Just eight more months and Bob Mcleod would be Dr. Mcleod and on his way; hell, he thought he could stand it for that long, after all knowing that pain is temporary makes it a lot more tolerable.

As he rounded the curve for the cutoff to the first sensor his thoughts wandered to the familiar desire of getting close to realizing the first step in his life plan. Once Bob earned his PhD in Atmospheric Science, he intended to apply for a teaching and research position at the University, or any other that may hire him. He thought the idea of teaching, having summers off, and doing research on the side, on his own schedule would offer him the security he always wanted and the flexibility and freedom he longed for all these years. To Bob Mcleod, these were the luxuries he could never afford, and they were the only things he really wanted out of life in the near term. Stability from a modest but comfortable job, and flexibility in schedule and pace. In a strange way, he envied Dr. Auster's station in life. He seemed to be set up just the way Bob hoped to be, yet they were very different.

Dr. Jim Auster was still a workaholic, not just spending his days and evenings teaching and conducting his research, but weekends, holidays, you name it. Auster always had his nose in his work. Mcleod thought that was extreme devotion for a project as seemingly inconsequential as this one.

Sure, it mattered but how much? If the pollutants harmed the trees, it would be over time and the state could reduce the emissions through higher taxes or legislation. If the pollutants were harmless it wouldn't matter, and if they helped the hardwoods grow it was only modestly because the growth rate in the region was not significantly higher than elsewhere in the state. The Doc's wife had died 14 years ago, the department secretary says he took it very hard, but you'd think he should be over that by now. *The Doc was a strange cat* Bob thought, rarely did he go anywhere outside his normal routine, he was more predictable than the weather. Bob knew this more than anyone else because he frequently had to find Auster to pass data on equipment malfunctions and try to get parts or money to fix the sensors.

The Doc was at his office by 6:00 a.m. Monday through Saturday which usually doubled as a quasi-lab so he only had to compete for lab space when he really needed it. He usually went out for lunch and to feed his dog at noon. He went to the same diner every day, and always got a piece of banana cream pie for his dog's desert. Doc never touched the stuff, but he swore that pie kept the golden retriever's coat shiny and clean; kept the fleas off too. Buck was the dog's name, his wife had given him to Doc as a birthday present the very year she was killed. Mcleod figured that Doc took better care of the dog than he did himself. After lunch he taught two classes and then stayed in the office until eight or nine p.m. working. Except Thursday nights, when he would leave by six to go to evening Mass at St. Michael's Catholic Church.

Besides his dog Buck, Dr. Jim Auster's only real friend seemed to be Father Gannon, the pastor at St. Michael. He had married the Doc and his wife many years ago and had performed her funeral mass just three short years later. The Doc seemed glad the diocese had seen fit to keep Father at the Cathedral for so many years. That is where he spent his Sundays. He attended the 7:00 a.m. mass, and then taught the children's Bible School during the homily of each mass that morning. After the last mass, he would clean up the inside of the Church, and spend the afternoon with Buck at his side working on the Church grounds.

Father Gannon used to tell him the Lord declared Sunday a day of rest and worship, he should not be working on the Church lawn, gardens, and grounds. The Doc always gave him the same answer, he said "I work every day except Sunday, and this is how I rest, by clearing my mind of my work and doing God's work on God's Day. If you don't like it Father Kevin Gannon, then you tell God His church grounds are in shambles because you won't let Jim Auster rest and worship on Sunday."

That was it; there it was; Doc Auster's predictable life strangely stable but Mcleod thought too much of a non-event for his tastes. No, Mcleod had bigger plans, once he got his security and flexible freedom. He didn't have anything against church. In fact, the only reason Bob knew this part of the Doc's life is because he, too, was a member of St. Michael's parish. Father Gannon introduced the two while Bob was still an undergrad in Meteorology and he didn't think that hurt him when it came time to find a research assistant. But Bob wanted to do something more with his life, not just have a life like he faulted Dr. Auster for having.

Bob was going to rely on his scientific skills in analysis and prediction for both his livelihood and his hobby. Mcleod was an avid stock market follower, he believed that predicting was predicting, whether it was the behavior of the atmosphere, people, or events of the stock market. He studied how to do the atmosphere and was pretty good at predicting what people would do. He almost had a sixth sense about people. He could analyze them, read them, and predict their actions pretty well, and he used to win beer bets all the time which was the only way he could afford a drink. He figured he could do the same with the stock market, a little at a time. Start with just a little bit of savings and invest it in commodities, or stocks and make a little money, make a little more, and *whammo* make a *lot* more. Some science with the right blend of skill and art and you've got one rich Bob Mcleod. He knew he could do it, all he needed was a way in. He was getting close...close…close to the turn off to the first trap…back to the business at hand; daydream terminated.

As he pulled off the gravel road into the field that held sensor number one, Bob saw a large coyote running back into the woods. The saving grace about this task was the opportunity to be outside, a lot. Bob Mcleod loved the outdoors, in fact this was the only part of his studies he would really miss, the opportunity to be out in the world he enjoyed most. Running the trapline he actually saw quite a bit of wildlife and some decent scenery. After all, his work was all in defense of the region's hardwood forests. It didn't hurt his opportunities during hunting season either, since he now knew the landowners who allowed the sensors on their private property, as well as, the government lands he could hunt.

Growing up in the state he hunted as a boy, sometimes it was the difference between eating or going hungry. It wasn't as bad now but every deer or turkey in the freezer saved a few dollars the next time he was in the grocery and it still mattered to the student in his eighth year of college. He was ready for the next phase of his life to be out of school and teaching or hunting his own research project. He had no interest in life outside academia. It was not for him, not now anyway, not until he had some money, some real money, but that would come later in life he knew, if he was smart and if he was patient. Patience he had learned as a child going without, as a hunter, as a student, and as a man. Yes, much would come later because that was the one thing Bob thought he had, time, and lots of it, he could wait for later, after all he had been waiting all his life.

Patience though was something Dr. Auster had a critical shortage of as far as Bob could tell. He was always in a hurry, always impatient...and for what he wondered? The man had such little variety in his life. Bob supposed the routine demanded replenishment in even greater doses than the adventure Doc lacked. He seemed to have a sense of urgency that was mismatched with his lifestyle; hurry up and do more of the same; feed the machine of monotony. It was more contemplative than Bob cared to be right now as he hurried to meet Dr. Auster to deliver the week's latest data runs from the trapline of sensors.

The good news was he'd be on time, the sensors were working fine, and the data appeared to be normal and contained no apparent anomalies. It was boring and just fine that way. This should prove to be a short meeting and Bob could get onto more important things, specifically his own research.

This morning's meeting went the same as the countless others preceding it. They met at the diner for lunch Saturday at noon, they exchanged idle pleasantries, ordered lunch, and discussed the data. Bob gave Doc some data disks. The Doc ordered Buck's piece of banana cream pie to go, and off they went. The meeting would end differently this week, and Bob Mcleod's life would change, he had no way of knowing it would not be in accordance with his plan.

"We do not know the place or time when God will call us to his Kingdom. We must always be prepared, as our beloved friend Jim Auster was prepared." Father Gannon's words grabbed Bob Mcleod by the nap of the neck and slammed his face foreword, back into the cold reality of life.

Plans are what you make when life is happening all around you. He remembered these words from somewhere in his past but couldn't place the occasion as he stood at the graveside and watched as the priest finished blessing the casket before it was lowered into the ground. There were only seven people present, including himself and the priest. The department chairman, the secretary and a few students. No family, no neighbors, no friends, just associates from work and Father Gannon. What a non-event.

Hell, it seemed like the Doc's whole life was a non-event—a brief marriage that ended too soon when his wife died and now a senseless end to his own life before he ever really accomplished anything. *Drunk driver.* The kid was too drunk to walk home so he drove, and Dr. James Auster, Atmospheric Scientist had the gall to be crossing the street in the middle of a sunny Saturday; the innocent victim of one of a million all-night parties in a university town.

One dead Doc, and one kid's life messed up forever, and come to think of it, one Bob Mcleod's life's plan in serious jeopardy since his own dissertation depended on the results of the Doc's research. He felt embarrassed by his selfish introspection as Father Gannon concluded the service and motioned for Bob to remain as the others began to depart.

"I believe you can help us, Bob," Father Gannon said. "Dr. Auster...Jim... has seen fit to leave his estate to the parish, and I am certain there are items at his home that belong to the University—papers, notes, disks and the like. Can I impose upon you to go through his belongings to gather up such items and deliver them to the appropriate people. I am not sure I would know where to begin."

"Certainly Father," Bob replied. "When would you like me to come by, it may take a while, the few times I was at Doc's house I saw mountains of paper, books, and notes."

Father Gannon replied, "Bob, it is I who am asking the favor, you select a convenient time and I will meet you, but there is one other thing."

"What would that be Father?" Bob inquired.

"Dr. Auster's dog Buck is in need of a new home. He is old now, and as much as I would like to keep him, I believe the last few days is about all I will be able to do. Will you take him and look after him as a personal favor to me. I know Jim would approve." For a few seconds Bob frantically searched for a way to politely decline the his pastor's request to care for the only surviving member of his recently passed boss's family. It was a brief and futile search which ended in, "Sure Father, I'll take good care of Buck, can I come get him this evening and start to look over the papers? The sooner I get started, the sooner we will both be finished."

"Thank you, call me when you are ready, and I will bring Buck to Dr. Auster's house and we can begin our tasks." Father Gannon blessed Bob Mcleod as he turned to leave, walking to his car he wondered what he was going to do with an old hungry mouth to feed, even if it was only a dog it was another thing he'd never had to do before.

The drive back to his apartment was a troubling one. Bob knew he needed the Doc's research findings to complete his own work, but he did not want to wait the months he knew it would take the University to hire a new professor, let alone the time it would take him to train the new guy on the project. Maybe the University would allow Bob to finish the

Doc's research and his own. It was not the first time since Jim Auster's death that Bob had had this thought. Reality started to rear its ugly head again as Bob reminded himself of his standing with the department chairman. They had *history* and none of it was good. Dr. Hugh Durbin was the Dean of the University's school of sciences. He was a physicist by trade, and placed the Atmospheric Science department at the bottom of his *gotta-love-it* list.

Mcleod had learned that Durbin was a rich kid, an only child whose daddy paid his way through school, bought him a new car every couple of years, and set him up in a nice apartment...the whole nine yards. When Dr. Durbin finally had enough of professional student life, his father used his influence to get him posted to the University faculty, and relied upon his daddy's generous annual contributions to move him right up the ladder to his current position in record time. Stepping on, or over good people to gain advantage was not something Hugh Durbin lost any sleep over and Bob Mcleod knew that all too well. Unfortunately for Mcleod, Durbin would have the final say in selecting a replacement for Doc Auster, and he would certainly see to it that Bob Mcleod's name would be at the bottom of any list. After all, they had *history. Screw him*, Bob thought out loud. The jerk cheated and cheating is cheating.

Their history began when Bob was a Junior, in his undergraduate Advanced Physics class. Professor Hugh Durbin was his instructor. Bob thought he knew more about physics than Durbin even then, but it was just another class and who cared as long as he got a good grade. Bob was making a little extra cash tutoring two of his classmates. Struggling to get through physics was common, struggling to get by as a starving student was even more common and good students frequently earned a few bucks this way.

The trouble started after a mid-term exam. Bob did reasonably well, one of the classmates he was tutoring did very well and the other did very poorly. Bob thought the exam was particularly difficult and was not surprised by the poor grades of his classmates, but he was surprised that the student he tutored did so well, even better than his tutor when he seemed unable to successfully get through the material in their sessions.

Bob congratulated him on a good grade but the following week slipped several of the more difficult concepts from the exam into the tutoring discussion and problem-solving session. The kid was just as clueless as before and that really made Bob Mcleod angry. He pressed the kid on how he got such a good grade on a mid-term when he knew squat about the material or concepts...nothing.

When Bob released the guy's shirt and let him down, unpinning him from the wall, he freely admitted that he didn't know the material and knew he wasn't going to get it before the exam. He went to see Professor Durbin to ask for help or extra credit, even an extension, but the teacher had a better deal in mind. Hugh Durbin offered a mid-term grade that would guarantee at least a C in the class if the kid would try to get his Dad to do a few nice things for him. "You get a passing grade; I get your daddy's help when it comes time; it's easy for you and everybody comes out happy. But, most of all, your daddy is very pleased his little boy passed this hard physics class. Save him the heartache and disappointment of flunking out of school. Show him you're a man."

The kid went looking for help in getting a real education and this *teacher* gave him a lesson in the *real world of ugly*. Mcleod didn't want to burn his fellow student. Even if he did, they would both deny it and the only proof Bob had was the kid's story right after he bounced him off a wall. But he was not going to let Durbin pull that again; it wasn't fair to anyone.

Stupid little Bob, Mcleod reminisced to himself, *"marching right into Durbin's office, telling him that I knew all about his little deal and he better not do it again or else.* It got ugly from there. Durbin had him thrown out of his office and their exchanges have been *equally cordial* ever since. No love lost there. They both knew the real Hugh Durbin even if others didn't.

No, it was unlikely Bob Mcleod would get a break from Hugh Durbin, unlikely he would be named Jim Auster's replacement even though he was the most logical choice. The Hugh Durbin that Bob knew would see this as a golden opportunity to screw him. Pass him up on this research project, significantly delay the research and subsequently Mcleod's work, and generally *get his goat*. Yes, Hugh Durbin rarely missed an opportunity and this was a good one.

Bob eased slowly past the diner where he and Dr. Auster had lunch the day he was killed, then drove a few more blocks past the very spot the kid ran Jim Auster down. Just seven houses further down the road was his home. Pulling into the driveway Bob noticed the newspapers and mail were piling up after only a few days and wondered what else he would find when he and Father Gannon went through Doc Auster's home.

He had been there before, but strangely couldn't remember the details of the non-descript decorations and clutter which filled Jim Auster's living spaces. The only things which really stood out were the pictures of his wife. They were all that seemed to hold special prominence in his simple world. Bob killed the engine of his old Ford pickup truck and waited for Father Gannon to arrive. It was a short wait before he noticed Father walking up the street with a big dog, Buck, on a leash. Bob sighed as he was reminded of the promise he made to keep the pooch.

Father Gannon opened the front door and released Buck from his leash. Bob Mcleod followed in behind and watched as the dog frantically searched the rooms unsuccessfully for his master. Buck laid down next to the recliner to await his missing friend's return as Father Gannon joined them in the living room. "As I said before, Jim left the house and its contents to the church, but I will leave you to recover and return any University property, or work-related items which you may need for your research. Jim dearly loved his work and I know he would want it continued. Please lock up when you leave and, if I may impose upon you to provide me a list of what you remove, I would appreciate it. We could use another computer in the school, and I believe at least one of these was Jim's personal computer. So, I would appreciate if you checked the electronics and their files at your earliest convenience. If you need more time than just tonight let me know tomorrow and we'll set another visit. I must leave now, but thank you again and I am sorry that we must engage in such an unpleasant task. He was my friend too."

All Bob could do was nod as Father Gannon departed leaving a lot of work to do, a dog to take home, and a priority list from the pastor with follow-on instructions. Process simplified and tasks passed, Father Gannon's closing comment was still processing and Bob was having a lot of trouble coming to grips with its true meaning. Bob had always considered himself Jim Auster's assistant. Doc always introduced him as his associate but Bob never consciously considered himself Doc's friend. That made him feel really guilty. Did Doc consider Bob a friend, one of his few friends, on a long list of acquaintances?

Had Bob really lost a friend in that tragic accident or had he simply lost a means to his own end of completing his research? Damn, was this really a dilemma or was Father just making sure Bob would keep his promise and do the job as outlined? Bob Mcleod figured it was some of both but it troubled him as he sat down to decide how to sort through the mounds of documents before him.

The best place to start is the beginning, so Bob proceeded to sit down in the recliner next to Buck and have a little chat. After exchanging a few pleasantries with his newly adopted pet, he proceeded into the makeshift study which was the second of the two bedrooms in the small house, and stared at the shelves. Each shelf contained neatly labeled rows of binders and notebooks. Bob recognized them as the data he'd recorded and notes he gave Doc each week after running the trapline. He knew these had to go so they were the first to be carried to the truck and packed into the front of the bed.

A few hours later the shelves were all cleared and five or six stacks of paper neatly piled waist high awaiting their own binders were also in the back of the truck. It was about time to quit being hungry so Bob, knowing the only place within walking distance was the diner, set out with Buck on a leash to get something to eat. He also knew it was the only place he could get Buck's favorite pie, and he wanted to get things off to a good start if he was going to keep the dog.

Half an hour later they returned and sat in the kitchen to eat—Bob at the table and Buck on the floor. He felt strangely comfortable here in spite of the circumstances that brought them together. Bob laid the pie plate down but Buck didn't move toward it, no worry he had eaten a bowl full of dog food shortly after they arrived, he probably just wasn't hungry yet. Or, perhaps he was only going to eat the familiar treat from the familiar friend absent today, not from a stranger in the master's house. The thought made him uneasy so it seemed like a good time to get back to the task at hand. The toughest part was still ahead, i.e. going through the computers and their vast contents of electronic files, analysis programs, and *stuff* atmospheric research scientists use to do their job.

Keeping with Father Gannon's directions Bob started with Doc's own PC and found only a couple of files that seemed work related so he copied them onto some blank thumb drives. There were the master copies of the code and documentation for some of the programs Doc had written to analyze the data they collected. Some of Bob's performance reports which had to be submitted every semester to the Dean were there but nothing new. There was an electronic banking program, Internet software, links and bookmarks to scientific and university sites around the world, a directory full of some weird recipes, but not much else.

No games, no address book, almost nothing but work-related stuff. It didn't take long to get through the little there was of that either. Bob copied the site's files to the thumb drives, and the recipes too. After all, everybody had to eat. The other computers took a little longer but there were only three of them, they were all University property and all the files seemed work related so Bob loaded the computers into the truck and would complete the rest of the file and data sorting at work.

It was a little after midnight when he decided to call it a night so he could get to work early enough to have a shot at an unscheduled meeting with the Dean, his *buddy* Hugh Durbin, to discuss Bob's proposal for the disposition of the files and completion of Doc Auster's research project. He knew he'd need more than a good night's rest to pull this trick off but it was a must do for Bob Mcleod. Buck willingly joined him in the front of the truck, Bob flipped the piece of banana cream pie up front too, just in case he changed his mind, after all every college student knows you don't waste food.

Monday morning, bright and early, Bob Mcleod sat waiting in the outer office of Dean Durbin's extremely comfortable suite. The department secretary seemed like the only thing Durbin couldn't taint with his personal odor of materialism, insincerity, and superficiality. Betty was in her thirty-second year at the same post, Durbin was the ninth Dean she'd served and, while she didn't like him, she smiled every day because in her heart she was sure she would outlast him. She was one of the few at Doc's funeral, they had known each other a long time.

Betty lost her husband three years ago, and Doc helped her through the toughest times by talking with her about how he made it after his wife died. She was grateful, and some thought they may even get together some day, but Mcleod thought not. They were wed to their marriages; their love transcended the deaths of their spouses. To get together would mean they'd have to move on and that, in his opinion, was more than either would ever be willing to do. Bob knew people and he believed those two were never going to get together and now Doc was gone. Daydream terminated...back to the business at hand.

"Good morning, Betty, I need about fifteen minutes with the Dean this morning, it's about Doc's stuff and his research project," Mcleod stated.

"Good morning, Professor Mcleod, he's not in yet, but I'll try to get you in before his first appointment. I'll tell him it was scheduled and he must have misread his calendar. You know he would never agree to see you first thing in the morning, especially on a Monday. Why you could stand to ruin his whole day, maybe even his whole week in just one meeting," she replied.

"Betty, what would I do without you?" Bob smiled.

"Why Sir, you'd certainly starve to death who else would hire an old man like yourself?" she quipped. Bob smiled. She was about as right as she was fun and Bob knew there was a grain of truth and some thinly veiled advice in her comment.

"Thanks Betty. Has he said anything about finishing up Doc Auster's state grant work?" Bob asked.

"Not to me...Good morning, Dean, how are you this morning, Sir?" she smiled at Bob.

"Fine, Betty fine, well, good morning, Professor Mcleod, what brings you in this morning?" Hugh Durbin queried.

"Why, our meeting this morning, Sir," Bob replied. "I am ready whenever you want to begin."

"Eight a.m. on the schedule," Betty supported.

"Well grab some cups of coffee, black, and come on in," Durbin grumbled.

Bob flashed a smile at Betty as he went to grab some coffee and try to secure his future. Bob Mcleod entered the office and placed a cup of coffee on the mahogany desk, then took a seat. "Sir, I'll get straight to the point, I would like the opportunity to finish Doctor Auster's research. I can complete the work to meet the requirements of the grant, and I need the results to complete my Ph.D. You know I am capable of completing the job. Bringing someone new in will cost at least a six-month slip, give me the job and I'll bring it in six months early. Dean?"

"Gosh Bob, I *am* impressed. You're still the cocky boy scout, huh? I'd love to oblige you, but I was thinking about just giving the state grant up and leasing out the lab, make a lot more money and get a corporate sponsor for some useful research with some commercial application. Now I have a way to do that without the trouble of defaulting a grant because there is just nobody around who can replace the uniquely qualified Dr. Jim Auster. Do you really think you can convince me that you can? Can you think of a good reason I should pass up this golden opportunity, Bob?"

"I doubt it," Bob steamed, trying to control his emotion. "I suppose you have no sense of loyalty to Dr. Auster, no personal or professional compassion to see his work completed for his good name or the good of the state that also operates this University and pays your salary. I suppose you have already made your decision long before I came here this morning?"

"Yes, Professor Mcleod, I have decided. Too sweet a deal to pass up. Blow the forests, this is business and Universities run on money, it is quite simple, really. But to show you I am not the complete jerk you believe me to be, I will allow you to complete the research if you truly wish; on your own time, and your own dime. I am terminating the grant. You can use the equipment, even Auster's computers if you need them. Shoot, I'll even let you use the lab at night, on a non-interference basis of course, for free. Bring it in six months early Bob, save Auster's good name and do him, the forests, the state, the University, and yes yourself a favor. You do what you asked me to do you hypocrite! You do it yourself if you can. I won't get in your way but don't dare come to me for help or I'll see you on your way myself. That is all and you may go now, and I mean now."

Bob turned on his heel to keep from belting the man across the room and silently walked out. "Thanks Betty, see ya later," he said as he slipped into the hallway. *Well*, Bob thought aloud, *that went pretty well. I get to keep using the equipment, computers, and data...and even some lab time at O-dark-thirty. I didn't get punched out of the program, and I didn't get punched in the nose either.* Not bad considering, but the real problem was the money. He now had no grant money, which also meant no stipend for the work he did, and an aggressive six-month deadline. At least he was still in the game, but the rules had just changed, and there was no grandfather clause. Time's a wastin'. There's work to be done. If it's too hard for you, Dean, it's just right for me.

Bob was working late for the fourth night straight going through Doc's computer files. It was mostly tedious work, he recognized the files, data formats, computation routines, and programs but there was just so much data to get through. Curiously though, Bob kept coming across some confusing reference notes in some of the files, and there was a whole directory on one computer which contained formulas, equations, and programs he didn't recognize. They seemed unrelated to the task at hand, but he would get to those later, right now he had all he could handle with what he did understand.

One mystery seemed to be solved though. Bob was really enjoying the companionship of his new friend Buck, who had yet to show even the slightest interest in the daily offering of banana cream pie. The many pages of handwritten notes Bob collected from Doc's house told a different tale. The first few pages of each section had spots from food, little stains where the paper had absorbed some foreign substance. Bob believed these consistent blemishes were caused by particles of pie crust and an occasional drip of pie filling.

Yes, it appeared Jim Austin had the love of banana cream pie, not his dog Buck. No big deal, but it made Bob wonder what other secrets Jim Auster may have been keeping. Some of the scientific research didn't seem to fit within the scope of the grant work. Was Doc doing some of his own on the side. That wouldn't be a first in academia by any means but, if he was, Bob mused, *I wonder what he was working on?* He'd figure it out later if there was anything to figure out. He had a project to finish early, a doctoral thesis to complete, and Hugh Durbin to put back in his place.

Only two weeks after Doc Auster's death Bob was organized, up and running. He had taken all the documents which were not directly related to the state grant research project and placed them in a box, surprisingly there was not very much which seemed unrelated. He was feeling pretty good about his chances to complete the project, and after a week of no sleep decided a break was in order. He didn't have much space at his place so Bob decided a functional break would be to go through the box of unrelated stuff and pitch out what he wouldn't need, and file what he found interesting. OK Buck, let's see what the Doc found interesting enough to choose as his hobby.

After several hours of pouring through the unrelated work, Bob began to notice references back to the data he had just worked so hard last week getting to know. Almost everything here was linked to specific days, events, or note pages from the data. The weirder the connections appeared the more intrigued Bob became but he couldn't discern a pattern. The formulas were all written using foreign variables. So, while they were scientific enough, Bob couldn't translate them from the language they were written in.

Why use a different language, Doc? What language is it? What other languages did he speak? Speak, what about write? Wrote code, yes computer code? What kind of code? Basic, C, Fortran, Unix, something from his school days, what is it, Doc? None of these, what kind of code, CODE, is it a coded formula Doc? What's the code, the key to the code? Keys, where do you keep your keys? Safe place, safe place, someplace safe from someone who wants your work? Home...at home Doc?

This was getting him somewhere, but it appeared he was going to have to look around Doc's house again. Bob decided to call Father Gannon in the morning to ask permission to do just that, but now he was hungry. Time to take a break from all this hard work research and new found sleuthing, and cook up some food. It was then Bob remembered the recipes he had copied from Doc's PC. Well Doctor Jim Auster let's see what kind of food you liked to cook, maybe I'll learn something else about you. Bob found the files and opened the directory called recipes. He didn't recognize the names of any of the files contained within, more curiously, they appeared to be named in the same coded variables as the mysterious research. "OK Doc, what ya got cookin', how 'bout cookin' somethin' up with me?" Jim sang out and proceeded to examine the files from Doc's personal home computer, *maybe this is where you keep the key* he thought aloud.

Bob opened the first recipe file and determined they were indeed recipes, but not for something you eat, but to create something he didn't understand. The first recipe was a design for what looked like a small machine, Bob recognized the primary component as some kind of laser, but the dimensions and key notes were in the same code he found earlier. Bob reviewed each remaining recipe and found them all to be recipes for creating something using the device in the first recipe. He knew he had to find the key to the code and look at Doc's house for the actual device portrayed in the first recipe.

What was it? What did it do? Did the device actually exist yet? Who else knew about it? Was Doc working with someone else, or alone? Was his death really an accident or did this have something to do with it? This was getting too weird, and it was already very late. He decided that three hours from now Bob Mcleod would be in the very first pew at the Cathedral's 7:00 a.m. daily mass. He and Father Gannon needed to talk.

Bob tried to concentrate on the prayers during mass but it was difficult. At the closing hymn Bob made his way to the rear of the church to meet Father Gannon. Once the rest of the people departed, Bob and Father Gannon walked back into Church to attend to the post-mass tasks while they talked. Bob showed the priest a printed diagram of the device he had discovered the night before and asked "Have you ever seen something like this at Doc Auster's. Do you know what this device is, Father?"

"Yes, and No, in that order," he replied. "I have seen such a device, in fact I have it, but I don't have any idea how to work it, and frankly I was too apprehensive to turn the darn thing on. It was in Doc's bowling ball bag of all places; the bag had a tag on it that says Thor's Hammer. I didn't think Jim was much of a bowler, let alone brazen enough to brag about it on a bag, that's just not like him. You know who Thor was don't you, Bob?"

"Yes, Father he was the Norse god of thunder, who forged the armor of the gods." Bob's reply came too sharply even for his own liking.

"Yes, that's close enough. I too was intrigued by Jim's reference to mythology and this strange device. I don't believe it is a new design for bowling balls. I found a few more references to Greek gods on Jim's PC you brought to me. I saved them to a disk; it was gibberish to me. Is this related to his research? You seem troubled?" Father Gannon asked in a higher tone, attempting to sound surprised.

"Yes, father it is University property and I really do need to get it back. The files, too, if I may. It's kind of a hush-hush thing Jim had been developing and I had completely forgotten about it but, when I didn't bring it in with me, our boss was pretty nervous about its absence. He doesn't want anyone else getting credit for Jim's work at university expense, I guess I can see his point." Bob was pretty uncomfortable telling half-truths to his priest, but he was half testing Father Gannon's level of knowledge, too, so he figured it would even out somehow.

"Very well, come with me to the rectory and I'll give you the University's hush hush new bowling ball and the files. I am pretty sure I got them all, I double checked before I reconfigured the PC for our school band teacher. It had an awesome sound card, a ton of RAM and video memory, and a stellar hard drive. I figured it'd be great for on-line music and video files. Catholic school just ain't what it used to be," Father grinned.

Bob called up the first of the files as soon as he got home. "Zeus" seemed like a great place to start and it was, there it was as he read intently. The leader of the gods file contained the gibberish Father Gannon copied and Bob was befuddled. There was a listing of all the symbols contained in the other documents, and each corresponded to a different scientific principle or law of physics. There were also numerical constants like the speed of light, PI, Avogadro's number, and laser light coefficients. This was some pretty heady stuff, Doc was into.

The next file was the Venus file, the goddess of love, Doc seemed to love his work all right. What was this stuff he loved? There was a plain text message, it was to his wife, and at the end of it he promised to make his life worthwhile. He would do something great for her to watch from above and be proud of him, and she would get the credit for inspiring the work she could not do herself because of her untimely passing. *Together we will change the weather, together we will change the world* is how it ended.

Holy cow! that's it, Bob gasped, **change the weather!** *Holy Cow! Weather modification? Could that be it? Where are those recipes...*he chanced a long shot and grabbed the printout from the night before and began to decode the name. FOG. Get another one, Bob, decode it, RAIN. And another, WIND, another SNOW. *Holy Cow*! Doc was trying to make the weather, or change it, or something.

Wait a darn minute, Bob thought, *why did he assume he was trying?* He may have already succeeded. What if Thor's Hammer already worked? What if he was already successful, after all there were many recipes in the directory. All the data in the boxes at his feet could be the results of his testing. The sensors, the grant, all that data could be the collection and verification data of his modification experiments. *Holy Cow!* Who else was involved in this? Who else knew? How could Bob himself not know if that was really the case? Who could he trust? Who is worried about Bob Mcleod finding out? Could Doc have done all this in secret, on his own? Too many questions, too much to digest.

Bob Mcleod needed a couple weeks to get through the data, to decode the stuff, assimilate it, and try to figure out how far along Doctor Jim Auster was in his ability to change the weather with this little machine. Bob figured the best place to run and hide from whomever may be watching him was right where he was...at home. He knew the best way to cover one's tracks was to walk in the ones you made before, so that was exactly what he would do, nothing different. Arouse no suspicion, make no changes, just focus, Bob, focus. The power to change the weather was something worthy of focusing on, especially if someone else had already figured out how to do it. Especially if anybody besides Jim Auster and Bob Mcleod knew about it. Now he was really hungry

CHAPTER TWO

TESTING THE SECRET

The next day found Bob Mcleod beginning his weekly run of the trapline. Driving out to the first instrument site, Bob's mind raced with the possibilities if Doc had really figured out a way to control the weather, even if only one event at a time. What if he could make it rain whenever, wherever he wanted? Select the wind direction and speed whenever he liked? Make it snow on a whim? The power and potential ramifications of such power were mind boggling. Did he really know how to do that already? Bob knew that he knew nothing yet. He only suspected and he would certainly need to collect the data no matter what. So, the only logical course of action was to keep the status quo and try to learn more to prove what he suspected.

As he listened to the stock market report—something he did every single day—he fantasized about how much money he could make trading commodities futures like corn, oranges, or soybeans if he could control the weather in these growing regions. Create perfect growing conditions for a bumper crop or wipe one out with an early freeze. Who would know? Who *does* know? That was a troubling question. Was Doc in it alone for the good of mankind, or was he working for someone like the military, CIA, some company, the Church, or a drug cartel. The possibilities of who could benefit from this were virtually limitless. Nothing out of the ordinary for an entire week except frustration!

Bob ran the trapline all week as normal...no incidents. He poured over all the data and Doc's notes and recipes repeatedly...nothing new. He was frustrated and enthusiastic at the same time. With no leads or strange activity in over a week, Bob decided the time for waiting was over, it was time to act. He had to assume that Doc was working alone and proceed in the same covered secrecy so not to arouse any suspicion or blow this golden opportunity. The possibilities were infinite, but so were the chances of blowing it if he let the cat out of the bag. All at once the Doc's lifestyle and indeed everything about him made perfect sense to Bob Mcleod. The Doc knew exactly what he was doing, and that deserved emulation. Bob didn't yet know exactly why the Doc was doing it. That would come in time, if at all. What Bob did know was through strange twists of fate the opportunity of all lifetimes had fallen into his lap and he was going to make certain to benefit from it.

For the first time in his life, Bob really believed the odds were in his favor. He had a purpose, and he was staring smack dab at a chapter in the world history book if he pulled it off. A chance at fame, celebrity, power, wealth and glory for the little guy, Bob Mcleod. A chance to put guys like Hugh Durbin in their place, if he could keep guys like Durbin out of the know...out of his work. The Doc had it all figured out. It was a damned shame that kid decided to drive drunk that night. Bob wondered how many other times the history of the world had been changed by such a needless act.

What did Doc intend to do with this capability? Bob's only real insight was the Venus file where the Doc promised his departed wife that he would change the world and make her proud. What did he have in mind? End world hunger? That would be nobly humanitarian. Conquer the world? That would be a distinct possibility if this power of controlling the weather worked over large regions. Pay me, serve me whatever or I will freeze you out, flood you, fog you in, like blackmail or environmental terrorism? Bob really doubted that was the Doc's motivation, but it was certainly a danger of the technology.

The more Bob thought about it the more worried he became. Then worry turned to out-and-out fear, for he realized that this could be the ultimate weapon, the irrefutable advantage over whole populations, civilizations, economies, indeed the global balance of power, distribution of wealth and...*wow*! His head was now throbbing. Good guys, bad guys, poor guys, rich guys...everybody would want this, and it would certainly be worth killing for if it worked. Maybe Bob shouldn't assume Doc was working alone. What if the state grant was just a cover? What if Durbin knew? He would have done just what he did to throw Bob off the real trail. No, that would be too risky, as he knows Bob is smart and would eventually catch on. No, Bob had to assume Doc was in it alone, but he would be extra cautious. Just because he was being paranoid didn't mean someone wasn't out to get him.

The device itself was a strangely normal looking thing, small like a hand-held vacuum. The trick now for Bob was to see how it worked, to see what it could do compared to what Doc's notes said it was supposed to do. The entire testing idea frightened Bob for lots of reasons but that fear was easily overcome. There was too much to gain, and too much to lose. Bob selected a clear day, and an isolated but open area in the woods near the center of the research sensors so he would have the maximum amount of data to analyze for his first test.

Bob decided to do something subtle but discernible for the first test, he would make some fog. At 11:05 a.m. he looked at Buck and said "Here goes," as he entered the recipe for Fog into the Thor's Hammer keypad, and set it in the middle of the clearing. Then he sped to the covered viewing area a hundred yards away. At 11:08 a.m. Bob's jaw dropped as the device began to disappear into a mist, *Holy Cow* it works, the damned thing really works. That was both good and bad for Bob Mcleod. The fog quickly engulfed the entire clearing and visibility dropped to zero. Suddenly, finding that thing in the middle of a fog bank presented a real problem to the only two-legged member of the experiment team.

Well done, Mcleod. Now get out there and find the darn thing and shut it off... As if things needed to get worse, Bob suddenly realized he didn't know the first thing about turning it off. Was there a built-in sequence in the recipe, did Doc have a timer on the device so it would only operate for a predetermined maximum time? This was not good. OK focus Bob, focus. "Buck, find that thing Buck, and bark 'til I find you," Bob pleaded to the dog.

Then he got out, walked one hundred paces and got on his hands and knees, and began to crawl in increasingly wider circles in a deliberate search for the device he could not hear or see. The fog was thick. After an hour of slow crawling in circles Bob heard Buck barking a few yards behind him. His patience gone, Bob crawled to the sound and found the dog sitting on alert. There in front of him was the familiar three red lights of the keypad; he had found it. Never did a dog receive such a grateful hug as Bob gave Buck just then. Bob had missed it in his crawling search but the dog had not. Half the battle over. Now Bob had to figure out how to make the fog go away, or if it would on its own.

Not good. Bob was starting to worry more, half past noon is not the time the area usually gets fogged in. The speed with which the fog engulfed his viewing area led Bob to believe he could have half the state fogged in from the hour-long search for the fog maker. His concerns were valid, but it was more than half the state; it was the wrong part of the state to fog in that day. Bob typed "OFF" into the keypad and the three lights went out, maybe it was just that simple, so Bob sat down and waited to see if the fog would lift. An hour and a half later the fog burned off very quickly as the midafternoon temperature climbed. Bob sighed in relief. Well, he would be more careful next time. Now it was time to take his sweat soaked body to the truck and go collect some data. It would be a long night running the trapline to collect and analyze the data.

Bob was right but it was going to be a long night for a lot of other people, too. Sergeant Andies, an Air Force weather forecaster was busy trying to find an explanation for the unexpected fog that blanketed the better part of three states for three hours in the middle of the afternoon on a clear day that just so happened to include the final test flight and refueling routes for an advanced training exercise for a helicopter assault with special forces teams. "The CG (Commanding General) is eating my tail, Andy, about this fog, we blew the forecast, busted the operation. The crews and helos are sitting in fields all across the state with no gas and it's gonna take a full day to get gas out to all of them and get them flown home! Man! My butt is ground sausage and the CG is making gravy, help me out here." Captain Lessur was in deep kimchee and knew it. "Andy, you don't miss many, but man we missed big this time. Guess what, everyone is reporting in now, the fog is burning off but, after three hours of unplanned loiter and ground time, nobody's got gas to get home. You can bet we'll have to explain this one a few times so get digging and see what we missed. We're gonna need an after-action report on this one."

"I'm looking, Captain, but there ain't a damned thing out there that points to fog! Dry air, windy, sunny afternoon, that does not get you fog, Sir," the Sergeant protested.

"I hear ya Andy but there are 27 gas-empty helos who got fog, and you can bet they will all be pointing at us when they get back. Keep hunting Sergeant!" Captain Lessur snapped as he turned to deliver the latest updates to the CG. He was right, his tail was ground sausage.

Sergeant Andies was one of, if not *the*, best forecasters in the business. Lessur swore by his hand-picked team and Andies was the best. He had to be for this team; the mission demanded nothing less. But there was nothing to indicate fog for that time anywhere in that region, and there was nothing to explain why it was there. Yet, there was no disputing its presence. The exercise was blown because of it and there were numerous traffic accidents reported to law enforcement agencies across the region. Insurance companies were paying claims already.

Even the TV weathermen were claiming ignorance on this one. Bob Mcleod knew he blew it too and he was lucky to get off undetected and unscathed...at least for now. The Air Force weather team supporting the Army special operations training exercise on the secluded range area of the military installation was 180 miles from the center of the trapline area

Doc and Bob knew as their backyard. But it might as well have been right next door because it was upstream from the military operating range. All good weathermen look upstream to see what weather is coming their way and this Air Force weather team was nothing but good weathermen.

Bob decided the next test would be a lot more subtle, he needed to determine how to stop, meter, or control the flow of the recipes. This was still a real dilemma for him, so he took a couple of days to plan the next experiment and examine all the potential problems while still getting useful data from the test. He decided on a wind test for the third afternoon past the fog debacle. Bob would start at the farthest northwest sensing station and blow a steady wind with three gusts to the southeast through the majority of the remaining traps. The strongest winds are usually in the afternoon, and they would be from that direction anyway. He would know the windspeed at his location so he could deduct that effect from the experiment and the resultant data would be both pertinent and accurate. It was a solid plan, he had covered all the possible flaws, so he and Buck set out for test number two with lots to learn. Meanwhile, downstream the weather team was preparing for a parachute jump with the assault teams from the helicopters.

"Looks great for the drop this afternoon, Captain," Sergeant Andies briefed. "Winds from the northwest at seven knots all afternoon...not a cloud around...temps in the mid-sixties. Let's get our knees in the breeze."

"I hope that's the only thing we get in the breeze today. Those guys are still hot about the fog thing. Hopefully, they won't use us as wind dummies," Capt. Lessur joked.

"Won't matter as long as they let us use our chutes boss. It's tailor made for jumpin' today. Time-over-target (TOT) is 2045 Zulu, 1445 local. I'm on chalk three and you're in chalk six. Sorry we aren't on the same pass but I didn't make the manifest. See ya on the DZ, Sir."

Bob Mcleod carefully typed in the recipe formula for wind. He set for sustained winds at 18 miles per hour for eight minutes, followed by three gusts to 26 miles per hour at one-minute intervals. Eleven minutes of wind, then back to normal conditions, while most everyone was inside at work. Few would notice, and those who did will probably barely notice such a brief episode. Bob entered the "Begin" command and the familiar lights went on; the laser device began its work. Bob held the device this time but felt no discernible change as it began a countdown on a screen labeled: *time remaining on activity.*

He hadn't seen that display before but thought it was a good idea as the wind began to pick up and he could see the leaves across the clearing rustle. He wondered how much the other sensors would actually record since the mechanical blocking of the trees and terrain could significantly reduce the downstream wind effects. He had selected the clearest path to the other sensors. That is why he used a pretty high wind on an otherwise relatively calm day...subtle but measurable.

The drop was a good one for Sergeant Andies, and as he stowed his chute into the *A-bag,* he could see chalk four on its inbound leg to the DZ. Jumpers away, good chutes, come on down and join the party boys. This was a non-tactical, *Hollywood,* jump. You don't get many equipment-free drops so everyone was enjoying the luxury and the nice day to boot. Sure did beat two days of pouring over weather data looking for phantom fog indicators. Chalk five inbound, jumpers away, good chutes, c'mon down boys and enjoy the ride. Captain's on the next pass, let's see how he does. He is not the best paratrooper in the Air Force which means he ain't very good when you mix him into the Army. Andies' hair stood up on the back of his neck as he felt the familiar pressure from behind. What's with the DZ smoke? Wind's picking up? What the....oh no, not now.

Thirteen-knot surface winds are the cut off for the static line paradrops, and right out of the blue we just busted that. Jumpers away, oh man this may be a bummer ride down guys, check the smoke. Chalk six used the same release point as the previous five chalks, but with the sudden winds they would be pushed much farther across the DZ than the previous chalks. Trees Captain, I hope you remember the pre-jump checklist for tree landings, you're all gonna need it. That's when the first gust came through and accelerated the jumpers drift toward the tree line. No doubt now...eight jumpers gonna get unexpectedly increased hang time, in the trees.

Sergeant Andies could only watch the chutes drift into the trees, the jumpers tried to steer clear but couldn't beat the wind. Then the second gust came and then the third, shortly after, the winds died down. Chalks seven and eight canceled for winds and DZ time to recover the jumpers hung in the trees. Another un-forecasted weather-related incident, Andies had that to look forward to once he recovered his captain. Hope he wasn't injured...but *man* would he be upset. Weather forecasting is a fickle business, but Andies rarely got fooled even on complex weather days let alone under such stable conditions. This was twice this week...by short-lived events with no meteorological indicators or explanations. He prided himself on his skills and had a great reputation which he was not willing to give up without a fight. He was gonna find out what he was missing, so he wouldn't miss it again.

Just as planned Thor's Hammer clicked off and the winds died down at the test site. Bob was pleased with the test so far, so he decided to collect the data right away to expedite his analysis. He and Buck climbed into the truck to go run the trapline feeling particularly successful, energized and filled with purpose.

Capt. Lessur was feeling particularly sore, pumped up with painkiller for his battered elbow, and equally filled with purpose. He felt bad about the jump; three others suffered broken bones from their tree landings. The CG chewed what little was left of his butt into freshly ground meat right there in the hospital, and then left him alone to suffer through his injured pride which now nicely matched his elbow. Two weather related incidents in a week didn't make him happy or look good to his boss either. He was right and Lessur was upset with himself. Also, his faith in Sergeant Andies had taken a direct hit as he was descending into the trees. He hoped he had a better explanation than he could find for the fog. They would find none for either event and he was starkly reminded that hope was not a course of action. They needed to find some explanation for all this.

All seemed to be going pretty well for Bob Mcleod's tests of the weather modification device Doctor James Auster had developed and built. Bob still didn't know what made it work but he was beginning to understand how to operate the device. He was able to decipher some additional papers he had overlooked before and was starting to understand the Doc's frame of reference when he wrote the software the system runs on. What he was not able to discern from the code, the programs, or the drawings of the device was exactly why it worked. He was beginning to understand the mechanics of how the device worked, even how the software interfaced with and operated the hardware components, but the concept behind what produced the result still evaded him. It had to be in the notes somewhere, something else he'd overlooked. It could be that it wasn't there because that was *the secret*, and the Doc was too smart to write down *the secret*; it could be that it died with him. The only device was the working prototype Bob had. For now, he had to assume that was the case and that made Thor's Hammer a priceless little contraption. It was then it occurred to Bob that his only opportunity may be short term instead of long-term. He started to look for a couple of ways to turn some weather into quick cash. The stock market is what he knew best so that is where he began.

CHAPTER THREE

A FORTUNE TO BE MADE

More than a few times Bob heard the phrase, "It takes money to make money." Well, he only had about two thousand dollars in his checking account, which also, sadly, doubled as his savings account. Bob had a lot of rainy days, and saving for them was never a priority. When savings came up against eating and tuition it seemed like it was always raining. Taking out a loan was out of the question. That was too risky and could arouse suspicion if he was being watched. No, two grand was what he had and that is what he would use to try to make some money to continue his work and maybe get a few things he'd never been able to afford. A few wagers on events to build up the two grand, then a timely placed acquisition of commodities would be the safest approach, he believed. He needed some local events, some local weather-related stuff because he didn't yet understand the range of the device he was depending on. There was one way to start, a local balloon race that weekend seemed promising. He found a *friendly local bookie* who covered this event every year. Two thousand dollars on the 11:1 entry seemed about as far as Bob wished to push his luck. The 27:1 turkey shaped entry was quite tempting but Bob thought that would just bring too much scrutiny on the event, and maybe onto him. As the race began, Bob sat on the tailgate of his truck, Thor's Hammer in hand. He waited for the balloons to drift some distance apart. About halfway into the race, as the balloons drifted over the open fields, Bob began to assist his unwitting balloonist meal ticket with a steady twenty knot tailwind. Bob realized it was a bit risky, but he had to follow some distance behind the balloon team's chase vehicle to keep the wind from the device from aiding the other balloonists. He knew the area well and managed to pull it off.

"Two thousand dollars at 11:1, makes twenty-two grand, buddy. I hate to see you win at my expense, but have a nice day," said the disappointed bookmaker. Bob was excited as he left but knew never to make another bet like this again with him because two big winning flukes were not a coincidence when you make your money the way he does. Bob took ten thousand to bet on the sailboat regatta at the nearby lake. Bob Mcleod knew all about this sailing event. After all, the pictures from last three years of winning this rich man's event were all over Dean Hugh Durbin's office wall. He and his Daddy's team were the hands down favorite and Bob was going to bet against them. Call it payback, machismo...even foolhardy but Bob knew he had a chance to get some evens on Durbin and he was not going to be denied even if it was risky.

You see Bob Mcleod had never had any form of power in his life...never been *the man* with regards to anything. He had always been a follower, a hard worker, but he had always been led. He felt he needed a shot at leading and thought this application of power was deserved. There were six other boats in the race, and Bob bet $10 grand on the fourth ranked boat, at 8:1. From a point on the edge of a cove Bob knew he could focus the wind gusts from the device to hold back all the other boats as his choice to win raced ahead, but only if it was in the rear of the pack like it should be. If not, there was no clear way to push it along ahead of the others. But this was gambling, and *it was ten grand he didn't have before the balloon race* he mused cavalierly. That weekend Bob set up his viewing area early assuming others might show up on the same spot for a better view of the race. He was not disappointed, when he was wrong this time, and was relieved to be the only one there when the race began. As the boats came around the turn, Bob cold see the two leaders neck and neck, and his boat in a surprising but distant third place. He leveled the now comfortable in his hands, laser-based device and fired up some wind. The two leaders began to encounter some serious crosswinds as they came into the turn. They initially bumped together, and the crews worked feverishly to adjust riggings and sails for the unexpected wind change. Momentum was lost, crew integrity was interrupted, and enough confusion was thrown in to disrupt their focus. The boat Bob had his money on was far enough behind to take advantage of the other's unfortunate circumstances, and cut in behind them to use the wind change to their advantage. The boat closed the distance on the leaders very quickly, and skillfully raced past the other two vessels as they were beginning to recover from their brief but undeniable bad luck. The wind now blew even stronger causing the first two boats to over correct their course while simultaneously pushing the new leader further away on its direct bead for the next turn. The distance between them widened, and the winds died down just as quickly as they had come up, not much more help for the remaining boats coming up alongside, but it looked like it would be a dandy race for second place. The leader had such a commanding lead it was doubtful anyone could catch her.

"Eighty thousand is a lot of cash, buddy, you better get it somewhere safe fast, before something happens to you and your money." Bob added this to the now growing list of places he was no longer welcome. Now he had enough to go after a stock market score which is what he really wanted, some serious money. There would be time to personally gloat over Durbin's loss later. He would see to that but he wanted to give the Dean some time to stop crying first.

Now Bob Mcleod was sitting on more money than he had ever had before...about one hundred thousand dollars in his bank account in two weeks. He was ready to spend it, too, but he knew this was only the beginning and he had to be patient. You need money to make money and he was setting up for a big score. It had been a pretty warm, wet summer, good growing conditions all through the Midwest. The pumpkin crop looked real good for fall sales; Halloween sales in and from the region were expected to be high because of the bumper crop. Futures prices were low for the same reason. Nearly sixty percent of the nation's pumpkin crop was grown in the valley region of the tri-state area. Bob knew this would be a problem for some people, but it was the best way he could make a controlled area experiment, and turn it into a money-making venture. An early freeze, while the pumpkin plants were all in blossom. Yeah, very uncommon but not unrealistic. A late summer freeze wouldn't be hard enough or long enough to damage the standing field grain crops, so the only real damage would be the autumn harvested gourds and some other flowers he rationalized. The blossoms would be irreparably damaged at about 31 degrees Fahrenheit, and the approaching cold front provided the right *natural cover* for Bob's plan.

He bought 100 thousand dollars of pumpkin futures and went into action. Three days later as the front approached, local forecasters were going for a low temperature of forty-one degrees, the first cool night of the fast-approaching autumn. Only two- and one-half months after Dr. Jim Auster's untimely accident, Bob Mcleod sat on a ridge line overlooking the tri-state valley area. A land rich in farmland, open spaces, pumpkin fields...not far from the western end of a vast military training area. As the winds shifted out of the North, and the cold air behind the front began to spill into the region, Bob Mcleod keyed in the temperature setting on the device the Doc had named Thor's Hammer. He had practiced in his house and in the trapline for two days before he bought the pumpkin futures and he was extremely positive that he could pull this off.

He sat at his post for two hours that night as the temperature fell to thirty-one degrees, it remained there for four more hours before the sun began to rise and slowly raise the mercury back into the upper fifties by mid-morning. Thirty-one degrees combined with the strong winds behind the front gave the pumpkins about a twenty-five-degree micro-climate for roughly six hours; the vast majority of pumpkin blossoms would whither by afternoon and fall, wasted by the abrupt freeze.

Bob returned to his small house about mid-morning to find Buck waiting for him at the door. "Well Buck, he smiled let's see what the TV boys got to say about that unexpected cold snap." Yes, the big freeze made the local news, and two of the regional airports, as well as the military airfield recorded near record low temperatures. It got a brief mention on the Weather Network. Fortunately, it was a very localized effect, probably enhanced by the terrain as the remainder of the region only dipped into the mid-forties. Bad news travels fast, and it didn't take long for the news of an expected bumper crop of pumpkins falling prey to a freak freeze to drive pumpkin future prices up. When they climbed about as high as Bob Mcleod thought they would go, he sold every share he had for nine times what he paid not a week before. Almost a million dollars, now he was getting somewhere, but he decided to lay low for a week or two and get some real science work done. The trapline needed running; the data needed analyzing; his research needed some advancing and Durbin needed some abusing. First Bob and Buck needed a celebration. *They earned it and they deserved it* he rationalized. Later on he would make it up tenfold for the pumpkin farmers for financing his research. There was much at stake here.

Bob wrapped up the trapline run by Wednesday and stopped by the department office with a bundle of flowers for Betty. This was a first, but Bob wanted to thank Betty for helping him with Dean Durbin a few weeks ago, and it was time to celebrate the Dean's regatta loss. As they chatted, Durbin came out and was startled to see Bob, "Still in business Bob, or have you given up saving Auster's time and name? I've got a great lead on a deal with the nuclear power commission doing some fallout and emission studies for the state power plants and University radiation research tied into a national network program. I have proposed we lead the effort and link everything to the lab setup you already have. I'll let you know how it turns out before the end of next month. I expect to need 24-hour lab time for a project of this magnitude, guess you better hurry along and be done before then. I don't believe I'll have any lab time for you, even in the middle of the night, Bob. How did you say your research was coming?"

"Better than your sailing career," Bob quipped too curtly. He regretted that before he was finished saying it and followed up with a big insincere smile. Without missing a beat, Bob continued, "Our research is coming along well, I can't take credit for what Jim Auster did, but I am picking up the pieces pretty well considering I'm not a doctor, yet!" Bob was still worried about ever getting that title, as he knew Durbin would be sitting on the board to which he would have to defend his dissertation. No matter...he would show them as opposed to telling them about his research.

"Well, I had my bad luck in the race to be sure, but at least I know my luck changes, I'm not so sure yours ever will, *Bob*." Durbin said Bob like a four-letter word every time he spoke it, and Mcleod wanted to put him down for good then and there, but knew that is just what Durbin was hoping for, and an easy way to get rid of him. *Not today, Dean, but in time you'll get yours, and it will be after I have mine*, Bob promised himself as he smiled and replied

"The odds are with me, my luck's been bad so long it's bound to turn good pretty soon, I can feel it. See ya later, *Dean.*" Bob said Dean like it was a four-letter word, just before he politely waved to Betty as he walked out the door. He had work to do, and the time had just gotten shorter. Not two hundred miles away, Sergeant Andies had a short amount of time to find another answer. Captain Lessur was really worrying about keeping his job right now. The CG had him for lunch with the latest busted forecast, this time it was an unexpected freeze. Not only were the guys in the field caught without proper cold weather gear for their planned maneuvers, the aircraft that went in to pick them up early were iced up enroute, an extremely dangerous condition, especially when flying low-level night operations. Extraction took the better part of the morning and a lot of training and money was lost. Lessur thought Sergeant Andies was the best in the business, but his confidence was deeply shaken. "Look Andy, all three of these were flukes. It stinks that they are so close together but get past it, learn from it, and don't let it happen again. Our credibility is taking a pounding these last weeks."

Andies was almost livid by now. "That temperature forecast was right on, and there should have been no clouds for any icing. I don't know why it went that low, but I know it's the third time this area has beaten me for no explainable reason. I don't believe in coincidences, Sir, something crazy is happening here and I will figure it out if it kills me."

"That's fine, Sergeant Andies. Just see that nobody dies before you figure it out! Keep the mission in focus, don't let this eat you up" Captain Lessur was worried. Andy would find a reason if there was one, but Lessur wasn't sure he could handle Sergeant Andies if he didn't find the reason, especially with a busted-up elbow.

Bob was afraid to take the laser device apart for fear he may never get it reassembled in working order. He knew he had to do something more to find out how it performed its magic, because right now that is what it was...*magic*. Bob knew it was science, not magic, that made this device work. What he did not understand yet was how it did what it did, or what it used to do it. Doc Auster had to have either bought or built every part inside, it was time to figure out which ones were bought, and from where, so he could determine what, if any he had built. He needed some quiet time after the early freeze in case someone was watching him. He needed some analysis time to get the research results tabulated and analyzed. He also needed some time to spend some of the money he had made the last few days. He remembered there were only 24 hours in a day. Everyone has the same amount of time. What he really needed was less to do in the time he had. *Prioritize Bob, focus Bob, focus.*

He carefully went after what he determined was the most important task, find out what the device did to cause changes in the weather. He decided his best chance for success was to disassemble the device, simultaneously going after both the what and the how. He had poured over every shred of documentation Dr. Auster had left at least five times and was no better off for his efforts. Examine the physical evidence and be careful were the two maxims for the next few hours work. Like peeling back an onion, Bob incrementally removed each piece of the device, carefully diagramming and marking the exact position, angles, and views along the way. Once the dissection was completed, he was elated to find that every single component had a serial number on it. Each of the parts were manufactured somewhere already. They were assembled by Auster, but he had not built any from scratch. Overjoyed at the prospect that the device could be physically replicated, Bob set out to determine what each component was, what the source was and how to acquire several of each so he could attempt to build another device. He would take on the software and coding for the components later. *Focus on the hardware first, Bob, focus.*

The internet proved the most useful and expeditious way to search for sources of materiel. As it turns out many of the components were fairly common laser-based technologies used in a wide variety of commercial and military applications. They would be relatively easy to find, and for the most part should be equally simple to acquire. There were three remaining components that posed him a greater sourcing problem. They appeared to be satellite sub-system related. They also appeared to occupy places of honor within the system, and integration schematics showed one to be the primary component, some sort of power conversion module. Now, the real hardware challenge began. This would be tough, but nowhere near as bad as the software challenges which were his next step. He searched all the big satellite companies and worked his way through their subsidiaries one by one. No help here and his head hurt, a lot. Trying military sites proved to be more challenging but using his academic credentials and system access codes he was able to at least get his foot into a few doors, from which he could do a little extra-curricular system navigation. BINGO! Somewhere in a space project schematic for a proposed, but scrapped, space-based atmospheric laser profiler program to measure atmospheric conditions was one of his components.

This may also be the break he was looking for, the clue to how or what set Auster on this path to begin with. Bob downloaded every single file he could find related to this profiler program and began to methodically, deliberately pour through each one for some link to Thor's Hammer. Time passed quickly, but progress was slow. Bob was absorbed—no — he was *immersed* in the work. Then he saw it, one of the remaining two components in a schematic for an obscure subsystem of one of the weather sensors aboard the spacecraft. *Yes*, he beamed as Buck began to bark. It was then he realized how much his life had become Doc's—a life he had strangely envied for some unknown reason. It became clear to Bob that it was more than just having a purpose, it was about having a passion. Doc's life was about searching and finding something he passionately believed in or wanted. The same could be said for searching and finding someone to passionately believe in or want. Doc Auster had found both but, for now, Bob Mcleod would settle for something close. There would be time later for the search for someone.

One more component to find and then he would have all the pieces of the puzzle to begin piecing together the context of the weather modification device dissected and on display before him in both physical and electronic forms. Bob tried lots of other places before he found another promising lead for the final mysterious component. It was a component used in an X-ray machine, common, but it took a long time for Bob's imagination to stretch the common medical applications of lasers into related areas. But what did lasers have to do with X-ray machines? They were different applications of some similar, yet decidedly different, principles. This could be a lead or a coincidence, but Bob would have to come back to it later. He now set out to add up all the pieces and parts and see what he had, look for patterns, similarities and find out what he had individually, to see if he could come up with some theory about what they did collectively. If nothing else, they were expensive. Three of everything cost him nearly four hundred thousand dollars. For once he wasn't even worried about money, he had some—still over half a million in his account. Electronic banking was pretty convenient, and he was able to order and pay for the components by credit card or electronic funds transfer. He should have known to be a little more discreet in his use of the internet for the last few days activities but he would learn this lesson soon enough. It was time to re-assemble the device and ops test it, but he needed to be well rested for both tasks, better get some sleep first. He had not expected such a drain on his finances so soon, so he recognized the need to hatch another money-making maneuver. What a great topic for a pleasant dream he thought as he drifted off, exhausted from his work. It was a restful, satisfying sleep. It would be one of the last such sleeps he would have for some time.

Waking up from a dead sleep with a good idea is something all scientists have experienced at some point in their lives, and Bob Mcleod was experiencing it right now. He had come up with a way to turn his half million dollars into a lot more if he could pull off this new plan. He was feeling pretty good but needed to stay focused. It was time to put the history changing weather modification device back together. Exactly eighty-four minutes later Bob tightened down the last screw on the final external panel, took a deep breath and turned it on. The lights came up in the now familiar startup sequence, and the control panel appeared to operate normally. So far so good. Bob still didn't understand how it worked, but he did know it had an internal, self-contained, and *somehow* self-renewing power supply. That he understood from the Doc's notes. What he didn't understand was how it renewed itself, because that was part of an energy transfer that took place during the modification process.

Doc had labeled all the software modules and documented them very well, especially the ones he wrote himself. He went into great detail about what the code did and how it related to the other software modules, but never mentioned why they needed to do what they were designed to do. Still a mystery but, if Bob had everything and loaded them correctly, when he assembled the *new Hammers* from the components he had just ordered, they should work...shouldn't they? *WAIT A MINUTE*, what made him think he had everything? What if he had missed a book, a stack of papers, something the Doc had that contained the missing information he needed. What if he hadn't missed it, what if the Doc *hid* it...what if he knew to hide the *why*? Where would he hide a secret, where could he hide it? Darn it Bob, what took you so long to get back around to this assumption?

Doc's house, the lab, the diner, and the Church where he worked every Sunday were the only places he spent any time. The Church...Doc was a very religious man, to keep a secret separate from the rest of the stuff he used, and that was all in his house. The best place to hide a secret in Church...*the confessional?* No, that is too easy, too predictable, almost cliché but that is Jim Auster; simple, predictable, cliché...at least on the surface. Time for an unscheduled visit to the church. It wasn't Sunday but it was time to get the spirit moving. Father Gannon was surprised to see Bob and asked him to come in for a visit.

"How is it going with the dog, is he adjusting?" Father inquired.

"Yes father, no problem. I was wondering if you found any other notebooks or other stuff from Doc Auster? Something that looked work related when you went through the rest of the house?"

"No," Father Gannon replied, "are you looking for something specific? Maybe I can help."

"Well, Father this is going to sound weird, but would you mind if I looked around in the Church? It is important, and I think Doc may have left what I am looking for in the Church, specifically in a confessional," Bob heard himself almost pleading.

"You're right, that request is weird, indeed, but let's go have a look. That is, if you don't mind the company." Father's words were a statement, not a question; Bob welcomed the company and nodded toward the door. Father Gannon unlocked the main entrance to the Church, and they entered, moving directly toward the nearest of the three confessionals. A thorough search of the first turned up nothing. Bob asked which one Father used the most, and which one Doc used when he came for the Sacrament. Father Gannon pointed to the next one, "Usually sat in that pew and used this side for his confessions."

Bob searched under the kneeler, under the chair, under the carpet, behind the small picture, nothing. Thor's Hammer? Check the panels, the woodwork, the wall! Check the wall between the priest and the penitent. *There*, a cut in the panel...Bob opened it with his hand and there behind the small panel was a thumb drive, a single drive that Bob just knew held the secret he was searching for. He had missed something, and now found it, right where Doc had left it, ironically, perhaps deliberately. Church is where many things are found; faith, hope, inspiration, knowledge, love, and secrets. It is where Bob Mcleod found what he was looking for and where he would someday return to find what he was really searching for.

"I must tell you; I am surprised by all of this," Father Gannon said as Bob emerged from the confessional with the small piece of plastic and metal in hand. "What is going on Bob?" he asked.

"Father, Jim was doing some highly sensitive research. It was imperative that he keep some of the documents separate from the others, just in case someone stole the ideas we were working on. They would be missing the critical parts. Kinda like hiding the brain from the body. One doesn't do you much good without the other," Bob explained.

"Bob, do you think this had something to do with Jim's death?" Father Gannon asked nervously.

"No, I don't. Jim's death was a tragic accident, but accident to be sure. That boy has nightmares about it now. He'll be messed up for a long time, paying for his mistakes over and over again. No, this is not something you'd send a kid to kill for, Father," Bob responded honestly. For this, he thought you'd do that yourself.

"Well Bob, what now?" Father queried.

"I get back to my computer and get started on this data. The sooner I get this done the sooner we can all get on with closing out his project. By the way, what are you going to do with Dr. Auster's house Father?" Bob wondered.

"Going to put it on the market next week, for sale. It is just too far from the Church for any functional daily use for the school or meetings. While I can manage money pretty well, I don't have the time nor the patience to be a property manager on the side," Father smiled.

"How much do you intend to ask, if you don't mind?" Bob asked.

"Fair market value against the closest comps, considering it needs some upgrades in the kitchen, but has gas heat not that darned electric crap, a nicely landscaped yard on a corner lot, unfinished basement, and is close to my Church in a wonderful neighborhood, with a fenced back yard for kids and a dog? About $172,680," Father grinned, "Why, you looking?"

"Not anymore. Look, don't list it with anyone, keep the Realtors out so you don't have to pay them 6% and I'll take it for what you're asking, just hold it for me for one more week. Then I'll have the money together, and I'll buy it, OK?" Bob spoke as he thought there may be more of Doc's stuff hidden in the house and if not, then someday the house would be famous so it would certainly appreciate in value. Doc would approve, and the Church gets a pile of cash, too. "Okay then, I've got to go, but I'll see you next week, and thanks Father."

"Next week? I better see you Sunday," Father said as Bob waved goodbye.

Bob examined the drive as he sat in the car. It looked plain enough, there was no writing on the label, nothing to set it apart from any other. When he got home and viewed the directory there were only two files listed. The first file was named **what**, and the second file named **how**. Bob opened the first file which revealed a long list of parts with stock numbers, suppliers, phone numbers, addresses, and points of contacts for each of the parts. Bob was glad to see that he was on the right track during his searches and was even happier to see a long dissertation on assembling the components and building out the device called Thor's Hammer. He would come back to this later, but first he just had to know the contents of the **how** file. He opened the file and began to read. About an hour later Bob smiled a conquering smile, now he understood, now he knew not only what was happening when he used Thor's Hammer, he now understood the *how*, and *why* of this remarkable machine. How Doc ever came up with the mix of sciences or the thought of combining these particular theoretical principles was truly the genius in him. Bob would give him credit for this work to be sure, but he would pick the time, conditions, and method. There was too much work to do before he could set anyone up to take credit for anything. It was time for making some more money so he could take care of the rest of what needed to be done.

Bob decided to use about half a million dollars for his next money-making move, which still left him well over 100 grand, enough to make good on his promise to buy Doc's house if he couldn't pull off his next job. Bob had poured through the files he found in the church over and again.

He was really starting to understand how this stuff worked. The parts he ordered were beginning to arrive, and he was feeling particularly successful these days. Bob believed that to win big you had to play big, so he was gambling almost everything he'd made so far on this next adventure. It was simple and would only take a few days, but it would score big if he succeeded. It could literally turn out to be a dream come true. He bought 500 thousand dollars' worth of gas futures for the next month. The price had crept up just a bit after the first cold front went through, but not too much, so they were reasonably priced shares. The next day called for another cold front to move into the region. Bob had selected a spot near trap number 13 to site his equipment. Thirteen was always his favorite number, and it was also his favorite trap location of them all. He set up for a three-day camp, just him and Buck. He had lots of work and reading to do, and Buck just looked like he needed to get out, but it was going to get cold. They took Thor's Hammer and set it up for a practice run, a late season thunderstorm. Well Bob had a pretty good one going about twenty miles away, right over traps number three and five, getting lots of rain and some wind. Then it died down about 70 minutes later and completely dissipated. Good it worked.

"Andies, where in the heck did that storm cell come from? And which way is it moving?" Captain Lessur called in from his secure cell phone as he was preparing for a live fire exercise in the northern portion of the training area.

"Sir, there are no dynamics to support any storm development today. It can't happen but I see it, too. It's the only cell on the radar and the only one for hundreds of miles. Next closest one is in Ohio," Sergeant Andies fumed. This was not happening to him, it was not in his forecast, and worse yet, it was not a planning factor in today's training.

"OK, so how about you tell the range fire control officer that the thunderstorm he's looking at just west of here can't happen? Better yet, you go tell the damn storm it can't happen today so it goes away and comes again another day! For now, just tell me which way it's moving!" Captain Lesser knew Andies was right, but they had to deal with what was happening, not what was supposed to be happening.

The trapline covered a pretty large portion of the state. It had to in order to accurately measure the downwind pollutants and their deposition rates at varying distances from the point sources. As a result, Bob knew the area pretty well. One thing he'd learned was that the natural gas companies used massive underground caves in the region to store their product. Bob knew where the primary pumping stations from the subsurface storage facilities into the pipelines were located. His plan would generate an impressive show for anyone watching with thermal imaging overhead satellites. The next thunderstorm he would generate, would contain a tremendous amount of lightning, one of those bolts had to hit the pipeline close to the pumping station. It was time. That night he got the thunderstorm up right where he needed it, and by his calculations initiated the lighting intensity and location within the storm. It wasn't GPS precision quite yet, but he could get into the right area with surprising accuracy. This was like hand grenades, he only had to get close enough to kick a good leak in the pipeline, the next bolt or two would fire it off once the break was made.

The intent wasn't to blow up the gas and the caverns, it was simply to get the pipeline lit off hot enough, close enough to the source to make it too hot and too dangerous to go in for repairs and just let the cleanest burning of the fossil fuels burn itself out. That is just what happened. Bob could see the glow in the distance after about twenty minutes of lightning and thunder. It was definitely a large fire, no big explosion, and nobody lived near it so there would be no chance of anyone being hurt even if there was a blast, the gas companies saw to that. Even security was only allowed within spotting scope range of the transfer sites to prevent any accidental catastrophe by a rent-a-cop having a mind fart and lighting a smoke. Bob knew the pipeline was hit, no explosion, no concussion, no huge flash or mushroom cloud. Just an increasing glow, and a lot of optimism from one Bob Mcleod. He had a couple of different ways he could have used the weather modification machine to make money on the fuel futures, but this one seemed challenging. Bob wanted to try out some new weather features to see if he could manage them to actually generate some significant weather. Wow, twice he made a thunderstorm. He'd generated lightning and now the entire regions supply of natural gas would be depleted through a freak act of God—*or not*—it was really an act of Bob. He sat there all-night thinking, alternating his gaze from the bright fire in the distance to the clear, starry sky above. He was pleased with the outcome because it had gone according to his plan, so far. The fire burned for several days, and could be seen from both weather and intelligence satellites with thermal imagers, some of these pictures even made the national news reports. With an early cold snap already, and the burning out of a large portion of the area's natural gas supply, Bob was just about ready to sell off his futures for a cool $4.7 million. Life was getting pretty good for Bob Mcleod, or so he believed.

"I don't know!" lamented Sergeant Andies, "Sir, there was nothing to support thunderstorm development in the area...no indications to even support a small storm if it did somehow develop...let alone one of that magnitude. There was enough steering flow aloft that it should have moved eastward rather quickly; not just sit there for an hour and a half and then fall down in the same spot it built up. I tell you, there is some really weird stuff going on, and it doesn't show up anywhere in the data, charts, observations...nowhere."

"I don't get it either, but you're the expert and you can't find any support, any reason? Well, don't feel too bad, I have been asking around and nobody else in the region has hit any of these events either," Captain Lessur consoled.

"Maybe not Sir, but their missions and reputation are not what I am concerned about. I missed them too and I don't miss stuff like this. There is something going on we need to worry about. If it keeps up somebody is going to get hurt, or killed. These are significant weather events that even a rookie should be able to pick out of the models, or the local analysis, but there is nothing there, Sir," Andies protested loudly.

"I've known you for years and you're right. You don't miss stuff this bold and, certainly, not this often. Let me get with a few alternate sources of information and set some stuff up. Maybe we are looking in the wrong direction. Maybe somebody out there has something going we aren't privy to; you are right about what is happening. So, let's go look at what's not happening." Captain Lessur had a few people and places in mind, he knew where to start.

"Hey JP, Lessur here, how ya been?" JP and Lessur worked a couple of operations together a few years ago and both had moved onto *bigger and better*, but they kept in touch. It was more important to know where to find an answer than it was to know all the answers yourself. "I need a favor."

"Fine Les, you only call me when you need something anyway. What can I do you out of today?" JP replied in his usual sarcastic style. That is one of the reasons Lessur liked him. He was consistent and straight up no matter what the issue or who it involved.

"Well, I need to know if God is working without authorization in my area. We have had several un-forecasted, significant weather events in the last few weeks. Nobody has hit them, even my man Andies is zero for all of them and that don't happen. Got us all baffled, man; got a feeling there is more of this on the horizon, too. I know the rule is nobody in DoD, or any other government agency does any weather modification work, but can you nose around and see if that's still a good rule? Might be good guys...or could be bad guys. I know you're still plugged in alot better than I am. Can you help me out on this?" Lessur sounded worried.

"You serious, Les? I mean c'mon, that's Sci-Fi stuff? Hell, you guys can't even forecast most of the weather you get asked about. There ain't a weatherman out there smart enough to change it. They tried that and gave up on it years ago. Just suck it up and admit you blew a few. It happens, even to the best of ya remember?" JP was testing him, and Lessur knew it, but it was okay.

"Damn it JP I am serious as a heart attack. Can you help me out or not?" Lessur hoped this would be enough to get his friend's help, and it was.

"I'll check around for ya sure, Les. How about a bonus too? I been working with this new Hacker Tracker stuff the information warfare guys picked up. Want to know if anyone has been spending a lot of time on any of the nets looking at weather data in your region? How about I check for any *unauthorized access* into weather center's forecasting mainframes? Maybe your data is being tampered with and not your skills? See who is really interested in the weather out there lately, stuff like that? Check around the edges just to assure you the only one messing with the weather is God himself...well maybe with a little help from Mother Nature? Sound good?" JP offered.

"JP, you da man! Thanks, I really need your help on this. Call me if you find something or need anything from me." Lessur hung up feeling better for taking some action, but uneasy about what he could actually find.

"Well now I suppose black fits the bill for a big truck; I'll take it." Bob Mcleod began to write a check for the new Ford F-250 XLT, extended cab, four-wheel drive pickup.

"You don't want to finance this rig?" the salesman suspiciously inquired.

"You do still take cash for sales, don't you? I can go somewhere else if that's a problem for you," Bob pressed.

"Oh no Sir...I mean...yes Sir, we do take cash, and no Sir; we want your business to stay right here. There is no need to go anywhere else. I just need to verify the amounts and account balance with our finance folks. Please have a seat in the lounge, I'll do up the paperwork and have the money guys do their thing at the same time. It should only take about fifteen minutes. There's coffee and soda's if you care for any. I won't be long. If you need a Mustang to go with that truck, we've got the latest five-point-zero convertible on the floor right next to the lounge, and is it sweet. Have a look, I'll be back in a few."

Bob was reminded of sharks in a tank, but it felt pretty good spending that kind of money without worrying about payments, interrogations from loan officers, or how he was going to pay for it. His truck was fourteen years old, and had too many miles to count. He deserved a new one, and Buck would probably love the smell of a new truck. Nobody he knew had to know he wasn't making payments on the new rig he rationalized as he sat in the Mustang. No, two new vehicles were a bit conspicuous he admitted, there would be time for all that later.

Ninety minutes later he was wheeling out of the Ford dealer's lot with one happy salesman waving behind him and yelling, "Come see us again Bob, and be sure to ask for Marty."

The new truck was great and he drove to the Church where he was to drop off a check for Father Gannon. After all, he'd promised to buy the house and that is what he was there to do. As he knocked on the door Father Gannon came around the corner of the rectory and greeted Bob, "I saw you drive up, Bob. Is everything OK? I didn't see you Sunday?" Father inquired.

"Yes Father, sorry about that but I was away all weekend. I am here to give you a check for the Doc's house like I promised. Well, here you go, a cashier's check for one hundred seventy-five thousand dollars, I figured when dealing with the Church I'd better round up from seventy-two," Bob smiled.

Father Gannon looked puzzled and smiled, "Bill Dawson is a Real Estate attorney; he's also a parishioner. I'll call him and see if he'll draw up all the necessary paperwork. I assume I can use some of the rounding up to pay him for his service?"

"Certainly," Bob replied. "Just give me a call and I'll come by to sign the papers and pick up the keys. Is the house empty or is there still stuff of Doc's in it?"

"Yes, it is empty and ready to move into once the papers are signed. That is a nice truck there...new?" Father was curious now.

"Yes, just picked it up today in fact," Bob said proudly. "She's a real beauty; drives great and feels good to ride in."

"Black beauty, huh, nice but I think that name's been used a time or two already. See you later Bob. I must be off but I will call you once the arrangements have been made." Father Gannon skipped up the steps and closed the big oak door behind him. Well two down, one to go Bob thought to himself, it was nice to finally have some money to spend. A new truck, a new house, and next some new computers. Not bad for a day's spending.

Bob drove up to the mall and parked his truck in two spaces so others couldn't get too near to scratch or hit *black beauty*. After all she was still very new, and very expensive. As Bob walked toward the computer store, he realized that twice today he had written checks for more than any amount he had ever written in his life, and it felt good to him. He was about to do it again.

As he walked in, he knew exactly what he wanted: top of the line laptops, docking stations, a nice laser printer, and a long list of high-end software. A large personal check later and he and a clerk were loading the goods onto the seat and floorboard of the extended cab behind the driver's seat. A tip to the clerk for his help and Bob was on his way home to set up his new systems and get to work. He had some satellite research to do and spacecraft data was not the easiest thing to get over the internet. But he knew where to start, and he could cover a lot more ground a lot quicker with the state-of-the-art system sitting right behind him. Time was wasting and he was starting to run low on time before Durbin began to put him and Dr. Auster's legacy out of business at the University. Bob Mcleod had other plans for Durbin, the University, himself and Dr. Auster's legacy. It wouldn't be long before all the parts he'd ordered arrived, and he could begin production of a few more Thor's Hammer devices. Only having one in existence was just too risky a deal for Bob to count on. He didn't want all his eggs in one basket, and he was betting on having lots of eggs in the not-too-distant future.

Once he got the new laptops set up, he needed to try it all out. Like the old saying goes, *the only difference between a man and a boy is the size and price of their toys*. He checked the weather online sites he frequently visited, got a stock market report to see what was particularly low for this time of year, and then went to the Air Force electronic library to dig for some more satellite data. He was not disappointed in the new system's performance but was disappointed in the results of his search. After what seemed like a million links later, Bob found himself once again at the schematics for the satellite which contained two of the primary hardware components of Thor's Hammer. He was able to find all the details he needed through persistence and a little creative typing, and perhaps some *not-completely-authorized* accesses he managed to create. If he was able to get to all this stuff via the internet, he wondered how many other countries or even bad guys could get whatever they were after by the same method. Orbits, nodal crossing times, downlink and transmission frequencies, data conversion algorithms, manufacturer's hardware and software documentation...he was able to find it all.

It was while he was sifting through some of the software code that he recognized a familiar sequence from Thor's Hammer. What if a lot of the software is out here already? The more he looked the more he recognized on one particular atmospheric temperature profiler. It measured vertical temperature soundings beneath the satellite by changes in the laser frequency tuning as measured aboard the space craft. That technology has been around for years. It was no secret; what was the link? Bob got really excited as a new idea came into his mind. What if he could use a satellite for his Thor's Hammer instead of the hand-held device? If he could use a geosynchronous satellite for a power platform, could he control the weather anywhere in the satellite's footprint? Why not, if he had enough power? A polar orbiting satellite could give him the same potential around the world perhaps. What other satellites had these two components and what earth stations controlled them? Was there potential to go global with this new power by simply applying existing technology? Bob was pleased with his brainstorming session but was quickly getting well outside his area of expertise. As a meteorologist he knew a lot about using the data from the satellites, even the rotation and orbital mechanics to determine where they would be at a given time to figure on when the next image would be available, but he knew almost nothing about satellite operations: controlling, steering, maintenance, internal configuration, etc. He didn't even know what he didn't know about satellites, but he knew they held promise for his new weather modification capability. Bob decided he needed to take it to the skies. Indeed, he needed to go global; in good time, but he would get there. It was time to end this session and get over to the Post Office. He had received a registered letter notice in his box yesterday while he was out. Bob didn't get much mail, but this sounded important. After all, who doesn't like to get mail that's not a bill? *Who ever said bills can't come via registered mail?* Bob corrected himself as the excitement waned. All his parts were shipped via UPS so he knew that wasn't it. Now curiosity began to get the better of Bob Mcleod.

As luck would have it, Dean Hugh Durbin was walking out of the Post Office as Bob was stepping from his new truck. "Nice wheels professor, did you borrow them or steal them?" Durbin asked, fishing for an emotionally charged response.

"Neither Dean. My old truck got sick and died, just too many miles so I got a new one out of necessity," Bob replied calmly.

"Lovely, Bob. Black is your color lately now, isn't it? Gotta run, please, be a stranger Bob, won't you?" Durbin sneered and with that climbed into his car and drove off.

Bob entered the post office to retrieve his mysterious mail. He should have listened to the little voice in his head when it spoke to him earlier... that little feeling he got when things just didn't seem right. Either you have a little voice and know exactly what Bob was thinking, or you have no idea how the little voice works. Bob was right, he should have listened to the little voice because, something was not right, and it was about to get a lot worse. The registered letter was from the securities commission to inform Bob that his substantial gains from the pumpkin futures netted him gross income substantial enough to exceed the federally mandated automatic report to the IRS of paid out securities gains. Translation: This was his notification they already sent the required reports to the IRS for tax purposes. Bob knew the general concept, but having never invested or made any significant money in the market he lacked most of the details about these processes. Darn! This meant someone could be—correction—someone *would* be watching his income now and for the foreseeable future. If they were already on the pumpkin thing, you can bet the gas futures would generate another one of these especially since the take on that was substantially larger. At least the income from the regatta and the balloon race weren't going to be reported by the bookmakers. He would have to be more careful in the future.

CHAPTER FOUR

THE "HEAT"

Meanwhile Bob's problems were getting worse. Any personal check over ten thousand dollars is automatically reported by the banking system to both state and federal officials. Eventually the two may talk to each other but, as with all government agencies, that usually takes some time even with today's computers. Computers only do what they are told and budget cuts and downsizing saw to it there were, indeed, fewer people around to tell any computer what to do next. The new computers, truck, and the house were three such checks Bob wrote the same day. With no prior entries for anything of such magnitude, with no previous account balance anywhere near these sums, and with the security exchange commission paperwork incomplete, state officials opened a paper investigation on Mr. Robert Mcleod. The usual suspected potential sources of income exceeding $100,000.00 were grand theft, drug dealing, or extortion.

Durbin knew Bob didn't have any money to speak of right now. How could he afford that new truck? That was a lot of rig to be running around the countryside checking weather observing stations at a couple hundred miles a day. Even if he had that kind of money set aside, to spend it now, when he knows his research funding is drying up, and his lab time is all but gone? Indeed, Bob's whole future was shaky at best right now. Hugh Durbin had personally seen to and enjoyed doing that.

No, this was out of character...out of line for the conservative but cagey Bob Mcleod; he was up to something. A priceless thought crossed his mind and then dug into Dean Durbin's psyche. *What if Bob stole and sold some of professor Auster's stuff?* A computer or two that belonged to the University but nobody really knew about, perhaps a few of the State grant checks or University stipends found their way to Bob's account by his own doing? Desperate times call for desperate measures Durbin mused to himself. Maybe we should have somebody look at your bookkeeping of university and state funds. Maybe you didn't swipe enough to pay for the truck, probably just enough to get them to float your loan? Even if he just moved it into and back out of his personal account, it would still be enough to be rid of Professor Mcleod for good.

Durbin too, had a little voice and he was listening to it. "Hello Sheriff Watson? Hugh Durbin here, I am deeply concerned about a situation I believe warrants your personal attention. Sir, could you please stop by my office at your earliest convenience, I will clear my calendar the moment you arrive? Why thank you, Sir, and yes, my father is fine. I will give him your regards, Sheriff. See you soon." As he hung up the phone Durbin knew at the very least, he would cast plausible suspicion upon Mcleod, and at best he would send him packing, disgraced with his tail between his legs ...destination unpleasant no matter where it was...prospects dim. This sounded better and better to the Dean the more he contemplated the possibilities.

Bob was heading back to his place to get cracking on his first attempt to build another Thor's Hammer while, at the same time, brainstorming ideas about spaceborne applications and potential satellite platforms to do the job. He was unaware that the letter on the seat beside him was only the tip of the iceberg for his troubles. A couple hundred miles away from Bob Mcleod the phone rang, "Lessur here, may I help you Sir or Ma'am?"

"Yeah, you can help me with a cold beer and a hot steak weatherman," JP chided his friend. "I know I have nothing for you, but I may also have something. So, you may get something for nothing, you follow?"

"No," Captain Lessur replied sharply. "I don't follow. I'm up to my neck in crap here JP so if you got something you have my undivided attention but, if you just want to flip me some grief, I'll take a rain check. Okay?"

"Gee Les, who pissed on your Wheaties, Man? Yeah, I maybe got something. You wanna hear it now or later?" JP asked.

"Shoot, I'll take good news or bad; either way it's more than I have now," Lessur lamented.

"Stop whining and listen up, Captain," JP directed. "First off nobody—and I checked everywhere—is doing any weather modification work in your area or anybody else's. That is, none of the good guys are, and we don't have any indications that any of the bad guys are either. Nobody I talked to even thinks it's an active topic anywhere, let alone being tested or experimented with—not since *Nam*.'"

"Okay, JP, I am not surprised but thanks for checking it out, Buddy…" Lessur was immediately interrupted.

"No wait, wait a minute Hot-Shot, there's more. That was only what I don't have, listen to what I might have for you. This Hacker Tracker program is really hot. I got two maybes for you here. There's one dude from Japan, been hitting all the local weather sites as well as the regional stuff religiously for about seven months so I checked him out. Dude's trying to get some business or industrial park deal lined up on the Tri-State expressway but can't get all the permits from the local governments. The guy is trying hard but not pulling it together. I don't think he is much of a candidate for changing the weather in the area. So, you bust a forecast but he is almost fanatical about knowing what the weather is out there. Got lots of hits around the events that you told me about, but almost all are repeated hits after the fact. He's a possible but not much of a probable. But the next one is a big interest to me. This guy is a probable in my book, I can feel it in *me bones, Laddie*," JP did in his best Irish, which was not very good.

"OK, wow me with your genius electron-man, because so far I still don't have much and you are ten minutes deeper into my afternoon. You keep this up and you will owe me the beer," Captain Lessur pressed JP.

"Right, chill my man, here it comes. There is a guy been hitting all the local products for some time, but goes super frequent around your event times. Exponential increase in taps and downloads on all the sites for local and regional weather products. Not just the one's you told me about but a few others too, but definitely isolated and targeted, including all the events you and your guy busted. So, I dig a little more on this guy and he's doing some serious net surfing, even a little looking in places he doesn't exactly belong. So, this guy is looking at everything like he's hunting for something right? Locks up in the satellite pages for days, all hours of the night digging into laser stuff, satellite, and x-ray stuff. Dude checks the stocks every day too...extra busy around the whole week of the explosion and the freeze but those were the only two real big market activities for this guy. He seems way too interested in the same stuff you're bumming about and almost obsessed with other weird stuff. I don't believe in coincidences, Les. I think this may be something to check out. The guy is registered to the State University academic instructor server, and one local Internet provider. Name is Mcleod, Professor Robert Mcleod, Ph.D. candidate...ought to be finishing up in about six months. Get this though; there's more. The guy just bought a house, paid cash. I got that in a public document search, deed and bill of sale. Over one hundred and seventy grand only weeks ago. I remember when I was in college, I owed a hundred and seventy grand I didn't have it to spend! What do you want me to do now, Les? How do you want me to play this?"

"I need some time to sort through this in my head, JP. How about can you just watch what he does like you have been without tipping him off that he's being watched?" Captain Lessur inquired.

"Bite me you weasel. Of course I can. How dare you question my ability as a sleuth. Shame on you, are you ready to buy me that beer yet?" JP shot back.

"Yeah, but don't plan on that steak until this turns into more than just your overactive imagination, Bubba. Keep in touch and let me know if anything new comes out of watching this guy," Les sounded off in an appreciative tone.

Bob Mcleod began to line up the parts and diagrams he would need to build another device. Little did he know, he now had the military, the Feds, the IRS, the local law enforcement, and the University all looking at him for different reasons...but all with the same idea in mind. Something about Bob Mcleod wasn't right at this point in time and they wanted to know exactly *what* it was and *if* it was legal. He carefully studied the diagrams and began to assemble the first of the new devices unaware of how quickly his plans were about to come apart.

The doorbell startled Bob. He laid down the third partially assembled device next to the original Thor's Hammer, closed the bedroom door and moved to the living room to answer the door. There were three men in suits, and they didn't look like they were selling anything. The shortest man produced a badge and an identification card that read Internal Revenue Service, and then began speaking, "Bob Mcleod?" he inquired. "Are you Mr. Mcleod?"

"Yes, I'm Bob Mcleod. What can I do for you gentlemen?" Bob asked nervously. "If it's about the letter, I just got it this afternoon."

"Well yes, Sir, in fact it is customary for an agent to personally notify individuals who make large sums of profit income that the federal income tax laws do apply and remind the individual...you Sir, in this case, that you must report this income on your tax return by the normal deadline. Sir, I consider it my duty to inform you, and inquire if you completely understand the verbal notice I have just delivered to you," the agent nodded.

"Well yes, I do understand and of course I will report it on my income tax returns, both federal and state returns. Yes indeed," Bob nodded in agreement.

"Good then, by the way Mr. Mcleod, my boss informed me you made all that money on pumpkin futures, is that right?" the agent asked inquisitively.

"That's right," Bob smiled "Was just investing in good old local pumpkins."

"Support your local economy kinda thing then, huh? Some people have all the luck I guess," the agent quipped as he gestured the other agents to the car in front of Bob's house. "Well Sir, congratulations on your good fortune, and don't forget Uncle Sam at tax time. We don't need to come back for another visit; we already have enough to do."

"Sure thing, you bet," Bob shouted after them and moved back into the house to watch them drive down the street. Now back to the business at hand, he may have less time than he thought. Certainly, he had to be more careful for a while he thought as he resumed work on the partially assembled device.

"He's lying," snorted the lead agent. "The guy's a meteorologist, doesn't have a dime for decades and suddenly invests money he doesn't have in pumpkins to support the local economy? Then turns huge profits on an act of God weather event? I'm not buying it guys. Open a file on him; let's work it from an insider trading angle. We've got plenty for that."

The FBI was in the process of spending taxpayer money to look at Bob Mcleod as well. Their lead agent was checking several large deposits exceeding ten thousand dollars each into a single account, all within a relatively short period of time with no apparent reason for an increase of income. That account belonged to one-each Robert Mcleod. The banking transactions and deposits exceeding ten grand are automatically reported to the FBI and the IRS; there were tons of them. These stood out though because of the source of funds, both from the securities exchange. *Too much, too fast for a guy with no money.* They suspected a new money laundering angle; most likely drug money had found a new way to enter circulation. The ramifications were worrisome, though. If the druggies could legitimately launder their dirty money into the stock market directly, a whole new series of problems were on the horizon.

This looked promising and Mcleod profiled like he would roll over on the next guy above him. He was certainly not the mastermind of this operation; probably one of several test cases to see how the scheme would shake out. It was sloppy at best, but the druggies had lots of time and money, and for every Robert Mcleod there would always be another hundred lined up behind him for the chance at easy money after he got caught. The local FBI field office wanted to get this early and shut it off. They didn't need this kind of extra activity nor the workload and caseloads it would bring if druggies connected directly into the market via goofballs like this Mcleod guy. "Shut it down fast and hard," Special Agent Miloc concurred. "Put somebody on this and make it stick. Work the computers on this guy; don't put anybody on him in person; we don't want to spook him. Just start a Hacker Tracker on him and watch everything electronic he owns or uses, services, cards, accounts, library checkouts, the works. Check with DEA and see if they are working this guy or have anything on him. I want him down and out of the game in less than a week." The regional FBI had both eyes on Bob Mcleod's activities.

"Les, I think we got something going on here," JP couldn't contain his enthusiasm. This weather guy at State I told you about, the Feds are watching him, too. They started a Hacker Tracker on him yesterday, and the IRS is doing searches and activity logs on all his accounts. He's got at least two other bad-guy catchers watching him in addition to us. Better get with the Office of Special Investigations and give them what we got. OSI better take it from here. I don't want to get too far into this if the Feds are on him. He's a local boy for CONUS law enforcement. Ain't a military intelligence bag without lots of legal mumbo jumbo. Brass gets way too nervous if DOJ or DOC come to us to do cop work for them. Hope it helps, but let's watch the next few plays from the sidelines before we ask the coach to put us in, OK?"

"Yeah, thanks JP. I'll call them. I owe you that steak now, but I'm gonna make Sergeant Andies go in halves with me. He may not be losing his skills after all," Captain Lessur grinned as he hung up the phone.

"Andy, you and I need to talk. Grab your lid we're going across the base to visit a friend at OSI."

Captain Lessur explained the events of the last two weeks to the Officer in charge of the OSI detachment, as both he and Sergeant Andies listened curiously. "You mean to tell me you think this guy can predict or maybe even change the weather with some new technique you guys don't have so we should investigate him? He's a civilian and he can do some stuff you can't. So you want me to open a military criminal investigation on this guy because your friend says the Feds are looking at him? You are joking right? Come on guys, think about it. What else you got...anything?"

"The Major is right, Sir; even the FBI is watching him. What can OSI do? Major, could you contact the FBI and verify if they are investigating this guy, maybe at least we could help them somehow if he's breaking any laws, and maybe he can help us connect to this guy if he's just a super forecaster. Worst case is he tells us to buzz off but we may learn something about forecasting techniques we don't use today. Is that doable, Sir?" Andies sounded off, sincerely.

"I suppose that is a viable, conservative course of action we could pursue Sergeant. I'll put someone on it and they'll be in touch; but don't expect too much out of this. The Feds like to tell us to keep our noses inside the wire and may not even discuss the matter. We'll see."

"Thanks, Major," Andies smiled. NCO's usually do have the best ideas he thought.

Special Agent Miloc of the FBI just got off the phone with the Air Force Office of Special Investigations agent and scratched his head as he began his trip down the corridor to the division chief's office. "Sir," he said as he knocked and entered his boss's office, "I just got passed a call from the Air Force OSI guys at the base, and they wanted to know if we were investigating a guy for forecasting the weather better than anyone else. So, we joked a little and laughed about weathermen and finally I got around to who or why and get this, they think the guy has some new forecasting gizmo that can tell him when this really weird weather is gonna happen. So, I say *big deal maybe they get a few right; be about time.* Sir, it's the same guy we opened on yesterday for drug money laundering through the market or securities, Mcleod. These guys say they think he's into something and they want to help find out what he can do. Maybe they can learn something about how he does his stuff so they can use it too."

"You're not kidding me are you Miloc? I can tell you're serious, aren't you?" the senior agent queried.

"Yes, Sir, serious...I told them I'd get back to them but I want to dig up some more on this guy. I'd like a few days to cover him good and then if we come up empty bring over the weather warriors at the base and see what turns from our little talks." Miloc was becoming intrigued.

"Okay, but make sure this gets to your team. I want them to look up and down this angle from our side. Maybe it's something we can spot or key on while we do our electronic surveillance on him. Treat it just like a lead from a known stooge and see what turns up. And Miloc, keep me in the loop on this. I want you to brief me up before we start bringing in DOD suits on this. It makes the brass nervous working with the military inside the states."

"Got it, Sir, will do," Miloc replied as he headed for the men's room.

Bob Mcleod had assembled the last of the new devices and they had all powered on okay. He was excited but anxious to test them to see if they actually worked. He was past due on running the trapline so laid out a plan to test each device at different locations along his run to make sure they all worked. He had no idea this would be the last time he would make this familiar trip through the countryside of his home state.

As Bob backed out of the driveway his mind began to race with excitement at the possibilities that awaited him if his newly assembled devices worked as he hoped. The opportunities to make money were almost endless. He could even hire himself out...sort of a fee for service enterprise to get the weather you wanted when you wanted it. He could guarantee it would not rain on your parade, or your wedding, funeral, whatever. Cool it down if it got too hot; refill your reservoir if it got too low; give you a burst of sunshine if you were depressed. Bob knew everyone was impacted in some way or another by the weather on a daily basis. Selecting what clothes to wear, bring an umbrella, plant the field or wait, pour the concrete or not, wash the car, drive or fly...you pick a scenario and you could find a potential weather impact on that activity. Be it direct or indirect, weather impacts everyone.

Bob believed with the proper patents, regulation, and control over a limited number of devices he could have an indefinite monopoly on the weather modification market. His device, his rules, his clientele, his power. *His* he thought, *thanks to the genius and hard work of Dr. James Auster*, as he recalled the man who had been killed only a couple of short months ago. What was the true story of why he had invented this marvelous application by merging these existing technologies? What did he actually intend to do with the capability? Because he had apparently not done anything with it while he was alive except test it. Bob had looked over and over everything Doc had left behind, and there was no trace of documentation that indicated what he intended to do once he perfected the device. Bob could only find a single reference on the subject, and it was embedded in the body of the notes he had read earlier, *that he would make her proud of him as she watched down upon him.*

As Bob cruised down the country road in his new pickup truck he wondered if Dr. Jim Auster might be looking down on him. If so, what did he expect? What would it take to make him proud of Bob Mcleod? What would Jim Auster have Bob do with this new technology? What was Doc planning on doing with this before he was killed by that drunk driver? Bob realized he would probably never know the answers to these questions, at least not for sure, but he did know there was a lot of money to be made and he was getting ready to make his share.

The first device was to be tested at the third trap. Bob set up a wind test which succeeded and followed that with a five-degree temperature drop. Both tests went well, were contained to the trap area, and convinced him that assembly and performance of this device were adequate. He now had two operational Thor's Hammers, one at his home and one in his hand. On to continue the trapline run. About an hour and a half later, he was preparing to test the second of the devices he had built in his house. It, too, successfully completed the same performance test and was deemed operational. The third test at trap number fourteen was equally successful. Bob was elated with the results so far; he now had demonstrated that the device could be built from existing off the shelf technology and components. Producing these things in quantity, at the right time of course, would be a snap. He made a mental note to buy stock in the corporations that built the key components of the devices in the truck with him. Bob set up his computer and began to download the data from trap seventeen. This was the closest site on his run to the military training area but Bob Mcleod had no idea of the significance this would have for him.

As he tested the final device, it too began to perform as expected. The temperature dropped by five degrees as planned, but this drop was also picked up by one of the military remote weather-observing systems operating throughout the live-fire ranges and training areas on the installation. The wind test was also completed, and Bob decided to put the new device through a few more paces before heading back on the homestretch of this trapline run. He thought a few clouds to shade the area would be a good idea and proceeded to set the device accordingly. He sat down on a stump and began to watch in amazement as the clouds began to swirl and puff and take their form in the sky above him. In awe of the small developing clouds Bob thought for a moment, *For the first time in his life, he thought he knew how it felt to create something.* He wondered if this was how an artist felt after creating a beautiful painting, or if a mother feels this way after giving birth to her first child.

He wondered if God himself had felt this way when he created the universe, our world, or man. He wondered if this would be a feeling he could only experience once in his life, or if he would have the same feeling, the same spiritual movement each time he used the device to create some weather phenomena that would never have occurred without his intervention. He wondered how many times in his life he would feel the way he did right then. He decided then to continue building that cloud into a tall majestic shower to rain down on the field of stumps and underbrush where he sat. Perhaps a little extra rain is just what this field needs to help it back on the path of the majestic forests all around it. The small trees restocked after the clear-cutting timber harvest which these acres encountered eight to ten years ago looked like they could use some rain. Bob felt great about himself today, and he felt like helping something, and this he thought was a good way of helping, a nice afternoon shower.

"There's no showers in my forecast for today, Sir, too dry in the mid-levels, and the dew point is way low all across the area. There's just not enough moisture in the atmosphere to wet your mouth. Not today, Sir, ain't gonna happen," Sergeant Andies commented somewhat annoyed by the captain's question. *If you'd get your head out of whatever operation you're planning and look at the darn charts once in a while you wouldn't have to bother me with these simple questions,* Andy thought. This was not rocket science, Sir, he mused, even if it was, a rocket is just a big bullet and we been shooting bullets for over a thousand years, how hard could it be he laughed to himself.

"Well, then Andy how do you explain this rain shower on the radar? It hasn't gone to thunderstorm criteria yet, but it sure popped up quick," Captain Lessur replied.

"The hell you say, Sir!" Andy was not amused and quickly stepped over to the radar scope. Sure enough, there it was small but still growing slowly, and it was not moving very much at all. "Well, I'll be…Sir, do you think this could be the beginning of another one of those BS events that we all miss and make me look bad? You think that guy we talked to OSI about might have something going on? I know it's wild but there just ain't no way this shower should be out there. Wait, maybe the radar is messed up, I'll check the satellite image, we should get another pass down in about four minutes."

"Andy, slow down man. You check the data while I make a few calls, I'll get you in about ten minutes. You watch this and if it starts to pop you put out a warning. That's right, skip past the advisory and go direct to warning if this thing clears twenty-two thousand feet. Just do it, okay? See you in a few," Lessur directed.

"JP? Hey Les here. Listen, I need you to drop whatever you're doing and look at this weather professor dude. What he's doing, where he is, where he's been what he's watching...all that stuff. I got a storm brewing out here again and the closest to a storm we should be fretting over is eight hundred miles away. I think our guy is busy and I think he's making a storm in my backyard. Can you help?" Captain Lessur's request sounded urgent.

"Hello? Hello? Les? Are you there? I just listened to some rambling idiot accusing a university professor of raining on his backyard without proper authorization from the local military meteorologist? Did you see the paranoid psychotic leave when you came in the room or is he still there holding the phone to his ear? Are you safe, are you armed with your umbrella? Geez, Les, get a grip," JP chided.

"I'm gonna get a grip...around your throat if you don't get on this. I don't have time to talk, just do it for me and call me if you get something. JP, this is hot, I can feel it and I need your help, now please get to it!" Les cradled the receiver and headed back to the radar.

"Just sitting there, Sir, not growing not moving. Check the sat pic, the only cloud in our sky is that little baby on our radar," Andy reported calmly.

"Good keep watching it, and let me know if it changes," I've got a few more calls to make. "Yes Sir, that's what I said. Will you just please call the Feds and tell them to record whatever this guy is doing right now? All right, don't tell them the whole thing just tell them this guy is busy doing the same thing he did last time. That could mean anything to them and it will pique their interest enough to get them on it. Thanks Sir," Captain Lessur concluded his phone call with the OSI.

"Andies, get me a radio and whatever spare batteries are charged. Is the Hummer fueled up and ready to go?" Lessur asked.

"Yes Sir, it is always fueled up and ready to go, unless it is already going," Andies replied. "What are you planning, Sir?"

"I am going out to see this storm firsthand, and whatever else I can see while I am there. Maybe he's there, maybe his equipment or something, anything. I am not going to sit here while somebody develops or tests weather modification in my backyard. They really should have invited me; now I am just gonna have to crash their party. Andies, keep the radio on, and let me initiate all contacts. I'll check in every twenty minutes. I'll have my cell phone too, but if I miss three reports, I am in trouble so send in some help. Keep an eye on that storm and make sure all the proper warnings are issued," Lessur's instructions were clear and received.

"Sir," Andies began, "Sir, be careful. This storm could go severe quick under these conditions, and if that guy really can change the weather ... Well, watch your back."

"That's what I got you for Sergeant. Thanks, now get to it," Lessur directed as he headed for the weapons storage area then to the parking lot.

Bob Mcleod now sat in his truck, watching the shower gently cover the meadow with its life sustaining supply of rainwater. He felt good about lending a hand to continue the natural healing process of the land, a land that was ravaged years ago by a clear-cutting timber operation. The earth, he thought to himself, is incredibly resilient. She takes whatever man and the elements dish out all in stride, all in a sort of natural order. For the first time ever, Professor Mcleod wondered if his device was capable of disrupting that natural order, indeed if his plans would have any permanent ramifications to the earth he so admired. After all, that was why he had chosen this profession of Meteorology, his love of the outdoors and the closed system known as the earth's atmosphere.

He loved the outdoors, being in the sun, seeing the trees, the sky, mountains, rivers, lakes and the animals that inhabit them all. Bob loved the peacefulness of being a part of nature. He concerned himself with its protection which was one of the biggest reasons he took the position working with Dr. Auster. In his own solemn but unspoken way, Bob Mcleod cared enough about it to work hard to find answers which could protect the land in his state. It wasn't saving the world but he could contribute to his own part of the world by taking care of his local area. He surely didn't become a meteorologist for the money but now he had an opportunity he never even dreamed about before. An opportunity to do both...to work in the field of study he loved and make money, lots and lots of money.

Bob decided at that point to take a closer look at the potential problems of using the Thor's Hammer. Would there be any atmospheric reactions to the weather modifications he initiated? If so, would they too be controllable, predictable, random? The problem was mentally challenging and the more Bob pondered it the more interested he became in the question. What would using the devices mean in the bigger scheme of the atmosphere, indeed, in the bigger scheme of human consequence? That was one he was not ready for. Professor Mcleod decided to work on the scientific question first. He was not prepared to entertain discussions about the future of mankind if they were able to control the forces of nature. *There would be time for deep consideration of that issue later*, Bob thought. That would take some time to work through; that would require some tough analysis and decisions and Bob wasn't about to go there for a while. This was too nice a day and too good a feeling right now to spoil with the mental toils of the future of mankind and weather modification. Bob had time to do that later, he believed, but he had not nearly as much time as he would have liked.

His chores of data collection and testing his new devices were not yet complete, but Bob decided the rain shower had accomplished its intended task. It was time to leave the peacefulness of the meadow near the sensors he called trap number 17. Time to get back to the business at hand, back to the house back to work, back to the computers and the numbers, and the research. All that indoor stuff paled to the calm he felt when he was out in the environment he studied. Bob thought it an injustice of monumental proportion to reduce the beauty and majesty of the environment to mere numbers and equations driving a plethora of computer models and algorithms. He smiled at the irony of that as he loaded his gear into the cab of his truck, and grinned once again, thinking, "Beauty is in the eyes of the beholder, and right now he *be-holdin-her*." As he set the last Thor's Hammer to end the peaceful rain shower he had created, he got a glimpse of understanding one possible reason Doc Auster had kept this device and its capability such a secret.

Captain Lessur kept one eye on the dirt road and one eye on the lone rain shower up ahead. This one was not growing in size or increasing in intensity as he knew it should under these conditions. He wanted to get there and find the people, equipment, and techniques involved in this experiment, or operation, or whatever it was. He was tired of wondering what was going on. It was time for him to know why these strange events were happening in his area of responsibility and he was sure this shower was his path to knowledge. He passed several cars on the dirt road, noting each of them for suspicious characteristics but there were none that he could detect. He checked in on the radio with Sergeant Andies, "Shower is stationary, Sir, like it's anchored. It isn't moving a bit with or against the flow. It topped out about twenty-four thousand feet and looks like it is starting to fall apart. It sure doesn't look like it is going to build into a thunderstorm. Sir, I recommend we cancel all advisories and warnings at this time. We are getting a lot of calls from all over the base. Sir, Sir, did you copy?"

"Roger, copy. Go ahead and cancel the stuff but keep watching this thing close. I'm about 10 miles from it so give me any indications you get, good or bad. Thanks Andy, out." Lessur was already disappointed that the small rain shower had not grown into a mammoth thunderstorm yet. There would be hell to pay with the flying guys and the maintenance guys about a false alarm for weather warning criteria on such a nice day with one piddly little rain shower so far away from the base. Credibility was posturing for another black eye and Lessur was out chasing a mad scientist in an alfalfa field. This was not good. As he closed in on the edge of the storm, Captain Lessur barely noticed the flash from the windshield of the black Ford pickup pulling out onto the road behind him. Two miles later Lessur turned onto a small road leading east, closer to the center of the dissipating shower. He was focused on what lay before him and paid little attention to what was behind him. The black truck continued down the road, and Bob Mcleod thought it a bit odd to see a Hummer out here, especially alone and with only one occupant. He made a mental note to check for any military exercises in the area. The last thing he wanted to do was raise anyone's suspicion, especially now when he was laying low, or so he thought.

Lessur found nothing except a wet area and a few clouds as the shower continued its natural dissipation into the dryer air surrounding it. The weatherman checked in once again and told Sergeant Andies he was returning to base, estimated time one hour fifteen minutes. A dejected and now angry Captain Lessur had a lot to think about on the way back. Andies had no luck getting the OSI or the FBI to react to the calls Lessur instructed him to make. Further, the OSI commander instructed Andies to have Lessur report to him immediately upon his return. Things did not go as the aggressive young captain had expected, and he was not looking forward to the rest of the day, indeed the rest of the week.

"OSI will have to wait Sir. The DO wants you in his office ASAP. I think he's a little upset about us going to warning criteria on such a small shower. A lot of people have to do a lot of stuff when you forecast winds in excess of fifty knots and three-quarter inch hail. He said he'd stick around 'til you got there, and I wouldn't advise keeping that colonel waiting any longer than necessary," Andies passed the information to his captain in equally conciliatory and advisory tones, displaying the experience and wisdom of an exceptional NCO. He felt bad for his captain, but they both had a lot riding on how Lessur handled the situation with the DO. He is after all, director of operations for the entire organization. He's the number three guy in the flying wing, but he's the doer of things. The commander and his vice make decisions and give direction, but the DO is the guy who takes those decisions from words and transforms them into reality. He has the commander's ear in all matters and Lessur didn't need to be on the DO's list of troublemakers and goof ups. Lessur intended to make the Air Force his career but he had hoped it would last longer than the eight years he served so far. After the initial shock of having his tail handed to him by the full colonel in what seemed like an infinite string of deafening questions beginning with, *Do you know how much...?* the DO began to settle back into his chair. Lessur stood there with a solid, yet disappointed, look on his face and the colonel, confident Lessur got the message, motioned for him to sit down.

"Now, tell me why you felt the need to run off across the county, with a loaded sidearm, chasing a rain shower. Son, you can't kill a rain shower with a bullet no matter how much you think it is threatening my base. What's up with that?" This is what the colonel was really after, he liked the weather officer, and wanted to keep him from getting deep into something he could not recover from. The DO knew, all too well, about the recent significant weather events in their area. He knew the CG and other staff members were losing confidence in their weather officer and, frankly, the DO was worried Lessur was on his way to wigging out over the ordeal. He had to be sure the captain wasn't having a nervous breakdown or some serious mental trouble.

Captain Lessur explained the whole story to the colonel who listened intently out of shear curiosity and skepticism. The DO called the OSI commander over to join them in their discussion when Lessur mentioned that he wanted to see the captain. The three had an interesting session which ended with direction to the OSI commander not to initiate contact with any law enforcement agency regarding Lessur's theory of weather modification in their area. If the OSI was contacted by any law enforcement agency regarding this topic the DO was to be informed immediately and, in concert with the OSI and the JAG, the DO would select a course of action appropriate to the contact. Lessur was not to deal with anyone except the DO on this issue. Captain Lessur was instructed to focus on forecasting and briefing the weather for the Air Force wing operations and the collocated Army command he served. He was further instructed to get it together because he was already getting attention at the higher levels in the organization. Forget about this changing the weather thing and focus on what he was being paid to do. The DO reminded the captain that, with regard to the brass, "A little visibility can be good, but you can die from exposure." With that Captain Lessur was dismissed. He headed back to the weather station to debrief Sergeant Andies. They were both ready for a beer.

Bob Mcleod returned to his home tired from the day's work but in a good mood, particularly pleased with his introspective sabbatical at the meadow. He tried to ignore the little voice that nagged at him, trying to cajole him into taking a hard look at his real motivations and the potentially devastating results this new capability could bring to mankind. The time to seriously consider the magnitude of even some of the impacts of using this technology were mind boggling. Bob knew he would make history but he also knew he would have to wrestle with, at some point in the near future, the context in which history would record the revelations and application of a man who can create and control the weather. There was the potential for great power and great charity; great benevolence and great terror; great compassion and great control. This moral dilemma began to creep into Bob's thoughts so he dismissed it as readily as possible. Oh, he knew he would have to come to grips with it in due time, and he knew he would have to make a big decision but he also believed he had time to figure it all out later.

He would get some help when the time came, starting with Father Gannon. He knew the priest was trustworthy and knew he would help for both Bob's and Doc Auster's sake in addition to the other obvious reasons.

Father Gannon was a good priest and a good friend to Doc. While Bob could not say that he himself was a good friend to either of the two, he knew their relationship would carry the day for him. He had time to figure this out. Right now he had more important tasks to accomplish or so he thought.

The IRS began the avalanche of events that was about to consume Professor Mcleod's future and change his life forever. A routine call from Special Agent Relltin to the local law enforcement agency to check for additional information on Robert Mcleod, including any pending or on-going criminal investigations proved fruitful. The sheriff explained they had just opened an investigation on the individual for possible theft of university property and embezzlement of both University and State funds. Special Agent Relltin explained, "Myself and two colleagues had just visited Professor Mcleod at his residence a couple of days ago because of the large financial gains he had made in the securities market. The encounter was brief, but all the agents agreed that Professor Robert Mcleod was keeping something from them So, they thought it worth looking into."

Sheriff Watson listened intently, and then explained to Special Agent Relltin the call from Dean Durbin requesting an investigation for financial and materiel improprieties beginning shortly after Dr. Auster's fatal accident. The Sheriff assured the IRS agent, "There was no link between Mcleod and Dr. Auster's death. That was a complete accident, tragically killing a good man and ruining the life and future of an otherwise fine young man of the local community attending his freshman year in his hometown University. No, this trouble began shortly after Mr. Mcleod begged to pick up the research of his deceased boss and the Dean, the big boss, told him to carry on in the tradition of the proud man before him. Obviously, this new power and authority, and trust of the University staff gave him the false impression he could steal them blind while they mourned the death of a colleague. I am looking into this mater personally," the Sheriff added.

"Well, then," Agent Relltin explained, "do you believe Professor Mcleod had access to large sums of money then, hundreds of thousands of dollars that he could move around? We are talking about a lot of money here. I don't think this is about some Professor pilfering from the petty cash bin or swiping a few computers. He's made millions in the last few months Sheriff. We know some of it was from gains on pumpkin futures, and some of it on gas. But we don't know how he financed the large sums up front for his initial investment. Do you think he could get his hands on half a million dollars of university funds without being noticed. I mean he's a meteorologist, right? A weatherman...not an accountant."

Sheriff Watson thought before responding, "No Sir, I do not. I don't think he could have gotten that kind of money through the University, and if he could, I don't believe he could have kept it hidden for long. No Sir, I personally know most of the folks in the financial and leadership roles in the University and they are far too careful, far too thorough to ever allow such a thing to happen. You say the man is a millionaire? Did you say that, Sir?"

"That's right Sheriff. The man has somewhere between three and six million that we are aware of now. There could be more, that is why I am calling," Special Agent Relltin went on. "Is there anything else you can tell me about your investigation thus far?"

"No Sir. Nothing I haven't already said. I was just beginning to formulate a strategy for my investigation when you called. Your timing was extraordinary I must say. What do you suggest we do from here, since this sounds like a matter perhaps best dealt with outside the local constabulary," the Sheriff conceded.

"Sheriff, if you don't mind, I'd like a few days to gather some more information on this guy; see what else I can find. I need to check with DEA and the Feds to see if they are working anything on him. Just sit tight and I will get back with you in three days...five at the max. Will that work for you?" Relltin requested.

"Just fine Sir, I will do my best not to arouse any suspicion on our subject's part. Anything you want me to do, or not do?" Sheriff Watson inquired.

"No, thanks. Just sit tight, you'll be hearing from me," Relltin concluded the conversation with a thank you and a smile. Sheriff Watson concluded by reaching for his phone book. Dean Durbin and his daddy may want to extract a little mileage from this news. Mcleod a millionaire, huh? That was news, and Hugh Durbin might be able to use that for something. The Sheriff knew better than to discuss, or even comment on the investigation, especially if it was IRS, but he also knew Durbin would be appreciative of what he could tell him. After all, Sheriff is an elected position and elections always come too soon when you are the incumbent.

Special Agent Relltin was pleased with his progress on the very first call of his probe into Professor Robert Mcleod. Never one to quit while he was ahead, he decided to see if the FBI had ever heard of this guy. After a few transfers and a couple of long holds, Relltin extended his winning streak to two in a row when he heard Agent Miloc on the other end of the phone. "Miloc here, who's this?" the FBI special agent inquired.

"Relltin, IRS. I'm looking into a guy named Mcleod, Robert Mcleod. Seems he's come into a lot of money, questionable origin maybe. Just trying to make sure Uncle Sam gets his share but I'm not sure Mcleod doesn't have something coming his way too. I'm just checking to see if you guys are watching him for anything. Seems the local cops are; thought maybe you guys might be too," Relltin concluded. He hated conducting business over the phone. His years taught him that the best way to share information was in person, face-to-face so you could see the other guy and read him. Easier to tell if he was giving you everything or if he was holding out, just taking from you. Relltin had a lot of experience doing this over the phone and he was good, which is exactly why he preferred to do it in person. There he was even better and it was easier.

Miloc replied, "Yeah, were working him, too. Think he might be laundering money through the market for some druggies. Started hitting him hard a couple of days ago. We're sure he's not the brains but we might be able to get to the man through our guy Mcleod. There are probably a hundred more just like him if our hunch is good, but right now he's the only one were on. What do the locals have on him?" Miloc wanted something back from his colleague on the other end of the line, a show of good faith if you will, before each of them gave away any of the good stuff.

"Local Sheriff says the guy's boss was killed in an accident. His new boss thinks the guy is stealing money from the University, and was having it checked out," Relltin offered. "Sheriff doesn't link him to the death but thinks he's worth checking out. Doesn't think the guy could get any large cash from the University undetected, but nobody ever wants to admit they are vulnerable. And besides, Mcleod could have somebody on the inside working with him or vice versa."

Miloc added another comment to the discussions, "I bet you won't guess who else is on this guy, one guess...bet you a beer?"

Relltin could tell Miloc was shooting straight with him and he wanted the rest of the story. "His lady? She's got a private eye following him to see who he's playing *poker* with? I like Michelob," he guessed quickly.

"I like it, too," Miloc continued. "The Air Force. The Air Force OSI, you know them? They wanted me to watch this guy about his ability to predict the weather. They call me up and say they got a guy on the base who thinks this Mcleod can predict the weather with some new system they don't know about. Want me to start watching him for them so they can learn how this guy does his thing. I don't really understand how they got onto him or why but it was about the same time we got our report of him spending some big cash. So, my boss had me check him out. Now I got four agencies that I know of looking at this guy. I haven't contacted DEA lately but maybe we oughta ask them too. Nothing like a full house when you're doing an investigation. We could all meet and have a big picnic while we sort out who's got what." Miloc seemed pleased that he'd won a beer. He'd learned long ago that in this business little victories were the ones that led to success. He liked his little victories; he depended on them.

"Okay," Relltin conceded, "one beer, soonest opportunity. What about records? This guy got a dirty past or what?"

"No, he's squeaky clean. A couple moving violations, but nothing your grandmother would be ashamed of. He's never had money, but never been too far in the hole either. Always worked, not married, no kids. School, work that's about it. This guy, until a short time ago was never even a blip on anybody's screen. You want to chat with this guy?" Miloc suggested.

"Already did, that's why I'm on with you," Relltin explained the brief meeting he and his team had on Mcleod's front porch and concluded with, "…and there is more to the story than he's telling. I know that, now I just need to find out what it is. I'll work with you on this if you want to roll him up and see what shakes out but you might only get one shot. He looked like he was holding out on me, but he did not look stupid."

"I think all crooks are stupid; otherwise, they'd be cops. Some say they think all cops are stupid; otherwise, they'd be crooks. Either way lets shake him up. If he is washing money for the druggies, he's new and just made two successful passes. He may roll over on the next guy up if you hook him and then offer to cut him loose for a name. My boss wants this game shut down fast and hard. If they are using the market with guys like him, you win too. If he's into something else we can turn it over to the locals or the base guys and it will be out of our hair. If he's clean we save time. If he's not, we slow the wheels of crime. Either way I think Mr. Mcleod needs a visit from some law enforcement officials like the FBI and the IRS. Let's do it in the afternoon so I can collect on that beer. What's good for you?" Miloc thought it rare to get an IRS guy who was good at field work and wanted to meet this Relltin character.

"I hate leaving things hanging, let's do him up today. You and I get together about one at your place, the FBI has better facilities and it gets me out of the office. We'll compare notes, get an angle, work the guys and then split for that beer. Sound good?" Relltin inquired.

"Yeah, that'll work for me. I'll have my guys roll him up and bring him in. He shouldn't be too hard to find, work or home. I'll give you a call and let you know if we have trouble finding him. If you don't hear from me, we are good to go. What's your number? Got a cellular?" Miloc reached for a pad of paper.

"Office is 609-6738, cellular is 609-7251. Are you on the second or third floor over there? Okay, see you around one. I'll be the good-looking guy looking lost," Relltin said and cradled the receiver. Let's see what else I can learn about Robert Mcleod before noon.

The rest of Relltin's morning was much less productive. He found nothing more about the innocuous Robert Mcleod. His tax returns were all filed on time, simple, straightforward, no money to speak of, not even enough to itemize deductions. There was very little to be learned from his IRS records. His credit history was much the same, very benign. Few large purchases, very little debt, only a couple of local credit cards, a phone card and a VISA. The phone card had provided few clues, too, mostly calls that appeared to be back to work while he was on the road. If this guy was hiding something he was doing a pretty good job, but Relltin wasn't buying it. All the paper indicated Mcleod was just a regular nothing kind of guy...a working student type.

That is hard to fake for so many years and Relltin had seen it all in this business. No, whatever Mr. Mcleod was into it was new stuff or it wasn't him. Wandering off the elevator on the second floor of the building that housed the FBI offices, he was glad they decided to meet here. The building was fairly new, and very nice, especially for this part of the Mid-West. It was a unique architecture for the region, a lot of glass in an oblong shape. It almost looked like a teardrop from the outside, and Relltin seemed to think the irony of having FBI offices among the many in the building was somewhat fitting.

"You Miloc?" Relltin asked accusingly of a man sitting behind a cubicle desk in a comfortable looking chair.

"You Relltin?" the man replied as he stood to greet the visitor. They each extended their hands which met in a hearty shake both exhibiting the firm grips they were each expecting in return. The two men were both consummate professionals. Both were exceptional performers in their respective fields and they could sense that of each other. Only luck could have put these two together on such a vague case as this one. And for Bob Mcleod, his luck was about to change in a very big way.

"Your guys pick him up yet?" Relltin inquired. The reply was satisfying, "They are on their way now. Should be at his home any minute. He usually goes home for lunch according to our surveillance; we'll pick him up there so we don't make a scene at the University. Trying to be a sensitive law enforcement agency. We don't want to get a reputation like the IRS has for being mean to our customers," Miloc grinned, looking for a reaction.

The two agents parked outside watched as Bob pulled into the driveway. As he stepped from the truck and closed the door, one of the two men approaching from opposite sides yelled, "Professor Mcleod? Sir, are you Robert Mcleod?" Bob turned to see who was calling after him but the next words he heard made it all too clear. "Sir, we are federal agents, please keep your hands where I can see them. I need you to come with me, Sir." Bob felt an empty pain shoot deep within him, a pain like the kind he felt on receiving the news of his parent's deaths. He knew this was different, but he knew, too, that no good would come of this and he wished for more time to finish his work.

"What is this about? Who are you?" Bob demanded.

The first man produced his credentials and reached for Bob's arm as he said, "Sir, I am Special Agent Hadforn, FBI, please place your hands on the truck. Do you have any weapons on your person, Sir?"

Bob's heart continued to sink. "No, no weapons; what do you want with me?" he countered.

"Sir, you need to come with us for questioning at the federal building. You are *not*, repeat *not* under arrest at this time, Sir, but you are obliged to come with me to answer questions. Sir, are you willing to come with us at this time?" the agent asked.

"You just told me I had to, now you are asking me. Do I have to or not?" Bob asked impatiently.

"Yes Sir, you have to come with us. I am going to check you for weapons now, Sir. Do you have anything sharp in your pockets, needles, knives, anything that may cut me?" the agent inquired.

"No."

"Any drugs?"

"No, I don't do drugs," Bob replied.

"Anything illegal on your person, Sir," the agent continued

"No."

"Sir, you are not under arrest, but we are going to transport you in our vehicle. You will be handcuffed and assisted for your safety, as well as, ours. Sir place your left hand behind your head please," the agent directed.

"Handcuffs, is that really necessary?" Bob asked sincerely.

"Yes, Sir. Left hand please, behind your head. Now the right one please," Agent Hadforn concluded as he snapped the bracelet onto Bob's wrist. He then took his arm and led him to the back seat of the plain, unmarked Crown Victoria and helped Bob into the back seat. As they began to drive off, Bob could see Buck barking through the window. He truly wondered what he was trying to say. Bob wondered what he himself would say. *It depends on what they ask me* he concluded as they began the short six-minute drive to the glass building. He sat quietly until they arrived, and then escorted him up to the second floor where he was processed and placed in interrogation room number three. There he sat quietly, thinking, and waiting, waiting to see if they knew anything or if this was just a fishing expedition. Bob was nervous, he was scared, but he was not a quitter. He was a fighter who never had to fight much but he was beginning to feel like he was being backed into a corner.

CHAPTER FIVE

CONFESSION

Special Agents Miloc and Relltin looked up from the paper covered table when Agent Hadforn entered the office, "Got him in room number three boss. No problem on the pickup. He didn't resist, but he hasn't said anything useful either. Real short trip in though. I don't think he's had much time to ponder why we picked him up and I didn't tell him why. Wanna let him sit and cool his heels awhile?"

"No," replied Relltin abruptly. "He knows why he's here. Let's get on him before he has time to think too much. We don't want the professor to think he can get cute with us."

Miloc nodded to Hadforn, and the three started down the hall to the third interrogation room. As the three walked into the room, Bob began to stand up. Miloc motioned for him to sit back down at the table. Bob did so, as Miloc began to speak, "Are you Professor Robert Mcleod, Sir?"

"Yes I am."

"Professor, I'm Special Agent Miloc. You've already met Special Agent Hadforn. We are with the FBI." Bob nodded as he glanced toward his captor.

"And this, Sir, is Agent Relltin. He is with the IRS. I believe you have already met him as well," Miloc continued as Bob nodded once again. "Professor, I think you know why we brought you in for questioning today. You are not under arrest for a specific crime at this time. However, if you wish to have a lawyer present for these questions that is your privilege. You want a lawyer for this professor?"

Bob thought for a moment. He didn't have a lawyer; he never liked lawyers; and he didn't know any well enough to trust, "No, I won't need a lawyer here today. What is it that I can do for you?" Bob tried to get some control of both his situation and his voice.

"Sir, you know why we are here, so how about filling us in on the details?" Miloc asked again.

"No Special Agent, I don't know why I am here. We might do a lot better if you tell me," Bob pushed. He worried that he'd pushed a little too hard.

"Okay, you got rich quick Professor. Too quick. We know how you did it, too. We know you are spending bunches of your new money on some very interesting things in some very innovative ways. We already have everything we need on you but what I want to know is who else you're working with, and who you're working for? It doesn't look very good for you, Sir, but if you help us maybe we can help you back. Help us get the boss and we'll make it easy on you," Miloc nodded to Bob.

"This is like a bad movie," Bob replied, somewhat relieved. He thought they suspected something but they were simply on a fishing expedition to see what information Bob would volunteer. He also suspected they didn't know anything definitive about his work, the device, or its ability. "What are you gentlemen talking about? Yes, I've made some money from my investments but I believe Agent Relltin and I have already had that discussion." Bob tried to remain calm.

Relltin appreciated the transition and immediately chimed in, "Professor, we are busy men. Just like you, we have lots to do so try this on; new house, new truck, new computers, numerous satellite components, in that order for starters. You been scraping by on beans up to a few months ago, now you are worth millions, and all shortly after your boss's untimely death. This doesn't smell good, Sir, and we both know why. I want to hear your side of it before we shut you down."

Bob was startled. Did they know about the Thor's Hammer or did they just know about his financial exploits? It was becoming painfully obvious that they knew what he was doing but did they really know how he was doing it? There was an incredibly important distinction between the two; history itself seemed to be hanging in the balance.

"Yes Sir, I haven't had much for a long time and I figured I deserved to spend a little bit of my newfound wealth," Bob tried to minimize the impact of Relltin's statement.

"I don't think you found this new wealth; I think you obtained it illegally. In fact, I know you did, Professor. So, let's start with how you got a few hundred thousand to invest in pumpkins. How bout telling us where you got that kind of cash?" Relltin pushed, as Miloc sat quietly, stoic in the chair carefully observing Mcleod's reactions. Of course, it was all being video-taped but you need to read the facial expressions and the nonverbal mannerisms during the questioning to know where and how far you can go in any interrogation. Both Miloc and Relltin were experts at this and they could tell they were already getting Professor Mcleod outside his comfort zone by a considerable margin.

Bob hesitated, contemplating the truth and then chose to lie but he chose a poor lie to answer the question he had not really given much thought to before now. "I've been saving my money," he replied with his eyes focused firmly on the table in front of him. Shifting in his chair and then looking up for the next question. Bob could tell by the fat grin on Relltin's face that he was not buying that story.

"Do I look stupid to you Professor? Why do you want to waste my time? Maybe you got time to waste looking at clouds or tornadoes, but I am a busy man. I work hard for a living and I've got more work than I can do in two lifetimes on my desk *right now*! So don't give me crap we both know is a lie or we can be finished right now. That would be bad for you, Professor, really bad, cause right now we are trying to help you. You jerk with me again and I will be out to hurt you instead and I can do that already. Don't mess this up; this is the *one* chance you get. What's it gonna be, you gonna talk truth to me or are we finished already?" Relltin stared at Bob with his cold blue eyes, hardened by years of seeing things on the street. Bob knew he had a problem and Agent Relltin was beginning to help him see its magnitude. Miloc was impressed with the IRS agent's skills. He thought they did mostly white-collar stuff, busting shirts that rolled over and confessed if you looked at them cross-eyed, but he was gaining a new respect for that agency. If Relltin was representative of the caliber of agents they had over there, he intended to solicit their help a lot more often than he had in the past.

"Yeah, okay," Bob began. "I won most of it. Won it on a bet, a couple of bets. Sports stuff. I needed to get some money up and that was the only way I knew how to do it quickly. It was risky for me. I had to bet everything I owned to get a stake, and it may not have been too smart but it was legal. I didn't rob a bank or anything."

"Legal? Betting book in this town is still illegal Professor. But you're right, it's not very smart. Still, it's smarter than killing your boss and taking the money from him. It's smarter than embezzling it from the University. It's smarter than laundering money for drug dealers. But you wouldn't know anything about those things would you now? Because you were gonna tell me the truth. Well, what happened Professor? Why are you still lying to me? I'll ask you again, do I look *stupid* to you?" Relltin was pushing hard now, he leaned over, getting into Bob's face he glared and fired again, "Do I look stupid to you? I'm no Professor like you are, but do I really look that stupid to you, Mcleod?"

Bob stood and his temper began to get the best of him. Miloc leaned forward and postured himself to react if either one of these two went hands on.

"No! No, you don't look stupid. You may act like you're stupid, but I know you're not. I didn't kill anybody! I didn't embezzle anything! I don't know a drug dealer even if I wanted to launder money for one. Hell, I wouldn't know how to launder money even if I needed to. I don't think you're stupid any more than I think I am. I got my money started by betting, I already told you that and it's the truth. I won enough to invest and you know the rest. I know how to invest money! I know how to make money but it takes money to make money and I didn't have enough to start out investing so I bet what I had. That's that, if you don't like it or if you don't believe it then tough. It's the truth and I can't—no—I won't be made to change the truth because it is not what you want to hear." Bob realized his emotions were charged, but the release felt good. He needed to yell at someone. He was worried, they all knew it and he was emotionally drained from the long hours and troubling events of the last several months. Bob tried hard to get control of his reaction, and the first thing he did was sit back down.

Miloc recognized the sign and stood up so Relltin would disengage. Time for a little good cop bad cop. So, he began, "Professor, what we really want is the guy you're working for. I'll be straight with you. I'd much rather have your help getting a bigger fish but if you are all we get? Well, we got to have something to show for our time and you'll get the whole heat all by yourself. Now, I don't think any of us wants that...least of all you. So, what do you say? Or do we need to go through this again?"

"I am telling you for the last time, I am not a killer, a thief, or a drug dealer. There is no bigger fish to fry. There is no other truth to give you and I am not going to make something up to make you two happy," Bob continued. "If you're not stupid enough to believe the one lie I told you, I can't believe you're stupid enough not to believe the truth."

"Okay, let's assume you are telling us the truth; it doesn't make sense enough Professor. You must not be telling us the *whole* truth. So, let's go there. What's the rest of the story Professor, what aren't you telling us? What have you left out, because it is an important part, otherwise Relltin would believe you. He knows the truth; been doing this a long time.

Give us the rest so we can believe you. After all, that's what we are here for, to get to the truth," Miloc concluded with an inviting gesture and raised his eyebrows in challenge to Mcleod.

"All right," Bob replied, "there is more. But, I'm gonna warn you, you probably won't believe this either," Bob said in resignation.

He wasn't sure why, at that moment, he decided to tell the two agents the whole truth. The strain of the last few months was a lot for one person, and one dog to bear. The exhausting hours of research, testing, and analysis. The strain of going it alone on a project with such magnificent potential and significance to the future, indeed, the future history of mankind itself. The pressure had been building on Bob for some time, and he recalled his time in the field watching the rain shower drop its life-giving liquid over the meadow. He felt an enormous weight lift from his shoulders as he succumbed to his desire to share his triumph, his new ability, with someone. The need to belong to something again outweighed the desire to maintain control of the power he alone possessed even if it was to the Federal law enforcement agencies trying to prove his activities were criminal. After all he rationalized, he couldn't continue his work or do anything else for that matter if he were in jail, or prison, or worse. Bob decided it was time to come clean, to clear his name so he could get on with making history. It was not the time nor the circumstance he would have chosen to reveal his weather modification abilities to the world, but he would have to make do. Just another day in the life of Robert Mcleod...dealt a tough hand...but time to make do, once again. If there was anything Bob Mcleod knew how to do, it was making do.

Bob began to tell his tale, "All right, here's what happened. I took the two thousand bucks I had and bet it on a balloon race at eleven-to-one odds. Then I took ten of that twenty-two thousand and bet it on a boat regatta at eight to one and won. That gave me enough to buy 100 grand in pumpkin futures. When the crop froze, I made a bundle, just under a million. I put most of that in natural gas futures, and when the pipeline and storage facilities were struck by lightning that turned into a lot more and, well, I'm not sure how much I have now, maybe you can tell me?" Bob challenged.

Relltin piped up at the tone of Bob's voice, "Well, you're right Professor, I don't believe you. You turned into a multimillionaire in a month. You expect me to believe you had such good luck that you turned two grand into a multimillion-dollar portfolio in a month?" Relltin laughed aloud, "You really do think I am stupid. Whatever possessed you to bet two grand on a balloon race, a boat race. Why pumpkins and gas? Why not pork bellies and ball games? I thought you were ready to work with us. Obviously, we are wasting everyone's time here Miloc. Let just cut our losses and smoke this bookworm. He can take the whole fall and we can get on with crooks who really appreciate what we can do for them if they cooperate." Relltin headed for the door and motioned for Miloc to follow.

"Look," Bob said beginning to worry again, "I warned you. I said you wouldn't believe me but it's true, I swear my oath it is. The reason I bet was because I knew I would win. I couldn't lose. They were sure bets, they were investments."

"What?" Miloc interrupted him, pushing at the sign of a breached defense, "You fixed the races? Insider trading? How did you know, professor?"

"I made it happen. I made the wind push both the balloon and the sailboat to victory. I made the temperature drop to freeze the pumpkins and lightning to hit the pipeline. I knew it would happen because I chose the time and the place and made it happen," Bob said triumphantly. There, it was out. He had done it; he had revealed the secret and confessed to being one of the most powerful men in the world. He felt great and he smiled with pride.

"I *am* stupid. We have God himself in the room Miloc and didn't even recognize him. I am sorry I mistook you for a common criminal university professor who steals and launders money for drug dealers. Please forgive, for I know not what I do! I have had enough of this crap. Let's go." Relltin was reaching for the door and Miloc followed him out. Bob sat alone in the room, confused and dismayed. They really didn't believe him. He told them the truth, gave them exactly what they wanted and they didn't believe him. Now he appeared to be in more trouble than ever.

He sat there amazed that they failed to understand what had just been revealed to them. The power and the potential were extraordinary. *Maybe they were stupid,* Bob worried, his mind spinning with possible outcomes as the agents discussed God only knows what outside the room.

"Can you believe this guy? I don't know who is the better actor him or me," Relltin fumed as they walked toward the soda machine. Miloc replied, "Yes, I do believe him, and you are a better actor. He came clean and he believes what he told us. Either he is one sick but lucky scientist or he's straight up telling us the truth."

"For a while there, son, I thought you had some potential. But I must be losing my touch because I can't believe you believe him," Relltin continued. Changing the weather. He said he makes whole counties freeze; individual boats and balloons catch wind and lightning strike. *Hello!* Are you okay? You already have those beers before I got here or what?"

"Remember I told you the Air Force OSI guys were watching this guy, too?" Miloc asked. "Well, the reason they contacted us was because they thought this guy *was* doing something with the weather. Forecasting with some new technique that their guys were missing. Wanted to talk to him, maybe learn how he was doing it. I don't think he's a better forecaster, although most weather forecasters don't seem to do very well on the news. I think maybe he was making the weather he wanted and that's why the guys at the base were missing it. It shouldn't have been there, and our Professor Mcleod was putting it there to get himself rich."

"You been watching too much TV, Bubba," Relltin looked concerned. "But, just say you're right. Just suppose you are right, that makes this guy one dangerous cat. If we turn him loose, he will be gone like a rat in a sewer. We'll never come up on him again. He's not stupid, that I know. He could wreak havoc, man! He could really screw with the world if this is true, Miloc. Either way we got a lot of work to do; beer may have to wait.

"Let's go in for a few more questions, see what we get from him and then call the base to see if we can get the OSI or whoever out there can help to come in and give us a hand with the right questions for this guy. Some techie, one of their weather guys, a physicist, whatever they can offer?" Miloc gestured to the soda machine, three buttons later they were on their way back into interrogation room three.

"Coke, Professor?" Miloc offered Bob a can.

"Is this a trick question? Coca Cola yes; cocaine no. I told you I don't do drugs. They ruin the mind. I'd just as soon ruin my stomach lining, so thank you," Bob tried to lighten the mood as he reached for the cold can.

"You gotta' admit Professor, this tale of yours is pretty tall. I'd like to believe that the only thing you're guilty of is illegal gambling and felony destruction of property, but I can't. It's too much to ask for me to take that on faith. Now, I might believe you are trying to help us now, but let's get diggin' where there's taters or we're gonna be in for a very long ordeal here. In case you're still not sure, I am not stupid." Relltin stopped, sat down, and challenged Mcleod anew, "You want a lawyer?"

"No. I don't need a lawyer, do I?" Bob asked seriously.

"Not yet," Miloc replied, "But let's not do anything to change that, okay Professor Mcleod? Why don't you tell us some more about how you make weather. I am certainly intrigued by that."

"There is a lot to tell there. That is why I needed the satellite components, which is why I needed to make the money so quickly. I needed to build the devices I use to modify the physical environment," Bob began.

"Wait one minute here...slow down for me professor. You built a thing that changes the weather out of some satellite parts you bought over the Internet? Do I have my stupid light on again? You're jerking us around again?" Relltin interrupted.

"No, and I'll tell you something else. If you want me to explain this to you, sit down and shut up. Quit interrupting me. This is important stuff, and if you think it's hard to understand, you ought to try explaining it to you.

Now if you don't mind, let me tell you what you keep asking me." Bob was straight up growing impatient and it showed. That is exactly where Relltin wanted to keep him, flustered but still talking.

"Yeah, okay, you tell us your story straight up. I'll pipe down for you, but imagine my skepticism as you continue. Be convincing Professor," Relltin motioned for Bob to continue.

"I made some machines that enable me to modify the weather. I built them. I can change the weather by programming in what I want to happen, when I want it to happen and the intensity level of the events. Simply put, I can change the weather to whatever I want it to be, whenever I want it to happen. That is how I got the early frost and the intense thunderstorm. I made them, and they made me rich," Bob paused. "What questions so far?"

Miloc asked, "How many of these machines do you have...have you made?"

"I have four devices. They are all the same. It only takes one to do the job, and I didn't want to risk breaking the only working one I had. I've built and tested them and they all work." Bob didn't want to get into the origin of the first one. That would come later; now he was explaining for the first time. He wanted them to grasp the concept then learn the details. Bob's student teaching experience finally appeared to be an unforeseen advantage.

"How do they work? Wait, never mind that. What can you do with them?" Relltin asked inquisitively.

"They can modify, even regulate all the physical characteristics of the environment. What I mean is: temperature, rain, snow, wind, clouds, lightning, pressures...duration, time, intensity, scale...all the parameters of the conditions. For example, I can make the wind speed increase by ten knots in a small area so the balloon I bet on moves faster than all the rest of the ones around it. That was exciting, so I did it for the boat too. I filled its sails after the other guys came around the point I was standing on while the two leaders met a stiff, unexpected, isolated headwind. By the time they realized it they were stalled to a stop. I turned the wind into my choice's sails and pushed it along. In thirty seconds, the race was decided and it looked like a tough break, nothing more." Bob realized he was talking too much. "What else?"

Miloc asked, "Who else knows how this stuff works? You do this alone or can somebody vouch for you? Got a helper?"

"Nobody. Just me. Too risky. Too complicated to bring someone else in to help. Not sure anybody would believe me, and not sure there is anybody I'd trust enough to help me anyway," Bob confessed, and for the first time the word struck him. That is in fact what they were getting from him, a confession. Maybe he should have a lawyer he thought, but it didn't really matter now anyway. Nonetheless, he would be a bit more careful with his comments.

"What's it look like?" Miloc asked. If these things did exist, he wanted them off the street now. He didn't want them out there any more than he wanted to let Bob Mcleod leave the building. But he could have a search warrant in an hour and confiscate the devices even if his boss wouldn't let him charge Mcleod and keep him more than twenty-four hours.

"Like a small vacuum cleaner really. Small enough to carry in one hand. Got a keypad on top and a fan vent looking thing on the front. Pretty benign looking device for being so powerful. Each one has a sticker of Thor holding his hammer alongside the keypad. Thor was the god of thunder, and the devices are called Thor's Hammers. Kind of symbolic," Bob explained without bringing Doc into the equation. He didn't want to have any stink on Doc Auster if this all went bad and Bob realized it could go really bad if either of the three of them took the wrong course of action. There would be time for Doc Auster to get credit when credit was being given, and that would be much later.

"I need a break, that Coke got me already," Miloc suggested. "Professor, you need the restroom or are you good?"

"I'm fine. But I could use some water, your guys picked me up at lunch time and breakfast is wearing thin," Bob confessed. There was that word again, Bob worried that he was becoming too comfortable in the discussion but it was hard not to reveal the work he was so proud of. Indeed…hard not to brag of his technical and financial accomplishments, especially over such a short time.

"We'll be back in a few minutes. You want me to get you a Snickers or something?" Miloc asked Mcleod.

"Sure, that'd be great. They took all my stuff before they brought me up here, I don't have any money," Bob replied.

"You can owe me, you're the millionaire," Miloc said as he left the room.

Bob didn't feel like a millionaire, he felt like a cornered cat and he didn't like the feeling. He had to keep reminding himself that he was still the subject of a criminal investigation but these guys were really good and Bob could tell. It made him believe they knew much more that they were telling him. He thought they had all they needed and that is why both agencies had their best guys on him. Mcleod would have been disappointed if he knew exactly how much of an accident the events that led to this session in room #3 really were.

As Miloc and Relltin walked down the corridor, they stopped at the third door and Miloc went right in and closed the door almost before Relltin was through it.

"Boss," he began, "We picked up that Professor, weather guy at the University who we thought was laundering dope money for some druggies, remember? He's the same guy the OSI at the base called about 'cause they thought he had some forecasting techniques they wanted. Well, he claims he can change the weather and that's how he made the money. Boss, this is weird, but we both believe him. He said he built four machines, little ones, that he does this with and they are at his house. I need a search warrant and a couple guys to go through his place to find them and bring them in here. I don't want to ask him for permission 'cause, if we have to spring him, I want them confiscated and not on loan from him. You got to go with me on this one boss. I'll bet my badge I'm right," Miloc said it all in one breath so his boss would hear him out.

"You that sure?" was all the response the senior agent could muster.

"Yes boss. A search warrant to get anything that looks like a small vacuum cleaner with a keypad on it. Can carry it in one hand he said. There should be four of them but make sure you get however many there are. He could be lying about the number," Miloc added.

"You want the OSI and that weather guy who made the original call?" the senior agent suggested.

"Great, that'd be good to get them up here. I want to keep this guy for the full 24 hours to wear him down and get as much as we can before we charge him with anything. We got enough for a felony hold but I don't want to play that yet; got a lot more to learn.

"Done. I'll let you know when we got the place searched. You better be wrong Miloc; if you're not, we're all gonna wish you were. Get it done."

"He's not wrong," Relltin added as they walked out the door. He considered what had just transpired and was keenly aware of just how much pull—make that respect—Miloc must have in his department for his supervisor to take him at his word on such a bizarre exploit as this. He was also aware of how much Miloc had just put on the line in his boss's office. That also meant he, too, was taking a great risk; he was just as convinced as Miloc when they walked into the room to resume their questioning of Professor Robert Mcleod. "So, Professor, tell me how this contraption works again. I am not sure I really understood it very well the first time through," he stated for effect. More to get Bob talking again, get him frustrated if possible, and look for loopholes in his story. Bob was wearing down a bit, and the idea of starting over again was supposed to get him a little more hurried and less cautious in the construct and perpetuation of this seemingly unbelievable story he was trying to sell the two agents.

Bob was not convinced the two agents believed him. In fact, by now he was relatively sure they were simply humoring him until they decided what to do with him. In their absence, Bob seriously considered calling a lawyer and keeping quiet for the foreseeable future but he dismissed that strategy after some analysis. He had already given them the truth and to dummy up or backtrack now would only serve to cast further doubt upon his claims. The effect he knew could be catastrophic. What he needed to do was get an opportunity to prove what he was saying...to actually demonstrate to his captors his ability so they would no longer doubt his story. He would be hard pressed to do anything from jail serving time for theft, embezzlement, money laundering, insider trading, or any of the other charges they could levy upon him at any time. Indeed, if he went to jail, there is no telling what would happen to the devices in his home. They may be confiscated then conveniently lost or discarded. Perhaps stolen from his home while he awaited trial, after all they looked valuable, and technology is easy to pawn even if you don't know what you have. Worse yet, someone could actually discover their use. He had already told the agents and they could do a lot of damage to people, property and even the reputations of both himself and Doc Auster. There was too much at stake to let some amateurs get their hands on these things, especially since Bob knew only how to make and use the devices by following the diagrams he recovered from Doc's files.

Professor Mcleod still didn't know all the concepts, theory, and mechanics of *why* the device performed its magic on the environment. There was still much research to do and many things to discover, refine, and exploit. The scientific ramifications in chemical and synthetic energy production alone were of the greatest magnitude. Life as we know it today could be changed forever and what Bob did in the next few hours would have a telling impact on how the future could play out. The weight of the situation did not escape him. He had known for some time the potential of the capability he had possessed just a few short hours before. He also knew that the longer he stayed where he was the worse his chances of getting the devices back or safely cached would become. He chastised himself for not storing them in a more secure location than the hall closet of his home and for not recognizing the situation he was in sooner. He rationalized he had more time but should have taken more drastic measures after the first visit from the IRS agents. This could have been avoided, and he knew it. He vowed not to make the same mistake again if he ever got the opportunity but, at this point, the chances of that looked pretty slim.

"Look," Bob offered, "if you didn't get it the first time you won't get it the next time. I can't make it any simpler. I can explain it to you but I can't understand it for you. I know you don't believe my words. I find myself not believing them sometimes but I swear to you they are true. I don't expect you to take my word for it. Let me show you."

Miloc looked surprised and glanced over to Relltin who was still standing near the doorway of interrogation room three, "Well, Professor, how do you suggest we go about this little demonstration. I want to believe you, but I have to admit, if I took this to my boss without some proof, he'd probably put me on leave of absence pending the results of my psych-eval."

Relltin grinned at the hypocrisy and added, "Yeah, well, I already think you're nuts even entertaining this story and I don't mind telling you both that. If it were up to me, I'd be filing charges right now." A good dose of tough guy, bad cop for the professor should keep him moving in the right direction he thought.

"Let me show you that it works. Take me to my house to get my equipment and I can prove to you I can change the weather. You can even pick what you want me to do, make it warmer, colder, windy, whatever, within reason of course," Bob suggested again.

Relltin jumped in, "Sure, take you to your home where you got something stashed or booby-trapped to kill me and my men allowing you to escape. Maybe your boss already knows we got you rolled up and you're expecting a rescue attempt. Escape in transit or something. I am insulted that you think I am such a dummy. I'm still not a professor like you but I am still not stupid. Do I look stupid to you, Miloc? Professor still thinks I'm stupid. Take the *I am stupid* sign off my forehead so he can quit wasting our time. Maybe you're stupid, and the Professor is just getting us confused but I know I'm not stupid."

Miloc offered a compromise, "Let me have someone go get your equipment and you can show us right here. How would that do for you Professor?"

"All right," Bob conceded. "Bring my equipment to me but we can't do the demonstration here. We will need some open space, and a relatively secluded area to operate. This capability should not be revealed to the general public for some time. Those are the conditions that must be met, they are non-negotiable." Bob worried that he had pushed too hard with that comment.

"Not negotiable? Do you really think you are in a position to be making demands, Professor Mcleod?" Miloc replied in a sincere tone to Bob's unspoken concern right on cue.

"No, Agent Miloc, I am not making demands," Bob quibbled. "I am only establishing the conditions I need to properly prove my story. You are the ones who will be disappointed and look bad if it doesn't work. You don't believe me now, so I have nothing to lose at this point and everything to gain. I want you to see this work and prove I am telling the truth. I want it to work and I need those conditions to make it work. It's up to you," he concluded.

"Let us go see what we can do. But it will probably take a while...several hours I suspect to put this together. We cannot release you during that time, you understand. While we have not yet charged you with a crime Professor, that possibility still exists and the probability of it coming true is very high. Stay here and think about that Professor," Agent Miloc's words were harsh and true and Bob recognized them as both. He leaned back in his chair and took a deep breath, recognizing his thirst again. He was extremely thirsty and began to value the simple freedom of getting up and getting a drink when he was thirsty. That and many other freedoms would be taken away from him if he failed to convince these guys his story was legitimate.

The phone rang late in the evening, and Sgt. Andies picked up quickly, "Weather, can I help you, Sir?"

The voice on the other end was loud and hurried, and Andies knew he would be in for a long night. He quickly called home and told his wife he would not be home for a while...maybe several days and hung up. She didn't like the short notice absences, but in today's military she was all too familiar with such calls. An immediate phone call to Captain Lessur followed. "Sir, I'm glad I got you. This is your lucky day," he began to explain, "I just got off the phone with an agent in charge of a Federal Investigation. He said they are looking into the case the OSI contacted them about. He wants someone from the OSI and the weather office to come down to the Federal building as soon as possible. Captain, they want us to listen to their questioning and help them with some technical questions and answers from a guy they are questioning!"

"Great! I hope they got something on this guy," Lessur proceeded enthusiastically. "I need to call the DO and get permission or he'll kill me. Stand by, and I'll call you back as soon as I can," he instructed the anxious master sergeant.

"Yes, yes sir, that is what he said. Come down as soon as possible to provide technical consultation during the ongoing questioning of someone they have in custody. Sir, it's our guy, I just know it is and I know we can help," the captain nearly pleaded with the DO.

"All right, but you wait for me there and do not, I repeat do not, participate until the OSI commander, the JAG and I are all there to hold your hand, Captain. Is that clear? This is more for your sake than ours, you be sure to stand by until I arrive and that is a direct order so make no mistake, understand?" Colonel Lincoln's demeanor left no doubt in the captain's military mind.

"Roger, Sir, will wait for your lead. See you there." Captain Lessur hung up and dialed the weather station, "Andies, meet me there, but don't talk to anyone on site until me and the DO, JAG, and OSI guys get there. Just call the Agent and tell him we are on our way then get your tail in gear and get down there."

In the evidence room lay a pile of electronic gadgetry that would make any electronics technician smile. The search of Professor Mcleod's home turned up all kinds of small vacuum sized things and lots of stuff with keyboards. Each item was tagged and inventoried...forty-six in all, including computers, calculators, and an assortment of electronic gadgetry that included the four Thor's Hammers. The search was quick, thorough, and productive. It seemed the search was the only thing to meet those criteria in today's events.

The military lawyer was the last to arrive at the Federal building. After a brief discussion, Colonel Lincoln, the DO spoke to the lead agent who called, "I am Colonel Lincoln, the operations officer for the Wing. This is Lieutenant Colonel Otto the Judge Advocate General, Major Naed from our Office of Special Investigations, Captain Lessur and Master Sergeant Andies from our weather office. Now, how can we help you?"

The group was led to the interrogation room #3 observation deck, where they could see Professor Mcleod sitting alone in the room below them. Miloc and Relltin entering through the doorway to the observation deck right on cue and began to address the group.

"Gentlemen, I am Agent Miloc, FBI. This is Agent Relltin, IRS. We have detained the man you see there, Professor Robert Mcleod, for questioning on a variety of charges. We have not charged him yet because he brings us a truly unbelievable story. That is where you come in. We think he may be telling us the truth and we need your help. He claims to be able to control the weather. Actually, he said he can change the weather and has made a small fortune doing it in the past few weeks. We do know he has actually made a fortune from almost nothing in just a few weeks but we need to ascertain how he did it. If he *can* change the weather, we probably don't have a case against him. Enter you guys. You contacted us a few weeks ago with an off the wall concern that someone was doing just this kind of thing. I don't believe in coincidences so help me understand this situation folks."

Captain Lessur spoke quickly, "If I may Sir?" Colonel Lincoln nodded approvingly, "We, Sergeant Andies and I, are both weathermen and had noticed several significant weather events in our area of operations recently. The problem was they were completely un-forecasted because they should never have occurred. The meteorological situation would not allow such events to take place naturally. The big freeze awhile back, and the thunderstorms that destroyed the gas reserves were two of the most noticeable. I asked a friend to look into some stuff and he came up with lots of electronic indicators that Professor Mcleod was possibly involved. That is when we called you." The captain noticed Colonel Lincoln's eyebrows raise as he realized it was the first time he had heard of JP's involvement. Although Lessur was careful not to use his name, he knew JP would get called on this and hoped the damage would be contained to just a good butt chewing from Lincoln although he knew it could be a lot worse in a big hurry if this got formal and ugly.

"So, you already think this guy can change the weather, Captain?" Miloc asked somewhat surprised, "Got anything to substantiate that...any proof?"

"Yes. I mean no proof but I think he can do something we can't. If it is changing the weather, it would solve a lot of mysteries for us. It makes sense regardless of how hard it is to believe. I'm surprised myself when I say this, but it is the most logical explanation," Lessur said unconvincingly.

"Well, he has offered to prove it to us and we want to let him give it a try," Relltin confessed. "We need your help to let him do just that. He claims that, with his equipment and a large open *isolated* area, he can prove his story by showing us that he can change the weather. Even offered to let us pick the things we want to see changed. Our problems are several. First, we are not sure what to ask him to do. And second, we don't have ready access to a place that is large enough and remote enough, but also secure enough, to meet his demands. We think we have all the equipment he claims to need, but I need some help. Time is on his side, and we can only legally hold him for about 14 more hours without charging him. I don't want to do that unless I have to. So, I got about half a day to get him to show us something and it'll probably have to be in the dark."

Colonel Lincoln looked at the JAG and offered a course of action for the group's consideration, "We have an isolation facility we use for exercises on the northern edge of our live-fire range. It is a secure facility, isolated and not scheduled for use until the end of next month. Tom, can we offer that facility and the use of the people in this room to help out?"

"Yes Sir," Lieutenant Colonel Otto replied. "It is uncommon to use military facilities for criminal investigations, but if we consider it a joint case with OSI then we should be on solid ground in doing it."

Colonel Lincoln hated the legalese but needed to make sure everyone was protected here. So, he looked over to Major Naed, "OSI in this investigation now?" he inquired in more of a challenge than a question.

"We're in, Sir," came the reply.

"I'll get the facility and security set up. Lessur and Andies you're with the agents, Otto you too. You guys work transportation, use your helos if you want to move quickly. Let me know and I'll approve the air space in the restricted military areas for you. Naed you work with them to get them to and in the isolation facility," Colonel Lincoln feigned a smile. "Sorry fella's this is your show. I'm used to making things happen not waiting for instructions. Your call," he invited.

"Like the colonel said, make it happen. Let's get the Professor down to get his gear, and move everyone out there. I want to be in place for our first strategy session and then a discussion with Mcleod in three hours. That should give everyone time to save the world twice enroute. Let's go." Miloc led the way out the door.

Bob stood as the agent entered the room. "Let's go get your gadgets Professor Mcleod, you have a show to do." Relltin led Bob to the evidence room where he was surprised to see his belongings spread out over several tables. "Point to what you need, and we will transport it to the test site," he instructed. Bob immediately stepped toward the table and felt a strong grip on his forearm, "Just point, don't touch or we open a new can of worms Professor. Don't mess with me now." His words were as cold and calculated as his stare. Bob knew he could and would back up those words and was a bit surprised at Relltin's paranoia. Then it occurred to Bob that he could use the Thor's Hammer twenty different ways to provide an opportunity to escape and he understood Relltin's challenge and concern. Bob complied and pointed out a laptop computer, and the four Thor's Hammers. He was not going to mess with them or mess up what he knew would be his only opportunity to prove himself. *No chances today my friend, we will save all our risk taking for another time* he thought to himself. Unfortunately, that time would come much too soon for Professor Robert Mcleod.

As they loaded him into the helicopter, Bob felt severe humiliation and he wondered if it would ever pass. Handcuffed, he made his way up the step into the helicopter and moved toward the seat with the floor shackles awaiting him. As he was secured, he wondered how much worse he would be treated if he somehow failed to convince them of his story, like if the devices were damaged in the search or in transit or if they failed for some unknown reason. Lack of preparation was not the least of many possible reasons for failure, including outright fear. He was about to go on trial of sorts without ever being charged with anything. His future depended on this demonstration and he was doing it without legal representation. The thoughts kept coming to him but he pushed them aside. A man who has done nothing illegal shouldn't need a lawyer he believed and he was one to act as he believed right. He may regret it later he thought but that would be later if it ever came. Right now, he had to concentrate on what he needed to do to show them he was telling the truth, and still be able to generate some phenomena to cover his escape if necessary.

Relltin, Miloc, Lessur, Andies, and Otto were in the second helicopter trying to discuss their next actions over the sound of the rotor blades moving them closer to the isolation facility on the Army range. "It's already dark. If he can change the weather, what do you think we should ask him to do for us, Captain?" Miloc strained his voice, the door was open and the cool air was rushing over them, whipping through the cabin of the helicopter.

"Wind is the safest, I think. Have him give us a twenty-knot wind from the Northeast. The wind should be from the Southwest at about six knots tonight. Have him give us that wind for fifteen minutes then turn it off. If he can do that, he's probably legit. Then let's get him to make us a thunderstorm. Should be none tonight so the only one around will be his. He claims he did the one that hit the gas storage areas; so, he ought to be able to do a thunderstorm with lots of lightning for us. We'll be able to see the lightning and feel the rain even if it is dark. Even a big thunderstorm probably won't hurt anything out there and we can get a good idea of what this guy can actually do with his stuff." Lessur was beaming with anticipation, this is the kind of stuff he relished.

He was an oddball for his career field in the military. He thrived on excitement, challenge, risk. Most meteorologists in the Air Force are the scientific minded, type B personality, detail oriented, analytical. Lessur was a double-A personality, outgoing, doer, not a studier and he was looking dead into the eyes of an opportunity to do something that may have tremendous ramifications to the service...maybe even the world. He looked over at Andies and grinned. They were both eating this stuff up; each realizing that, at a minimum, they had regained both the confidence and respect of their DO. They were asked to participate in a Federal Investigation based largely on the things they had taken so much grief over the past several weeks. The DO had personally set up the help and they were both in the thick of it all. At a minimum they were in the game and having fun. The best-case scenario included making history and they both knew it. They all knew it and it scared them...to the person it scared them.

What if this guy really could change the weather like he said he could? The possibilities were endless. Professor Robert Mcleod could easily find himself the richest, most powerful man in the world. What weapon could you possibly use to counter the forces of nature unleashed upon you in a controlled, orchestrated attack? That thought had occurred to Colonel Lincoln, too, and inwardly he was horrified at the potential if the capability did exist. He was afraid, if it did, that even the mighty United States military would be unable to match the forces of nature in an all-out battle, especially if the enemy was as malicious as some of the international terrorist organizations which existed today. Colonel Lincoln had a lot to do and a lot to think about as his helicopter screamed toward the isolation facility to link up with the rest of the group.

CHAPTER SIX

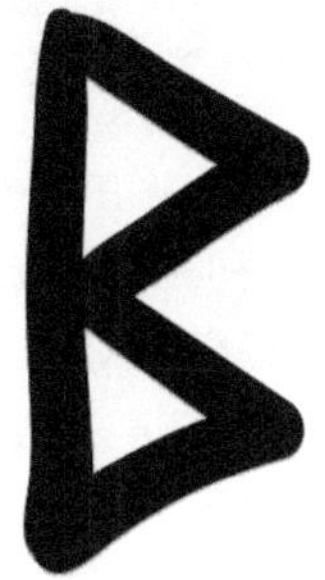

DEMO'S ARE US

Just before 2200 the last helicopter, carrying the investigation team set down at the helipad and it's passengers dismounted. They were met by Major Naed, the OSI officer and led to the mission planning area where he had Bob's equipment in the weapons storage facility in the east corner of the building. "The Professor is in the commander's office with two FBI prisoner transport guards inside, and two at the door. The compound is secured by a 10-man, armed security force on the gate and perimeter, three of my guys are roving patrol inside the wire. The county Sheriff's office has been notified of an exercise so they do not come snooping around. That's all I've gotten to so far," he concluded.

"Good job," Colonel Lincoln began. "Gentlemen, we have restricted airspace for twenty-five nautical miles in all directions until tomorrow at 1000. We have clearance from the Wing Commander to assist with the investigation for now, but it has gone no further than that. I don't want any more exposure on this than is absolutely necessary and, for now, that means the people in this room. Agent Miloc, I'm asking you for this as a condition of our participation. Agreed?" Once again, Lincoln was not really asking but Miloc knew he was also right again. He liked the man's attitude and he appreciated the man's ability to deliver on what he says.

He agreed and nodded for the colonel to continue. "I have secure radios and night vision devices for everyone. That's all I have...Agent Miloc?"

"Thank you, Colonel, it looks like we are in good shape then. Security, communications, wide-open area, isolation, and authority to proceed. That about covers everything for now. Your Captain Lessur suggests we have Mcleod do winds first to see if he's just blowing smoke up our skirts or not. Bad pun was intended gentlemen," Miloc grinned but all in the room could sense the seriousness of the situation and the poorly timed joke was not going to carry the agent. He continued, "Okay, we get him to gin up a Northeast wind at twenty knots and see what he can do. If he succeeds, we get him to give us a thunderstorm...see the lightning and feel the rain. Dark or not, night vision or not we'll know what we are dealing with by then. I am extremely concerned about executing this little test. If he can change the weather, I don't want him hitting us all with lightning or something and escaping. Be alert and be watching him. There is no telling what type of plan he has, who is involved or even what we may have inadvertently disrupted by picking him up today. Let's get this right the first-time people because I don't know if we'll get a second chance with this guy. He has time on his side if he decides to clam up and wait us out and I don't want to find myself in that position. Everybody clear? Let's get to it then." Miloc and Relltin followed Major Naed to the office where the guards were holding Bob and followed him into the room. It was Miloc who was running the investigation, the FBI had the lead and the IRS was supporting with Relltin as their only agent for now. Miloc started the conversation.

"Professor Mcleod, we have transported your equipment here, and it is ready for you. We are at a remote site on the Army's training range. We have a twenty-five-mile radius closed off to air and ground traffic, with the obvious exception of a security force for your protection, until 10:00 a.m. tomorrow. I am prepared to give you the opportunity you requested, but it is conditional. The terms of the condition are these: A. You demonstrate to us your ability without injuring or endangering yourself or anyone else in the area. B. The same goes for property, don't break anything, Professor. C. You don't use your equipment in a threatening manner, or an attempt to escape or secure your own release. My terms are also non-negotiable and, if you cross me professor…if you violate my terms, I will assume you are lying to me. I swear to you, I will prosecute you and with what we already have and you will go to prison. I will destroy everything we took from your house in our search and I will make it my personal business to see to it that you never get a chance to screw with anybody again. Your funds will be confiscated and you will be sunk. Not threats Professor Mcleod; just the way I do business. Do you accept my terms or do we call it a day and just head back to the city?" Miloc finished his oration six inches from Bob Mcleod, right in his face and Relltin admired the way his new Federal law enforcement companion had just ensured the complete cooperation of the Professor. He could see it in his eyes before Bob even began to speak.

Bob could tell, once again, that the agents were taking him seriously. He wasn't exactly sure what they knew but he could tell that Miloc's speech was from the heart, coldly sincere and Bob Mcleod didn't want any part of Special Agent Miloc on a personal vendetta against him. He made a mental note to try to get him on his side after all this was over. Miloc was the kind of guy you wanted on your team and not working against you. Bob sat uneasy for a moment before he responded, more for effect than anything else because he knew by now his nonverbal uneasiness had sent a clear signal to the agents that the message they were sending was received loud and clear.

"I'll do it just like you tell me to Agent Miloc. I agree to your terms, and you have granted me mine. Let's get to it then, shall we? I am getting extremely hungry." Bob thought the remark would add an increased sense of urgency, but instead drew a chuckle from the two agents.

"You guys didn't bring any pizza, did you? We'd all probably do better on a full stomach, maybe they keep some beans out here, MRE's or something?" Relltin was quizzing the OSI officer who scurried off immediately checking for some sort of chow as he too was pretty hungry. A case of MRE's, meals-ready-to-eat, were brought over and they all sat around the planning table as the pouches were pitched to the men. Bob was uncuffed and brought over to eat with the rest of the men. Relltin wanted to build a little rapport before the test to see what came about.

As Bob joined the crowd, Captain Lessur asked of him, "Professor, how does it work? How do you do it, change the weather I mean?"

Bob was a little uneasy with the mixed crew of military and law enforcement and gave the captain a good looking over as he began to open his MRE, trying to decide how to respond to the young man.

"Excuse me," Lessur corrected himself, "I am Captain Lessur, Sir. I run the weather office here for both the Air Force and Army missions. I am a meteorologist by trade. This is Master Sergeant Andies; he is my best forecaster. I'm curious, Sir; how do you do it?" Both Colonel Lincoln and Agent Miloc decided not to curtail the young captain's ambitious questioning of their subject and all waited to see how Bob would respond.

After examining the contents of the MRE and deciding the Bar-B-Q Pork with rice sounded pretty good, Bob opened the green envelope, took a bite and looked up at the young man to reply, "It is a complex process broken down into simple tasks. The machine does all the work, I simply make the inputs. Have you seen it, the device I mean?"

"No Sir, not yet," Lessur responded, his disappointment evident in his tone.

Bob quickly picked up where he left off, oblivious to the rest of his audience, pleased to have someone with a glimpse of weather background to finally be able to discuss his achievement. He knew to be careful what he said but he was already giving them everything so he wasn't worried too much about anything other than contradicting his own story. He remembered the words of Mark Twain, who said, "If you always tell the truth you don't have to remember anything." He hoped they would hold true again today as he continued on for the captain, "The device is built to send energy pulses through the atmosphere, in just the right amplitude and frequency, to incite the desired phenomena. I input the instructions through the keyboard and the software does the work.

The device fires until the desired activity level is reached, then continues or terminates the activity based on operator input. The device itself is very complex, very delicate, with *sensitive* components. Hope they weren't damaged in transit." Bob shot a glance over to Agent Miloc just to introduce the concept in case there was a problem with his first attempt.

"What is the governing principle that enables you to modify a variety of conditions with the same device Sir? How does it produce the end result?" Sergeant Andies question was right to the meat of the matter. He was an excellent weatherman, forecaster, and meteorologist. There is a subtle but important distinction between the three. That he didn't have a degree was never a hinderance to Andies. His practical experience and passion for the science far exceeded anything formal schooling could have provided him. He was capable of teaching almost any topic in the weather curriculum and was justifiably proud of his expertise. Many a military operation succeeded because he was putting out the forecast, and many a time those conducting the operation requested him by name when others were already there to do the job. He was very good. Key people in operations knew it and they made sure he knew they knew.

"Fair question Sergeant Andies," Bob smiled. "Right down to business then; it seems the best explanation is kinematics. Added energy changes the temperature, which in turn affects the pressure. From here you can effect changes in moisture, vapor pressure, and this induces ionic charges. The frequencies and durations can be tuned in complex patterns to trigger and quell the molecular changes and produce the desired conditions. All these atmospheric properties are changing concurrently but, by synchronizing each incremental change, one can produce a selected outcome from any set of starting conditions. A lot of math and relative solutions to get the proper algorithms in synch and off you go. I have simplified the explanation for our purposes here but you appear to be able to follow the concept," Bob complimented the NCO. "For the rest of you, it's a lot like individual musicians and instruments playing in an orchestra. Alone they are just okay but working together they can be amazing. They just need the right music, timing and conductor," he grinned.

"How do you control the scale, the magnitude of the event or the change?" Andies continued as he took another bite of his dehydrated peaches.

"The strength and speed of the energy bursts determine the distance and duration of the modification, and thus the scale and intensity of the event. It's a combination of synchronizing laser and X-ray bursts that allow you to focus the appropriate energy at the right intervals. Fascinatingly simple really once you see it in action," Bob was stretching it here. He believed that was the process, but he himself was not yet certain. It may not have been nearly that simple, and he hadn't cracked all the codes yet on the inner workings of the Thor's Hammer but credibility was a must right now. He didn't think either of the two weathermen in the room could argue enough theory to prove him wrong and, even if they could, something had to be responsible for the events he was about to demonstrate for them. For now, anyway, he was still the expert in the room and everyone needed to believe that, including himself. Master Sergeant Andies seemed satisfied for now with his answer. He at least had enough to consider the possibilities.

Bob paused to eat some more of his MRE, which wasn't as bad as he expected. Under the circumstances he was feeling pretty good about a lot of stuff, eating included. He looked over as Miloc asked him again, "Who has been working with you on this project, Professor? Who else knows what this thing can do, or how it works?"

Bob's reply was sharp, "Nobody. I told you before, I am working alone on this. I picked up some important information from Doctor Auster's research after he died. He really deserves the credit; without his research I would have never gotten this done." He was trying to give some credit where it was due, but Miloc made a note to check into Doc's death and the work he did. If this really worked, it could certainly be motive enough for a murder. He decided now was not the time or place to pursue that line of questioning, and noticed Relltin picked up on it too. He really liked this IRS guy.

"It seems I am doing all the talking here; I better eat up. Colonel, what do we have around here, where are we? I didn't get too good a view on the flight in, a lot of dark is about all I could see," Bob posed the question to the—up to this point—quiet senior military officer in the room.

Colonel Lincoln's reply was subdued, "Nothing but low rolling hills and lots of trees Professor. Not much else. Lots of unexploded ordinance on the range from years of use, misfires and such. Nobody looking and nobody listening, just like you requested. What do you say we get started?"

"Okay by me. Agent Miloc are you ready?" Bob inquired.

"Let's do this. But here is what we are going to do," Miloc continued, "Professor we are going to do this in a crawl, walk, run approach. I need you to do some winds for me. You said that you did that for the balloon and boat races right? Can you give me twenty knots from the Northeast for fifteen minutes?"

"I can do that," Bob claimed matter-of-factly. "I just need my equipment."

"Does it matter which one? Are they all the same?" Captain Lessur asked

"They are all the same, just bring whichever one you like, Captain, and we will give it a go," Bob replied, needing to keep his confidence—both actual and perceived—as high as possible. He was about to begin a new chapter in the history books.

The group exited the isolation facility and entered the cool night air. It was fairly still, and stars were numerous in the clear night sky. *A beautiful night for a demonstration of weather modification* Bob thought hopefully. As they stood on the concrete helicopter parking pad, they could make out Captain Lessur and one of the escort guards making their way toward the group. Captain Lessur handed the device to Bob and immediately offered to help. Bob explained as he went, "First, we check the power supply. It is almost self-sustaining. Good, fully charged. Then the startup sequence, which is fairly complicated, you type in S-T-A-R-T."

Bob smiled, not really visible to the crowd, but Lessur saw the glimmer of his teeth and returned the gesture.

"It will tell you when it is ready, the display will change from W-A-I-T to R-E-A-D-Y. Good, now it's ready. I make my inputs," Bob stated as he typed quickly into the keypad. He wasn't ready to reveal the input codes, nor explain Doc's simple recipe system to the audience just yet. There would be time for that later and he hurried past the sequence hoping the omission would go unnoticed; it did not.

"What are the input parameters?" Captain Lessur asked somewhat hurt by the hurried entry. "What do you type in to set the desired outcome?"

"That is fairly complex; I will explain it later. For now, let's just see if we can make it work," Bob sounded demeaning. Although unintentional, it was taken that way.

"I usually set the device on the roof of my truck at this point; I suppose out of convention more than any real operational need. Can I set it here on the ground, in the open area?" Bob requested.

All around were a bit nervous at his request. *Why set the device down now? Was it unsafe to handle? Should they take cover? What was in store?* they all wondered silently.

"It's not dangerous, just works better on a stable platform. The output is more precise. I'm standing here with you. All that will happen is we'll pick up a Northeast wind for fifteen minutes," Bob tried to comfort the crowd as he walked farther out onto the pad and placed the device on the ground pointing to the North. "Wait a few minutes and you'll get your wind. Mind if I sit down?" Bob inquired as he sat down on the cold concrete about thirty feet from Thor's Hammer. He faced the Northeast and waited to feel the wind to pick up against his skin. He didn't have to wait long and was elated to feel the breeze coming from its new direction, increasing intensity until it was steady at twenty.

"Good Lord above, protect us all," Colonel Lincoln said softly. The group exchanged apprehensive glances as they witnessed the twenty-knot wind, sustained from the Northeast continue for several minutes. Relltin was the first to speak to the smiling Professor Mcleod.

"Well Professor, it seems you have succeeded in impressing us all. I may start to believe what you've been telling me. You really did this? What else can you do with that thing? What *can't* you do with it?" he asked with escalating concern in his voice.

Bob addressed the group, "Gentlemen, in about eight minutes the winds will subside and return to their natural flow, likely from the Southwest. Hopefully seeing is believing and I have shown you just enough to gain some credibility. I'm not making this story up, it's real. Let me show you some more so you're convinced. How about..." he was interrupted in mid-sentence.

"A thunderstorm, a weak one, but a thunderstorm. I want to see rain and lightning, Professor. You show us a thunderstorm over that field, just like you did a few weeks ago. All by itself, stationary, pop up, sit there, and die down. That was you a few weeks ago just west of where we are now, wasn't it?" Captain Lessur was persistent, excited, and exuberant about what he was participating in right now.

"Yeah, that was me," Bob submitted as he remembered the lone individual in the Hummer driving out on the dirt road, "was that you in the Hummer racing around out there, Captain?"

"Yes, it was. I was looking for you. I knew someone had to be doing this. Andy and I both knew it was artificial and I went looking for the source. And now here we all are. Can you do the thunderstorm Professor?" he asked in an almost challenging tone which did not go unnoticed by Colonel Lincoln.

"Yes, I can. I'll do twenty-seven-thousand-foot top. Given the conditions Master Sergeant Andies, do you agree we should get some decent rain, a little lightning, but won't get out of control? Don't want to mess with any aviation by going too big. Don't need the undue attention now do we?"

Bob consulted no one in particular. He went over and picked up Thor's Hammer, entered the proper recipe and sat back down waiting for the cloud to develop. "Take about ten minutes to get it going. Relax, you'll know when you're about to get wet. It will build up and dissipate naturally, according to normal physical laws. The device simply acts as a catalyst to the desired event. Kinda kick starts mother nature really. Should last about forty minutes if that's okay with everyone," Bob concluded. "Let's watch, shall we?" he said almost smugly, hoping he hadn't come across too cocky.

"What had you hoped to accomplish by building this device?" The voice was Colonel Lincoln's, and Bob was surprised by the somber demeanor with which he asked the question. Bob silently considered the question as he mentally reviewed the chronology of discovering the Doc's research and cracking the code, testing the device, then building his own. He never really sat and contemplated an end state for the device and its power. The immediate needs were always financial and that is about as far as he had considered to this point, with the exception of his day in the meadow where he satisfied his urge to help something...to bestow the gift of rain from the sky to aid the thirsting meadow. Bob didn't have a good answer for the colonel but it was a good question.

"Well, Sir, honestly, I never gave it too much thought, really. A lot has happened to me in the recent past and I have spent most of my time getting the devices to work, building and testing them to make sure they do what I tell them to do. I had to make some money to buy the stuff to build them, and I guess I spent the majority of my time focusing on the immediate needs...the near term. I don't think I did anything illegal, but maybe you all think I did. I don't know. I do know this capability has a place in the history books but I don't know yet what that chapter should say. I didn't get much past my midpoint analysis before our friends here decided to make a federal case out of my activities. What do you think Sir? What should I do with it?" Bob inquired almost relieved to have asked the question as he watched the cloud continue to grow both vertically and horizontally. Before their very eyes the group was seeing the birth of a cloud, that was growing into a rain shower that would grow into a thunderstorm. They knew they would not be disappointed; they knew Bob Mcleod was for real. They were witnessing history firsthand and they knew it.

"I am not sure what you should do, but I know what you should *not* do," Colonel Lincoln responded. "You must not advertise this capability. This must not become known in a haphazard way. This capability must be protected, at least for the time being. Gentlemen, you all came out here under the agreement of cooperation and security. I must insist that we discuss at length what to do next. The ramifications of this capability are extremely serious. Look up at that storm building before you. The ability to create the weather of your choosing is a weapon of enormous potential. In the wrong hands, this could threaten our very security as a nation. Render our weapon systems or defenses ineffective. For now, we must treat this device as a weapon and we must keep this weapon a secret."

Miloc suddenly became very uneasy as he recognized the corner the colonel had neatly painted him into...and very smoothly he thought. Great place, great condition, certainly military home court advantage to keep this thing under wraps regardless of the status of an ongoing Federal investigation. The rain began to fall slowly onto the small group standing out on the helicopter landing pad. As it increased, so did their acceptance of the fact that Professor Robert Mcleod's invention had complicated their lives beyond their wildest dreams. They would be involved in this from now on whether they wanted to be or not. They were about to write history, and it seemed like at least the first chapter in this story was going to be classified, for now anyhow.

As the lightning began to flash from the growing thunderstorm outside, the group looked at each other as they rejoined inside the isolation facility. The thunder clapped loudly as the rain fell faster against the metal rooftop of the building. Bob smiled a satisfied smile as he looked at the expressions on their faces. It was as though creation itself was the art they were appreciating but he knew it was not the creation of the storm and its application which held the power, rather it was deciding when, where, and how to apply the weather that made this such a powerful thing. The very thought of being able to summon up the wind itself, the rain, the heat and the cold to serve one's own purpose was mind numbing. Colonel Lincoln was right, in the hands of an enemy this power could be used for terror…to dominate through fear and by force. What force could a nation call upon to battle the searing heat, flooding, or cold? They could not counterattack such a force with a conventional military force. Getting to the person controlling the device would be the only effective counter-measure to such an offensive. Controlling the device or its operator would be the only way to counter. That meant him. At least for now, that meant only him. Professor Robert Mcleod had just become public enemy number one without ever displaying any malicious intent whatsoever.

Bob had cooperated and demonstrated his willingness to do what they asked of him. For the first time he felt threatened. At this point in time, this could all go away by destroying the devices and eliminating their source, him. As simple as that, the problem, the *threat*, would cease to exist. No more to worry about except the people in the room and they were few enough to ensure cooperative silence which, even if broken, would be impossible to prove without him. The feeling was unnatural to Bob. He had never been a threat to anyone before—except perhaps Hugh Durbin—but now he felt like a threat to all mankind. A threat and an opportunity…both perspectives carried a heavy weight and Mcleod was starting to feel that weight pulling at him as a crack of thunder brought his mind back to the immediate tasks at hand.

Miloc broke the silence, "Well Professor Mcleod, congratulations. It appears you have shown us twice this evening that you can indeed change the weather as you said. I still don't understand how or why, but that doesn't really matter right now. What does matter to all of us is what we do next. Honestly, gentlemen, I am open to suggestions. I agree with Colonel Lincoln that we need to keep this quiet for now, but we can't all stay here forever either."

Relltin piped up, "If we believe you did get your money from investing and not drug dealing, or stealing from the University, then we may be in good shape, legally. I don't know of any laws prohibiting the use of lightning around natural gas storage facilities but we could probably come up with a way to charge you with something like felony vandalism, or arson, if you confessed to intentionally destroying that facility...which you have not actually confessed to yet. Did you want to confess that to us now, Professor, so we have something to charge you with...or would you rather say nothing and be released without charges at this time?"

"Given the choice, as I understand it, I believe I'd just as soon be released without charges being filed because there is nothing for me to confess to," Bob responded.

"Fine, then. As long as you pay your taxes on your financial gains on time, the IRS has no further need to continue its investigation into this matter. Agent Miloc, without a confession of a crime, does the FBI wish to continue its investigation of the Professor at this time?" Relltin continued.

"No, not at this time. The FBI does not intend to press charges at this time, nor do we see the need to continue our investigation. Apparently, no federal laws have been violated in this case," Miloc cautiously followed Relltin's lead.

"Well then," he continued, "I suppose that leaves it up to the military. I think our investigation is just about completed, no crimes to prosecute at this time. However, we do have the sticky wicket of national security to deal with; now, don't we? Colonel, I think you guys probably ought to take it from here, don't you?"

"Yes, Agent Relltin, I suppose you are correct. It would appear that we should take the lead in dealing with this situation. Do I understand correctly that Professor Mcleod is no longer under Federal investigation, and that you will no longer be detaining him for any alleged criminal activity?" the colonel pursued.

"That is correct Sir, but should you feel the need to detain Professor Mcleod in the interest of national security, we may assist your troops until we are relieved, if you desire. This is a military installation, and federal agents are required to assist in law enforcement duties of military officers, if requested, in the execution of their lawful duty," Relltin finished.

"Okay, so now I am passed over to the military? Your time is almost up and you're not going to charge me with something you cannot prove, unless you figure a way to prove it later. So, in the interest of national security, the military can detain me for how long? I still have my civil rights, don't I?" Bob wasn't very happy with this good-news bad-news situation.

"Indefinitely, we can detain you indefinitely if we need to Professor. It's rare, but it can be done. We need to keep you and your devices under wraps for a while to figure out what to do next. As for you two, I appreciate your situation, but how quiet can you keep this?" the colonel asked the two agents.

"Quiet as mice until you tell us otherwise. I can eat a little crow with my boss, and the rest of the transport agents will either be quiet or unemployed. It will stay mum until you break the story, however long that takes," Miloc assured the colonel, and Lincoln believed him.

There was lots to do, but nobody really knew where to start. Colonel Lincoln was the senior officer on the scene and he knew the lead was his, and he knew they were about to embark into uncharted territory. His primary concerns were to protect the information they had—at least contain it—and not break any laws. The first was an area he was familiar with; he'd had lots of special operations experience and many of the missions he had participated in were still classified. The legal part was outside his comfort zone, though, and what he did know about the laws seemed very difficult to apply to this set of circumstances. After all, even the law enforcement guys were stepping out of this tar baby. It was going to be tricky and they knew it. He decided to start with what he knew. "All right, here's what we are going to do," Lincoln boomed so there was no doubt he was driving the train. Confident in tone and demeanor he continued, "Everybody might as well get comfortable cause we are going to stay here for at least a few days. OSI, get on the horn and set up around the clock security, tight, single-entry point, armed patrols.

The only people in are people I clear; the only people out are those under my personal escort. That starts right now. Have them arrange four-meal chow for the whole crew, including us. Naed get to it."

The colonel scanned the room as the OSI officer headed for the secure phone. "There's a dorm across the sidewalk with bunks and showers, probably not much else, but make do. We'll get some flight suits and towels and stuff sent out so you don't have to go home for uniforms or such. You can each call your wife or family, if you need to, and tell them you'll be out of town for a week or so. I guarantee it will be the truth. No mention of where, what, or why. If you'd rather I do it for you, just let me know. It's late, everybody get squared away with those things and get a bunk and some rest. In the morning, we'll start fresh. I know it'll be hard to sleep but do it anyway; you're all gonna need the rest. Professor Mcleod, Sir, I would like you to stay with me this evening. We have some things we must discuss. The handcuffs can go with you guys. Now, Agent Miloc, I cannot stress to you enough how important it is that you and your people keep a lid on this. It is against my better judgment to let anyone leave but I'll take you at your word. You have been extremely professional; I have been very impressed with you and your team. Please maintain that for me. I know how to reach you, and I may need you but, for now, you and your team are cleared to go. And Thanks," he concluded sincerely.

"Agent Miloc. I have a favor to ask you," Bob spoke as the agents were headed towards the door. "Since it looks like I might be gone from my home even longer now, would you please have someone stop to feed and water my dog. It's been a while now and you guys have already been through my home. I'd hate for the poor guy to get hurt in all of this. His name is Buck."

"Sure, Professor. We'll take care of him," Miloc nodded, and he and his crew headed for the door. He couldn't help but wonder what they would do next. He didn't want to leave, but knew it was the right thing to do. He still had a mission to do with respect to this case which he had just blown wide open. It seemed to go against all his training but keeping it quiet was the easy part of what had to happen next and he knew it. He and his team would do their part. He turned at the doorway, "Good luck gentlemen, and I'll be seeing you. God speed." As he walked into the night, the sky clearing as the recent thunderstorm gave way to the otherwise cool, starry night. He felt a deep chill which he knew wasn't from the cold air.

As the agents left the isolation facility, Colonel Lincoln took a look at the remaining people in the room. The two weathermen, the JAG, the security detail, and the professor each looked at the colonel awaiting their instructions, "Professor, please come with me. The rest of you, make your calls and get some rest. We'll meet in here for breakfast at 0730. Questions? Good then, goodnight gentlemen and thanks for your help."

Colonel Lincoln led the professor over to the kitchen area and grabbed a couple of coffee cups, handing one to Bob. "Black?" he suggested as he offered to pour some of the strong brew into Bob's cup.

"Fine, Colonel. Black is fine. How much of this are you not telling me? Sir, I gotta admit I am getting more than a little worried about how this whole thing is starting to go here," Bob expressed himself a bit more openly than he'd really wanted to but he was really worried he'd be stuck out here for a long time, or maybe worse.

"Frank, Professor, my name is Frank, please. We need to discuss some things tonight that we will both tell stories about for many years. I'd just as soon be as informal as possible if that suits you?" Colonel Lincoln offered.

"Okay. Works for me, Frank. Please call me Bob. I prefer it to Professor every day of the week," Bob reciprocated. He could spot sincerity and differentiate it from a load of crap and Bob could tell this man was smart. He could sense the colonel was a man of honor and was willing to let him prove it.

"All right, Bob. I'll get straight to it. We have a serious problem here. I want to help out as much as I can, but I gotta tell you that very soon this will be out of my hands. The brass, and I mean the big guns, Chairman of the Joint Chiefs, Secretary of Defense, those kinds of big guns are going to be involved in this almost immediately. CIA, everybody is going to want a piece of what you can do with those things. I want to help you get out of this in one piece. Hopefully, you'll accomplish something you set out to do when you built these things. Bob, do you know the magnitude of what you possess?" Colonel Frank Lincoln asked.

"No Sir, I do not. I don't think anybody can understand the magnitude of what could happen with these things. I can change the weather to anything I want, whenever I want. The opportunities are limitless," Bob appeared to be defending himself a bit with his answer.

"Opportunity, Bob, if viewed from a positive seat. Threat or weapon, if viewed from a negative seat. I will tell you that perspective matters and so does the perception of your intentions. I don't know how much thought you have given this, but you may have invented the most powerful weapon on the planet...the most awesome offensive arsenal in the world. A weapon to economically ruin entire regions of the world. Destroy property, rearrange the entire geography of the world perhaps. Governments, businesses, militaries, farmers, terrorists, utility companies, the list of people and motives for wanting this capability is endless. If you haven't given this matter much thought, we need to decide pretty quickly what we're going to do here, Bob."

The words were strong but true. Everybody could think of a way to use this to their advantage but it's destructive potential had not really sunk in until this very moment. Bob sat quietly and let his mind race through the virtually unlimited negative possibilities he knew existed somewhere but had avoided considering until now. The idea of a terrorist using it to strike fear into the hearts of the innocent...for an enemy of the United States to use it against Bob's own land...these were unthinkable outcomes that Bob Mcleod considered unacceptable if they were ever perceived as possible. Bob wondered if Doc had foreseen such applications of his work. He wondered if they contributed to the air of secrecy that Doc had maintained. Perhaps he knew all the time that mankind was not ready for the purely peaceful application of this device for the common good.

Competition, power, and fame are driving, motivating forces difficult, if not impossible, for some to overcome. Bob wondered if that is why Doc had such a strong friendship with his priest. If Father Gannon had perhaps known all along of Doc's work. What if he did? Had he thought it best to let his secret work die with the Doc? Bob found himself wishing he knew the answers to these questions, wishing Father Gannon was there to ask. It wasn't an issue of whether Bob would do good or bad. He had already decided to use the device as a positive force. The issue was really how to keep others from being able to apply the power in a negative way, or for negative purposes. *But who decided what was good and what was negative?* Did Bob have the right, or the expertise to declare one need or desire more valid than another? Did anybody have the right to do that? Who could decide such matters? Right now, it was Bob Mcleod and Frank Lincoln setting the stage for just those decisions and Bob felt woefully under-qualified for the task at hand.

"Frank, I know I don't want this used as a weapon against my country. Against anyone for that matter. I don't want it used as an offensive weapon by anyone's military or government. You are right, lots of people could use this to do a lot of bad stuff. Flood, freeze, or burn up crops; Defeat radar systems; break stuff with hail, winds, or even tornadoes; interrupt commerce; regional stability...I got the picture. I don't want any of that, but how do we prevent such negative things and still accomplish the positive? Enhance agriculture; improve forestry; fisheries and harness energy. We could feed and fuel the world in a few short years if we all work together at it, I suppose, but I don't think mankind has it in 'em right now for all that stuff. The competitive advantage and the almighty dollar run the show right now. Sure, there would be a seat at the big table for the man controlling the weather but there is no telling how it would turn out if only one man knew the deal. That's a problem for me, isn't it? I'd be target number one for everybody's collective defense? But, if I tell everyone how to use it, then there is no real way to prevent an all-out weather war when conflicting desires cannot be negotiated. We are between the proverbial rock and a hard place aren't we, Frank?" Bob concluded without really expecting a reply.

"Well, it's going to be a little worse than that for you, Bob. As long as you are around, whether the devices are destroyed or not, there is always the risk that you will make another one. Then we start all over again. There is also the risk that someone gets to you and, whether you want them to or not, gets the technology from you. Proliferating this type of technology is a very real threat to everyone. That is how most governments, militaries, and power-seeking organization will see this once they know it exists," Frank warned the professor.

"You mean, if they destroy the devices and kill me, they eliminate the threat...to the best of their ability anyway. Eliminating the opponent's potential offense becomes the best defense. Holding onto the secret could backfire, so the best weapon is no weapon at all?" Bob submitted the theory to see if they were singing from the same sheet of music.

"That is indeed one course of action. But there are certainly others and those are the ones we need to concentrate on right now. I learned a long time ago to *plan for the worst, prepare for the most likely, and hope for the best.* We have three ranges of options. I think we should focus on finding something that lets us use these things for what they can do without giving the bad guys something to hold over our heads. I sure don't know what that is but we need to find it Professor, and soon." Colonel Frank Lincoln looked concerned, he was worried, and Bob could tell. "Let's get some rest and go after this in the morning. That's only a few hours away so try to get at least a little sleep Bob. We are all going to need it... especially you."

There was very little sleeping done in the few hours before breakfast. They were marred by fitful sleep, as Bob Mcleod tossed and turned thinking about the events of the day and worrying about things to come. He was tired, dog-tired, but relieved in the knowledge that he was no longer in this thing alone. That same relief was a source of concern, as well. Now he had more people involved than he had previously hoped. He was fairly sure Relltin and Miloc would hold up their end...at least for a few days if not longer. Sooner or later one of them or, more likely, the transport agents would begin to talk. At a minimum this would draw undue attention so Bob expected the relief from the Federal agencies to be temporary at best. He was equally concerned with the players that were not yet in the game, especially the CIA. Bob cringed inside when Colonel Lincoln predicted their involvement but he knew Frank was right about everything they discussed last night. And, more importantly, he was shooting straight with Bob. He could tell and he admired the colonel for that. He was certainly in a tough situation, too, and Bob appreciated his candor and honest assessments. If there was one person in this that Bob thought he could trust it was Colonel Frank Lincoln.

There was another person Bob thought he could trust but he wasn't involved in this just yet and Bob wanted desperately to bring him in now. Despite his desire, Bob knew it would be best to keep Father Gannon clear of the situation for now. He could be very helpful perhaps but later in the scenario if it started to turn sour for Professor Mcleod. If things went bad, he would need some help on the outside and Father Gannon was the only one Bob could think of to go to in a hurry. He wasn't sure what the priest could—or even would—do for him but it was a comfort just knowing he had an option to try if everything here turned south and Bob had to make a run for the hills. He hoped it would never come to that but he remembered Frank's point that *hope is not a course of action* and he was beginning to think about some pretty unattractive options some of the evil players could decide for him.

It was the colonel, himself, who interrupted Bob's fitful solitude by tossing a green flight suit and a bag of toiletries, a towel, some socks, underwear and boots onto the floor next to the bed. "Time to get to it Bob; breakfast in fifteen minutes. Grab a shower, get dressed and I'll see you for chow. Got a busy day coming up. My boss will be out here by 0930 and he is bringing lots of questions. We'll go from there. Welcome to the Air Force, Professor Mcleod." Bob could only manage a grunt as he rolled out of the stiff bunk, collected his gear, and headed for the latrine area. He was not very pleased when he realized there was no hot water but the cold shower really washed away the grogginess and kicked his brain into gear despite how tired he felt. Everyone was already seated and talking when Bob got to breakfast. They sat on both sides of a long table and the seat at its head awaited the professor. A simple but adequate breakfast of cereal, some fruit and bagels, hot coffee and milk was set up on the counter with a pile of scrambled egg MRE's.

The chatter quieted when Bob walked into the area and Colonel Lincoln gestured for him to sit at the head of the table. That made him a bit uneasy but he took the chair and sat down, greeting them all with a hearty "Good morning, everyone," as the colonel poured him a cup of coffee from the pot at the table.

Captain Lessur spoke first, "Professor Mcleod, I was wondering, how big of an area can you affect with only one device? And, can you use them together to affect a larger area, kind of like in tandem or something?"

"I don't know really," Bob replied honestly. "I have never really had the opportunity to measure the total area effectiveness of the devices. I do know that the first time I used it I affected the entire area of my sensors —nearly the entire state actually—for only one parameter, though. I don't know if multiple parameters decrease the effective range or not."

"Would that have been an unexpected wind or cold snap by chance Professor?" Sergeant Andies inquired, remembering the first couple of mysterious missed forecasts which prompted him and the entire senior staff to doubt his forecasting skills.

"Yes, in fact they were two of the first events I did. I suppose they did get the attention of quite a few folks around here, though that was certainly not my intention. The first event was a dense fog, and that covered an extensive area," Bob said somewhat apologetically.

Colonel Lincoln decided to focus the conversation on the tasks of the present and future since they would have time to discuss the past when there was more past available to them all. "Bob, you said earlier you are the only one who knows about the capabilities of your new technology. Aside from the people who were out here yesterday, is there anyone else? This is very important, so take your time thinking about it." The words came across like a warning and, though they weren't intended to be threatening, they accurately conveyed the seriousness of the colonel's question.

"No, I'm it. Nobody else knows as far as I am aware. I never told anyone. But you guys found me out so I suppose someone else could have. I really doubt it," Bob said truthfully, and he had already decided not to tip his hand concerning Father Gannon. He might know from his relationship with Doc but Bob didn't really think so and he wasn't going to get him involved in this right now anyway.

"Well then, there are a few things we need to attend to this morning," Colonel Lincoln continued. "I intend to stay here for at least a few days while the bureaucracy works itself into a tizzy about the whole affair. We will keep this area and this information at the top-secret level. You are not authorized to discuss this with anyone...period. Only the people in this room and only using secure communications with each other if we do anything electronic. Bob, we need another localized demonstration for the general this morning. The wind thing worked pretty well last night. Let's start with that. No thunderstorm today; we don't need the attention from anyone right now. Captain Lessur, Sergeant Andies, put your heads together with Professor Mcleod to come up with a few more low-profile ideas to show the old man when he gets here. The last thing we need is for our little show of proof to him to get fouled up. He'll think we all flipped out. You've got about an hour to get it together and get back to me on what you plan to show us.

"Major Naed, I need to see you right after this to get some security stuff in line. I want non-disclosure statements from everyone, I want the JAG to review them, and I want some legal leg-work on weather modification. Formal treaties, international agreements, laws, whatever could apply to what we are doing here. We are going to need all this stuff fast gentlemen. So, get it on; the clock has already started. Questions?"

There were none as the men bolted for the doors to get cracking on their tasks. Frank was pleased that everyone was eager and focused. He was equally pleased that a reasonable plan came from his mouth this morning because when he started talking, he wasn't sure what he was going to say. He'd always had the gift of thinking on his feet. Analyze the problem, check your resources, evaluate your options, pick a course of action, and implement. The process seemed to work no matter what the subject matter and he had been able to recognize and hone his skills in that area for some time now. His superiors recognized his talents too, as the colonel was already promoted ahead of his peers and on a fast track to making at least his first star. He knew, if he handled this well, there could be a few more in his future. That was the least of his concerns and he knew it. There was too much to do and a lot more at stake than anybody's career. This group was lucky to have a man of integrity and honor at the helm right now.

Bob began thinking about what the colonel had said as soon as it came out of his mouth. What if he had nothing to show the old man? What if he denied the whole thing to the general? What if he claimed the whole thing was a scam or that he was kidnapped and the whole thing was a conspiracy, a hoax, and he was no longer willing to play along? The idea had half a chance of working and it was about all Bob could come up with to try to get out of this situation before it got too ugly. The thoughts raced through his mind for a few moments as they walked into one of the briefing rooms to try to figure out what to show the general in less than two hours. Bob dismissed the idea after considering the risks to his improving credibility and the slim chance of actually discrediting his new colonel friend. No, Bob decided earlier to shoot straight on this deal and, even though it was getting tough to do, he knew he must finish what he started. Even though it appeared to be much more difficult than he originally believed. No, he needed to work a real solution to this real problem. This was no game and it would be disastrous to begin to treat it like one. He needed to shoot straight and get the important, powerful people on his side, and he needed that right away. He needed to start with the general this morning. He needed to get started on what to show him.

"Well Captain, what do you think we can do to impress your general?" Bob asked politely. He knew he was not too popular with the two weathermen and this was his opportunity to make it right. "If my work has somehow caused you some discredit, I apologize. I hope you weren't hurt by it in any way. If there is a way to get you back in his good graces just say the word. We'll do what you think will impress him the most. What do you suppose that would be?" Bob asked.

"Seeing is believing. But with this stuff feeling is even better. I think the wind direction and speed of his choosing. A localized temperature change, up or down; he gets to pick. And, since three is the charm in most cases, let's make the man whatever kind of cloud he wants. However big, however high, however he wants it. Can you do that Professor?" Sergeant Andies asked. "That will make a believer out of the old man and trust me, you need him on your side. He's a fighter and if he's for you then you'll win. If he's against you, then you will lose. It doesn't get any simpler than that, Sir."

"I can do that. I know I can show him that. Then we can talk about the rest and give him whatever kind of show he needs. Those are simple recipes and they don't take too long either." Bob cringed inside and reprimanded himself for using the word recipe.

He'd hoped they wouldn't ask him to explain the input codes and it seemed he had just handed them the perfect opportunity to bring up the issue. Both weathermen looked at each other, noticing the clue they'd just been given but not being too sure what to do with it. Captain Lessur decided there would be time to pursue that when there was more time. Right now, they had the general inbound and they needed to get ready. "What are we going to need to pull this off, Professor?"

"Well, I suggest we set all of my devices out for him to look at. Get a feel for the size and transportability of the things. Then let him pick one and we'll use that one for the first demonstration...the wind. Let him pick direction and speed. Then go from there to the temperature and, if we still need to, next we'll do the cloud of his choice. If that's not enough then I give him a thunderstorm he won't soon forget. Does that still sound okay to you guys? You are the experts on this guy," Bob responded quickly, hoping to put some time and distance between his previous recipe comment.

"Yes, I think that will do the job. Let's pitch it to the colonel so we can get a decision and start setting it up." Captain Lessur led the way out to find Colonel Lincoln.

As they entered the room, Colonel Lincoln was just hanging up the secure telephone and motioned them to continue in and have a seat. "What do you guys have?" he asked the group. The colonel nodded approvingly as Captain Lessur proposed the course of action they developed earlier in the morning.

"Looks like a beautiful morning out here; I kinda hate to mess with it. Sounds like a good plan...escalating intensity as required. Good. The old man will come in this building first. We'll all sit around the table and give him the story. I want him to get the whole story...and complete, concise answers to all his questions. Once we're ready to stop talking and start showing, we take him out that door over to the helipad. Then, Bob, it's up to you. Take the lead and explain each demo to him as you're doing it. Don't get ahead of yourself but keep it moving, too. If you don't have any questions, then get your gear set up and get ready. If you have a chance grab an MRE or something for later because we may be with him for quite a while today," the colonel advised the three.

"Sir, what happens after we water the general's eyes?" It was Sergeant Andies looking ahead and hoping the colonel would give him some insight as to what they could expect. He knew better than to expect the boss to explain it to them, but he was hoping for some kind of vector to posture for. He was disappointed.

"That's going to be up to the general. Let's focus on the task at hand for right now. Get to it gentlemen," he instructed and they all complied, each wondering the same thing. What would the old man do? What would he have them do? There were so many possibilities that there was no point entertaining them anymore. They set off to gather up the Thor's Hammers from the weapons storage area and get them in place for the demonstration.

By 0920 they were assembled in the large area of the isolation facility that had become their informal operations center. It was the room they met in the first night and they were sticking with its positive aura for the general's visit. They settled into their places as the helicopter's engines were shutting down. Colonel Lincoln waited for the general to emerge from the door of the Blackhawk. He greeted him with a sharp salute and a smile as the two-star stepped down to the pavement. The general returned the gesture and stretched out his hand to greet the colonel. They had worked together earlier in their careers and Frank was glad to have been selected by him, by name for his current assignment. He enjoyed working for someone he respected, and continued to learn from. Major General Peters was a great mentor and a friend to Frank. He was glad it was General Peters who got the first crack at this dilemma. Frank knew he was a level-headed problem solver, politically astute but a true warrior. That is exactly the mix they needed to lead them through this maze of potential disasters.

The room was called to attention as the general entered, and he quickly put them at ease and waved them back into their seats. He walked directly to the man he didn't recognize but could tell by his hair and beard was obviously not in the military. "Professor Mcleod?" he boomed, the voice was deep and fit the six-foot heavy framed man from which it came.

"Yes, General, I am Professor Mcleod. Bob Mcleod, Sir." Bob hoped he came across okay as he shook the general's hand.

"Bob, I am Major General Jim Peters and I command the post here. I know it may be kind of confusing having an Army two star and an Air Force colonel in your business but we'll need to work through that. I understand you have quite an amazing new technology to show me today. Frank tells me you can make the weather do whatever you program into your gadget. Bob, I gotta tell you I need to see that for myself. But, if you can—and I'll bet you can—then we got a lot of issues to work through very quickly. I hope we can do that collectively, and cooperatively. I apologize for having to detain you even this long but I know Frank has already explained why we must. I also know that you all have had an exhausting past 36 hours and I appreciate all the work the whole team has put in. So now I am going to sit down, shut up and let you continue. Frank?" The general moved to the head of the table as Colonel Lincoln stepped up to the small briefing area at the front of the open room.

"General Peters, you are here because Professor Mcleod has developed a way to modify the weather on-demand, Sir. By entering a code into the device you see on the table, Bob can affect any atmospheric parameter. Intensity, duration, and spatial resolution can be controlled, adjusted, or terminated by the device operator. The Feds have terminated their investigation and for now are quiet but eight of them did see the first demonstration and know what Professor Mcleod's device can do. The FBI lead agent and an IRS agent are the two running the civilian show. They are the ones who brought us in and we ended up here. The only folks that know what's up out here are the folks inside this wire. Sir, I think it best that we let you drive the discussion from here. Bob has assured me this was a solo project and nobody else knows that he can do this. The technology is only documented on his computers and in his head, and the devices are all out here with us...Sir?" Colonel Lincoln concluded, passing the lead to the general.

"Thanks, Frank. Bob, I already know this is an amazing feat you have accomplished, my congratulations on achieving what can only be described as an historic accomplishment. But there are many things we must concern ourselves with regarding this capability. Let's have a look at what you set up to show me and then we can take it from there. Do you have any questions for me right now, Bob?" the general asked in an encouraging tone.

"No Sir. If you step over to the table, you can have a look at the devices I have built. They are the same and they have all been tested to varying degrees. So far, they all perform properly and I believe are safe to operate. Yesterday I showed the folks here a wind event, a temperature change, and then a small thunderstorm. Prior to that, I have accomplished similar events over both large and small areas. General Peters, I gotta tell you, I don't think there is any event I cannot initiate from my device. But I haven't done them all yet. Deep freezes, blazing hot, rain for weeks on end, flooding, drought, winds from whatever direction for however long...everything we know in terms of atmospherics can be initiated, sustained or terminated from this device.

"The potential good is overwhelming. Ending world hunger, sustaining solar or wind energy sources, ending pollution...just some of the possibilities. And there is, of course, the other side. The side I don't want to see like weapons, terror, the whole offensive use for political gain. I know these are weighty issues, Sir, but I want you to know I am aware they exist. My desires and goals in showing you this capability today are so we can eliminate or minimize the negative uses and apply this capability to the positive. This was developed to do good for mankind not to be a weapon for a single government. There is still a lot I don't know about the long term or counter effects generated by using the devices.

"Sir, I want your word you'll help me do good with these. I need your word on that. We can't go any further without it. I believe you and Frank are both men who will stand by their word. Men of honor who can be trusted. Well General, I am in a position where trusting is going to get pretty tough to do pretty quick. So, if you are inclined to promise me your help, then we'll get to the demo and figure this out. But, if your inclination or motivation is weaponizing these for the US and using them as military and political bargaining chips, then we are going to have some problems. I ask you to be as honest with me up front as I have been with you all already. I just need to know, and honestly Sir, I need to know now."

Bob surprised himself with the oration, but he meant it. He knew it was long overdue for him to vocalize the thoughts that he harbored but never really dealt with before. He was glad that he had waited until now to voice them to the group. He could tell by the general's face that his comments had made the impression he had hoped for. The general's reply confirmed what Bob read in his eyes and on his face. He could tell it wasn't simply because he'd hoped to see it, the agreement was genuine in word and expression.

"Bob, you have my word. You may not know that the military man is the most peace-loving man in the world. He loves peace, hopes and prays for it daily whether he recognizes it or not. After all, we are the select few who must fight the battles for the masses. We love our country and freedoms enough to fight to the death for them if called upon to do that. But our hope is to never reach that point. Our families, friends, and countrymen should share that hope. I am glad to see you share that view with us. We can work together; on that I promise you. Now let's see what you can make this thing do out here." The general gestured for Bob to lead the way outside. Bob suddenly felt good about the situation, as if a big burden had been lifted from his shoulders. As he headed for the table of Thor's Hammers his confidence began to build and, once General Peters selected one, they headed out to the helipad for demonstrations.

It only took twenty minutes to complete the wind and temperature demos for the general. There was not much discussion during the shows really. Everyone was focused on the events, and the magnitude of what they were witnessing was sobering; each person contemplating some variation of the outcome they were building together. General Peters indicated that he needed no more convincing and motioned to the others to follow him back inside.

As they began to settle back into their seats, General Peters excused them to take care of whatever they needed to and invited them to return in half an hour. He wanted a chance to talk privately with Bob and asked Frank to stay as well. Once the room cleared, he addressed the two remaining men, "Guys, we got a hell of a thing here. Like you said earlier, there's a lot of good and bad thrown in here, but I think we can pull this together. It's too late to bury it. Too many people already know about it and, even if we wanted to keep it quiet, the Feds would eventually come at us from some angle. Not a good plan at all. I think we take it right to the Chairman and the Secretary. Sorry Bob, the Chairman of the Joint Chiefs of Staff and the Secretary of Defense. I think we should also have the Secretary of State there too. We get a vector and then we'll end up doing the same kind of thing for the President and a few others. The crowd will be small but very powerful. Initially it will feel like *death by demo* but it won't take too long to get you set up in a lab, refining your processes and devices while the administration decides on a strategic course of action on how to utilize and proliferate this capability."

"There is going to be a lot of high-level help on how this gets done in the interest of national defense and economic stability, Professor. You understand that, Bob? I don't believe you and I will have autonomy on what to do with this. But for quite a while you will be in the driver's seat. That is, as long as you are the only one who knows how to make this work or how to build another one. Don't be cocky about it but remember they only need you as long as they need what you can do for them. If someone else can do it cheaper, faster, or more to their liking, then you are no longer an asset. We just need to be sure you don't turn into a liability. Are you okay with all this so far, Bob?"

"Yes Sir, and I appreciate your candor. Well, the sooner we start the sooner we get to the good parts. I'll be ready when you are, just tell me what to do and where to be," Bob conceded his appreciation and support. It felt strangely like surrendering to a friend but he knew he had just made a powerful ally and that is exactly what he needed right now. It felt good and it reminded Bob how long it had been since he'd felt good about anything.

It was just that simple really. General Peters left the room for a private spot with a secure telephone as his executive officer got busy dialing phone numbers at the Pentagon. Others began to mil back into the main briefing area eager to learn what the old man had said. Time began to crawl along for the team members outside the room where the general, his executive officer, and Colonel Lincoln were talking among each other and on the secure phones. Forty minutes seemed like forty days to the folks standing by but that's how long it took for the three to emerge from their private session. The general approached Bob and said, "We are on for tonight, 2230 local, right here with the Chairman and the

Secretary of Defense. They want to wait to bring anyone else in just yet. Besides, the Secretary of State is overseas and won't be back until next week. We'll see how it goes here, discuss the impacts, then go from there. They are blocking some time to brief the President tomorrow afternoon on their recommendations. Folks, I don't have to tell you what the ramifications of this capability could be. You've all had time to stew over that already. I want you to do the same thing tonight that you did for me this morning. I also want you to look at the weather forecast and plan something that is completely contradictory just to hammer home the point. Be a little conservative but get the point across. Frank, I'll leave that up to you to figure out.

"We don't need a hurricane or anything to bring a lot of attention, but something the Chairman can impress the President with in his debrief. Gentlemen, you've done an outstanding job so far. Now you've got some more work to do. I expect results just as good as you've provided already. Frank, I'll see you all again this evening. Right now, you've all provided me with a lot of work as well. So, I'm going to get to that. Does anyone have any questions for me?" The question was more of a formality than a request for inquiries, but Bob spoke up.

"General, are we moving too fast? I mean, those are some heavy hitters right up front." Bob was justifiably intimidated, and it showed.

The general recognized his concern but focused, "Professor Mcleod, this is heavy stuff you have brought to our corner of the world, Sir. It demands the immediate attention of our nation's leadership. And our nation's role in the world order demands we deal with this issue from both national and global perspectives. Security, economic, and political systems can—indeed will—be affected by this technology. Bob, big stuff gets big attention in a big hurry. Right now this looks like the biggest thing since electricity. Let's keep our perspective folks. This is important stuff. Anything else? Good. Gentlemen get to work and I will see you all this evening." He turned and left the room. Both he and his executive officer climbed into the readied helicopter and the entire team watched them take off and disappear over the treetops.

"Gentlemen grab some chow. We will rally back here in forty minutes to plan for tonight. Professor, stick with me please. We'll talk while we eat." Colonel Lincoln wasn't sure how Bob was going to handle the situations he was about to face so this was going to be a pep talk.

The team just stood there in disbelief. How could the colonel think about eating? The general just told us to get ready to impress the Chairman of the Joint Chiefs of Staff and the Secretary of Defense so they could prepare to impress the President of the United States! Captain Lessur looked at Sergeant Andies whose eyes were as big as saucers. "The Chairman and the Secretary will be here tonight for a demonstration of your new technology, Professor. They are going to brief the President tomorrow. Holy cow, welcome to the big leagues, Professor Mcleod. You are the man now. I guess you are about to help decide what kind of country my kids will be growing up in. Let's do it right, okay?" Captain Lessur cheered the group on as he began to grasp the gravity of General Peter's words. The visit, the immediate reaction, the lightning response from the Pentagon...these things were not commonplace in the world in which the men in the room dwelled. Sure, they appeared routine to the Washington insider but even Colonel Lincoln, who had a fair amount of time inside the beltway as well as the rings of the Pentagon, was impressed with the attention and speed of the senior leaders. They either understood or feared the magnitude of the issue if it proved to be true. Frank hoped—for everyone's sake—they feared it more than they thought they understood it.

"Gentlemen, if you don't chow now, you will miss your only opportunity to eat before tonight's demo. Now get to it we've got lots to do. Bob, how about a chicken and rice MRE? I'm buying!" Frank gestured for the Professor to follow him into his temporary office. The same area where he and General Peters had spent their time on the phone setting up tonight's activities.

CHAPTER SEVEN

THE HEAVY HITTERS

S it down, Bob," Frank said as he closed the door behind him. "I'll get you that MRE in a minute but first I want to make sure you are okay with all this. I know we are moving out fast, and we have the attention of some key leaders tonight. We need to have this level of attention, Bob, if we are going to deal effectively with this technology. There is a lot of good that will come from using your devices but, to make the good a reality, we have to prevent the bad from overshadowing it—from taking over. We can't do that with just the people on this compound, Bob; you know that. We need a lot more help and a lot more stuff than we have here. The way to make that happen is to get the big guns in the game. We talked about that before and now it's happening. I just don't want you to be overwhelmed by this. These guys are just men like you and me. They hold high positions in our government but they are just men, Bob. You with me on that?"

"Yeah, thanks. I know but I thought I'd be the one to pick the time and the place and the conditions when I revealed this gift. The further we go with this the more it appears to me that I am the commodity. I don't seem to have a say in it anymore and I am not comfortable with that Frank. I don't mean with you or General Peters, or anyone else...not individually. In fact, you both have been great and I appreciate your help.

But I am talking about the circumstance, the process, the conditions. The military...the government...the President for crying out loud! We are talking about the United States' position on weather modification and its influence on the global economy and balance of power. I was not exactly prepared for those kinds of words when I went to work three days ago and now they are all that I can think about because that is everyone's focus. We need to remember that it is more than that. This technology, as you guys keep calling it, is a great thing for mankind and we need to keep the good of the world in our plan as we push through this process.

"This is not a military technology developed for the Pentagon. This is a capability to enhance the lives of everyone in the world. That is the perspective I want everyone to keep. It is great that the US is in a position to lead that effort. In fact, no other country is anywhere close to being able to do it better and that is super. But I need their help, not their permission Frank. What I am looking for here is their assistance in doing this the right way. I am not looking for their decisions on whether I can do this or not. I don't mean that to sound threatening or anything but I won't be bullied about who will benefit from this either," Bob concluded with a questioning look to Frank as he digested the comments.

Bob was surprised at himself, once again, by the conviction with which he spoke those words. He was beginning to appreciate what Doc must have thought through long and hard during his time as the only person knowing about Thor's Hammer. Doc Auster probably had all the answers, had a plan, had everything all worked out and written down somewhere. Bob never saw it though and he looked everywhere.

No, Bob knew better now. No one could have a plan for how to spring this technology, this capability onto the world and all its occupants. Nobody could have devised a plan to please each government and their people on what they could have and what they would have to sacrifice for the common good. Not Bob, not Doc Auster, not anyone. He knew that now, and he understood why Doc had kept the secret to himself. He didn't know how long Doc had known how to change the weather, but he believed he now knew why he hadn't told anyone about it. It was *too* scary and it was *too* dangerous. Bob had to face his fears now, as well as, the danger. He wished he could talk to the Doc right now to see if he had any good ideas about what he was going to have to do tonight. Bob was used to not getting his wishes but he was starting to get pretty good at hope, and *that* was fairly new to him.

Bob found himself thinking about Father Gannon again. He wondered if Doc had been searching for answers, guidance, help or something of the sort from his priest. Could that be part of the reason they were good friends? Part of why he spent so much time there taking care of things. It was possible. If Doc was having as much trouble thinking about possible scenarios for applying his work as Bob was having right now, he may very well have consulted his spiritual leader and friend for guidance. Bob decided he could not rule out the possibility that Father Gannon did know about the device and its capability. He made another mental note to visit Father Gannon at the earliest opportunity. Right now, he had to concern himself with the gaggle of national leaders who were coming to visit him at their earliest opportunity.

"Bob, I have to tell you, I still think it will take some time to work through this," Frank tried to address the Professor's worries. "The ramifications are global as you know. But I don't think anyone is looking to tell you what you can or can't do with this technology. I believe the greatest concern we all share is that it gets used in a positive manner rather than negative one. And that is going to take some time to ensure. That is how we are viewing this, Bob. We need some time to prepare and proactively establish some conditions that will preclude anyone from using this against us or anyone else. Time to evaluate potential threats and develop effective counter measures to ensure any would-be enemies don't use this as a weapon against us. That is what we are talking about, Bob...not permission to do good. Am I on the right track here?" Frank concluded.

"Sure Frank. But how will you ever get to what you are looking for? How can you possibly develop an effective countermeasure against the force of nature's most violent activities? Tornadoes? Drought? Flooding? Winds?

It won't happen. We both know the threat is from the user not the technology or the device itself. You would have to eliminate bad will in the world to do what you are suggesting. It's like guns. Guns serve a useful purpose in society. For protection, deterrence or something even simpler like hunting or target shooting. Their presence enables protection because they help deter people from doing bad things to others they believe may also have a gun. Simply because they might be armed there is hesitation, not because the gun is there, but because the person holding the gun may decide to use it to kill you."

"The gun is the instrument, but the person is the issue here. Will they use it on another human being in self-defense? Probably so, if they were sufficiently threatened. That is what we are talking about here Frank in the defensive role. But guns also have the offensive application many people choose. They abuse the positive by accentuating the negative. Use guns to murder, rob, or maim for some gain or just a perverse sort of sport or fun. It is not the gun that kills for pleasure it is the twisted person using it for a twisted purpose. You know the old saying, *guns don't kill people, people kill people?* That is what we are talking about here. You can't take that out of everyone and then use the device for the common good because someone declares the threat is gone and the all-clear has been sounded.

"This technology has to be used in order to sound the all-clear and maybe people will see that they can all have the things they need; that they no longer need to use the negative side of things to get what they want. That is the difference. We may be talking about the same end state but I think our courses of getting there may be extremely different right now Frank. I don't want to keep this a secret until mankind has fundamentally changed. No, I want to get this out to the world so we can fundamentally change mankind." Bob was now standing, upright, and making his newly articulated views known to the colonel. Once again Bob found himself taking a passionate view on something that just came from within, something he hadn't ever consciously considered or spoken before now.

For a moment he felt inspired as if by some great force...perhaps by God himself intervening. Bob knew they were really his own words and thoughts though. He had been suppressing these weighty issues for some time but they were always there in his subconscious throughout his work on Thor's Hammer. He knew, eventually, he would have to deal with such issues but put the idea off because of the sheer magnitude and endless permutations the scenario could present. But he did know he had to do the right thing. He had to do what Doc would have done. *Make her proud of him,* were the words Doc wrote concerning what he would do with this technology. Make his beloved—gone before him—wife proud of him. He owed Doc at least that much. He owed everyone that...at least that. At a minimum he had to do the right thing and Bob Mcleod was not used to doing the minimum.

"Bob, I agree with you, and this won't be an easy thing we start tonight. Easy was Major General Peters. He recognizes the issues and pushes this up to the next level. But after tomorrow, when the President gets his briefing, there is no higher place to push. We need to get on building the plan. The hardest work is still ahead, Professor. Tonight, we are demonstrating and verifying the technology. That is easy. The hard part is deciding *what* to do with it, then *how, when* and *where.* That is where we will earn our money Professor. So, as we discussed before, that is where you had better have a good plan and sell it well if you want your way. I am not the one you need to convince here. I am a nobody in this game. I have no authority...no pull. You do though; you're the man with the technology. You are the one they must listen too whether you like it or not. Whether they like it or not. For now, the only person who knows how to do this is you. So, for now, you have their ear Professor...for now.

"General Peters convinced them you are for real so there's no fooling around now. No *just a hoax* or *it must not be working anymore.* Time to write that chapter in history you were talking about before. I know this is not easy, Bob, but it is important. It is probably the most important thing we will ever do. Let's do it right. I promised you my help and I meant it. We need to do this right and I will help you the best I can. Remember though, I am a colonel in the United States Air Force and I will—I must—do my duty to my country. So, I will obey the orders of the officers above me. You know that. But know that I will help you in the future just like I have the past two days. I have done my best and I have been honest and straight with you. I will continue to be so and I ask you do the same. We've got to do this right. We all have a lot riding on this," Frank concluded. Bob smiled, he knew Frank was right and he trusted him now more than ever. It was comforting having him as an ally and Bob knew he needed every one of those he could muster right now.

"Now where is that MRE you promised me, Colonel?"

The rest of the afternoon went by slowly for the team. There was not much new to do really. They met after "lunch" and discussed the upcoming events. The weather forecast for that evening was virtually clear skies, unrestricted visibility, cool with light winds. Anything they chose to generate tonight would be easy to show as an un-forecast condition. So, they decided to basically stick with same show they gave this morning to Major General Peters. Start with modifying the wind, by letting the Chairman pick a direction, speed and duration and Bob would make it happen. They figured temperature would be a good one tonight. Let the Secretary of Defense see how much heat he could stand. It was kind of poetically fitting they thought in light of his recent testimonies before the Congress. He was already getting a lot of heat over Defense spending and personnel issues so it seemed symbolically appropriate. The clear skies would let the night air cool quickly. So raising the temperature to a relatively high level selected by the Secretary of Defense would be easily recognized as not normal. It would also be easily verifiable by a simple thermometer, and of course, they would feel it too.

The last thing they planned, which hopefully would not be needed, was a thunderstorm. They agreed a fairly good sized one with lots of lightning was a sure-fired convincer of even the most skeptical critic. They didn't expect to need it to convince the men but they might need it to show them the scope of the technology they possessed. It was more to make them think than to convince them of the legitimacy of the technology.

Bob didn't believe it would take them long to start thinking about the potential applications of this new capability once they saw it in action. He knew they would already be considering and discussing both the positive and negative sides of the whole thing.

That is why they were coming out here, he thought, quite simply to confirm their fears. Not to see how wonderful a technology has been developed, rather to verify the existence and relative magnitude of a weapon against which they are not prepared to defend. They would bring a threat assessment to the President tomorrow, not a vision of potential applications for the common good. Bob knew from the discussions he heard between the legal officer and Frank that weather modification research was restricted by treaty and convention. The United States Department of Defense does not engage in such activities. But now, out of the blue, they possess the ability to do just what the treaties were designed to prevent from happening. A single nation's government would possess the technology to change the weather anywhere in the world at the time of its own choosing. Not a thing could be done by the target country if and when they ever discovered an event was not a true act of nature. There was always plausible denial. It could have always been the true course of nature that brought on the weather event in question. Conversely, the US could be blamed for every little weather condition which caused some inconvenience, financial loss, or natural disaster which occurs. It was pretty unnerving to him as Bob played out a few possible scenarios in his head.

They had decided what to do, made the necessary preparations for the demonstration, and now simply sat back to wait for the dignitaries to arrive. Most of the distinguished visitor preparation that normally accompany a visit from such high-ranking officials were not necessary for this trip. The security was tight, and there were only a few people on the post who knew they were coming. Major General Peters, the post Air Traffic Controller who was sworn to secrecy and would not make the calls required in his checklist when he heard the aircraft's notable call sign. The chief of the Air Force Security Forces and Army's Military

Police were both notified and instructed to double their patrols but not to interfere with the movement of the official party. That was it. Nobody else knew they were coming and only General Peters knew the purpose of the visit...except, of course, the few men still out at the Isolation Facility.

They could hear the helicopter before they got the one-minute-out call from the pilot. It was already dark and the team assembled inside the dining area had a sense of déjà vu as Major General Peters emerged from the helicopter. Outside the door on the well-lit helipad, they could see Colonel Lincoln greet the men as they climbed down from the large helicopter. The blades were spinning progressively slower as the aircraft's two engines were quickly shut down. It was obvious they intended to stay for a while. The Chairman exited first; he was wearing the standard Army field uniform. Immediately behind him, the Secretary of Defense, clad in jeans and a chamois shirt clamored out of the big machine.

They proceeded directly toward the side door of the isolation facility where the remaining few men awaited their arrival. That was all there was to it. No fanfare, no Aides, no protocol, just a security detail and the three of them rolling up their sleeves and getting in it personally. The team took that as a very good sign. Their visitors were interested and cautious, had made it their personal priority, and looked like they meant business. Bob was as worried about that as he was pleased as they entered the room. Everyone popped a rigid posture when the area was called to attention but the four-star general quickly ordered everyone to be at ease as he moved toward the waiting men. Colonel Lincoln led the three men over to the waiting team and introduced each of them by name. The last man standing in the row, wearing a flight suit with no patches or name tag was introduced...Professor Robert Mcleod.

"Gentlemen, it is my pleasure to meet you," Bob said as he extended his hand to the Secretary of Defense.

"They haven't been making you eat any of that lousy military MRE chow have they?" he asked with wry smile. "That stuff always binds me up something fierce. It's supposed to I guess but it always takes me two or three days to get back to normal after I eat one of those things. It's my pleasure to meet you, Sir. It is some extraordinary things I hear you are going to show us tonight. This is General "Dutch" Charles, Chairman of the Joint Chiefs of Staff. Everyone tells me he looks bigger on television; do you think?"

Bob appreciated the attempt to put him at ease and smiled, "No Sir, the general looks pretty big in person. Right now, he looks pretty big to me," Bob said as he extended his hand to meet the outstretched hand of the six-foot five-inch Army four-star general who leads the greatest armed forces in the world. Bob was never in the military but he had a lot of respect for them and this man had risen to the top of his profession. He knew that usually took a lot of hard work, motivation, and sacrifice in the military and he could tell by the man before him that was how he got there. This was no Hugh Durbin riding the coat tails of his Daddy kind of general. No, General Charles was the real deal and you could tell it quickly and easily.

"Professor Mcleod, it's good to meet you. I've heard a lot about what you can do, and frankly it scares the tar out of me. We don't have a whole lot of time, so how about if we skip the formalities and get right into why we are here. I don't want to sound pushy but no point in beating around the bush or jockeying for position. Let's get to it, shall we?" the Chairman requested.

Bob thought for a minute and decided that he would return the two men the same courtesy they showed him. They were important men in the country—in the world in fact—and Bob was about to become a player in world events whether he wanted to be or not. He thought it best to take his lead from them and operate in their realm as best he could. He knew he was outclassed, outgunned, and essentially out of his league in lots of ways but he could tell these two important men in front of him had gotten to their stations in life because they were men of conviction and purpose. That, Bob knew he could relate to. These two men who had to take worldly views and make recommendations from a tremendously broad and complex set of conditions were simply two men.

Bob knew how to be a man, how to stand up for himself and what he wanted, and he knew what he believed in. So, that would be the basis for dealing with these two. He knew they would understand that and he hoped they would see it and appreciate that in him. So, it was at the very fundamental level of manhood that Bob addressed them, "All right General, I'm prepared to work this way. I can change the weather. Make it *what* I program it to be and *when* I tell it to be however *good* or *bad* I want within the natural environmental parameters. Temperature, wind, rain, snow; you name it and I can make it happen. Takes a small machine—there on the table—a couple of commands into the keyboard and that's it. No more complex than that; anybody can do it once they know how to operate the device. We are prepared to demonstrate that capability to you any time you want to see it.

"I did this on my own...well, the man who deserves all the credit was killed by a drunk driver but I am the only living person who understands the technology. This is not a military project; got no military money; no University money. Nobody's invested in me and I'm not working for anybody on this deal. We can do a lot of good things with this technology but a lot of bad could be done with it, too. You are here to help me see that *bad* doesn't happen. I don't know a lot about world politics or the stuff you all do at your level. But I do know, at the fundamental level, that my technology can make your job a whole lot easier or a whole lot harder. What do you hope to accomplish tonight gentlemen?" Bob thought he was straight up with them and they deserved that from him. He was direct and honest and hoped it would carry the tone of their meeting.

"We appreciate your candor, Professor Mcleod. I like that very much. I hope to get an idea of what you can do and how difficult or easy it is to do. I also hope to discuss with you some possible courses of action on how and when we can use this technology. Frankly, if you can do what Major General Peters tells us, we are going to have lots to discuss and that scares the crap out of me. Mr. Secretary here also needs to get enough information to brief the President tomorrow afternoon. And, believe me, the President will have some very simple, direct questions that we don't know the answers to right now. Did I miss anything, Mr. Secretary?" the general concluded.

"No Dutch; that about covers it, I think. General Charles and I are very concerned about the ramifications this technology could have on our national security, as well as, that of our allies and enemies around the world. Professor Mcleod I am sure you have considered at least a few possible negative applications of this technology which could damage our military posture, both offensively and defensively. We are very concerned; the President is concerned; we just need to learn how concerned we must remain."

Secretary Fitzgerald was a complex man indeed. He could relate with the simple folks and blend like cream in coffee with the highest of diplomats and royalty. He was extremely diverse in both knowledge and experience, remarkably so for a man so young. He was a very capable Secretary of Defense. Some thought him better suited for Secretary of State. Still others believed there was a Presidency of his own on the horizon for the forty-three-year-old. Bob was very leery of him and after listening to him for this brief period could tell there was something about the man that made him uncomfortable. He couldn't put his finger on it right now but that sense of people had never let Bob down before. So, he wasn't about to stop trusting it now. Bob decided on the spot to deal as much with General Charles as possible and let him handle the Secretary. Bob needed every advantage right now and letting the Chairman of the Joint Chiefs of Staff deal with his Secretary of Defense seemed like a good idea to Bob.

"All right gentlemen, shall we go outside and show you what you came to see? No point in wasting everybody's time." Bob walked to the table and took two of the devices from it, handing one each to the Chairman and the Secretary. "Just to give you an idea of how small and lightweight the device is but please don't press any buttons. The commands are entered through the keypad, and coded language inputs enable, instruct, and disable the device. It only takes one of these little guys to get the job done, I haven't tried two of them together with opposing instructions. Honestly, I don't know what would happen in that case and I wasn't in any hurry to find out. Then I met these guys and, well, here we are. I tell you there is still a lot of stuff about this I don't even know yet. I was not completely finished with my research when the Feds scarfed me up a couple of days ago," Bob continued talking as he led them onto the helipad for the first of the demonstrations. "Secretary Fitzgerald, it is about sixty degrees right now. Captain Lessur over there has a thermometer...sixty-two he's signaling, thank you. Sir pick a temperature you want the air here to be and I will make it that way for five minutes and then it will revert back to the natural temperature. What would you like?"

"How about fifty? Is it easier to warm it up than to cool it down, Professor? We don't want a gimme on this, now do we?" the Secretary answered in a politely challenging tone. He seemed like the kind of man who could give you a good ass chewing and make you feel good about it and that really worried Bob Mcleod.

"Doesn't matter Sir, the same amount of work for both really," Bob replied as he made the appropriate entry into the keypad. Almost immediately Captain Lessur announced sixty degrees, and counted down as the air noticeably cooled to fifty degrees. He passed the thermometer for all to see and five minutes later it began a slow climb back up. "Fifty-one," he called out, "fifty-two"...and so forth as the temperature continued to rise back up.

"That is amazing," the Secretary of Defense remarked. "What is next Professor? You are off to an impressive start."

"Well Sir, you can see there is little or no wind tonight. If General Charles will pick a direction and speed, I will give him whatever wind he chooses," Bob said matter-of-factly.

"Northeast at twenty knots if you please, Professor." The general knew wind from that direction rarely occurred in this part of the country unless it was associated with bad weather. Plus, he was facing that direction with a clear field of view and knew any kind of trickery would likely be visible in that direction. The general was a graduate of the *trust-but-verify* school of experience.

"Very well Sir," Bob replied. "I can see you know a little bit about the weather here. We rarely get wind from that direction unless we are on the back side of a low, which we obviously are not tonight. Any significance to twenty knots, Sir?"

"Yes, in fact that is how many different knots I had to tie to get a merit badge in Boy Scouts." The general's smile was visibly warm, even in the darkness of the evening. Bob had already entered the recipe for the winds the general requested and almost instantaneously they picked up from the odd direction until a few moments later they were stiff from the Northeast. Captain Lessur passed around an anemometer and each of the visitors held it up and read for themselves as the display held steady at twenty knots.

"Well done, Professor," the general said. "I gotta tell you, this is a most impressive technology. It is also *most* concerning, indeed. Professor, this is all neat stuff but I get the impression you are just toying around with these. Kind of like little parlor games or something. Just how much can you really do?"

"I have never gone for all out devastation or anything, General, but I am convinced I can produce up to level five tornadoes, category five hurricanes, and maybe even tsunamis. I have never done any of those but the theory is the same no matter the application and I have done all the calculations. They are within the capabilities of the device in my hand. Would you like to see a strong thunderstorm, without the tornado of course?" Bob offered.

The general looked impressed, but before he could reply, the Secretary spoke up, "No Professor, I don't think we need to see a thunderstorm, *unless* you can do the tornado with it." He was looking for a reaction and that comment drew one from everyone there as they all began to speak at once. General Charles' voice boomed above the rest, "All right everybody. Settle down. Listen up. Mr. Secretary, please elaborate on your request, Sir." The general was just as curious at what he would say as the next person but thought he was pressing the limits of testing the Professor. After all, that is what they came to learn.

"I'd love to see a thunderstorm on such a clear night. I'd be most impressed if you could do that for us professor. What I would be amazed by is if you could spawn a tornado from that thunderstorm somewhere on this small part of our military reservation. Now, don't get yourselves all in tizzy here gentlemen. I don't want to put anybody at risk, especially any of the local population. But if you can drop one down near that forested area right over there—the one we flew over coming in, we could really get a feel for the magnitude of what we are dealing with here. After all, that is what we came out here to do. If you can't or if you believe it is too risky, professor, then I want you to tell us. This is your technology. You are the expert; you make the call." The Secretary meant it, not as a challenge, as much as a test of Bob's courage, both physical and moral.

Bob Mcleod nodded at the man, as he stared into the eyes of the civilian leader of the most powerful military on the face of the earth, he calmly replied, "I can do that for you Mr. Secretary, and I will. You'll get to see what you came to see."

With that he retrieved his notebook from the pocket of his flight suit and began to enter the recipe and parameters to meet the Secretary's request. He was extremely cautious, as he wanted to make sure he entered this exactly right. *It was like calling in artillery on an enemy during close quarter combat* Bob thought. You want it to be close and effective but you don't want to hit your own folks. Unlike a battlefield, though, it was silent on the helipad. You could hear all the sounds of the night right then, including the quickened breathing of the man typing codes into Thor's Hammer. Bob thought to himself, *Doc if you ever made a mistake on these recipes, let it be a different one than this one I am typing. I need all the help you can give me now. If you're watching, please help me out right now.*

"Okay then gentlemen, here we go. All we do now is wait and watch. It will take a little while for the storm to develop given the current conditions but once it gets whipped up you'll see your tornado or at least the damage it did. Either way, you'll get the idea. Sure hope there's nobody in those woods tonight. It is going to turn ugly in there pretty quick. I suppose that is one advantage mother nature has over us, she always knows what is going to happen and we can always chalk up things we don't expect to her being fickle. That has just changed folks.

"This technology will let mankind decide for itself what natural events should occur and when. No more droughts or famines, if we choose to avoid them. It is possible to end world hunger, for example, by ensuring a few good years of growing conditions in regions of agricultural plenty. Our Midwest region for example. Perhaps increasing fresh water supply in the Middle East by a nearly continuous period of rainfall whenever needed to keep the growing population from killing each other over the scarcest commodity over there. Loads of oil but not enough water to drink. Sure beats the high cost of de-salination plants everywhere don't you think?" Bob was nervously rambling and decided now would be a good time to stop. He had made his point about the positive application of his technology and needed to see the response.

"You raise an interesting point Professor," Secretary Fitzgerald conceded. "In the interest of national defense, I suppose we could solve all the world's pending crises over a period of time and that would greatly reduce the risks and potential threats from overseas. In fact, it could do the same from an internal perspective, as well, I suppose. I know the FBI and Justice Departments are up to their necks in worry about the rise in violence and what they claim to be domestic terrorism. We could all benefit from this technology to be sure. But as I'm sure we all agree, so could the enemies of our great nation. This technology could really hurt us, militarily, but also economically, physically, politically, even emotionally. We need to ensure these things don't happen. Professor, you stated that you are the only person who understands this technology? You are the only one who can create one of these devices or even operate the ones that currently exist, is that right?"

Bob didn't like the tone of the question or the possibility of where this discussion could go, but he pressed his luck. After all, the clouds were beginning to form up nicely and he figured he had their attention now. Surely they wouldn't do anything drastic with a tornado about to hit near them and, certainly, not before they saw what he could do and briefed the President. Bob began to think he was getting the hang of this. That was not nearly as true as he would have liked to believe at this point. "Yes, that's right. I am the only one right now. You guys have me and my machines and nobody else knows what they are capable of except, of course, the FBI and IRS guys who handed me over to you. They have some idea but no real proof they can demonstrate.

"That puts me in a pretty precarious position, don't you think? If you want to use this stuff you need me and my machines both. If you want to cover it up and throw away the whole thing, it's sitting right in front of you in one nice, neat bundle. Easy to get rid of and no way to prove it ever really existed outside a few overzealous imaginations and a few coincidences. Yes, General Charles, you folks have the upper hand and I know that. I respect your position and your concerns; I really do. In fact, I have given this considerable thought over the last couple of days and I still don't have a good answer for any of these dilemmas."

"Wait a minute Professor, nobody has any intention of burying you and your tools in some desert and pretend you never existed. We don't kill people or their technologies like I think you are suggesting. Rest assured; we are not here to silence you, Sir." The Secretary had spoken up immediately as Bob's comments struck a nerve, apparently, not too far from the surface. "Bob, this is some tough stuff to deal with and you know it. If you don't know it yet, you are obviously catching on very quickly. So, let's get it right, shall we? We can do this the easy way, together, or the hard way which is not together. I can speak for all of us here, it will be much easier for us if you work with us.

"We are not in an enviable position either, Professor. How can we say with any certainty that we can protect our nation from this technology... ever? I don't know how we can; so let's get together on this. That is why we are here. Are we all clear on that now?" He was mad now, he obviously felt like he was viewed as the sinister civilian spy sent by the

President to deal with the situation. Nothing was farther from the truth. This man was the real deal and he cared genuinely for the military and the nation. He had never worn the uniform but inside the man beat the heart of a true warrior. A pride and sense of duty to country and fellow soldier that would have been fitting of any career military member. That was good to know and Bob could see that now.

"You're right. I didn't mean to offend you, Sir, but I needed to know. This is some scary stuff we are dealing with here and I didn't ask to be brought here with you guys. You brought me here, remember? Neither of us like it much but for now we are stuck with each other. I think we should head over to the building and get our rain gear. We have about ten more minutes by the looks of things before we start getting wet out here. I think we'll want to be outside to see your tornado. But let's have a clear path to some shelter, just in case things go awry. Better safe than sorry; lets err on the side of caution. I need you folks around to keep me out of trouble."

Bob led the way toward the isolation facility. He meant what he said and they all knew it. They had reached another milestone for the team of folks that was writing the first few chapters in the history books that would talk about man's ability to control the weather. They had added the two highest ranking military men in the world to their team. They all knew it and they were all glad about it. The rest of the evening was going to be the easy part, just stand out in a torrential thunderstorm and watch a tornado less than half a mile away chew up the forest...*what could be simpler?*

They could hear the rain begin falling onto the roof of the isolation facility as they were finishing up a quick break and donning their rain gear. The sound of the rain beginning on the previously clear night was in itself enough to convince the two distinguished visitors beyond a doubt that the technology was legitimate but the degree of capability was the remaining question to be answered. The hurried side conversations between participants quickly ceased as all eyes turned upward, responding to the increasing tempo of the rain falling onto the rooftop. Colonel Lincoln led the group to the door and ensured each man had a functioning flashlight before heading outside to witness the rest of the storm. The group huddled together against the side of the building which offered the best view of the forested edge of the clearing. It was also the side with an overhang to deter some of the heavy rain which was beginning to swirl in from virtually every direction.

The rain and lightning continued to intensify while the wet drops became bigger and colder. The winds increased steadily from seemingly every direction as small hailstones began to pop all about the ground around the group. They began to get visibly nervous as the weather around them intensified. Major General Peters asked Bob loudly, "Is this what you expected? Does this look like it is supposed to or should we head for cover?" They were all thinking the same thing, and each appeared equally relieved that someone had the sense and courage enough to say what was on each of their minds. Bob was standing at the edge of the overhang looking up into the hail when the general voiced his question loud enough for all to hear.

Bob yelled loudly to ensure he was heard by all above the pounding rain, hail, and wind, "This is what you asked for gentlemen, enjoy it while you can. It is supposed to look like this. We have the advantage of knowing what is coming, and when. Enjoy your advantage gentlemen; this is nature at work for you!" It was almost scary hearing the words. Bob compounded the eeriness of it all by stepping out in the rain with his arms up, looking skyward as the rain and hail fell upon him. He was basking in the success of generating a thunderstorm on a clear night. It was obvious that this was his victory over nature and he was invigorated by his triumphant achievement. It would only be a matter of minutes before the rotation in the clouds above him would yield a small but devastatingly powerful tornado right on cue.

Bob began to see the funnel cloud dropping from the storm cloud after he heard the train-like roar of the rushing air only a thousand yards away. He didn't have to point it out to the group massed behind him under the overhang. They were all pointing out toward the woods, in the direction of the sound of the rushing air, now swirling to the ground ready to destroy the timber in its path. They could hear it, too, and in a few short seconds they would see the funnel cloud as it contacted the earth and became a tornado. It was an F-1...the smallest Bob could generate and still make an impression. It was to be very short lived—only about two minutes before it dissipated—but long enough to do serious, indisputable damage to the wooded area they were watching. There would be no doubt to anyone inspecting the area that the damage was from a tornado.

That was the order, and that is what Professor Robert Mcleod and the Thor's Hammer delivered, on time, on target. It was impressive, and several intense flashes of lightning served to guarantee each spectator at least one clear view of the rotating cloud and the flying debris around it as it tore through the forest. They all stood there for several quiet moments after the tornado had completed its deadly run through the trees. The rain was still falling and the lightning flashed but they could already tell the storm's intensity was beginning to decrease. It was Secretary Fitzgerald who spoke first, "Why don't we go inside guys? I think we've seen all we need to see." And that was all anyone needed to hear as they headed into the dry safety of the isolation facility. Bob was the last one through the door and, as he entered, the team began to applaud. The small group clapped and whooped like they had won a hard-fought battle. In a manner of speaking, they had. For the first time ever, a person had created and controlled one of nature's most fierce entities. A man created a tornado; his team was proud of him and they were showing it with applause. Bob was surprised by their response. He was pleased with himself; in fact, he was proud that it had worked as advertised. He was genuinely surprised at the applause, but it set the tone and reflected their appreciation for the capability of the new technology.

"Professor Mcleod, for the first time in a long time I am speechless. Well done, Sir, that was most impressive," Secretary Fitzgerald was honestly taken by the experience. It would take some doing to repeat the impression this demonstration had made on him, and that was not likely to occur any time soon. In fact, the same was true for all members of the team. None had ever witnessed a tornado in person before. They had seen them on television, but that is like seeing a picture of the Mona Lisa or the Grand Canyon. Each is indescribable; it must be experienced to be understood. The fact that this tornado was called up on-demand made it all the more spectacular to them. It was remarkable. Those were the words but the experience was much more than words could describe.

"Sir, I suppose the next thing we need to do is figure out the next thing we need to do." Colonel Lincoln was the group's real problem solver and the suggestion was aimed at no particular *Sir* in the group. But since it was a target rich environment, he knew the formality would not be wasted.

Secretary Fitzgerald responded to the question, "Professor Mcleod, I'd like you to accompany us back to Washington tonight. I want you to explain what you can do with this technology to the President tomorrow. Will you do that, Bob?"

"You ask me that as if I have a choice Mr. Secretary. If I have a choice, then yes, I will go with you. If I don't really have a choice then no, I won't go with you and you'll have to take me against my will." Bob's response was unexpectedly complex. The team was a little bit surprised by it in fact but Bob knew he had to establish right now his status in this situation before he could continue. He couldn't afford to get caught up in the moment. After all, he was the one who had his freedom at stake here not anyone in else in the room...just him.

"Yes, Bob you have a choice. You don't have to go but I would prefer you come with us instead of after us. Once we make our report to the President, he is going to want to talk to you in person. I'd just as soon have you there already; have you involved in our report from the beginning. That is my preference. Will you go with us to discuss this with the President?" the question came from the Secretary a second time, but it was sincere, not threatening or demeaning in tone. That is what Bob wanted.

"Sure, Sir, I'll go with you. I'd like to stop at my house and get some of my own clothes and stuff. See my dog. It won't take long but I've been gone for days now and, no offense Frank, but I don't like wearing flight suits.

I'm not a pilot and I don't want to be one either," Bob smiled a genuine smile. It was a simple request but an important one and Frank looked over at Lieutenant Colonel Otto, the JAG, who had his hands full so far trying to find legal ground for all this recent activity. He nodded because there was no real reason he knew for not letting the man return to his home.

"That should be fine Professor but given the circumstances I must insist you be escorted by bodyguards at all times." The lieutenant colonel was a good JAG and had gotten the spin just right.

Frank smiled an approving smile at him as he spoke next, "Very well then. Major Naed, please arrange the security detail and transportation for Professor Mcleod to and from his home. Back here in two hours for a departure from the airfield with the Chairman and Secretary. I also need you to store all the devices in the weapons facility vault. I want an accountability trail and positive control measures on everyone who sees or touches these things. Same procedures we use for storing and transporting nukes and I want this activity to be classified top secret. Only people with TS clearances will be assigned any detail or activity concerning these devices. Do you wish to classify it in special access channels, General?" Frank asked the question, realizing that he was getting on a roll. He decided to stand down a bit in deference to the generals in the room.

"Frank's right, General," Major General Peters spoke up. "We should treat this as Top Secret, with special access required, until we get a better grip on where we go from here. The President's guidance will be the first step but implementing that will take some time even after decisions are made. I think a TS special access program is the way to go, Sir, and Major Naed can get us squared away in that department. These always have names Professor...care to give us a name for this project? After all it is your baby," Major General Peters offered.

"Thor's Hammer Sir. That's the device's name. Will that do?" Bob smiled.

"Thor's Hammer it is. Major Naed, set it up. Everyone in the room, and Colonel Lincoln personally controls access to this SAP. Nobody gets anything until he approves it. Sorry Frank but this is going to be your baby for a while longer, at least until we move the devices. General Charles, we will wait until we hear from you personally, Sir, for our next instructions regarding Thor's Hammers. Gentlemen, do you have anything else for the group?" The question was directed to the Secretary and the Chairman.

"That sounds like a good plan; go ahead Frank. Captain, you're a meteorologist aren't you?" General Charles addressed Captain Lessur.

"Yes Sir, General," he replied confidently to the four-star's accusation.

"Are you a good one then?" the general pressed.

"No Sir, I am a lousy meteorologist but I am a damned good weatherman," Captain Lessur smiled, hoping the general understood the difference.

"All the better then," he replied strongly. "Frank, I'd like to bring the captain along with us for tomorrow's session. We might need a translator to de-geek some of this stuff for us. No point in getting any more people involved in this than already are. Can you spare him for a while?"

"Yes Sir. I think we can spare him for a while, as long as we get him back eventually. He's the best one I've come across in my twenty-three years in the Air Force; I'd hate to lose him," Frank took the opportunity to plug his young officer. He knew Lessur was chomping at the bit to find the answer from the very beginning and they probably wouldn't be here right now if it weren't for his enthusiasm early on. He was glad the Chairman asked for the young man to accompany them. "But, Sir, one thing if I may? I don't recommend giving him a vehicle and a weapon at the same time Sir."

"Captain Lessur, you can explain that to me on the airplane. Right now, you better get your gear ready. Plan on several days at least. If you've got your class A uniform handy you better bring it. Get busy son; you need to be planeside in two hours," the Chairman nodded at the door and the captain took his cue, heading for the door at a trot. He didn't want to give anyone the opportunity to undo this trip for him. He was more excited now than he was after the first demonstration. He was in on the ground floor of this technology and the Chairman of the Joint Chiefs of Staff had just asked him to accompany him and the Secretary of Defense to DC to brief the President of the United States. Yeah, he had plenty to be excited about but not much time to get anything except ready to go.

"Frank, good work, keep it up. Thanks to your entire team. I don't have to tell you the magnitude of all of this. You guys did well, but the hard part is coming up. Keep your mouths shut on this. That is a direct order from me, the Chairman of the Joint Chiefs of Staff. You talk about this to anyone without Colonel Lincoln in the room with you and you will find yourself in Leavenworth forever. Everybody understand that order?" The Chairman was loud and clear and so was the response. A resounding *Yes Sir* came from everyone in the room. "Mr. Secretary, do you have anything, Sir?" General Charles invited.

"Just a thank you, Gentlemen...outstanding job. Keep it up and keep it quiet. I will see to it that the general keeps his word and I am pretty good friends with the Governor of Kansas. Let's get on that helicopter so these men can get some rest, General. Thanks again, you did a super job here tonight." With that, the Secretary headed for the door, Generals Charles and Peters on his heels. The rotors were already beginning to turn on the Blackhawk as the three approached. They climbed aboard and two minutes later disappeared over the treetops. The helicopter would circle overhead, surveying the damaged forest for ten minutes before heading back to the airfield to talk about whatever men of that rank discuss in their private sessions. Every man in the room wished they could be a fly on that wall, especially Bob Mcleod.

"Thank you, gentlemen, you did a great job. You really knocked their socks off. Professor, I got to hand it to you; that was awesome. But you better go with Major Naed right now and get your gear. You've got to make time to get home and back to the airfield. But be safe, Naed.

No Hollywood stuff; you and your bodyguards are carrying precious cargo. I want him delivered intact and on time. Better get moving, Bob, and remember...do good!" Frank shook his hand and headed him toward the door. "Call me day or night if it doesn't feel right, Bob. If nothing else, I can always give you my opinion if you want it."

"Thanks Frank, and thanks for keeping your word. I hope to see you again soon."

Bob meant that as he stepped into the night. It was cool and damp thanks to him. Now he was heading home because he had a plane to catch. His night was a long way from being over and he was already tired, but it was a good tired. The kind of tired that hard work and success bring and that kind of tired he could learn to handle.

Major Naed led him to a suburban with a driver and two men already waiting inside. He explained it was one of the vehicles they would have used to drive the Secretary and Chairman back to the airfield if the helicopter could not be used for some reason. They drove on to Bob's house, following his directions. The drive was virtually silent as both Bob and Major Naed considered the events of the evening and what was to come. They couldn't really talk about them because the men in the vehicle with them were not cleared. They saw the storm but had no idea the man they were transporting had created it. That is how it needed to be for now but they would likely figure it out eventually. As they approached Bob's house, he could see there was a light on inside but the front porch was dark. Bob sat patiently inside the suburban as two of the men entered and secured the house, making sure it was empty and ready for the person they were protecting. The driver remained in place, engine running the entire time, prepared to make a hasty exit if the need arose. One bodyguard returned to the vehicle and told Bob the house was clear and he would escort him up to the house now.

Once inside Bob felt relieved to see things were very much the way he left them. He was sure the house had been thoroughly searched but was glad they hadn't torn the place up in the process. He could hear Buck barking in the back of the house somewhere and went to see the pet he had missed the past few days. The bodyguard had closed the door to keep him in the room and as Bob opened it Buck came jumping out, obviously glad to see him. He petted the dog and played with him for a couple of minutes and then walked down the hall to his own bedroom. He noticed there was still food in Buck's bowl and fresh water in his dish and he knew that Agent Miloc had kept his word about taking care of Buck. He knew the agent was a man of his word and he was glad to see he was keeping it for Bob. He hoped the agent was equally successful keeping a lid on his discovery. Bob grabbed a suitcase and threw in some clean clothes, then added some toiletries and a couple of notebooks. He didn't particularly think he would need them for this trip but he didn't want to leave them in the house. He couldn't afford to lose them if he never got back here. Bob said goodbye to Buck and the three men were out the door and quickly on their way back to the airfield to begin the flight to Washington DC.

As they pulled onto the post and began to head to the airfield, Major Naed commented to Bob, "I hope you get to accomplish what you set out to do Professor. I've got four kids at home myself and it would sure be good to know they will grow up in a safer world than we have now."

Bob wasn't sure how to respond to the comment, so he just smiled and said, "Me too." Then stared back out into the night. He really never set out to do anything great with the device but Doc Auster had. Bob was going to get rich by it but Doc Auster had a different view of what rich meant and Bob was getting large doses of that the last few days. He felt guilty that he hadn't protected the secret better and that there remained the possibility that it would be years before the technology could be used for its original purpose. But Bob had already decided to do his best to allow all mankind to benefit from this technology, not just one man or one nation. He wasn't much of a philosopher really but he had grown up knowing the difference between right and wrong. He knew he had to do the right thing and that is what he intended to do.

He couldn't help but remember his encounter with Hugh Durbin over the grades of the student Bob was tutoring. That little encounter had nearly cost him more than he could have ever imagined at the time. Now, it was clear that many times we don't know why things happen but everything *does* happen for a reason. Bob knew he had been chosen to deliver this technology to the world for a reason and he was going to do his best to accomplish that task. He had to do it right for himself, for Doc Auster and his wife, for his country, and now it seemed for Major Naed's four kids and millions of others he has never met. He would do his best.

The suburban pulled up to the flight line gate and proceeded directly though. Bob could see the jet was ready to go and Captain Lessur was already there, unloading his bags from the back of a suburban just like the one Bob was riding. They pulled up and got out of the vehicle. Colonel Lincoln greeted them, "Glad you could make it and on time no less. I'm impressed; it will be reflected in your paychecks," he grinned. "They're on their way out. Go ahead and climb aboard; the steward will get you settled into the right spot. Good luck gentlemen; I'll see you both back here." With that, Frank turned and headed back into the building. Bob and Captain Lessur climbed aboard the executive jet and were told where to sit. They were both admiring the impressive, and functional interior of the jet when they saw the Chairman bound up through the door, the Secretary of Defense right behind him. They both smiled at the two already seated as they made their way to other side of the table set between them. "What a great aircraft," Captain Lessur commented. The men smiled as the steward closed the door, almost immediately the aircraft began to roll toward the runway.

They were airborne a few minutes later and the Chairman spoke first, "Once we land there will be someone to take you both to Andrews Air Force base. You'll stay in the DV quarters there, guarded, and we will transport you both to the White House tomorrow afternoon for our meeting with the President. Be ready to go by 1300, Captain, class A uniform if you got it? Professor, look as good as you can, you only get one opportunity to make a first impression." Both men nodded they understood their instructions. "Relax, and get comfortable, it takes a couple hours to get back. Is anybody else ready for a drink?" he offered. Everybody nodded and the steward made his way over to them to talk about what he had available. The four men's preferences known; the steward headed back to prepare their drinks.

"Now Captain, let me know why Colonel Lincoln advised me not to give you a weapon and a vehicle at the same time. What's that all about, son?" The general smiled at the now blushing Captain Lessur.

"That's how we got involved in his thing, Sir. The Professor had generated a rain shower when there really shouldn't have been one. I was sure somebody was messing with the weather since we were missing some no-brainier forecasts on some significant weather. So, I took a Hummer and my sidearm and went out looking for whoever was messing up my weather," the captain explained.

"Did you find him then?" the general asked

"No Sir, not that time. We put out weather warnings for thunderstorms on the entire installation and the only thing that happened was that shower popped up and down in the same spot. Lot of work for folks when we give them a false alarm. Colonel Lincoln called for me to come explain it to him but I was out chasing the storm and whoever made it. The colonel thought I was nuts but he came around, especially after the FBI called us to help them," Captain Lessur concluded his story.

"Well Captain, try not to do anything like that in Washington, okay?" The general's comment came with a smile as big as the ones it drew from each passenger. The steward arrived with their drinks and the Secretary spoke, "Gentlemen, I propose a toast. To the greatest technology I have witnessed. Let us all be wise and steadfast in applying it. Professor Mcleod, the weather is tamed! Good job, Sir." The men raised their glasses and drank their caramel-colored liquids. "Now, I am going to get a nap. This has been a helluva long day, and tomorrow starts when we land. I suggest you all do the same." Nobody needed to be told twice. The jet was comfortable and in minutes each man was fading into their own dreams. The next thing they knew, the steward was tapping them to get ready to land. They were five minutes out form the airport and they were about to begin the next leg of their journey.

After they taxied to the private terminal area, the men were greeted by several uniformed men and a crowd of what appeared to Bob to be security or secret service. The officers saluted the general as he exited the jet and all four passengers huddled together as the others shuffled about them performing their duties. "You two gentlemen will come with me," a dark suited, middle-aged man with an earpiece and a stern look instructed Bob and Captain Lessur. The Chairman nodded and said, "See you this afternoon. Try to get some rest and look good, okay." With that, they were led off to a waiting vehicle with several guards inside. Two other vehicles accompanied them the entire way to their quarters. They were escorted to a large suite on Andrews Air Force base and instructed not to leave their quarters until they were called to do so. It was a cold type of security...formal and secretive. The two could tell they would be well protected but knew the real objective was to keep them well guarded.

"I am going to get some sleep," Bob announced as he headed off to one of the bedrooms. "I'm beat. I'll see you in a while. Maybe we can get something to eat later," Bob said as he closed the door and headed for the bed. He noticed there were no phones or phone lines in the room; there were none in the whole suite. He knew that was by design and he hoped he wouldn't have to stay in this place very long. He already didn't like it but he was very tired. He could protest later if that became necessary. Right now, he wanted some sleep and the bed looked very comfortable; indeed, it was. He slept for a long time.

The knock on his door came at noon. It was Captain Lessur letting him know he had one hour before they had to be ready to go. Bob hadn't even unpacked yet but it didn't matter; he felt rested for the first time in a long time. Bob grabbed a shower and put on a pair of jeans, a sweater, and boots and came out of his room. Captain Lessur was sitting on the sofa watching television. He looked sharp in his service dress uniform, the jacket hanging on the chair with a surprising number of ribbons for such a junior officer.

"Good afternoon sleepyhead. I don't know how you could sleep so long. We are going to meet the President of the United States in a couple of hours."

Bob replied, "Good afternoon, Captain, you look sharp today. The reason I slept so long is because we are going to meet the President today. I was tired, dog tired and now I feel good. I feel ready. Do you feel ready young man?"

"I was born ready," the captain smiled. "Ready to go and itching to be there."

"Where are you from Captain?" Bob inquired of his new roommate. "Ron. Call me Ron, Professor, I am from California," Captain Lessur replied. "Born and raised in San Diego. Saw the Navy there my whole life and decided the Air Force was the Service for me. How about you, Sir?" he inquired.

"Born and raised in Missouri. Midwest kid then and now," Bob replied as the knock on the door disrupted their getting to know each other.

"It's time gentlemen. Are you ready to go?" the agent inquired.

"You ready Ron? I am. Don't forget your jacket," Bob said.

"Ready to go. It's a blouse Professor. The Service dress coat is called a blouse. Just in case you ever need to know for later...like if you join the Air Force or something," Ron Lessur smiled as he headed for the door with the blouse draped over his forearm. They were led to the curb where another Suburban was waiting for them. They climbed in and off they went for their meeting with the most powerful man in the world, the President of the United States. Captain Ron Lessur wondered to himself who really held the most power now, the President or the man who could control the weather. For now, it was the President he thought but, if Bob Mcleod decided to turn evil, it wouldn't take him long to give even the United States military and the President a run for their money. After all, that is really why they were going to this meeting. Everybody knew it, but nobody had said it yet. Ron wondered if Bob knew what he was doing or if he was just shooting from the hip. It was hard to tell; it really seemed to be a little bit of both really. In fact, it was both. Bob sat wondering what he was going to do this afternoon during his discussion with some of the most powerful men in the world. He knew they would be wondering what Bob intended to do and, if they didn't like the answers they got, they were certainly in a position to change Bob's plans, if they chose to. That is what worried Bob the most. Should he be straight up with them or tell them what he thought they wanted to hear.

That was an easy decision for Bob Mcleod. If they didn't like it, that was too bad. He'd spent his whole life telling people what he thought—not what he thought they wanted to hear—and he wasn't about to change now. Not even for—no, *especially* not for the President of the United States. The man deserved the truth and that is just what he would get. Now, all Bob had to do was figure out what he really intended to do with this technology. He already knew what he intended to do, but he needed a hand figuring out just how to do it. His thoughts were interrupted as they turned onto Pennsylvania avenue. Before them, on the right-hand side, was the White House and they just drove on up to the gate and wheeled past the guards onto the drive that took them to the visitor's entrance. They were met by the press secretary and taken through the maze of security check points and searches. Finally, they were seated in an outer office area and instructed to wait there. They were both getting nervous now.

"Ron, your tie is crooked." Bob pointed to the young officer's Windsor knot which began to disappear under his blue collar.

"Thanks, Professor," he said urgently.

"Bob. Call me Bob, okay? You think I should have worn something more formal, don't you? Truth is, this is the best pair of pants I own. I sure didn't have time to go shopping before we left. I never needed anything but jeans for what I do," Bob confessed as they waited nervously.

"You're fine. At least you'll be comfortable and that will be an advantage for sure. What are you going to tell them, Bob? What are you going to do with this technology?" Captain Lessur asked sincerely.

"I honestly don't know what I am going to tell them. I guess it depends on what they ask me. I know I'm going to do some good with this technology; we just need to figure out the best way to do it," Bob finished with a smile. Bob's answer confirmed Ron Lessur's suspicion that he was shooting from the hip more than he was working from any plan. He both admired and pitied the meteorologist. He wished he could be in his place but, at the same time, wouldn't trade places with him right now for the world. Ron was glad he was wearing the uniform of his country and not the jeans of Bob Mcleod. With that thought, the door opened and the President's personal secretary came out and escorted them into the office. Before them sat the Chairman, the Secretary of Defense and the President of the United States. Two other men sat across the table and Bob immediately recognized them as the Secretary of State and the President's National Security Advisor.

Bob stood still momentarily, not sure where to move to or who to address first, so he waited. The Chairman of the Joint Chiefs stood and walked over to the two new arrivals. "Bob...Captain welcome. Come on in and let me introduce you to the gentlemen in the room." General Dutch Charles led the two across the plush carpet to the man seated at the head of the table. "Mr. President, this is Professor Robert Mcleod. He is the man we have been speaking of...the man who invented this remarkable technology. Professor, the President."

"It is a pleasure to meet you, Sir," Bob said as he extended his hand to greet the leader of the free world.

"My pleasure, Professor Mcleod. My pleasure, indeed. I have heard some remarkable things about you today. I can hardly wait to discuss them in greater detail. Welcome to the White House. And you must be Captain Lessur, welcome son it's good to meet you," the President said as he extended his hand to the youngest man in the room.

General Charles made personal introductions of Bob and Ron to the remaining men in the room and then invited them all to be seated so they could get started. The leather upholstered chairs and the highly polished cherry wood meeting table gave the room a feeling of warm strength and comfort. This was where much of the business of the country was conducted, and the most important business Bob had ever dreamed of participating in was about to start.

The President wasted no time. He started the meeting himself, and got right to the heart of the matter. Bob thought he liked that approach. "Professor Mcleod, the Secretary and General Charles have spent the morning with me discussing the demonstration you gave them last night. I must say, that is a remarkable technology you developed. Congratulations. You created a tornado for them right when and where they asked for it? Is that something you can repeat, Professor?"

"Yes. I can do that again, Sir, or any other naturally occurring weather event," Bob answered pointedly. He had a feeling it was his little voice telling him that this was not going to be what he had hoped. There were no real indications of anything he could see or hear, but he could tell. That little voice, that sixth sense, whatever you call it, it was warning him right now. Bob decided then and there to be direct and cautious. He was being hunted; he could feel it. He wondered for a second if it was the same kind of feeling a deer might have as it sniffed the air, knowing that something wasn't right but not being able to detect anything immediately threatening as the hunter watches from his tree stand only yards away. Bob knew something wasn't right; he could just tell.

"Well Professor, I believe you can and I haven't even seen it yet. Those who have were astounded by your ability. So, let's cut to the chase then Bob. We need you and your stuff a lot more than you need us; that is for sure. You could do some real damage to our economy, even our political system either deliberately, or unintentionally with those devices of yours. Or worse yet, some of our political adversaries, or enemies of the States get a hold of them and we could have ourselves one disaster after another. The military experts tell me there is no way they can defend against that kind of technology for years if ever, Bob, and we just can't have that and still meet our national strategies. So, I am prepared to make some deals with you right here...today. I want to buy your technology, turn it into a national program to continue your research, and put all of our resources into developing and advancing this capability. I'm told you said yourself there is still work to be done and stuff you haven't tested yet. What do you think is a fair price Professor, what are your terms?" the President concluded his statement.

So, this was the best they could come up with? Buy me out, pay for my silence then off to do who knows what with their new toy? Pacify me with reasoning that so much more can be done if someone else is doing it while I sit back on the beach and drink Margaritas? What does he think I am, a pawn in his game who can be bought out after delivering the goods to the highest bidder? Bob decided to see what kind of man they thought he was and test out the President's resolve at the same time. He knew he only had one shot and this was already going all wrong. Bob was about to buy into a game even he didn't think he could win.

"Well now, Mr. President, that is quite an opener. I am not sure you have all the facts yet though. You are correct, Sir, that this technology is quite impressive and, yes, it would be virtually impossible to defend against if it were used in an offensive role. I guess you are right, though, you need me more than I need you. I suppose there are lots of folks who would spend scads of money to buy this technology if it were on the market, which it isn't, just yet. You want to buy me out, is that it? Let's make sure we are saying the same thing then? You want the whole enchilada, tax, title and license? I'm out and you got the ball. You'll call me if you need anything, more for consultation but won't expect much more than my silence and loyalty? Is that what you are asking Mr. President?" Bob inquired.

"That's one way to put it, Bob. I don't want anyone but my people to know about or work on this technology until the United States government is ready, able, and postured to reveal it to the world in whatever forum is most advantageous to our nation. This is important to our country and our national security. I want it, and I am willing to pay for it, Professor," the President countered.

"How much are you willing to pay for it, Sir? Surely you discussed it before I came in. I don't like to haggle. So let's get right to it, best offer only, how much are you willing to pay for it? What are your terms Mr. President?" Bob hadn't broken eye contact with the President since he gave his opening remark, and he could see that man was not used to being in the position he was headed for and that suited Bob just fine. Bob wasn't about to look around the room for reactions because he didn't want to give the President a chance to deflect this to his advisors. The answer was swift in coming.

"Five billion dollars, and you turn over everything. You never work on anything like it again. We get the patent, documentation, the devices and you retire to do whatever you dream of doing in your spare time. We do this thing our way, and you get enough money to do whatever you want, Bob, except anything that even smells like weather modification again. You take that knowledge with you to your grave. Those are my terms, Sir, and they are not negotiable." The President was standing, glaring at Bob by the time he completed his words

Bob knew he had no place to go right now. If he declined the President's offer, he had no chance of getting anything done. They would keep the devices; they already had them. Bob recognized fear on the President's face and he sensed it was fear of what decisions he would have to make if the Professor decided to cowboy this technology on his own. Bob couldn't chance the limits of fear, especially if that fear was within the most powerful man in the world. He knew, if he refused the men in this room, there was little recourse for them to take except to deal with him as an enemy of theirs and an enemy of the state. He didn't need that kind of pressure, not now, not ever. What he needed was some more time, a better plan, and some help. None of Bob's friends even knew where he was for the past few days and certainly none of them knew he was meeting with the President.

It was easy to say, but hard to do, "I'll take your offer Mr. President. Five billion dollars is a lot of money but we both know you'd have spent much more than that trying to duplicate this technology. But I think we should agree to the specifics and write them down. I'd like a contract Sir," Bob's reply was unexpected. He finally decided to break eye contact with the President and look at the others in the room. Their faces showed emotions ranging from pleasure to amazement. Captain Lessur was dumbfounded at the entire happenings. Truth be known, there turned out to be no real reason to have him in the room but he was present just in case there were some technical questions about the demonstrations the Professor had given. The President smiled at Bob as he reached for his chair and regained control of his emotion. Sitting back down he said, "Good then. We can have a contract Bob but this will be complicated. We'll have to bring in military lawyers to draw up some classified papers for that," the President began to explain but Bob interrupted him.

"Excuse me, Sir, but, with all due respect, I don't think that will be necessary. I'm a simple man and all I am after is your offer on paper. If you'll just write it down and sign it that will be fine with me. The United States gives Robert Mcleod five billion-dollars, tax free, lump sum payment for his weather modification technology and four Thor's Hammer devices. He is not to work on this technology in any way, ever again without the personal permission of the President of the United States. You write it out we both sign it and get a copy. Sweet and simple Sir, I don't need a lawyer for that unless you do, Sir," Bob offered.

The President pondered for a brief moment. This had become personal with him now and he didn't even consult the others in the room. Bob could see the man hated to be challenged but he was not one to back down from a fight. It appeared to him that this blue jeans-clad young scientist was challenging the President of the United States and that could meet with nothing less than a quick, decisive response from the man the world looked to for leadership. "Okay, Professor. We'll keep it simple and I'll write it up just like that for you. But know this, Bob, it will be simple on paper but our lives are no longer simple. This technology you bring to the world will make sure of that. This is great potential for both good and bad. That is why I am willing to pay such a price for it but you, too, will pay a price for your work. We will have to watch you all the time. *Trust but verify* is the name of the national security game we play in here. We will trust you to do what you say. But we will verify that you are keeping that trust. That is not a threat or a personal vendetta; it is a requirement. We watch others that could threaten our government or national security, so it's not just you, Bob, but certainly you understand why this is now necessary?" The President leaned over the table, awaiting Bob's reply as he reached into his pocket and pulled out a pen. He nodded to General Charles for some executive letterhead from his desk.

As the general brought the paper over Bob replied, "Yes Sir, I understand. My life just became our life, right?"

"That was well put, son; I guess you do understand," the President smiled as he began to write. Bob watched as he wrote word for word, exactly what Bob had spoken. He was impressed with the President's talent for recall and knew by the writing that the President had heard and acknowledged every word Bob had spoken. When he completed the one-page writing, he pushed it over to Bob and said, "There you go, Professor. If it's okay, just print and sign your name there on the left and I'll do mine on the right. After all, I am the President. His mood had lightened, and it was obvious to all that he was pleased with himself. He had gotten the best of the deal and he and everyone else knew it.

Bob signed it and smiled back, pushing the paper and pen back across the table, "There you go Mr. President." The President printed his name and signed it next to Bob's signature.

"Somebody make one copy of this please," the President instructed, holding up the letter. Before he knew it, Captain Lessur was taking the paper from him and walking toward the door. "Hold on son; right there is a copier. Don't leave the room until the Professor has his receipt," he smiled as the silence in the room was broken with laughter. "Bob, tell me a little bit more about what we are getting for our money," the President asked.

"Sir," Bob began, "You are getting weather on-demand. You name it and it can be done. Change the temperature, wind direction, speed...make it rain or snow. Pretty much the entire spectrum of natural phenomena. I hope you put it to good use, Sir. There are a lot of hungry people in the world who are counting on you now." Bob's words bit hard into the conscience of each person in that room and he knew it; that was his intention. He continued, "Gentlemen, this technology was not developed for weaponry or with malicious intent. It is intended for the good of people, people all over the world. Our country is uniquely postured to deliver that good and that is what I am counting on. I know it will take some time to make that happen and I understand that defense is critical. But once you work all that out, I am counting on you to bring the good of this technology to the world. I hope that doesn't take you all too long. You bought a lot of good with this money, Mr. President; that's what you bought. I hope that is what it brings us all," Bob concluded.

Captain Lessur handed the two papers back to the President, who in turn pushed the original across the table to Bob. "Nobody gets to see that but you, Professor. We'll see to it that IRS, FBI, banking commission and everybody else stays off you. You can't hide billion-dollar transactions for long, but suffice to say it will be where you say you want it. If the word leaks out from you that we have this technology or that letter shows up anywhere, your assets will be frozen and you'll be in prison so long we won't remember where we put you. The only way that letter is good is if it never sees the light of day, Bob. Do you have anything else for me Professor?"

"No Sir, that's it," Bob said.

"Very well, then. You'll be escorted back to your rooms and someone will let you know when to be ready to fly back. It has been a pleasure doing business with you, Professor...an honor to finally meet you." The President stood and shook Bob's hand, as the rest of the men followed suit. As Bob was nearly to the door, he stopped and turned, "There is one other thing, Mr. President. The pen? Would you mind terribly if I kept the pen you used? You know, kind of like a souvenir? I always see it on TV when you sign stuff. Would you mind?"

"Not at all. Here you go, Bob, I wouldn't have figured you for the sentimental type. Enjoy your fortune and keep your promise." The President smiled as he opened the door for the two of them and they exited on cue. That was that. Bob and Captain Lessur were met at the door and the agent was instructed to return them to their room at Andrews. They walked through the White House to the waiting Suburban silently, both their minds still racing over the events that just occurred. It was a quick ride back to the suite and they both were silent the entire drive, staring out the windows of the moving vehicle but not really seeing anything as they concentrated on the meaning of their meeting with the President.

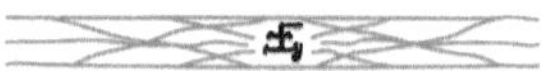

As the President returned to his seat at the table his National Security Advisor spoke first, "Sir, with all due respect, we are going to need him to do a lot of the work to get us up to speed on this technology. I don't believe this will be a simple case of reverse engineering like we can do with some simpler weapon system."

"You're right. But we don't have him, not now. You guys take as much time as he will give you and pick his brain as clean as he will come, but don't press him too hard or he'll clam up and we'll be screwed. Make sure you get him to show you how to operate and maintain the devices we already have; then focus on learning the technology. We can't afford to have anyone using this against us, especially him. And make damned sure we know where he is every second of every day. I will personally call down there and ask when the last time he brushed his teeth and you guys better know. We lose him into the ether and he becomes public enemy number one until we got him clamped down again. Every electron from his computers, finances, telephone...*everything* gets recorded and filed. We are going to need him later, when he cools off, and I want to know everything,

I want to have something to leverage him with. Gentlemen, I think we are going to need it if we hope to get his help weaponizing this technology for us if we ever need to. I don't think there is going to be any other way with him except coercion. Am I wrong?" the President concluded.

"No Sir, I believe you are exactly right," the Secretary of Defense replied. "He told me this was for applications to better mankind, just like he told you to do good with it. He won't help us much to weaponize it. He'll probably even work to prevent it if given the opportunity."

"We need to weaponize it first so we can be around to do good with it. We'll have to convince him of that. I still believe that and I think I can convince him over time with the right motivation. Does anyone disagree that we weaponize first?" The President's question was more of a challenge and the edge in his voice clearly indicated that his question was rhetorical. "Good, then. Gentlemen, you know what to do so go do it. Thank you and remember how important security is on this thing. General Charles, I am counting on you to clean up everything from those demos and the Feds. I don't want the Justice Department involved in this at all. That's all gentlemen, have a nice day." General Charles nodded and the men stood to leave the room. As they departed the office and headed toward their waiting vehicles it began to rain. *How fitting*, General Charles thought to himself, *how poetic this rain seemed to be as they drove off the White House grounds.*

Bob and Captain Ron Lessur walked into their room and closed the door behind them. "Holy cow Professor! I knew that meeting would be memorable but I didn't expect anything like that; maybe you shouldn't have worn jeans!" Ron tried to lighten the mood and it worked.

"You think that was it? Maybe I'd have only gotten half a billion if I dressed nice. I figured this way he'd know I needed the money," Bob smiled. "I don't think he likes me very much."

"What do we do now? I guess hurry up and wait huh? You get used to that working with the Army," the captain continued.

"Be careful there, Captain, I'm sure we're being recorded, you don't want to say anything to get you into trouble now do you?" Bob warned. Ron got a sullen look on his face when he realized Bob was certainly correct. Then he understood why Bob slept so long the night before and commented only on the things he did before the meeting. Ron was disappointed that he didn't give that a thought himself and made a mental note to watch closely what he said from then on.

Three guards were posted at their quarters last night and there were now three new faces on duty. Bob believed the President would keep his end of the deal and did not think he was in any immediate danger. On the way back to Andrews, Bob had given a lot of thought to just skipping out at the earliest possible opportunity but had thought better of it after contemplating potential outcomes of that option. No, better to continue to sit tight, help them along, collect his money and then glide off in as low a profile as he could maintain. That course of action would give them the greatest confidence that they were still in control, and Bob knew that was important. What he didn't know was who *they* were now.

He had to assume the military, the FBI, CIA and who knows what other organizations would be tasked to keep tabs on him. They needed enough information to be satisfied that all was well, and Bob could use little holes in their satisfaction to do whatever else he decided. That would take some time but they would be all over him very soon—if not already—so he knew he needed to be more patient and hope for some complacency to creep in down the road. There would be none at first, not after the President issued a directive to the men in the room that Bob's life was now their life...at least for now.

"Well, Ron, how long do you think we'll have to wait here before we go back home?" Bob asked the captain.

"I don't know, Sir. They'll probably fly us back under guarded escort; so they'll use their own transportation. Probably tomorrow afternoon." Ron had no sooner spoken the words when he heard the knock on the door as it swung open. The man wore a gray suit and stepped inside leaving the door wide open, "Gentlemen, pack you gear we're going to the airport. We leave in ten minutes." And back out the door he went, closing it behind him.

"Bob, for two months I haven't been able to forecast anything right, and I'm starting to think it's because of you," Ron Lessur smirked at Bob, "Let's get packed up; we don't want to be late for our bus." The two moved to their rooms to pack up the items they brought. The trip was much shorter than either of them expected and they assumed they were heading back home, but neither of them had the inclination to inquire about the destination and they weren't sure they really wanted to know the answer.

They loaded up into the Suburban and headed off to the flight line. They could see a small jet landing as they drove toward the gate. "Are we flying out from here?" Captain Lessur inquired. "Yes," was the only response from the driver, and they made their way through the flight line checkpoint and proceeded to a signal man and stopped. The small jet that just landed was taxiing in their direction; it was their ride. It bore Air Force markings. It was one of the small jets they use to transport senior general officers and dignitaries around to avoid the attention, hassles, and risks of flying the commercial airlines.

It pulled up and, with the engines running, dropped the door and a crewman stepped out. He conferred with the man in the gray suit, grabbed up their bags and loaded them into the aircraft, then motioned for the passengers to come up. Bob and Ron were loaded in first, and the two passengers in the suburban followed them into the aircraft. The suburban departed after the aircraft door was closed and they immediately began to taxi out to the runway. They were on their way but they were not sure where. The trip was quiet. Both the travelers knew whatever they said would be either recorded or reported by their escorts, so they took advantage of their comfortable digs by napping and reading some magazines onboard.

A couple of hours later they noticed indications of preparation-to-land activities in the cockpit. They began their descent through the now dark sky towards their destination. Almost immediately after touchdown, the pilot applied the brakes hard and the aircraft shook momentarily in an obvious effort to use as little runway as possible for the landing. As it turned out, that was because there was very little runway to use here, and the small jet needed all of it at maximum performance just to take off and land. There were a couple of sets of lights on and they both recognized their location as the isolation facility they had just left the night before. It was nice to be back to more familiar surroundings, even if they weren't nearly as fancy as the ones they had just left. They could see two men waiting in the lit area and it didn't take long for them to recognize them as Colonel Lincoln and Major Naed.

As the aircraft taxied over and stopped, three more men in suits appeared. The plane stopped, the door opened, and the two men stepped down to the pavement. Colonel Lincoln extended his hand to Bob, "Welcome back. How did it go?"

"Very well Frank, very well. Thanks," Bob yelled over the engines of the aircraft. The group walked over to the nearest building as the plane began to taxi back onto the small runway to depart. The three new agents picked up the escort duty, while the two that flew down with Bob and Ron remained on the aircraft. Two minutes later it was gone into the night sky.

They walked the short distance from the small flight line to the chow hall area of the isolation facility, just making small talk about the flight and how quickly they had to open up the runway so the jet could land here. That was no small task and Colonel Lincoln took the opportunity to let them know he had to jump through hoops so they could get back in here and not have to endure another transload or a long drive from somewhere to get back out here. It had been a while since an airplane had used the strip. It was used to helicopter traffic, and it had been a while since there was even any of that out here before this week.

The men entered the dining area where they had all stood in awe the night before when Bob had produced the tornado for the Chairman and the Secretary of Defense. "A lot has happened in twenty-four hours," Captain Ron Lessur said to the anxious crew all seated together as they walked in and saw the men all sitting around the table sipping coffee. "You aren't going to believe it."

Ron gave the curious men his version of the happenings of the past day as he remembered them. He was accurate but a bit more emotionally charged than Bob would have liked. Still, he sat quietly and did not interrupt the young captain's dissertation. Ron spoke for more than thirty minutes about their trip and Bob decided to take in the captain's perceptions of the events to see if they interpreted the events the same way and maybe pick up a few things he didn't see from his own vantage. Bob had eyes locked with the President almost the entire time he was in the room and he was interested in the reaction of the other men in the room. Ron offered some information but, apparently, he was watching Bob and the President most of the time. Bob was a bit surprised that the information Ron was sharing hadn't been deemed super-secret or something. It wasn't the kind of stuff you wanted blabbed around, especially if you were the President of the United States. That thought was just about on cue as Colonel Lincoln finally interrupted the young captain who was nearing the end of his tale.

"You all know, of course, that the description of the day's events that you just heard is your compensation for a job well done here. That story, and every shred of what you have heard and done these past few days is classified top secret, compartmented, code word *Thor's Hammer*. You cannot discuss it; you cannot even acknowledge it exists outside this room. You may as well not even remember it after tomorrow, just like it never happened. We finish our work here tomorrow and then we get on with our own business. We will meet in the morning at 0700 for teardown instructions and we will de-brief each of you by 1400 and you'll be home for supper. Get some rest; I'll see you all at seven. Professor Mcleod, Sir, I'd like you to join me in my office to go over a few things before you turn in if you don't mind?" Frank concluded.

"Yes Colonel, no problem. But I have to warn you, I've gotten my second wind listening to Ron tell me about yesterday," Bob replied. "Good night gentlemen." Bob followed Frank into the small office and closed the door behind him, taking a seat on the small but comfortable chair across from the table the colonel was using for a desk.

"Sounds like you had quite an adventure," Frank opened the conversation.

"Yeah, we did. It wasn't what I had planned, but I guess what is done is done, and all that is left to do is go on from here." Bob was being direct but he had to test the waters a bit with Frank before he offered any details.

"General Charles talked to me several times today, Bob. It is not normal for an Air Force colonel to be getting detailed orders directly form the Chairman of the Joint Chiefs of Staff. But this is not a common situation we find ourselves in," Frank continued.

"Okay Frank, I'll spare you the pain. What's next? What did he tell you to do with me and my gadgets?" Bob dug right into the meat and potatoes of the conversation he had become pretty good at that the past few days.

"A plane arrives tomorrow morning. You and your devices will be loaded and taken to a top-secret Army research facility in the Southwest US. There, you will do technology transfer and training to a scientific team. That will take as long as it takes them to understand how the devices and the technology work. In the meantime, someone here looks after your house, your dog, and all your stuff. If you need something you don't have, they will get it for you. If you have something you don't need, they will return it for you. A series of bank accounts have already been set up for you— in your name only—in a variety of banks here in the US. Your entire five billion has already been deposited but you can only get to a small portion of it. When the technology transfer is complete, the remainder will be released, but none of it is transferable outside U.S territories. That way, they can freeze all your assets anytime you fail to live up to your end of the bargain. That is about all I know right now but that is a lot for one afternoon. Anything you want to tell me about the trip or your deal?" Frank asked.

"As a friend or as a colonel reporting directly to the Chairman of the JCS?" Bob asked seriously.

"I guess it looks like I had that coming, huh? I don't know myself if I can separate the two anymore, Bob. But let's try them in reverse order," Frank responded sincerely, but a bit unsure of himself.

"Nothing else for the colonel. But for my friend of the past few days, I'll say thanks for your help and your caring. I don't believe the President will do anything with what I give him except weaponize it and use it for our national advantage. I think he believes he bought himself a power that cannot be beaten and he might be right. I didn't start this thing for anyone in particular except maybe myself. But I know a lot of people can benefit from it and I'd hate to think that will never happen because of one man. No, because of two men—him and me. I hope he can see the good in all this and use this technology to make the world a better place and soon. I really *hope* he intends to do that, but I really *doubt* he will," Bob smiled. "That's about all I have for either of you. If you don't have anything else, I think I'll turn in too," Bob smiled again and headed for the door. It wasn't really a question; he was finished and so was their conversation.

"Good night, Bob, and thanks," Frank waved to him as he left the room. He wished there was more he could do for the man but he knew there was nothing left to do. He had his orders and he was to carry them out. They weren't bad but he wished he could have a more positive forecast for the events to come. He too believed that Bob was right and both of them had become pretty good at reading people over the years. They both had the same feeling. It was hard to see it any other way given the outcome of the meeting in Washington and the turnover plan. Tomorrow would be the beginning of another chapter in the history for bringing this technology to the world and neither man felt very good about the way it was shaping up.

CHAPTER EIGHT

MAKING GOOD ON THE DEAL

Morning came quickly for the entire crew, but especially for Bob who just seemed to put his head on his pillow when Captain Lessur was rousting him. They ate a quick and quiet breakfast knowing it wouldn't be long before they were all to be debriefed and released to their lives...the lives they knew before their involvement with Professor Bob Mcleod. Bob felt obliged to say something, as he knew he would be departing sooner than the rest of them, "Gentlemen, I'd like to say something to you all. Can I have your attention please?"

Bob stood up and looked around at the small group of men assembled in the dining hall. "I'd just like to take a moment to say three things to you all. First, I'd like to apologize to you all for getting you involved in something without your knowledge and disrupting your lives. I hope you will forgive me for that. Second, I'd like to thank you all for your help in getting us all through this so far without anyone getting hurt; so, thanks. And lastly, I'd like to wish you all good luck. I probably won't see any of you again, if all goes well, I suppose. So, best of luck to you all and, once again, thank you," Bob concluded his comments by walking to the exit and heading for his bunk to pack up his gear. As he headed for the door, the men in the room clapped and stood for him. He had earned their respect and, to Bob Mcleod right now, that was worth more than the billions of dollars he had waiting for him in his new bank accounts.

For the second time in ten hours, a small aircraft landed on the airstrip outside the isolation facility. Bob knew it was his ride. The devices were already packed in weapon containers and marked as extremely hazardous material. Bob had his few things already packed, as the three agents summoned him to catch the taxiing aircraft. They began to load the weapon transport containers; each housing one of the Thor's Hammer devices. Bob's bag went in behind them and the three agents and Bob Mcleod climbed the steps to the passenger compartment. Almost immediately the aircraft began to taxi back to the active runway while the steps were still being lifted and secured for the flight. Bob waved unceremoniously out the small window but knew there was little chance of anyone really seeing him. It seemed anti-climactic in a sense...the way he departed the team. Like it was no big deal...business as usual and, perhaps, it *was* that way in the military Bob thought. He had never been in the service, so he didn't know. Maybe it was that way all the time but it was new to him. They were very professional; that was just their way; do the mission the best they could then get on with the next task at hand. It made sense but it appeared strange to Bob and doing it was very different than saying it. The aircraft was off quickly after a short take off roll.

"So, where we going fellas? You have to tell me otherwise it's kidnapping and we don't need any of that now do we?" Bob asked nobody in particular.

"To the desert, Sir, specifically a part of west Texas even the Texans don't care about. You might as well settle in and get comfortable. It is gonna take a few hours and at least one stop for gas. I sure hope the weather holds; they are calling for some rough stuff this afternoon," the agent reported to Bob.

He smiled. "At least that I can help you with. Let me know if you need a hand. Meanwhile I think I am going to get a nap. I am beat—didn't get enough sleep last night—maybe I can catch up," Bob replied, and a few minutes later he was asleep again. The airplane shuddered as the pilot landed and applied the brakes. Bob woke with a start and looked immediately out the small window to see what had happened. He knew all was well as he saw the ground and the small buildings speeding by outside the aircraft. He didn't even concern himself with where they were. He could tell it was not a major airport. In fact, it was probably not even on the map but it was where they chose to land. Bob reasoned this was the fuel stop the agent had mentioned earlier and he was correct.

The jet was fueled with the passengers onboard and fifteen minutes later the plane was once again airborne, heading southwest into Texas. Bob decided to continue his napping. After all, the first one had gone so well. This time he fidgeted and couldn't get comfortable but it was more mental than physical. He was having a hard time accepting his decision and his fate even though he really had no choice in the matter. That was the real concern. He could do nothing if he were dead and that is exactly where Bob truly believed he would be if he had not accepted the President's offer; he could see it in his eyes. The man would have had him killed before he allowed him to threaten the country with such a device but it troubled Bob because he thought he would have done the same thing if their roles were reversed.

It was bothering Bob Mcleod that he despised the man for what he did but Bob knew that was the only option. So, Bob did the only thing he could have done, *right?* If it was the right thing to do, then why was he so troubled by doing it? Bob knew Dr. Jim Auster had already provided him with the answer to that question and now he was not in a position to deliver what the Doc had worked so hard to gain. That was what the real troubles were, not the fact that the seats were uncomfortable or that there was too much light coming into the cabin through the too-small windows.

Bob knew he had to deliver the weather modification technology as promised or there would be no chance of any good ever coming from it. Unfortunately for Bob, he didn't have a plan yet for how to make it right with Doc and the rest of the world. He knew a rich man with good intentions had a better chance of pulling it off than a dead man who took the secrets but not the devices or the technology with him. No, he had to give it up as planned, convincingly and completely or there would be no new opportunity. It would take some time and some thinking to change the course they were on now. But Bob knew with his new wealth he could bide time and posture for his next move, even if it took decades to make. Eventually, the entire world would benefit from Doc's technology and Bob Mcleod would see to it if it was the last thing he did. He was equally determined to see that it was not the last thing he ever did and that was the hard part.

Now, he had to deliver the Thor's Hammers, explain the technology as he understood it, and provide the recipe codes to people he hadn't even met yet. He wondered if this was how a prostitute felt, taking money for something they could never get back. Knowing they were going out to do something they didn't really want to do but had to in order to survive. Getting paid for giving something that should be given freely out of love rather than bought; their hearts not in it but their needs or desires overcoming their knowledge of good and bad.

It was a tough pill to swallow for the man who had always believed it was more important to do the right thing than to do things right. He would deliver the goods as he promised and get the money. He would buy lots of things with his wealth and do good stuff with his money but the one thing he vowed to himself was to somehow make good on his posthumous promise to Doc and his wife. He would make them both proud but it would take some time and now a much more indirect path. It would be difficult, but he would find a way because not doing it would be even more difficult for Bob Mcleod. Sleep finally came.

The aircraft was taxiing down the long black asphalt strip when Bob was awakened by the agent announcing they had arrived. "Welcome to Texas," he said, sarcastically, "Of course this part of Texas nobody really cares about, that's what makes it great for us." Bob could see two Suburbans waiting at the end of the taxiway, facing toward a dirt road that led off into the vast desert. There was an air of familiarity in the scene, mostly from Bob's imagination because he had never spent any time in the desert.

The blue sky was a sharp contrast against the brown of the desert, and the long black asphalt ribbon of road that disappeared over the horizon. The plane stopped near the two big vehicles and the engines shut down. A fuel truck was approaching the plane from one of the two buildings across the runway as the door opened and the warm wind blew into the cabin of the small plane. Bob was glad to be out, even if it was in the middle of nowhere. He and the agents climbed out of the small plane and surveyed their new surroundings as the doors of the Suburbans opened and several men dressed in casual clothes approached the suited men who had just deplaned.

They conferred for about ten minutes as Bob milled around checking over the cargo and his bags now lying on the pavement. Several of the men from the suburban began to load the cargo into the first Suburban and the agents who accompanied them on the flight began to climb back into the small jet. Bob was momentarily uncomfortable as the two men who had been talking approached him. He thought *if they were going to kill him, now would be the right time and a great place.*

"Professor Mcleod, this is Agent Zach. He will be taking you and your gear from here. Good luck, Sir," the lead agent said, then he turned and began walking toward the waiting aircraft.

"My pleasure," Bob replied to both agents, then extended his hand to Agent Zach.

He shook Bob's hand and invited, "This way, Sir, we have about a two-hour drive ahead of us and the sooner we are on our way the better. How was your flight?"

"I slept through most of it, so I guess that makes it a good one. I doubt I'll be able to sleep through the drive though. Where are we off to?" Bob replied.

"Work, Professor; there is much to do and the team is waiting for you. They are very excited and anxiously awaiting your arrival. I must warn you, though, they will want to get started as soon as you arrive. Just consider yourself warned; these guys are real geeks and they get excited about a lot of stuff. But I have never seen them this fired up about anything. You must have quite a treat lined up for them." Agent Zach seemed nice enough but Bob decided that he was not going to get too friendly with anyone from this point on. He had confided in Frank and, although he felt safe enough in what he had told him, he didn't want to put anyone in a position where they would have to choose between loyalties to their employer or Bob. It was like Frank said, he had a job and a duty to carry out even if it meant choosing mission over friendship. He didn't need that now and he didn't want to put anyone in that position. Cordial—but distant—would be Bob's rule of thumb for this phase of the operation.

He climbed up into the second Suburban and they drove out into the desert. The entire trip the landscape never changed. Nothing but rolling hills of scant vegetation and sandy soil on both sides of the road for as far as the eye could see. It was the same view he had at the airport but there was no runway here. Otherwise, it was the same. There were spots along the road where it was covered with sand blown across from larger fetches with no wind breaks, much like snow in the winter where Bob grew up. It was clear the road got very little traffic. It seemed to go on forever leading nowhere and Bob thought that was an interesting way to describe the path he had found himself on lately.

Finally, after a long quiet ride through the desert, Bob could see some small, flat buildings on the horizon. As they came closer, Bob could see that they were surrounded by several layers of razor-wire concertina fencing. The area was surprisingly small—about half the size of a football field—with two small buildings inside the wire roughly the size of gas stations to one side of the road. Bob was surprised to see that one of them was indeed a gas and water station and the other building was a small building with a discrete sign that read visitor's center. "Visiting what?" Bob said aloud, but he soon noticed the armed guards at the dirt road entrance to the small compound containing the two buildings. "This is it? No wonder they were excited about getting company; you guys must be kidding. Are you staying, too, or what?" Bob's voice began to demonstrate his ability to speak a few octaves higher than the tone he used for the small talk they shared on the drive through the desert.

"Relax, Professor, we are almost there. A lot more to this place than meets the eye," Agent Zach commented. Just then, the Suburban pulled off the main road onto the dirt road leading into the compound. They cleared the small, guarded gate, as the rent-a-cop waved them through. They drove under awnings covering the gas and water pumps and headed for the visitor's center. The vehicles made a hard left turn down a small ramp that led to an underground parking garage. It was, indeed, much larger than Bob had expected and he could see that it continued down for several more levels. They stopped for another guard. This one was heavily armed and the security point was much more forbidding than the one at the gate. Large caliber automatic weapons permanently mounted on turrets and heavy moveable barriers were the most visible of the first level of defense to the underground facility they were about to enter.

They passed four similar security points on their descent to the main level of the underground facility. Steel and concrete pocket doors were the standard entry to each of the large and small doorways leading into the main structure. Each was guarded by robotically controlled mini-guns with complete lanes of fire covering every possible avenue of entry or escape. This place was deep underground, secure, heavily defended, and very hidden from the world above whether you happened to drive by or be looking for it from an overhead satellite. Bob was beginning to feel more and more like he was where he expected to be...inside the hidden world of technology development and exploitation. He understood he was there to be exploited and this place looked like it would live up to his expectations.

They stopped in front of the largest of the visible doors and turned off the engines. There were no parking places anywhere near the entrances. The closest one was sixty feet above them at the last check point. An escalator and moving sidewalk descended steeply from the parking lot's personnel entry point to the main sidewalk adjacent the series of doors. An easy shot from the security point or the door guns, regardless of which direction you were trying to go, in or out. There was no path for vehicles to crash into any doors. Bob climbed out of the Suburban and looked around the surprisingly cool, but dry area he was standing in. There was little to see, and the agents were busy unloading the cases and gear Bob had packed and brought along. Bob had some of his own computers, files, and other belongings packed and sent here too. He asked if Agent Miloc could continue watching and feeding Buck, and that request was begrudgingly granted. Bob wanted someone Buck knew to be taking care of him...and to have someone he knew be able to verify how long Bob had been gone.

He trusted Miloc more than most men and hoped if anything went tragically wrong, at least some outside influence was possible. He just hoped he hadn't put him in any danger by keeping one of the original men involved in the disclosure still a participant in his activity...and, perhaps, seen as a threat. Bob felt like he had to take that chance. Even if they went after Miloc, chances of getting that cagey guy were slim. He had that going in his favor.

They easily gathered up the gear and walked toward the entrance, where Agent Zach entered a numeric code into a keypad, and then stood motionless before a flat plane of glass that scanned his retina as well as his photograph and handprint to ensure and cross-check his identity. The place was as secure as any in the nation—the world for that matter—and they were about to enter and get to work. The door opened and all the men walked inside, still burdened by the bags containing Bob's gear.

Once inside, there was a series of metal detectors, scanners, X-ray machines, and explosive residue detectors to clear before they entered a holding area where they would obtain badges and security codes for the areas they would be permitted to access. This place was tough to get into for sure and Bob believed it would be even tougher to get out. The security cameras recorded every activity. They were everywhere and they were motion sensitive. So, if you were moving, at least one of the many cameras focused on you. It was a truly remarkable place and quite abuzz with the latest in electronic and physical security gadgetry.

They walked down a long corridor, passed only by the occasional person wearing a white lab coat with a few identification badges hanging from their neck. The place was clean, stark, and devoid of any decorations. The floors were carpeted and there was ample lighting, artificial sunlight in a place that was never intended to see the real light of day. There was nothing that differentiated it from any other sterile building interior, except for the knowledge that they were hundreds of feet below the surface of the earth. It was secure, isolated, armed, quiet, and largely invisible. There were no interruptions unless they were invited; there were no visitors unless they were scheduled. The men entered a large auditorium and, to Bob's surprise, it was nearly filled by over one hundred people sitting in the theater style chairs stretched out before the podium on stage. They all began to talk among themselves as the small group of men entered. Their presence had caused quite a commotion it seemed and it appeared they were all assembled to greet, meet, or otherwise witness some activity involving Professor Robert Mcleod.

As they walked toward the front of the assembly, Bob became much less comfortable than he had been before. He could feel the eyes of the group upon him. He could tell they were here waiting for him, waiting for something he had not yet been told about...something for which he'd have no time to prepare. Bob could tell he was going to be in the hot seat and he didn't like it—not one little bit.

Agent Zach motioned for Bob to follow him onto the platform that held the podium. He began to address the group immediately, "Ladies and gentlemen, I appreciate your attendance and your interest in our new project. I have with me Professor Robert Mcleod, the man responsible for R&D as well as prototyping the Thor's Hammer. He will be with us for a while." The group applauded staring at the man standing before them at the podium. Bob waved and smiled an insincere smile at those in the auditorium. "If you'll excuse us now, the good Professor has had a long journey, and we must get him in-processed and settled in so we can begin our work as soon as possible. Thank you for taking the time from your busy schedules to welcome our new colleague, Professor Bob Mcleod."

Agent Zach led Bob back off the podium and up through the small auditorium into the hallway.

"What was all that?" Bob asked in an agitated voice.

"You just met your new partners in weather modification professor. You'll meet some of them individually of course but, for now, they needed to meet you more than you need to meet them. We must in-process so you can get your prints entered into the access computers. We haven't much time," replied Zach.

"This is one high-tech weird place you have here, Agent Zach," Bob said.

"Well, I am in charge of security but it is certainly not my place. I really don't know who runs it officially. Lots of agencies I suppose have some stake in it to ensure we have no shortage of funding. I can assure you we have no shortage of funding. A staggering number of technological advances have been developed here—many of which you may be familiar with—but many you will never see until it is useful to reveal them. But yours...now there is a unique and elusive technology. Controlling the weather, on a whim...Now, that is a useful but dangerous capability don't you think?" Bob thought Agent Zach had to be more than the head of security, although that was itself impressive enough in this place. No, he had too much knowledge, insight, and curiosity. He had to have a broader role to match the interest he was showing and being the first one engaging with Bob...but he would learn more of that later he thought.

"You know a lot and ask a lot for a security guy. What else do you do?" Bob surprised even himself with the question and Zach was a bit surprised as well.

"You are very observant aren't you, Bob? I am indeed more than head of security. Although I do perform that function, I am not limited to it. I also own several of the advanced technologies this place works on. You could say I am sort of a partner in the firm. But rest assured, your stay here is only temporary and then you'll be on your way to enjoy the small fortune your work has earned you. By most standards five billion dollars is not a small fortune but it is not the largest one I've been involved with either. We need to get your eyes and hands printed and your body imaged before we do anything else. Then I will rejoin you and we will get something to eat. I'll give you a tour of our facility and explain the rules and emergency procedures. Don't worry...we have never had to use the emergency procedures. Our underground facility is the *most advanced* and operates the *most reliable* systems in the world. Nothing but the best for our people. See you in a little while."

Zach turned and left Bob at the entrance of a room filled with contraptions Bob had never seen before and three technicians who motioned for him to enter. The remaining agents were standing in the hallway and, although Bob was certain there was no worry in them about him trying to escape, he was surprised that they were still very diligent in their guard duties. He reasoned they were now tasked to protect him or, more appropriately, protect the government's investment in him more than anything else. Probably to protect them more from Bob hurting himself than any other threat. It made sense given all that had happened. The President hadn't gotten his five billion dollars' worth yet and Bob was still as valuable to national security as he was a threat to it.

He moved over to the first station on the largest machine and followed the technician's instructions. Half an hour later he was, printed, scanned, photographed, badged, coded and ready for lunch. Almost immediately, Agent Zach reappeared and they headed for the cafeteria just down the hall. A beautiful dining area; china plates and silverware, real glasses and cloth napkins were the standard. Several cooks stood behind the entry line and you ordered your selection. It was then prepared for you on the spot. It was impressive and the selection was virtually unlimited, cross cultured and impressively exotic. Zach ordered a Maine lobster with a side of curried rice and Asian prickly fruit. Bob ordered a medium rare T-bone steak with baked potato and carrots. Then they sat down to await their meal.

"I really love eating here. I have become spoiled about dining and I have to work out much more frequently since coming here so I can maintain my weight. It is more difficult, but certainly worth it," Zach confessed to

Bob as he laid the napkin across his lap. "So, Bob, what do you want to know about this place and what your role here will be, or is that just it?"

"Let's start with that; what will my role be?" Bob countered. He felt like he was being toyed with in a little one-on-one with his new shadow Zach, but smartly assumed they were being monitored and recorded for others to evaluate as well. He learned that lesson the hard way at Andrews and he wasn't going to assume anything different. He wasn't going to make that mistake twice but perhaps could leverage it somehow while he was here.

"Your role is very simple really; tell and show us all you know about modifying the weather. Show us how to build, maintain, operate, and repair the Thor's Hammer devices. Impart your knowledge to us and make sure we know all that you know so you never have to come back and do any of the work yourself. Keep your deal with the President. That's it really." Zach's reply was more than matter of fact, it was cold and calculated. It was, in fact, strictly instructive in nature.

"That, like most things, is simple, just not easy," Bob jousted back too quickly.

"Spirited? Yes, Professor *simple* but not easy. Well, that is your role here. The duration of your stay is entirely up to you really. The employees here are all committed to their work and are very well taken care of. They like it here. Their lives are simplified by the structure, security, and their work. Many of them are far more comfortable here than they ever were with their lives in the world above. It can be cruel; people can be cruel to those they think are different...those they don't understand...the geeks, the brilliant but brutalized geniuses of our time. Not everyone gets lucky like celebrity billionaires who make fortunes from their ideas whether they deserve to or not. No, we have quite a group of folks here who prefer it to the outside, who would not be too disappointed if they never left a place like this where they are respected, treated like royalty, and accepted without hesitation by those around them just because they are here."

"You may find you also like our complex enough to stay with us for quite a while and, of course, *if* you follow the rules, you may stay as long as you like. It is simple Bob but, as you say, it is not easy. I predict you will not want to stay with us, though. You are too passionate. You still hold the freedom to demean our activities and principles. You would find us too confining and restrictive for your more boorish behavior. We rather see our rules as freeing us from the confinement we endured while living with the masses. No, I think you won't stay long but we are, nonetheless, most glad to have you, and we have much to learn from you. Ah, let's eat. They are as good as they are quick when it comes to preparing a wonderful meal my friend; dig in," Zach concluded as a man in a white serving jacket brought out two large plates with their orders. He placed the food before them and immediately left them to their discussion.

"Looks good. Let's see how it is; you should never grade things on appearance. It's what's inside that matters," Bob replied metaphorically and could tell by the smile that it was not lost on Zach. "So, my role here is simple and, when you get what you need, I am free to go?"

"That's it really. Is the steak to your liking? It is Angus, my favorite beef," Zach added.

"The steak is excellent, thank you. So, what kind of stuff will you and your band of merry men do with the technology I am bringing you?" Bob got right to the heart of the matter.

"Well, that depends on a lot of things really. How it works for starters. What the ramifications are in terms of stability and applications to other problem sets...economy of scale, range limitations and the like. I suppose the options are many. That is what we will learn in the days ahead," Zach answered truthfully.

"But your primary task is to weaponize it for them?" Now Bob was really hitting at the heart of his own concern.

"Bob, you have been reading too many bad novels. You have already weaponized it for us my friend. It is small lightweight, easily transported and concealed. They require low power input and appear to be made from parts you bought off the shelf and kludged together. How much more weaponizing do you think we need to do to put this to practical use? Instrument for good or weapon for bad; all depends on your perspective."

"No, we need to further refine and test the systems. Baseline the results and establish the operating thresholds, parameterize the effective ranges, write operating procedures. We do all that detailed scientific analysis that takes things from good ideas to wonders of modern technology for our nation. Our job is the *what, how, and why* parts. Somebody else decides *the who, the when, and the where* of the problem set here my friend. We supply them with options and technology exploitation from our diverse group of subject matter experts. What they decide to do with them is an entirely different process that takes place elsewhere." Zach was eyeing Bob intently now, hoping he didn't have to come right out and slap him with the common perspective that these men simply worked R&D on stuff they really got into and left the use and technology applications up to others. Bob got the picture...and it was all too clear to him.

"Who are *they,* in this case?" Bob asked

"The President and his National Security advisor. We have some high-ranking bosses and no middleman; it is like buying beer directly from the brewery without having to pay the distributor's markup. It is much cheaper and much more productive this way my friend," Zach replied.

"Come now, enough talking and eating. There is lots of work for us to do here. The sooner we get started the better and the sooner we all have something to celebrate," Zach prodded.

Bob knew to this point his suspicions were being confirmed. It appeared, if Zach was telling the truth, that the President himself would decide what to do with the technology once it had been examined and documented sufficiently. This was not unreasonable given the magnitude of the impacts controlling the weather could have but Bob was still uneasy about the deal he had made with the President. Not because of the money, but because he could tell a lot about the man from how he dealt with Bob. He didn't trust him to do the right thing on his own. Bob was going to have to help that man along the path of doing right with this technology. The best next step was indeed to get all these geniuses as smart as they could be on the technology and to document and parameterize the processes so they could be published, shared, and exploited when the time was right.

Bob was diligent in his turnover efforts with Zach and the other members of the secret community beneath the Texas sand. He was careful not to offend them and answered all their questions the best he could. Bob knew there were few opportunities to work with such a great pool of scientific talent as was assembled here and he was going to take advantage of it. After all, there was still so much he himself did not know about how the devices worked and he was intent on learning as much from these people as they learned from him.

The first two weeks went very smoothly and very quickly. Bob had covered just about all of the information he knew they needed to operate and understand the theory behind the devices. His next task was to instruct a group of technicians on how he built the devices and the functions and relationships of the mechanical components. This task would change his life forever. As the new group assembled for introductions and a task review, Bob was feeling very comfortable working in this setting. He estimated another two weeks, and he should be finished with his part and be able to return home. There was light at the end of the tunnel on turning over this technology and it was very appealing to him. The thought of getting back to his own life was inviting.

His little house, his neighborhood, his dog...even his truck were beginning to become fond memories and they hadn't even been his very long. He missed his friends at the University but doubted that he even had a job there anymore. After such a long unexplained absence, he was sure Durbin had already removed him and his stuff from the University completely by now. Bob was homesick and it was a new feeling for him. He had never really had an identity that he could miss until now and he found it strange that it wasn't really his, rather it was inherited from Doc Auster. Bob wanted this phase to go quickly so he could get back to the things that were waiting for him, not the least of which, was the freedom that five billion dollars would bring him.

The group had assembled and was milling around when Bob first noticed her. He found her stunning and couldn't help but stare at her for what seemed to him like a very long time. She was one of a surprisingly large number of women in the facility but there was something about her Bob recognized even before they met. She was tall with shining blue eyes, brown hair and a smile that could melt a man. She was chatting with a few other technicians but Bob could tell she was the light in the room. She was indeed something special he thought even at a distance. There was much more to learn about this lady and why she was here. His mind raced back to his warning to Zach, "Looks good. Let's see how it is, you should never grade things on appearance, it is what is inside that matters." He decided then and there he was going to try to get to know her. It had been a very, very long time since Bob Mcleod had a woman in his life.

As the group assembled and settled down, Zach began the introductions accompanied by a brief explanation of the person's specialty and expected role within the group. Bob was both pleased and impressed when he introduced the young lady as team leader for the mechanical development group. She was an exceptionally talented mechanical engineer and an experienced machinist. Her task was to design and build any custom parts required for the devices. She would also have a voice in deciding if the commercial parts currently used in the devices were suitable or should be replaced with other materials for strength, durability, safety or a myriad of other reasons.

Her name was Ann; everyone there went by a first name only and Bob wondered how many of these were their real names. It was another way to curb any deliberate or unintentional prejudice. Bob smiled and shook her hand as was the protocol for the facility. He was careful to do the same for each member of this new group so not to offend anyone but, more importantly, not to reveal to anyone, especially Ann, that he was particularly interested in getting to know her.

The work of the morning went quickly, mostly overviews of what they would work on and the processes they would follow for the next few days. Bob was pleased to learn that Zach wanted the three team leaders and Bob to join him at lunch to continue discussing the plan for diagnostic and mechanical checks for each component of the Thor's Hammer. That meant Bob would be having lunch with Ann and he thought he could tell a lot about a person by what and how they eat. He was thrilled inside and agreed; so they all headed down the hallway toward the dining rooms. It was on the walk down the hall that Bob noticed that Ann appeared to be in excellent shape. Her long legs were lean, although he could only see her calves. Her waist was small and her shoulders were wide enough that her flowing brown hair could not cover them across her back. She walked with her head up, always looking around and making eye contact with those who passed the group. She didn't fit the profile of most people who worked here who walked around with their heads down completely introverted. Many even seemed afraid of personal contact or interaction with others.

Many of the people Bob had met and worked with over the past two weeks were much more comfortable staring at a computer screen or working with machines than with another human being. They seemed to prefer it because it was safer; it was not threatening; and it was much less work than having to deal with human thought, emotion, and cruelty. She was not this way and he could tell that right away. She was smart but alive, vibrant, and outgoing and he wondered why she was here among some of the walking-dead geniuses of our time. She was a light among them and Bob found himself drawn to her. There was more to know about her. She had a story that he hoped she would be willing to share with him.

Throughout the lunch Bob was dutifully attentive to the discussion, but he would have rather given in to his desire to stare at Ann and talk alone to learn more about her. Her apparent outward disposition made her being there even more mysterious and attractive to Bob. He had already considered the notion that she was a plant to watch him but he dismissed that on instinct. He could tell she didn't have the disposition for that kind of work and deceit. Bob Mcleod knew how to read people. He knew she was special and it made him optimistic about the future; it felt good.

After lunch they went back to work on explaining and understanding the physical components of the machine Bob called Thor's Hammer. The name was appreciated by most of the group because they were familiar with the mythical figure it was named for. They were enthusiastic about learning and worked together for many hours. Bob was enjoying himself today, having fun, and imparting his knowledge with a new enthusiasm. It was already late when he began to feel hungry. A few in the group had already quit for the day but many were still there, willing to match the pace of their briefer on this their first day with the weather modification machine and its inventor.

When Bob looked at the clock, he was surprised that it was almost eight p.m. Much to his delight, Ann was one among those still there with him. He approached her, and with a new air of confidence asked, "Ann, would you like to join me for something to eat? I'm about ready to give it a rest for this evening and grab a bite; I'd really enjoy your company." Bob motioned to the door with a sincere tenor is his question.

She smiled at him and nodded, "Sure Bob, it would be my pleasure, thank you. It's not every day I get invited to eat by someone who has changed the world with their invention—every *week*, yes, but not every day." She smiled a coy smile and walked through the door Bob was now holding open.

"Thanks everyone, see you tomorrow," Bob said loudly to the remaining members of the group as he and Ann walked out the door. A ring of *goodnights* followed them into the hallway as the others in the work area responded. They were alone at last and Bob was thrilled to be in her presence. "What would you like to eat this evening; I'll buy," Bob said jokingly as they walked toward the dining area. Everything was free; there was no money in the facility because there was no need for it there.

It was a sort of Utopian model existence with a high government budget. After all, some of the technologies they had discovered or refined had generated or saved billions of dollars for the United States, so the place and its people had paid for themselves many times over. It was in the government's best interest to make the small community as simple and enjoyable as possible in order to keep it staffed with such talented people.

"To be honest, Bob, I'm not all that hungry but I really wanted the opportunity to talk with you some more," Ann confessed as they made their way into the dining area. The words were like a sweet song to Bob's ears and his ego got the best of him for a short moment before the alarm bell sounded a caution that he could not assume she wasn't there to keep an eye on him. There was that possibility so he could not let his guard down...not yet—perhaps—not ever. "Well Ann, I am flattered. I am also hungry. How about some ice cream then? Surely, they keep lots of that around here," Bob smiled and she agreed. A few short minutes later they were sitting alone in a small booth waiting for the server to bring them each a banana split. "So, what was it that you wanted to talk with me some more about Ann?" he asked her with a smile.

"If I ask you a question, will you promise to answer it; I mean truly and honestly answer it for me?" She looked sincere. She also looked concerned, as if she was taking a big risk and knew it but just had to proceed anyway. It was the most concerned she had looked all day, and Bob knew that because he had been watching her, secretly but intently, all day.

"Okay Ann. You look concerned. I'll promise, if you will. Quid pro quo, one-for-one until you are ready to quit. Fair is fair; do we have a deal?" Bob answered.

"Deal then, but ladies first." Ann was cautiously pleased that Bob agreed but equally nervous that he would be so interested in her in return. His reply pleased her more than she admitted to herself that this man would be interested in her but she was also aware it could just be a defense in case he needed a mechanism to derail her questions. Worst case was that he was either smart or charming; best case was that he was both. She continued, being very careful about how she phrased the question, "I'll be direct. I find it keeps things simple. You don't know anything about metals or the physical composition of your invention do you, Bob? You had help building it," she asked him as she stared him right in the eye to gauge his response and read his nonverbal behaviors.

"No and yes, but that was two questions; one disguised as a statement. My turn." His reply was immediate and honest, and she could tell. Bob could also tell he had caught her off guard with his reply and he saw he had a momentary advantage. So, he fired off two quick questions in return. He had been wondering about them all day, so he didn't have to waste any time selecting his words. "Why did you choose to stay and work here? And what would it take to get you to leave?" Bob knew the second question would be the most awkward for both of them because there was an implied intention that he wanted her to leave and was willing to do something about it. It could also be explained away that he was curious, really meaning what would cause her to leave, not meaning what would he have to do to get her to leave with him.

"I see you believe in being direct too, Bob. Okay, fair is fair. But I want you to know these are things I don't share with others. I appreciate your honesty, I do, but I want your word as a gentleman that you will respect my privacy. I'll be honest with you because I have a lot more questions of you now but know this; I am an honest person and you are treading in very personal space here so please respect what I tell you as personal. It is not for discussion with anyone else; you are asking a lot of me already. I need your promise."

She looked at him as if he was the executioner and she had just requested mercy, a strong hand and a quick, accurate, and lethal blow to spare her pain. Bob knew she was sincerely concerned; he could see that she was indeed vulnerable to him and this was plainly no act. On one hand he regretted asking these two questions because it made her so uneasy. Like a bull in a china shop he had gotten to the core of the lady. It was where he wanted to be but it was not how he wanted to get there. He would do better but he was glad she was willing to continue. Worst case she was too smart or too trusting; best case was she was both.

"I promise. Quid pro quo, Ann. Your words will stay with me as long as mine stay with you. You have my word, as a gentleman," Bob smiled. He was sincere and she could see it in his eyes that he would keep his promise. The banana splits came and the server left as quickly as he appeared.

"Okay, Bob. My dad ran a machine shop. When I was little, I begged him to take me to work with him every day. If things were slow, he would take me. I loved the smells, the sounds, and being with my dad. He taught me to respect metal, to understand it, to work it. He showed me how to get it to do what you asked of it. He was a great machinist and he loved to teach me. The men in the shop kind of adopted me as their mascot. I had a lot of 'uncles' after a while. I loved it. I went to college and double majored in metallurgy and mechanical engineering. Dad worked his tail off to keep me in school. He said this was just taking his turn and mine would be, when I graduated and got rich, I could pay his way through retirement like he paid my way through school."

"It was our joke but it was also his dream, really...for me to be that successful. I never knew my mom; she left before I turned two. She couldn't handle a baby, being saddled with a kid when there was so much more out there for her to learn and do. She died when I was six. Drugs. A friend of hers told me she regretted leaving us and that whether she OD'd by accident or on purpose didn't matter. She used drugs to ease her pain and said she regretted leaving us that's why she used so often. I don't know if that was true or not but that's what she told me." Ann wiped a tear and smiled, forcing a weak laugh before beginning again.

She took a bite of the melting ice cream and began to speak, "You asked the question. Well, anyway, Dad and I were close. I got a good job out of school in my hometown—well *city,* actually. About half an hour from Dad's shop. I used to go there whenever I could; after work...even at lunch sometimes to see my dad and my *uncles*...to remember what it was like when we were all together. That was the only home I remember.

Well one night, when I was twenty-four, not too long out of school I went to Dad's shop after work. It was late but they had a big job in and were working long days. Dad had hired some part-timers to help him on this job and one of them was leaving as I was coming through the parking lot. He assaulted me right there in the parking lot of my dad's shop. I fought him off pretty well was holding my own and screaming loudly as we went at it...but he was a big man."

"Ann, I'm sorry, Ann. You don't have to," Bob interrupted her but she cut him off.

"It's okay. You asked; now listen. One of my *uncles* heard me scream. He yelled for my dad and then he came out to help me. It all happened so fast. The guy tore my blouse and had me on the ground before I knew what happened but I got in behind him and was grappling for position when my Uncle Gary bowled him over and started fighting him. The guy pushed Gary off of him then pulled a gun and shot him. Right in front of me, he killed my friend, a man whom I had known since I was a little girl. He loved me like his own daughter. Then that worthless bastard turned back to me and he was ready to kill me next. I was crying, I was scared but I could see it in his eyes."

"Then that man fell down dead right beside me. My dad walked up to him and emptied his gun into him. I lost my *uncle* but my dad lost a lot more than that. It's hard for a simple man to explain to a judge why six bullets to the head of a man is the right thing to do for the ones you love and to make it clear to others on the street that his was not the place to attempt such treachery. They charged my dad with a bunch of crap and it took a whole lot of lawyers a whole lot of time and a whole lot of money to get him through it. They did their jobs but it cost my dad his business, his shop, and all my *uncle's* their jobs. Everything we had. We all pitched in and helped him the way he taught us to help others. He gave me a gift and I am giving it back now.

"I make a lot of money here and now he has his shop back and my *uncles* are all working for him again. Because I am here, they get lots of government business and he's doing well financially, too. I've got two more years on my contract here and then I will be done. That is what it will take to get me to leave...two more years, Bob. I think that covers both of your questions. Who helped you make the machine?" She took a deep breath and started for her melted ice cream when Bob reached for her hand and stopped her. She looked up with a start at Bob leaning across the table.

"I am sorry to have put you through that—I had no idea—but thank you for sharing it with me. I can only imagine how hard that was for you. I will respect your privacy, I promise." She knew he meant it and he did... clearly, he did. He could not fake tears.

"Thanks, now it's your turn; answer up," she pressed him with a sense of urgency in her voice. Bob answered agreeably.

"Doctor Jim Auster. He was my boss at the University. A meteorologist, as far as I know he built the first device himself shortly before he was killed by a drunk driver. That is how I came to be here. I studied it and copied the others from the original. I believe they are identical; I didn't know what I would affect if I changed something. So, I changed nothing. At least that is what I thought until now." Bob's answer was short but accurate. He wanted to ask another question, but was interrupted by Ann. "The last one. The last one on the table is the first one; the rest are the copies. They are not identical, Bob, they are subtly different. Like art, it's easy to tell the original from copies. Bad copies are even easier to spot. No offense, but it was easy to tell."

"None taken," Bob replied, "What do you intend to do in two years when your contract is up?"

"Go back home and make up for lost time with Dad. That was too easy; you're not getting soft on me now, are you?" Ann smiled.

"Is that your next question, Ann?" Bob smiled

"Yes, it is," she volleyed back, surprising herself and Bob with the challenge.

"Yes, I am getting soft on you. You are an amazing woman, Ann," Bob stopped.

"My question. Do you like it here? You seem to and that doesn't seem to be what one would expect from someone who is here against her will."

"Incorrect assumption my friend. I am not here against my will. They gave me back my father and for that I am eternally grateful. I am working with some of the most brilliant people in the world and the scientist inside me is in heaven. It is the daughter inside me that has to take a back seat for a while. My dad taught me that every situation is what you make of it, both good and bad. So, I am making the best of this and learning and teaching as much as I can. I am doing my share to make this world a better place for me, my family and my friends. That part I like. Not being able to leave and see them; that part I don't like. What did you intend to do with the devices when you built them?" she returned to the Quid pro quo.

"I didn't know really when I was building them what to do but I knew I had to do something. I set out to make the world a better place. I under-estimated the power and competition for such technology until after it existed and then it was too late. I know the good that can come of it; economic, political, and social stability. Over time we can provide food and shelter for everyone who wants it but I am afraid that, like Doc Auster, I may never see this happen. There is much time and many obstacles between now and that vision. Do you want to quit keeping score and have a normal conversation now? Stick with one subject for a while because I do. I want to talk about you, Ann. I would really like to get to know you better...I really would," Bob confessed, partly because he was getting tired but mostly because he just couldn't *not* tell her how he felt. She had to know so he could relax.

"Okay Bob, I think I'd like that. Yes, I would like that very much. But I have to ask, who named the Thor's Hammer? You or was the first one already named when you got it?" she asked.

Bob explained, "Doc Auster gets all the credit for naming them, all the connections to Thor and the references to the old stories and commanding the thunder and lightning and all. It is a bit ironic I suppose that my last name is Mcleod and my heritage is from somewhere in that region."

Ann responded with a smile, "*Ironic* maybe...*fate* maybe? Either way, given where you are now, I guess that makes you *Thor's Apprentice*. I hope you paid attention to all those old stories. Now, I am hungry. They make a great Ruben sandwich...interested?" Ann smiled invitingly.

"I'd like that a lot." They smiled at each other as she waved for the server and placed their request for sandwiches and iced tea. They continued their discussion about the origin of the device and Ann's memories and plans with her father and *uncles* from his shop. The clock quickly showed eleven thirty and they both admitted being tired. Neither wanted their time together to end but they knew they needed to rest. Tomorrow's schedule was a long one and there was much work to do.

They parted at the door and each headed for their rooms which were on opposite ends of the facility. There were strict rules against sex among the employees and they were diligently adhered to. There could be no competition among scientists for the intimate favors of other employees without destroying much of the non-threatening, collegial environment they all enjoyed. There was a *special staff,* who worked there specifically for that purpose and some even had long term sexual relationships with these *special staff* for years. But it was all private. There were no relationships between the R&D professionals there and they were housed as far apart as possible to prevent such activity.

"Goodnight then, see you in the morning. Bob, thank you for listening and for being honest with me. I guess I didn't realize how long it had been, or how much I missed having someone to really talk to. I had a good time—a little tough—but good, thanks." Ann smiled that big smile for him and Bob nearly melted into the hall floor.

"You're welcome, Ann, but it was my pleasure I assure you. I had a great time, thank you. Good night." Bob turned and headed down the hall with his smile fixed, his heart racing and his mind swirling with images and thoughts he tried to impress upon his memory so as not to forget. The camera followed him down the hall and he wondered how much of their discussion had been recorded. He knew probably all of it but it didn't matter. They both knew where they were and the time they shared was worth any risk that might come of others in security knowing some of the details of her past. After all, someone already knew them and that was how she got here. He hoped his revelations were equally harmless. They should be but he wasn't certain on either account.

What he was certain about was that she was not there to purposely get information from him, although they could use her for that if they let nature take its course. He was certain that he liked her a lot, he cared about her, and she seemed genuinely interested in him too. It had been a long time since there was a woman in Bob Mcleod's life and he was glad to see that might be changing soon. He was too excited about replaying the night's events in his mind to worry too much about any of that. He was excited about Ann, he was excited by Ann, and he couldn't wait for the opportunity to see her again. It was a short walk to his room but it was a long night of tossing and turning, thinking, remembering and wondering about her. Morning couldn't come soon enough for Bob Mcleod.

The team had a busy schedule the next day and they accomplished quite a bit. Professor Mcleod was particularly upbeat and informative, paying close attention to the portions of the work that centered around the physical composition of the components. These were the efforts that afforded him the best opportunity to be close to Ann. She could tell he was interested in her and it both flattered and frustrated her.

On one hand she was flattered as a woman that the smart, powerful, and, presumably, wealthy man had taken such an interest in her. On the other hand, she had much work to do and much to learn from him on a professional basis so she could do her job. Separating the personal from the professional was hard for anyone but particularly difficult under these circumstances. Honestly, though, she didn't really mind. Ann could tell she liked Bob from the first time he looked at her. It was the way he looked at her. It was nothing like the ogling leer she had seen many times before from men chasing women like dogs in heat. The look she saw was a kind, warm, sincere look of desire and caring.

It was hard for her to describe. Though it reminded her of the loving way her father looked at her, it was different. It contained a discernible, recognizable flare of both physical and emotional wanting and that pleased her. She had been living there for two years now and had two more years to go on her contract. Ann had never really had a serious relationship before. Although there were a few times that what she thought was love turned out to be everything but, she was excited about Bob. He was all the things she envisioned the man in her life would be, and he was real now. He was there and he was interested in her and that made Ann very happy.

It also concerned her because she knew that, even if Bob was really interested in her, what kind of guy would wait around for two years before they could even start a normal relationship? Even if he stayed there for her, which would be too much to ask, what kind of relationship would that be anyway? No, she knew it would be tough but she was used to tough. The situation is what you make of it. View every challenge as an opportunity. Attitude is everything. You miss one hundred percent of the shots you don't take. The little rules her father taught her flooded her brain every time she thought about Bob and she decided that contract or not, tough relationship or not, whether he was serious or not about her, she was going to get to know him better. She was going to find out who he really was, what made him tick, and what he wanted from life.

She was interested in Professor Bob Mcleod as a man as much as, perhaps even more—much more—than as a scientist. Ann wanted to get to know Bob and she was used to getting what she wanted, no matter how hard she had to work to get it. She was used to hard work; she had been doing it most of her life so that didn't scare her but starting a relationship with this particular man did. Their situations were both tenuous at best and that scared her but not enough to make her dismiss her desires. She knew the looks Bob had given her because, through his expression, he was reflecting what she was feeling inside.

The day's work had passed very quickly and the teams all made significant progress as the clock ticked quickly into the evening hours. It was nearly seven by now and Bob approached Ann during a break as the materials team was wrapping up for the day. "I really enjoyed our discussion yesterday, Ann. I was wondering, well, if you'd be interested in continuing it tonight during dinner?" Bob asked. The invitation was vanilla enough that anyone within earshot who heard it could take the remark innocently enough, but Ann recognized—or perhaps hoped—that there was more in the question than just a casual observer could note. She saw in his eyes that he really wanted to spend more time with her and she was not about to let the opportunity slip away.

She had spent most of the time last night telling him some of the most personal things in her life while all she could do was quiz him on the secrets of the technology he brought to them. She had all last night and all day today to regret not focusing on learning about him but instead spending so much time listening to the scientist in her rather than the woman. She would strike a balance tonight, even if he was hesitant, because she knew her smile could melt glass under the right conditions and she really wanted to get to know him. "I think I'd like that very much Bob. About forty-five minutes in the dining room?" Ann replied, and returned his warm smile.

"That'll be just fine. I will see you there, then," Bob stumbled a bit.

"Great. Oh, Bob. If you get there before I do, please get us a booth, okay?" Ann smiled as she looked down and resumed her task.

"Sure, no problem," Bob replied as he began to bid good night to the rest of the team. He was elated that she agreed to join him and on top of the world that she made it clear to him she wanted their dinner together to be private. That sounded great to him and he was feeling good about life today. Dinner that night was quite a treat for the two as they talked and ate for hours. They dined together every night for the next six nights, laughing, talking and learning about each other. They discussed their pasts, their presents, and their goals and futures. They bonded over dinners and worked hard during the day to get the work done. They had struck a mix between personal and professional that seemed to be working.

A natural balance that others noticed but didn't seem to mind. The only one who even mentioned or seemed to notice their routine was Zach, the head of security. His comment was to both Ann and Bob at the same time and simply reminded them that being professional in the workplace was of the utmost priority. It was thinly veiled but it was noted. They made a concerted, successful effort to be the epitomes of professionalism at work and not to make a scene while eating together. They obeyed the rules and they were allowed to continue spending their time together. They grew closer every day over the weeklong period and enjoyed each other's company tremendously. It seemed that Bob had not only found someone who shared his interest in making the world a better place through scientific advances, but also shared his interests in the world he was trying to better.

Bob realized while he was here talking to Ann over the past week that, until now, he never really set out to understand the reason for the goals he set for himself. They weren't really financial. Meteorologists don't make much money by comparison to other degreed professionals, especially research meteorologists. No, he knew now that his goals were driven by something simpler than money. He was driven by the need to work hard and help those who couldn't help themselves...whether they were the trees and animals of the forest, the kid who was failing Durbin's class, or the people of the world who could benefit from the weather modification technology but would likely never know it even existed. Ann helped him see that about himself and, if for no other reason than that, he felt like he owed much to the lady. She was extraordinary and for the first time in a very long time, perhaps for the first real time ever, Bob Mcleod was falling in love.

The pace of the work with the teams over the past ten days had gone remarkably well and was ahead of schedule. Bob felt like he had given them everything they could possibly need. Certainly, he had repeatedly covered everything he knew. The next and last phase of his technology handoff was supposed to be working with both the physical and theoretical groups to marry up the seams between how it should work and how it actually did work. They all needed to understand the technology in its entirety, not just their portion of it, to prevent any oversights or accidents. Bob would miss seeing Ann every day at work but took solace in the thought they could still have their dinners together.

He knew though that this phase should only take a few days and then he would be free to leave, his work here completed. He truly wanted to get out of the underground facility, but he dreaded the thought of leaving Ann behind. He would bring up his leaving at dinner tonight and ask Ann if she would leave with him if he could arrange it. He hoped and believed she would, but he couldn't make such a move without her complete approval first. He would do almost anything to have her by his side but she would have to want to be there. It must be her decision without pressure or fear. He wanted her to love him too but, because of who he is, not what he can do.

At dinner that night Bob asked her early in their conversation, before he lost his nerve, "Ann, I will be free to leave in a few days when the teams are content that they have all the information they could squeeze out of me. I would like to ask you something, and I want you to be honest and answer with the first thing that comes to your mind, okay?"

"Okay, Bob," she replied softly, seeming a bit concerned and nervous as she fidgeted in her chair anticipating the question.

"If you could, would you leave with me?" His question was simple, and the words chosen carefully after an afternoon of mental deliberation on both what and how to ask her. Bob almost felt like a trial lawyer in his analysis, but this was important stuff, to both of them, and he wanted to get it right.

"Wow, that is quite a question Professor Mcleod. But the answer is yes, if I could, I would leave with you, Bob. I don't know how, especially down here but I think I'm in love with you. Please don't stop me because this is really hard for me to say. I need to say it now or I might never have the nerve again. I say I think I am because I don't really know. I have never felt this way about anyone before—not even when I thought I was in love but really wasn't. I don't know if this is how it is supposed to feel or not. I've only known you for a brief time and I feel like I've known you my entire life. Oh no...I think I heard that on TV once. I don't know if it is this place. Being here for two years may have flooded me up with emotions I don't understand.

"Bob there is so much I don't know for sure right now but there are some things I do know for sure. I really enjoy being with you and I admire you. You are a man's man inside where it really counts; you are brave and strong and honest and sincere. I love that about you and you're a pretty good man's man on the outside too if I may say. Well, I just did say...so there. I know I don't want you to leave because I would really miss you. I would feel like I missed my chance at the man who I was meant to be with and I would never have a way to prove myself either right or wrong. I would always wonder and I can't stand that. Yes, Bob, I would leave with you; I would like nothing better than to do just that.

"You have changed me inside, and I don't know whether to be thankful or angry with you because now you are going to leave me and I don't know what to feel. If I listen to my heart, it tells me I love you. If I listen to my head, it tells me to appreciate our time together and get back to work. I like what my heart is telling me a lot better than what I hear from my head but I don't think I can do both. I can't stay here for two years and love you the entire time and still do my work and I can't leave my work for two more years. I think I love you...but I don't think I can." She was smiling as the tears were dropping from both her eyes.

She looked so fragile for a woman so strong in both spirit and body. Bob was elated at the words she spoke but heartsick to think he had caused her such pain. He knew that he loved her and, if there was any doubt before dinner, her words cleared his head of any which may have lingered in the recesses of his subconscious. He reached across the table and took her hand in his; holding it softly up to his mouth, he kissed the top of it and looked up at her.

"Ann, that was a wonderful and courageous thing you just did. Thank you for being brave enough to tell me how you feel. I am not that brave but I feel the same way about you. I know I love you. That is why I asked the question but I was too much of a coward to hope that you could feel the same way about me after so short a time. I was afraid to ask you what I really wanted to know for fear of what you might think or say. I want to stay with you, and I will for a while. I will find a way to free you from the rest of your contract, if you want me to. If you want to come with me, I will find a way."

Bob smiled and kissed her hand again; it was still holding tightly to his as he spoke. Ann nodded and stood up, her eyes locked onto his the entire quick, fluid motion. He stood, too, and they held each other as she cried a joyous release of emotion and fear. He held her as if it was the first and last time he ever would, drinking in the sensations and scorching them into his memory. She backed away and smiled, still holding his hand. She looked into his eyes and could see the sincerity, the caring that she had recognized a week before. She began to walk out of the dining room, their dinner half eaten, and motioned for him to follow her which he did. When they were in the hallway she turned and pushed him gently against the wall and kissed him for the first time. It was the same way he had held her, as if it were the first time and would be the last time they ever would.

She smiled and said, "I knew you would kiss me like that; I knew you would." She took his hand and led him down the hallway, in the opposite direction which he had grown accustomed to walking over the past few weeks. When he realized they were both headed in the direction of her living quarters he stopped for a moment, looking surprised at her. She calmly smiled and said, "Let them try, I am a woman in love. Will you stay with me tonight?" Bob smiled and his eyes revealed his answer as he continued to follow Ann down the corridor.

Neither of them slept much that night, and the morning found them sharing breakfast at the same table they had revealed their feelings to each other the night before. Bob had a full day's work planned but was in no mood to discuss technology this morning; he had other things on his mind. Not the least of which was figuring out who he needed to talk to about getting Ann released from her contract. It was time to use some of his money and he couldn't think of a better way to spend however much it took to allow her to leave with him in a few days. Bob left Ann in the hallway and headed out to find Zach. He had a schedule change and a new mission this morning.

Chapter Nine

What Money Can't Buy

H e knocked and entered the security office Zach used throughout the day and found him sitting in a large, comfortable chair staring at a computer screen full of text. "Come in Bob, please sit down. What can I do for you this morning?"

"Zach, I'll get right to the point. Who is the personnel guru here? Who hires people and gets them to come and go; does their contracts that sort of stuff?" Bob asked.

"Bob, I am afraid that is classified information and I am not allowed to share that with you. Have you decided to stay with us?" Zach asked sarcastically and grinned a menacing grin. "Or does this have something to do with our friend, Ann? She is a nice girl don't you think?"

"Okay, let me try this again. For weeks I have done everything I said I would. I have followed your rules and provided everything you have asked of me. Now, I am asking you something *my little chief of security* and whatever else you do for this place. I want to talk to the person who holds the employees and their contracts and I want to do it this morning. You are the person I am supposed to work my issues through so now I am asking you to do your job. No, I'm not asking anymore. I will wait here until you have me speaking to them. Did you get it this time?" Bob's nostrils were flaring, and it was clear to Zach that this was not the time to mess with Professor Mcleod.

"All right Bob, no need to get all bent out of shape now. I am the person you want to talk to. I am the one who hires, fires and maintains our recruits. What do you want to know?" Zach countered.

"Not good enough. If you are the man—which I seriously doubt—no offense, then I want to speak to your boss. Who would that be?" Bob demanded.

"Can't tell you, my friend. That is why you go through me for all your stuff. That is why you were instructed to do that from the very beginning. It's my way or the highway. Is this starting to sound familiar?" Zach said, tiring of this verbal sparring. After all, it was still early.

"I don't care who it is or where they live, or what they do. You don't need to tell me any of that. Get them on the phone and we are going to talk about a personnel issue if I have to break your fingers one at a time to do it. I am not asking you Zach. I'm telling you; now do it!" By this time Bob's voice was loud, his emotion was clear, and he was no longer concerned about making a scene in the security office. There were two men standing in the doorway but Zach held up his hand and waved them off. Bob turned to see them and was pleased when they backed up and left the room on Zach's silent order. "Look, I am dead serious about this. I hope you have figured that out by now. Who do I need to talk to?"

"Bob, do you really think you're doing the right thing? Thinking clearly? I mean a few weeks underground; you get a little attention and piece of ass from some cute widget maker and now you want to feel important by springing her from her deal?" If Zach was looking for a reaction from Bob, he got what he was looking for as McCleod rose from his chair and pinned the small man against the wall. With his forearm against Zach's throat and his weight leaning into it, Bob said in a menacingly unstable voice, "Look you little piece of garbage. I asked you nice, and I asked you not so nice. Then I told you nice. Now I'm gonna tell you not so nice. You are on very dangerous ground here my friend, you have crossed the line.

You have one chance to step back over that line to where you want to be. Now pick up that phone and make the call." Bob was wild eyed, and hell bent now, as he lowered Zach to the floor by letting off some of the pressure against his throat. As the air began to flow back into his lungs Zach stood on his feet and walked over to his desk, sat down in his chair and shot a defiant glance to Bob. He picked up the phone and dialed a long string of numbers, an access code, and then spoke, "This is Zach, I need to talk to him." After a long pause he spoke again, "Of course it is urgent or I wouldn't be calling him there. I need to speak to him and I will hold because I need to talk to him now." He rolled his eyes, "It is so hard to get really talented help these days and now you want to take one of my brightest prospects because you couldn't keep your zipper closed last night. You are really trying to torque me off this morning aren't you, Bob?"

"Let's just say up until this morning I didn't think you were all bad but I have since changed my mind about that," Bob replied, still fuming. He was interrupted as Zach spoke into the phone.

"Sir, it's Zach. I apologize for breaking in, but I believe this is very important to our project and I need your level of approval. Sir, Professor Mcleod is in the office with me, and he would like to speak to you. It is only the two of us, Sir, I will put you on the speaker," Zach concluded as he activated the speaker phone so they could share in the discussion.

"Good morning, Bob, how are you enjoying the accommodations?" the voice on the other end inquired.

"Fine, they are first rate. Everything here, in fact, is first rate. The project is going well. We are ahead of schedule and I expect to be wrapping up here within the week. That is why I must speak to you; I have a request and I hope we can come to terms with," Bob stopped, awaiting a reply.

"What is it? Wasn't the five billion enough?" the voice on the other end laughed jokingly and Bob was now certain that his suspicion was correct.

"Mr. President, I would like you to release one of your mechanical engineers from the remainder of her contract. She has two years remaining but she is ready to leave. Sir, I'd appreciate it if you allowed her to do just that." Bob was direct because he knew he was at a significant disadvantage.

"Bob, what does that get me except one less mechanical engineer, a recruiting problem, and a bad precedent? She knew what she was getting into and she signed a contract. She made a commitment; why should I let her renege on that?" The reply came slowly and deliberately.

"Sir, because it gets me out of your hair. It keeps your project going and it keeps this place a secret," Bob replied

"It seems to me I already have those things and this place is already a secret. More importantly Bob, what does it get you? Why are we having this discussion?" The tone was inquisitive but impatient, the man obviously had other things pulling at his attention.

"It gets me my wife, Mr. President. I wouldn't bother you with any of this unless it was that important to me. We both want me happy, Sir. This gets me there," Bob stated coldly.

"All right then; two weeks to turn her work over to a replacement and she is free to go once Zach is satisfied the turnover is complete. She doesn't have to stay until the project is complete but concoct a good cover story for the others. I don't want anybody thinking they can just walk out of their deals. Is this the girl whose father shot that guy all up?" he asked.

"Yes Sir, Ann," Zach replied before Bob could speak.

"I never was comfortable bringing her in there; she was just too cute. Not geeky enough for that crowd. I'll need to listen to my instincts next time. Well, good luck gentlemen; I have a meeting to get back into. And Bob, congratulations are in order I suppose. I hope it all works out great for you and I hope I never hear from you again; I really mean that. I want both of those things for all our sakes," the President concluded by hanging up the phone.

Zach looked at Bob and smiled, "Congratulations Bob, you got your wish. You do know of course I am going to get my head handed to me for this? But in a way, I don't really mind because I have developed a lot of respect for Ann. You can tell her if you wish but not the others. I will need some time to make all the necessary preparations for her departure and build the cover story for her dismissal. It probably won't be anything flattering for her reputation because there are very few things one is dismissed for here and falling in love isn't one of them."

"I am leaning toward a security disclosure that warrants removal. It will tarnish her integrity in the eyes of the team here and her sudden departure will be quite a topic of discussion no matter what...but it is the quickest and the simplest. Neither of you gets a say in how I do this. I just want you to know that there is some necessarily negative baggage with the result you requested. It won't mean anything on the outside but it must cast a negative image for those remaining here for what I hope are obvious reasons by now. Is there anything else. I now have a lot more work to do than I had planned for today so if you'll excuse me?"

"Yes, there is something else," Bob replied hurriedly. "Thank you. And I am sorry I got rough but this meant everything to me. She means everything to me."

"If you hadn't, you would have never gotten me to make that call. I am not intimidated by violence. I have seen lots of that but I am moved by passion. It was the wild look in your eye that convinced me, not your threats. I needed to see it and it was there. Now, if you don't mind, there is one other thing. Your departure should go as planned in a few days. I don't want the two of you leaving together. It will add far too much credibility to rumors. And by the by, please spend your remaining nights with us in your own quarters and not hers. In less than two weeks you can do that for the rest of you lives but, for now, keep the rules so we can get her out of here with the least impact to all of us."

Zach's instructions were backed up by a look that could deflect bullets and Bob knew he was right. He would need a normal environment to sell

Ann's release to her colleagues and maintain the order and discipline inside their underground world, however twisted it might be. So, Bob nodded and walked out of the office. He had waited his entire life for someone like her. Certainly, he could wait a couple of weeks to begin their life together. Besides, he had some things he needed to do as soon as he was free from this place and Ann would be much safer where she was. He was pleased with his morning's work as he walked down the corridor towards the lab area they had been using for this phase of the technology transition. He wanted to jump up and down, screaming in jubilation on the outside just as he was on the inside, but he knew that he couldn't. He had to tell Ann, though, and he hoped to do that at lunch.

The next two hours passed slowly, like a father waiting for news from the delivery room he worriedly anticipated a wonderful event. But she was nowhere to be seen. The team members weren't sure where she was. So Bob went looking for her in all the normal places he had seen her working or studying. Finally, he went to her room and knocked on the door. She answered after a quick look through the peephole and let him into her room. She was crying and, after he closed the door, she put her arms around him and sobbed into his shoulder. "I just couldn't stay out there this morning. After last night, knowing you would be leaving soon. I don't want you to leave. I know it is selfish but I want to be with you. I don't want to be alone here like I was before I met you."

Bob replied while still holding her gently, "I have to leave, Ann. I have to get some stuff together and squared away before you join me. After all, two weeks isn't all that long, is it?"

"Two weeks?" She replied jolting upright. "What do you mean two weeks? I have two years on my contract not two weeks! This is no time to toy with me, Bob. What do you mean?"

"I got you released from your contract. You turn everything you have and everything you are working on over to your replacement over the next two weeks and you're out of here. You can leave; you can come with me Ann. We can be together just like we talked about. We don't have to wait; you don't have to be alone; we can be together. That is what you wanted right? I know it's what I want." Bob wasn't sure how to take the blank look on her face, staring at the door behind him. Then he could see it winding up inside her and the smile broke across her face from deep within her as she lunged toward him and hugged is neck, twirling him around and around in celebration.

"How? That is wonderful, I am so happy, but how did you do it? That just doesn't happen here. Everyone knows you don't leave until your time is done. That is the deal and nobody has ever left early. In fact, everyone usually stays longer and works out a new deal. How then?" She needed to know and he told tell her, about the call to the President, and also explained the story Zach would have to concoct to pull it off. "Do you trust him? Are you sure they will do what they say?"

"I don't really trust Zach but I believe he will do what the President told him, as long as, he doesn't change his mind and give Zach new instructions. I do know the only way they will let you out is if we do it like he says. So, you are going to have to go along with whatever he comes up with to get you out, even if it tarnishes your reputation and your credibility within this underground community." Bob was honest. He promised himself he would always be honest with her. The cost of losing her trust was far too high for him to sugar coat any of this. Ann agreed with a smile. It was a small price to pay she thought for being freed early to be with the man she now loved. "There is something I need to ask you, Ann. I guess the best way to do this is to just come out and do it. So, I want to know if you would consider being my wife?" He looked at her expecting to wait for the shocked look to hit her face and drain all the color from it, but that didn't happen. She looked up at him and smiled.

She took his hand and said, "Nothing in this world could make me happier. Yes, I will consider being your wife. And yes, if you are asking me to be your wife I say yes...yes...yes. I have never been so sure of anything in my life as I am about the fact that I love you. I know that sounds cliché but it is true. I love you and want to spend the rest of my life with you, I hope I can make you happy. I would absolutely consider being your wife."

Bob smiled and held her close for what seemed like a long time. He knew they both needed to get back to their work and didn't want to make Zach's work any harder than it was already going to be. Bob needed him as an ally now more than ever and, if they stayed in her room much longer, they might not come out all afternoon. They agreed to go back to work and get as much done as possible so they both could leave on time. It was a small price to pay for the abundant riches of the budding relationship they both saw awaiting them. They had both heard that good things come to those who wait and it was time to put that to the test once again.

That evening they shared dinner together and talked about what they would do together when they were free of the underground think tank they shared tonight. Bob agreed to move from his place for a while and start fresh in Ann's hometown nearly eight hundred miles from his home. He knew there was nothing left for him back there by now anyway. He was sure that Durbin had seen to the demise of the work he and Doc had begun years ago. At the very best it would be completed by someone else if it were ever completed at all. Durbin would certainly take this opportunity to spread manure on Bob's reputation. He could hear him now preaching about responsibility, commitment, and loyalty and Bob's lack of them all.

What kind of man doesn't show up to his job and his research for nearly two months and expects it to still be there for him? No, he was certainly finished at the University...at least for now anyway. Bob decided to go back collect his things...his dog...his truck and drive up to Ann's to find a place to live convenient to her father's machine shop. Ann would help out there for a while until she could find something else if she wanted. Bob had not told her yet that he was a multi-billionaire. Though he suspected she knew he had some money, she had no idea how much and he would keep it that way for now. Bob had some business at the church to tend to, as well. He intended to donate Doc's house—well, his house now—to Father Gannon's parish. They could keep it or sell it for cash.

He didn't care which but he thought it was what Doc would have wanted for his friend, the priest, so he would make it so. Bob would move his stuff and settle his affairs the week Ann was doing her turnover with her replacement and they would meet up the following week and surprise her father with the good news. They had plenty as far as Ann was concerned.

The remainder of the technology turnover tasks were wrapped up in three days and Bob was longing for sunshine and to get going on his plans for him and Ann to be together. He approached Zach and asked him how the plans were coming for his departure and Ann's early release from her contract.

"The old man nearly bit my head off that I allowed this to happen you know?" Zach began. "He thinks it is pathetically romantic and that I am an idiot for not seeing this coming a mile away. It was Truman who used to say, *Farming is easy when your plow is a pen and the nearest corn field is a thousand miles away.* Well, this President can bite me! Seems he should read Truman because I don't think he has a clue how hard it is for me to arrange the miracles we do for him here. He thinks, if he throws more money at us, we can do anything. I suppose we have proven him right on that more times than wrong so perhaps it is partly my fault but it wasn't easy to see this coming. Did you see this coming Bob or was it a surprise to you that you two hit it off the way you did?"

"It was a surprise for me yes but, as soon as I saw her the very first time, I knew. I knew without a doubt Zach. It was easy for me to see once I saw her. Go easy on yourself; this is much more difficult to deal with than farming. Truman would be proud of you," Bob consoled. "So how is the story on getting Ann out of here coming along?"

"I took the easy way out this time. Even though the easy path is always mined, I am a softy at heart so don't let this blow up in my face, Bob, or I will hunt you down. Am I clear on that?" Both his tone and demeanor changed instantly and Bob remembered that this was one man he didn't want as an enemy. There was so much about him that was just not right that Bob didn't think a team of psychologist with a month of Sundays could ever understand—let alone fix—all that was wrong with Zach.

"She will be transferred to another facility to work on a new Department of Energy project...a by-name request from the President. It keeps her reputation intact and mine too. After all, it's true. I figure you two will be spending lots of your own energy doing personal research on each other and I was directed by the President to make it so. There it is all nice and neat in a little package with a bow of truth surrounding it. I get my change-over to a new technician, you get your little wife to be, and I never see either of you two again. What could be better? You know the answer to that is nothing, so don't waste a brain cell on it Bob. You'll be leaving day after tomorrow at 0900 and she will be exactly one week behind you. Now, was there anything else?" he asked with a non-question tone to his question.

"Sounds great to me. Thanks, you old softy you," Bob tried to lighten the mood but that went over like a fart at a church dinner so he smiled, left it hanging in the air, and walked out. The time passed agonizingly slow as he finished some final details and said his good-byes to the people he had worked with these past several weeks. Ann got the same public goodbye as the rest of the folks but, privately, Bob bid her a passionate farewell early that morning. It would be a long week before they saw each other again.

Bob waved to the group and was led to the passageway to the main door he had entered. There Zach handed him off to three waiting security transport agents who walked Bob and his bags to the waiting Suburbans that stood by with their motors already running. The bags were loaded quickly and Bob bade Zach an appreciative thank you and asked him to make sure Ann was well taken care of the week he was gone. Zach could read the thinly veiled threat beneath Bob's comment and smiled and waved as the windows went up on the vehicles and they headed for the guarded gates and the sunlight. It was morning and bright as the sunlight bent around the corner of the spiraling ramp while the cars climbed to toward the surface. Finally, they were free, *free* to see the sky and feel the warm sunlight. The freedom flooded back. They headed toward the airport and Bob quickly nodded off to sleep so he could dream of Ann for the two-hour drive to the airport. He awoke to the sound of roaring retro burning jets across the airfield. They loaded the plane with the passengers and the bags they carried and were airborne a few moments later.

It was time for another good nap. He was exhausted but he had lots of work to do once he got there. Problem was, he was airborne but had no idea where he would end up. The suspense decreased as the aircraft began its descent to the small runway Bob recognized as the isolation facility where they conducted their demonstrations. He was near home at least but had a sinking feeling there was more to his being here than just a convenient transload point to for him.

As the plane taxied back up toward the dining area, he could see both Colonel Frank Lincoln and Major Naed standing by with a couple more men in suits. Bob presumed they were a fresh security detail to relieve the men who had flown up with him. When the plane stopped, Bob could see a couple of Suburbans parked beside the building. They were running and positioned to pull up along the aircraft to move its cargo and passengers. The door swung open and Bob climbed down the small steps and walked toward his Air Force friend. "Good to see you, Frank," Bob smiled as they shook hands once again. "To what do I owe the privilege?"

"I had to open up the airstrip and asked permission to see you home safely. The general agreed so here I am. You remember Major Naed." Frank smiled as the young officer stretched out his hand to shake Bob's.

"Always a pleasure to see someone so good at making sure I get where I need to be all in one big piece. How you been?" Bob asked.

"Great, Sir. We have two vehicles standing by to take you to your residence. Those were my orders, Sir. Once we get you there, we are mission complete but I believe the Feds are going to tail you for quite some time. They have set up a watch house near yours so they can monitor your movements...keep you safe. I suppose to both protect their investment and ensure you live up to your end of the bargain," Major Naed smiled and rolled his eyes.

"Okay fellas, you can let the boss know his message was received loud and clear. But I do appreciate hearing it from you. It softens the sting a little bit, even though I knew it was coming. Frank, you gonna ride with me out to my house? You need to know where to collect the beers I owe you and, honestly, I am ready for a mess of them today," Bob smiled as he waited for the colonel's reply.

"Sure will. I'd like to hear about your trip, too. I think we can get these guys to stop along the way and pick up a few groceries and some beer. I make a mean Ruben sandwich; go great with those beers. I'll fry if you buy?" Frank offered.

"Deal, let's go. I'm hungry and thirsty and never did care too much for either one of the two. Gentlemen shall we get moving?" Bob motioned to the security detail and waved a goodbye to Major Naed as they climbed into the Suburban. "He seems like a good officer, Frank."

"Top shelf. We've done a few operations together before this one and I have to agree with you. I try to keep guys I know will do well around; it makes everything go better. Builds some loyalty and a good working relationship. I hope he stays around a long time; he is a good one to have on your side, Bob," Frank smiled.

They mostly chatted about stuff in the news and what was going on in the world. Bob explained that he was not in a position to hear any of that where he was and was anxious to catch up with the real world. Of course, he knew the transportation detail was recording their conversation so he wanted to keep their discussions generic and unhelpful to whomever would be listening to them.

He also knew his house would be bugged and wired, too, but some loud music and a few quiet comments would be all he needed to tell Frank what he wanted to say. After all, he couldn't tell Frank too much without putting him in an awkward position and Bob was not willing to do that to his new friend. They stopped and got enough groceries for the next few days: a couple of cases of beer, a bottle of champagne, and a huge rawhide bone for Buck, then proceeded to Bob's house. Frank asked about the champagne but Bob put him off and offered to explain later.

They pulled into his driveway where Bob saw a car he did not recognize parked behind his truck. The security detail knocked and entered the house while the passengers waited for clearance to enter from the driveway. The agents appeared quickly and waved them in. A man emerged behind them, and Bob immediately recognized him as Agent Miloc. Bob smiled and Frank recognized the man as well. "I'm glad we got a couple of cases, I owe him a few beers, too," Bob smiled as they wheeled into the driveway.

"I was just here feeding Buck on my way home. I guess my timing is good, but I almost shot the first idiot who came through the door. He had his gun drawn for Pete's sake," the FBI agent chastised the group walking toward him as Bob tossed him a beer from the stack he was carrying.

"Good to see you again, and thanks a whole lot for taking care of my dog while I was gone. Sorry I couldn't call and let you know how long I'd be gone or that I was coming back, but I'm sure you understand all that better than I do. Come on in and visit awhile, if you have some time. Frank is going to cook us up some Ruben sandwiches and I owe you more than a few beers. Can you stay awhile?" Bob's invitation was immediately accepted. Miloc had been keeping an eye on things here for weeks and he wanted a full debrief on where Bob had been and what he had been doing.

"I wouldn't miss it. What in the world have you guys been up to lately? It's been a long time since we've seen you? Me and Buck were starting to worry. Come tell me all about it...well, whatever you can." Miloc released Bob's hand and shook Frank's next. "Good to see you, Colonel," he said with sincerity and conviction.

"Frank. Please call me Frank. I hear colonel so much at work sometimes I forget that it isn't my given name," Frank smiled. The three men went inside and walked through the house dropping bags in the bedroom and groceries in the kitchen. Then they took turns in the bathroom after petting a very excited dog. They all settled into the living room to work on their beers. Bob turned on some music, louder than he liked, but he needed it to cover some of the conversation he knew was being recorded from somewhere in the house.

His first order of business was to tell his two new friends he had met Ann and was going to be married. He wasn't sure *when* yet but he was sure *to whom,* he joked. They all congratulated him and Frank got the champagne from the refrigerator. He now understood why Bob had bought the bottle. He popped the cork and handed the bubbling bottle to Bob and the three took turns drinking from it just like they were at a college party. Frank carried the bottle into the kitchen and began to look around for what he needed to begin cooking Reubens.

"I don't know about you two but I am starving. I missed lunch to get that airstrip open again so the Professor here could get himself home in low profile. Sometimes it is hard for these guys to understand that opening an airstrip that is almost always closed isn't necessarily in keeping with the lowest of profiles, even though it keeps the boys from the watchful eyes at our airport. They mean well and I guess it's okay once in a while." Frank was hoping whoever was recording this would hear and consider his comment before they messed up the good security they had going out there.

The men chatted, ate, and had another beer. Bob explained what he could to them. He explained to Miloc, who preferred to be called by his last name, that he was pressed into selling his technology to the US government for a large sum of money. He couldn't give him the exact details but he could tell him the gist of the story without breaking his security agreements.

Frank added, "The agreement was with the President himself and the sum was ten digits with a lot left over, but Bob can't tell anyone any of the details and neither could he." Now Miloc couldn't tell anyone either. Bob looked surprised at Frank but was glad he shared the information with the agent. Bob went on to tell them he had been working in a classified underground research facility and met Ann there. The two of them hit it off and never looked back. He told them he was planning on moving and wanted to start new somewhere. He was happy and they could tell by the look on his face and the gleam in his eye that she meant a lot to him. They all smiled and toasted good fortune and happiness. Bob offered the two men his thanks and added he would never have made it through without their help and open mindedness.

He added, "I have never been very good with sentiment but I intend to make it up to you guys. If there is ever anything I can do for you guys, I want you to know you can count on me to help you out. I owe you more than any money can buy. If money can help, I know where I can get some." He smiled, laughed, took a drink and continued, "I know you probably can't take any money and I'd bet you wouldn't even if you could because you are both men of principle. But I offer just the same anytime you might need it. College for the kids, Frank...whatever...just ask. Miloc, same for you. I really mean that and I hope you know it. I had to offer or I wouldn't feel right. I hope you consider my offer in the spirit it is intended," Bob finished.

"It's nice to know I have a rich Uncle if I get into a bind. Thanks," Frank smiled. "After all, you are much older than us. I guess it is only right that you are much wealthier," Frank added trying to lighten the mood a bit.

"I'm nine years younger than you are! How'd you make colonel without being able to do simple math or tell the truth?" Bob asked, then added, "Oh never mind, I guess that question really answered itself, didn't it?" They all laughed and then decided it was time to break up their party while the two men were still safe to drive. Three beers over three hours with a meal was okay but none of them were inclined to drinking and driving. Bob shook their hands and asked them to keep in touch. He hoped to be moving in a week or so and wanted to keep in contact. They agreed and wrote their phone numbers and addresses down for Bob. He waved goodbye as the men both climbed into Miloc's car and drove off. Bob went to his own bed climbed in. Exhausted from the trip and mellowed from the beer and champagne, he quickly drifted off to sleep hoping for dreams of Ann.

The next day he woke with Buck licking at his hand dangling over the edge of the bed. It was well past sunrise and Bob had already decided to go to the University today and see what his status was there. He really wanted to see Durbin one last time but, more importantly, to say goodbye to Betty whom he was sure was worried about him. She was the only one on that staff who cared more about people than they did about the business of learning. He would miss her but he made a mental note to make sure she would be financially secure for her retirement in three years. She would never take his money either but she would work for him he thought. Bob figured he could use someone back here to keep his affairs in order and take care of some things. He didn't know what or how yet but he would take care of Betty and get her out from under Durbin's wretched thumb.

CHAPTER TEN

UNFINISHED BUSINESS

The University was today's business. Tomorrow Bob would stop by the Church for a meeting with Father Gannon. Bob had a hunch they had a lot to talk about. At a minimum he wanted to go to confession, because all that was discussed in confession was sacred and secret between the priest, God, and the penitent. He had a hunch the pastor may have a secret or two of his own he would be willing to share after he heard what Bob had to say. Right now, it was time to greet the beautiful day with a run with Buck, a shower, breakfast at the diner, and a trip to the University.

Bob had decided all that time underground hadn't helped his health any, so he had a slow two mile run with his dog. Buck had no problem keeping up and enjoyed being out of the house and out of the yard. A quick shower and a quiet breakfast at the diner where he had learned to relax and slow down were all he needed to get his head right. He felt good. Now, in familiar surroundings, he felt renewed. He left the diner and began the short walk to the University and Dr. Hugh Durbin's office. Bob entered the building and sneaked up behind Betty, who was seated at her desk in Durbin's outer office talking on the telephone. He spoke clearly, "Hey gorgeous, have you been true to me?" Betty wheeled around in her chair, dropping the phone with a start at the unexpected voice behind her.

"Bob Mcleod, I ought to smack you. Where have you been? I have been worried sick about you...up and run off for months at a time without ever so much as a word. You are done as far as he's concerned. He personally packed up all your stuff from the lab. He's got it in his office waiting to give it to you personally. He hired another grad student to collect the data. He gave someone else your job and the lab time to finish the work on the grant Bob. You really screwed up. I don't think there is any way he is going to let you back here. He even placed you on academic suspension. So, you'll be lucky to finish your PhD let alone get your job back. Hello Bob...are you listening to me? He hates you and now he's got you in a trick. What happened; where have you been? Will you say something?" Betty finally took a breath, excused herself from the phone call and hung it up. Bob stepped over and gave her a hug.

"Thanks for caring about me, Betty. I expected as much from him but it really doesn't matter anymore. I've got a new job and it pays well. I won't have time to finish the grant project but it's important, so I am glad he's got someone on it already. I expected that; it's nice not to be disappointed. A lot going on in my life now Betty. Can you have lunch with me today, or do you already have a date? I'd rather meet you after I get done with Durbin. I don't want you to leave with me. That might hurt your good standing with him if he thinks you still like me. I've got great news and a deal I want to talk to you about. How about the student center half an hour after I leave. I doubt I'll be long in there? I know I don't have an appointment but I think he will want to see me...right?" Bob asked.

"Okay, but you have a lot of explaining to do young man. You are no quitter and, as far as I can tell, that's just what you're doing. You worked too hard to quit now. You better have lots of good reasons or you and me are gonna have it out. You go in and deal with him now but you'll have to deal with me at lunch," Betty promised him, and she meant it. Bob knew she would come to lunch ready to tackle a bear and he appreciated her. She was the closest thing to a Mother that Bob had in his life, and he was kind of proud to see her so upset at his recent behavior.

He smiled at her and rolled his eyes just to throw a little gasoline on the fire she was already building. Bob had decided he was going to be perfectly mannered, calm and polite while he was here with Durbin. After all, Bob had the upper hand and he wasn't going to stoop to the low level that he was sure Durbin would want to take this encounter. Betty buzzed the intercom to tell him Professor Mcleod was here to see him at the same time Bob knocked on the closed door and gently pushed it open. "Dean Durbin, got a few minutes?" Bob inquired.

"Well, well, well. The prodigal son returns. Come in and sit down, Bob, we have much to discuss. I've missed you...literally for months. I thought you might be dead but I can see that is not the case. I really wish you would have called. So much has happened since you left us. Where did you go? What happened?" Hugh Durbin was as genuinely interested as he was sarcastic. The sheriff had told him that Bob reportedly had made a few million dollars and was under investigation by the FBI and the IRS so the dean was intrigued.

"Shall we dispense with the sarcasm Hugh and get right to the point?" Bob asked politely.

"We can dispense with the sarcasm but you are to address me as Dean Durbin. I am not your bar buddy I am your academic Dean and your boss," he shot back.

"Does that mean I still have my job and my student status, Dean?" Bob added quickly, but politely?

"Unofficially yes, for now. Officially, no. You are on academic suspension and you have been replaced on the grant by another graduate student who is serious about their loyalty to the university and protecting the environment. I am the only one who can reinstate you in either capacity. I have collected your personal items and held them for you. They are in that box in the corner. You are pretty pathetic in my eyes today, Bob Mcleod. What would you have me do with you now? What did you come here to ask me?" Durbin piled on the *superior being about to pass sentence on the prisoner* attitude a bit too much for Bob but he managed to keep his cool.

"What would it take if I wanted to come back?" Bob asked the question because he had to know and he wanted to get something on the mini tape recorder in his pocket just in case he needed it to protect Betty or himself.

"It will take a lot my friend. You see I am still confused by your extended absence and reappearance two months later. You must tell me all about that and about the money someone told me you had made under less than honest pretenses," Durbin stopped and waited for a reply.

"I had another job offer and I took it. It was temporary. The money was good but now I'm back. I can't tell you any more than that. That's it. There are no other-than-honest pretenses. Am I back in, now?" Bob asked penitently.

"No! You are not! You keep any of that money you made? You got a new truck, paid cash for it before you left and it sat at your house the whole time you were gone. You bought Doc's old house for cash. You do this with my money? Drug money? I won't have a criminal in my employ, nor in my school," Durbin lashed out at him.

"I see you've done your homework. The sheriff tell you this?" Bob asked.

"I have my sources and he is just one of many, Mister. Don't underestimate me, Bob. I can crush you if I want to but I'd rather you just cut me in on whatever scheme you've got going on. I don't even need to know what it is. It will cost you fifty grand to get back as a student but I won't let you back at your job unless you give me a damned good reason why you need that job to make your scheme work. I don't want to be party to any of that. What is done is done but you ain't breaking no more laws working for me. I want compensation for all those laws you broke before I knew about it and that will get you back to finish school and be on your way.

"That my friend, is what it will take to get you back, fifty thousand dollars. Sell the house and you'll make more than that. So, I don't want to hear any whining about not having it. I'm letting you off easy, too. I could ask for a lot more given all the pain you have caused me but I am a reasonable man. I know how important it is for you to finish your education so just think of this as repaying a student loan."

"You really have me all figured out don't you, Hugh? Well, you can take your offer and stuff it. I am not coming back and you can keep both my education and my job. I am not about to pay you anything, let alone fifty grand to come back and be under your thumb for the rest of my life. I have more pride, dignity, and morals than that. You don't deserve to be the Dean of a kindergarten, much less one at a respected University. I'll just take my things and be on my way. I hope I never see you again but I suspect someday I will." Bob shook his head and began to walk to the door.

"You'll be back, Bob. Don't you walk away from me. You'll come crawling back on your belly before you know it and it will cost you a lot more next time you come back. You think about that before you walk out this door. You need me and you need back in. You better not blow your one opportunity. It may not be here next time but, if it is, you can bet it will double in price, Mister." Durbin was speaking loudly now, almost threatening, Bob.

"You are the pathetic one. Sorry to trouble you; I can see you have a lot of important things to do. Try working on yourself for a while. You might find it a valuable improvement project. You certainly appear to be a fixer upper." Bob walked out and smiled at Betty. "See you at lunch in half an hour," he whispered as he walked past her and out the door. Durbin stood behind his desk with the look of failure across his face. He wasn't sure exactly what had just happened but he was knew he wasn't happy with the unexpected outcome.

Bob strolled across the campus to the flower shop and bought a dozen long stemmed red roses to bring to Betty. He began to walk back toward the student center with just enough time to make his lunch date with the lady who had looked out for him for years. He slipped a card into the tape recorder as he walked and dropped it back into his pocket. As he entered the student center, he saw Betty sitting at a table waiting and looking around for him. Bob walked up to her and smiled as he presented her the dozen roses, "For the woman I love, Thanks for taking such good care of me over the years." Bob laid the roses down in front of her and hugged her.

"What is all this about? What has gotten into you, Bob?" she demanded.

"I am leaving Betty. I am going to Indiana. I am moving at the end of the week and I am getting married to the woman of my dreams. It is time for me to move on from here. So, I wanted to say goodbye...maybe," Bob said matter-of-factly.

"What? Married? Moving? Why?" Betty stammered all the words out one at a time as she stared at Bob in disbelief.

"The short version is I met Ann on this new job and we hit it off, fell in love, and now we are getting married. You'll like her and I hope you meet her soon," Bob added. "The flowers are for you and I have another proposition for you if you'd like to hear it," he inquired.

"Sure, why not? You're full of surprises today!" she exclaimed.

"I want you to quit your job and work for me. I can't stand to have you working for that snake. I'll pay you a hundred thousand a year and you don't have to move. Frankly, I won't need you to do much either. Are you interested?" He waited for her reply.

"How are you going to pay me a hundred grand a year...let alone for doing nothing? You don't have that kind of money...do you? Wait, she's not some heiress or something is she? Are you into something illegal Bob?" she asked all her questions in the same breath, obviously, overwhelmed by all this. Bob suggested they grab something from the line and talk while they ate lunch. He answered her questions as they proceeded through the line.

"She is not an heiress and I am not into anything illegal. But I did make a lot of money on this job I was on. It is all legitimate but I can't tell you much about it. It was a government job and it is classified. I did some work nobody else can do and they paid me handsomely for my work. Trust me, I can afford not to come back here and work. I can afford not to work another day of my life if I chose to stop working. I can afford to pay you a hundred grand a year for as long as you want to work for me. I might even give you a raise once in a while if you do a good job," Bob smiled at her as they sat back down at their table.

"Okay, let's say I believe you...which I don't yet. What would I have to do to earn my hundred grand a year? I am only making fifty-one now and I have been at the University since dirt was new...and you're right about Durbin. I don't care for him one little bit." She took a bite and waited for Bob's answer.

"Well, that's just it. I don't have a great job description yet but I know I will need some secretarial work, some typing, some letters and some file keeping for what I am going to be doing the next few years. I don't know when I will need it but, when I need it, I will need it on the spot...like immediately. I won't want to keep any of the records at my home and I need someone I can trust.

"That narrows it down to you or me. I don't do that stuff; Ann will need some help, too. I thought you could do it from here and keep some of the records here as well. When I need you in a hurry, I'll buy you a plane ticket to where I need you to be. You'll work a few days and then you can come home if you want. Some work we can do online so you won't have to travel a lot. But, when I contact you, I will need you to trust me to do *what, when and where* I ask. Again, I need someone I can trust. This is more of that government work I had before so it needs to be closely guarded. Are you interested?" Bob tried again.

"My Dad always told me if it sounds too good to be true it probably is. He also told me if it looks like fish, smells like fish, and tastes like fish, then it probably is a fish. This sounds too good to be true, Bob, and it sounds shady and sneaky. I love you kid but you're asking me to quit my lifelong job for a lot of money doing very little of something I don't even understand. I can't tell you yes...not now." She was right and he knew it. He expected this to be her answer, so he moved to his backup plan.

"I figured you'd say as much. How about we compromise? You keep your job and work for me, too. I know you have a lot of vacation saved up. So, I'll pay you the same amount of money and when I need you just take a few days' vacation. You help me out and then go back to work. I'll pay for everything and, if you don't like it, you just tell me anytime and you can quit. I want you to be able to leave when you just can't stand working for Durbin. He can ruin you and I don't think he would blink an eye doing it if you got in his way. He might get wind of my new job and come after me in some way. I am afraid he may go through you to get to me and I don't want anything to happen to you. If he gets ugly with you on anything, use this to send him back where he came from." Bob set the small tape recorder on the table. He pressed the play button and listened with Betty to the conversation he had with Durbin. It was enough to convince her.

"Okay," Betty agreed, "I intend to keep my job at the University, and for your information that slime bag isn't big enough to drive me out even on a bad day...but I'll keep the tape for backup. You're right; that may come in very handy if we ever come to blows. I will also take you up on your offer on one condition. You actually call me sometime and have me do something for you. It doesn't matter what it is.

"We both know I can use the money and I'm pretty sure this is just a thinly veiled effort on your part to help me out without offending me by just giving me some money. Well, Bob, I appreciate that because I wouldn't take your money just to take it. The only way I will keep any of it is if you actually have me do something for you. I don't want you out running around doing something without a wise old woman looking over your shoulder once in a while. Do we have a deal then?" she smiled and pushed her hand across the table to shake his.

"We have a deal, my dear. Thanks." Bob shook her hand and reached into his pocket and pulled out a checkbook. It was a new leather cover with crisp paper inside. He wrote her a check for one hundred thousand dollars and handed it to her. "This is your first year's salary. Can you meet me at my house this weekend? Saturday anytime would be better than Sunday for me. It should only take about two hours and then I will have kept my end of the bargain, even if I don't need you the rest of the year. But I suspect I'll have more for you to do...maybe even more than you'll want to do. You might even want to quit your job at the University so you can spend more time working with Ann and me. But, that will all have to be determined later. Is Saturday okay then? Saves you a vacation day, right?" Bob smiled.

"I'll see you Saturday, boss. And thanks, Bob. You have no idea how good your timing was. He was really starting to get to me and I didn't see any smart way to fight back and win. See you Saturday," she smiled and got up to leave. She needed to get back to work and didn't want to stir Durbin up any more than he already was after his morning meeting with Bob.

As Betty headed back, he realized it was still early, barely afternoon. He had accomplished all he set out to do here much quicker than he expected. So, he decided to walk over to the Church and see if he could spend some time with Father Gannon. *Never put off until tomorrow that which you can accomplish today,* he heard in his head. He couldn't walk Betty back to her office because he knew, if Durbin suspected she was helping him in any way, he would try to get rid of her. It sounded like a good plan, actually, but Bob knew if he got rid of her it would be from the University altogether—not just out of his office—and he couldn't risk that. It was a pretty good walk to the Church but it was a beautiful day and besides, his legs were stiffening up from the run this morning. He had no idea how out of shape he was until he got out there this morning thinking he could just pick up where he left off three and a half years ago.

It was time to go find Father Gannon and learn what he knew. It was time to share and see if Father had anything to share back. Bob set off for the Cathedral and mixed with the students scurrying between classes. He wanted to make it as difficult as he could on anyone who might be following him. He walked this morning mostly because it would be much more difficult to follow him than if he were driving and older men loitering around campus were easy to spot if they followed him.

Just because he was paranoid doesn't mean they're not out to get him he thought as he headed down the sidewalk toward the church. He needed to be careful; there was a lot riding on him now. He now had Ann and Betty to consider and he believed he was the only man in the world who could see to it that the weather modification technology was used for the good of all. He was hoping his time with Father Gannon would increase that number to two men.

It was quiet along the streets he walked and it took him some time to get to the Cathedral. Bob didn't notice anyone following him as he rounded the corner where the large building stood. He went past it and walked around the block to see if anyone followed or looked familiar on the way back, but nobody did. Bob thought, either they were very good or they were just not there. So, he walked up to the rectory door and rang the bell. It was the middle of the afternoon by this time and Bob hoped to catch Father Gannon with no appointments. The priest was home, and answered the door with the same smiling face and question he asked of everyone he greeted, "Hello there, Bob, what can I do for you today?"

"Good afternoon, Father. I hope I am not interrupting anything but I was wondering if you had some time this afternoon to hear a confession and talk with me awhile?" Bob asked.

"Certainly. Come in. I have to leave in about three hours to go to the hospital to visit some of my parishioners this evening but, until then, I am free. I haven't seen you at mass lately; have you been traveling?" Father Gannon asked as he led Bob to the room in the rectory that he used for an office. He motioned for him to sit down in the chair as he did the same.

"Yes, in fact I have been gone for a couple of months...a new job of sorts. In fact, that is why I am here. I plan on getting married soon and wanted to talk about that with you. But first, I'd like you to hear my confession," Bob stopped and waited for the priest's reply.

"Very well. Just a minute, then. Is here, okay?" Bob nodded and Father made a few preparations so they could both be a bit more formal for the sacrament. Then he nodded and motioned for Bob to proceed. After he spoke an act of contrition, which is a general request for the forgiveness of sins, Bob asked the priest before he continued, "Now, Father, anything we say must stay between you, me, and God right? I mean this a confession and it is protected by your vows and the Church, right? You can't tell anyone what I am about to tell you, correct?"

"That's right. There is no legal way for anyone to compel me to disclose your confession and my vows prevent me from ever speaking a word of it to anyone. I guarantee the confidentiality of what you tell me. It is one of my roles in our church. Are you in some kind of trouble or have you done something illegal that you are concerned I will talk to others about?" the pastor asked him.

"*Trouble*...perhaps; *illegal*...I don't think so; but *wrong*...maybe. I have been away on a job. I had to deliver something to someone that I don't think is going to do the right thing with it. I feel party to something that may hurt a lot of other people instead of helping them. And Father, I got paid a lot of money to do it so I am not sure I didn't sell out my friends and myself and others I don't even know who could benefit from this." Bob was beating around the bush, half hoping for a reaction, and half not being able to say exactly what he had done.

"You are speaking in generalities here. Maybe if you were more specific, I could help you understand if you have committed a sin or not. Do you want to try that?" The priest asked. He was a seasoned veteran at helping people heal themselves by admitting their faults and failures, then finding a way to overcome them. He knew it was a three-part process.

Admit that what you did was wrong, determine the reason you did it, and then take some corrective action so you don't do it again. He first needed Bob to admit to him what it was he was concerned about doing so they could figure out if it was wrong or not.

"Sure, I can do that. I discovered that our friend Doc had found a way to modify the weather. He built a machine that allowed him to change the weather and I found that out, too. I figured out how it worked and built some of my own. I made some money with them to finance some more research but got twisted up in the FBI, IRS, the military, and the government. I had to prove to them I wasn't crazy; so I had to show them the technology to stay out of jail."

"They were afraid I would use it or sell it as a weapon, so they bought everything from me for five billion dollars. Now I can't work on the technology to help people with it anymore and I am afraid they are going to use it to hurt people or, at least, not help them. I think I did the only thing I could have done at the time but I don't feel right about it and I need your help to fix it. I think you may know some things that can help me fix it Father," Bob got it all out in one breath so the priest couldn't interrupt him.

The priest sat there in amazement and thought for a moment before he spoke, "So, you know about Thor's Hammer? Doc's secret is out?" Father Gannon spoke with a clear tone of mixed disappointment and fear. "Doc worried about how to deliver that thing to the world and couldn't come up with a good way. So, he decided to do nothing instead. Frankly, I doubted you would figure out what it was but couldn't bring myself to end Doc's work and the technology he was so proud of developing. Who knows of its capability now; how far has it gone?" Bob reached into his pocket and handed Father Gannon a copy of the signed agreement between himself and the President. "Wow, you didn't waste any time with the middlemen of the world, now did you?"

"Just a week or so Father. You knew about it all along then?" Bob asked.

"I knew what Doc told me it could do but I never saw it work. I knew what you were asking about that day you came by but I couldn't tell you about it and, frankly, I wasn't sure Doc would have wanted anyone to know so I kept mum and waited. Now my wait is over. I don't think you have committed a sin here, Bob, but I am curious about how it came to pass. I am still hearing your confession so, if you'd like to talk about it, I would like to hear about it," the pastor offered. Bob accepted his invitation and spent the better part of an hour explaining the entire ordeal to Father Gannon. They had two drinks of Irish whiskey along the way to help the discussion along. Bob told him about the demos, the White House meeting, the underground facility and about Ann. It was clear to the priest that Bob was here to try and figure out what to do next.

Even more importantly it was clear to Father Gannon that Bob was intent on getting the technology used for the good of mankind. He made no bones about the fact that he didn't trust the President to keep his word about using the technology for everyone. He knew the President couldn't spend enough time in office to weaponize it, develop defenses, and then commercialize peaceful applications that would benefit everyone. Bob was going to find a way to keep his contract with the President and get the technology out there without risking this or any other nation. He just had no clue how. But Bob had convinced Father Gannon that was what he intended to do.

"Bob, that is truly a remarkable story. I don't know whether to hug you or hit you upside the head. You probably deserve both so we'll consider them offsetting penalties and I won't do either. Wait here a minute; I think I might have a suggestion for you," the priest instructed as he got up from his chair and left the room.

Bob stood to stretch when he noticed through the window a man outside milling around the bus stop. It was the same man who had gotten on the bus an hour ago when he was walking up to the church. Bob didn't know for sure but he was fairly certain he had just spotted one of his tails. Bob was feeling particularly proud of his discovery when Father Gannon came back into the room carrying what looked like a bowling ball bag in his right hand. He set the bag up on the desk with a soft thump.

"Doc was afraid one of the things wouldn't be enough. So, he built two of them. I have been holding it for him for several years now. I know he will never come for it but I didn't know what to do with it. I have never used it; he never showed me how. I guess he wanted to keep me afraid of touching it so I wouldn't end the world or something. I don't mind telling you it worked. I'm afraid to look at the thing actually. The potential damage it can do is as great as the potential good. I can tell you have thought long and hard about this, which is why you are here. Well, I have too...for years, in fact. It really weighed heavy on me after Doc died. I am glad you came today, Bob. It feels as if a great weight has been lifted from me. We may not have the answers yet but, at least, we know we are no longer alone in the fight. The question now becomes, what do we do about it?"

Bob stared at the bag lying on the desk. It was exactly like the one he had found the first device in. He walked over and opened it without saying a word. It was an exact replica of the machine he had found. Doc had built two and kept one in reserve with Father Gannon. This changed everything as far as Bob was concerned but they would have to work together and work smartly. Bob couldn't help but feel like he had been given a second chance...another chance to do correctly what he had blundered through the first time.

He had less time but more money than before. More importantly, he had a partner now. And, if he needed Betty or Ann, he was pretty sure he could count on them to make a team. It was a small, scrawny team at best but Bob was used to being the underdog and knew sometimes appearances could work to your advantage. Bob sat and contemplated his position for a moment. According to his contract with the President, Bob could no longer work on anything related to weather modification, but it didn't expressly forbid him from counseling Father Gannon on how to use the device he already had in his possession. And what he did with it after that was strictly up to the priest, right? The President of the United States had no authority over how the priest used items he owned, and Bob's contract certainly held no weight over Father Gannon's activities. Bob suggested that the priest would have to do the dealing if they were going to do anything with this device in order to avoid giving the President any grounds to reclaim Bob's money for breach of contract. And Bob had no idea that another device existed, let alone that Doc had actually shared his secrets with anyone. They would be fully compliant with the letter of the contract. A little gray by the intent of the agreement maybe, but certainly in the right by the letter.

Bob knew the president would understand that logic because he had used it in his own defense several times since taking office. Bob and the priest talked for another hour trying to come up with a scenario in which the technology could be exploited without jeopardizing themselves, their loved ones, or Bob's contract with the President. They had a thin concept going by the end of their discussion and Father Gannon agreed, in principle, to give it a try. He would have to do all the work but that didn't bother him, as long as, the technology got out safely and was used for the common good—not just the good of one President—even if he was the President of the United States of America. Others needed to benefit from Doc's discovery and hard work and Bob and Father Gannon had hatched up a scheme that might have a shot at making it possible.

Bob left the rectory, agreeing to return in the next couple of weeks with his fiancée, Ann. Father Gannon was to study the recipes and operating instructions Bob had written down for him. He was not to attempt to use them or operate the device; that would come later. Knowledge first, application later he was instructed.

Bob followed Father Gannon through the rectory and watched him place the device on a shelf in a linen closet and closed the door behind him. Well, all appeared safe and, with instructions already given, Bob felt comfortable enough to leave his new partner. "Father, be careful. And be good," Bob warned as he bowed his head and asked if he had been forgiven his sins. Father Gannon ended Bob's reconciliation sacrament with the appropriate prayers but decided not to assign him a penance. After all, he had been through enough just getting this far. Bob thanked the priest and bid him farewell as he stepped out into the darkness and disappeared down the street.

He had accomplished a lot today, and was proud of himself as he noticed the man huddled in the covered walkway still had not gotten on a bus. Bob headed back to his house, being careful to stick to the busy streets and stay in well-lit areas. He returned home and found Buck glad to see him. There was a message on the answering machine from Ann. She called just to check and see that he got back okay and to say she really missed him already. It would be a long week waiting for her to meet with him he thought as he listened to her voice on the machine.

Bob used the next couple of days just to relax and chill out around the house. He watched television, cooked, and drank a few beers, and occasionally sorted through some papers. He used the quiet time to clear his head and think about what he was doing and, more importantly, what he was about to do. When Betty came over Saturday morning, he gave her stacks of paper to arrange into files for him. He couldn't tell her what they all meant yet, but it was easy enough to sort them by topic and author. Most of it was Doc's or his own notes and research stuff. None of it explicitly talked about weather modification but it was all the research that went into the discovery. She sorted, separated, stacked and divided the documents until they were all accounted for and labeled with little yellow sticky notes.

This took about two hours and Bob was surprised at how efficient Betty was. She was really good at this stuff. He was upset with himself at being surprised by her skills. Bob handed her three one-hundred-dollar bills and asked her if she would go to the office supply store and get some color coordinated binders to put the stacks of paper in. They would also need a heavy duty three-hole punch. He wanted paper copies of everything in a separate and secure location as a backup for all the digital files. He then wondered if Doc had already done the same thing. He would fix them lunch. Then they could finish up afterwards, load some of the paperwork in his truck and take it to Betty's house. She agreed and was off in a flash. Bob prepared a taco salad, which he knew was her favorite lunch. After she returned and they unloaded the stacks of binders, the two sat down to eat.

"Bob, what can you tell me about what you are doing? I know you told me there was lots you couldn't tell me...and I'd have to trust you...and I do. But what can you tell me that you haven't already?" She was genuinely concerned and Bob had already taken some time to reconsider his position.

He leaned over and said very softly, "I'll tell you in your house, mine is bugged. Let's just enjoy lunch and talk about stuff you wouldn't mind your mother reading in the newspaper." Bob smiled and gave her a reassuring look. They finished up lunch talking about the good old days at the University and reminisced about Doc. When all the papers had a new binder for a home, Bob loaded some into his truck. "Let me take you out for a nice dinner, Betty. A thank you present for helping me so much today." Bob held up his hand to stifle the protest he knew she would make about already being paid way too much for doing so little. "Unless you already have other plans for dinner, I insist," he smiled charmingly.

"You know I could never turn you down. You always had a smile that could melt rubber, you jerk. That is not playing fair. Okay, I'll go to dinner with you but you have to pick the restaurant. I'm not doing any more thinking today," she whined as she smiled at him.

"Let's get this done and get on out of here," Bob added.

They climbed into their vehicles and drove clear across town to Betty's house. It was a small, modest place but very comfortable. She had plenty of room for herself and her treasures from her long marriage and Bob could tell she still loved her husband very much. Even though he was gone, he was still very much part of her life in the most positive of ways. She wasn't holding on unwilling to acknowledge he was gone like some do. No, she was secure in his absence, knowing it was up to her to keep alive all the good that he brought into her life. She was basking in the positive aspects of their long relationship, keeping them alive in her life even though he was gone, unlike many others who dwell on the negative, bemoaning all the things they will no longer have in their life when their spouse is gone. As they carried the first load of binders into the house and placed them in the spare bedroom, Bob stopped and asked Betty to sit down so they could talk for a few minutes...and she did.

"I am working for the government now. They are paying me not to do stuff. Not to do anymore work in the area of weather modification research. That is what all this stuff is. Work Doc and I did—separately, by the way, never together. We both did parts of it and I want you to keep all Doc's stuff here at your place." Bob paused to allow Betty the chance to speak what her face revealed.

"I don't understand, really. Why would they pay you not to do stuff?"

"Because I already know how to do it and they don't want me selling it to anyone else and that is how I can afford all this stuff and to pay you. I can't tell you much more. There really isn't much more to tell. I will occasionally need some of these notes and, if you have them here, you can read me the part I need or send it to me. You'll need a fax machine and a computer, won't you? Of course, you will. I know you can use both. So, here is some money to buy them when you get some time. There's no rush. I shouldn't need anything from here for a week or two at the earliest. Put this somewhere safe and get yourself really good ones," Bob said as he peeled off forty one-hundred dollar bills. "I learned the hard way you need to do all this stuff with cash and not checks or credit cards. I keep lots of it around now so the banks don't have it all when I need it in my hands. Now let's finish up getting this stuff in the house and see how much space it is going to take up. I don't want to impose on you too much." Betty took the cash from Bob and put it up in a cabinet. They unloaded the rest of the binders without saying much. When they were finished storing them neatly in a closet so she could easily access them when he called, they sat down for a drink and more conversation.

"Is any of this dangerous, Bob? For you, for Ann, for me? For anyone?" she worried for the both of them.

"No, I don't think so. There are too many people who are aware of the technology now for them to kill me. I think they are far more concerned with keeping me safe so, if they have any problems making it work, they can come get me to help them again. I wouldn't have gotten either of you involved in this if I thought there was any risk to you. But, if anybody ever does come for this stuff—I don't care who it is—just give it to them. It is not worth getting any kind of hurt over. There is nothing here that can help anyone but me, but you don't need to worry about that," he assured her.

"You mean they know how to do it already? Change the weather I mean?" she asked in amazement. After all, she had been working with meteorologists practically her whole life.

"Yes, I showed them how and gave them the equipment to do it. You can't tell anyone this, Betty, especially any weather people—especially at work. Doc figured it out in his spare time, I think, and I managed to finish up what he started. It is a national security issue and my orders came from the President of the United States himself, in person. I had to tell you Betty but you can't talk to anyone but me about it, not now anyway. Someday you'll be able to tell stories about how you helped me, but not now. I need that from you and I am going to make you promise because I know your word is good enough." She smiled at Bob's words.

"I promise. I knew Doc was a great man. He always said one day he would make his wife proud of him; one day he would make us all proud of him. Well, I'm proud of him and I hope he knows it," she finished by looking up, as if waiting for a reply from heaven.

"Well, I haven't always said it but I am going to make you all proud of me, too. It may take a little time, but I will keep that promise to you, as sure as, I know you will keep your promise to me. Now, go put on something comfortable for dinner. We are going to Tony's Mexican for lunch and Italian for dinner. I know they are your favorites and, the last time you were at Tony's, dirt was new. My treat; take your time; I'll just watch TV until you're ready if you don't mind?" Bob stretched out his legs and flipped the channel to the news to see what was happening.

A band of much needed rainfall was lingering over a drought threatened portion of northern Texas and Oklahoma providing crop saving relief just in time. Bob thought how odd that was for the system to linger under the upper-level flow pattern they showed. Then it hit him. They were already using it! Surely it was too soon. Surely, they would do more testing. Then it occurred to Bob that this was their testing. They had nothing to lose and everything to gain. It was close enough to the facility to be convenient but far enough away not to arouse suspicion. It was used to prevent a financial disaster from striking a region in our country so that was a positive application. Bob was proud and worried at the same time. They were already using the device in live tests and that meant he had a lot less time than he had originally hoped for. He would have to step up his timeline but first he had a dinner date with one of the ladies in his life.

They went out and had a nice evening of conversation, pasta, and red wine. Bob and Betty had always been nice to each other, shared lunches, and wise cracks but this was the first time they had ever gone to dinner together. She was a good twenty years his senior but they had a great rapport. They spent more of their time talking about the people who weren't there than they did about themselves. Bob told her all about Ann, almost everything he knew about her. He shared how much he looked forward to spending his life with her.

Betty shared the highlights of her marriage to her late husband, hoping it would help Bob understand how strong the bonds between two people who really care about each other can be if they work hard at keeping them strong. She told him that successful marriages don't just happen. They take a lot of hard work, dedication, sacrifice, and understanding. Bob had all that in him. He just needed to make sure he applied it in his new relationship if he really wanted to make it work. She counseled him like a son and he listened to her like a mother. They probably both filled a void in each other's lives. Bob had been a long time without his parents and Betty and her husband could never have children. *They tried* she told him but were never able to conceive. *What a shame* Bob thought, that a woman who could have been a great mother to her children should go childless in an age when so many terminated their pregnancies. It didn't seem fair.

Bob counted it as a blessing that he was benefiting from her counsel even though he knew she could have been so much more to many others. He suggested she volunteer at one of the area children's centers or volunteer to be a foster parent, or something to fill the void she confessed to have. Betty said she would consider that because, honestly, she needed to do something with herself besides work. Her lifelong hobby was her husband and the television was a completely insufficient substitute for filling the void. She thanked Bob and Bob thanked her. The evening was a great time for both of them and Bob was considering some of the things she said as he drove back to his house after dropping Betty off at hers. She was a great lady and he was now able to keep her in his life even after he moved.

The next day Bob found himself in the pew at morning mass listening to Father Gannon's sermon on giving and sharing. Bob thought it was appropriate given the endeavor they were about to embark upon together. They had lots to do and now even less time to get it done. If all went well, they would complete their efforts in a few weeks, Ann would be with him, and the world would be a better place for all to live.

The optimistic view overshadowed the realist inside him while he sat in the place of faith. Deep inside he knew he would succeed but he wasn't nearly as confident when it came to how he was going to be able to pull this off. He was counting on some divine intervention and he was pretty certain having a priest on his team wouldn't hurt any when it came to that. Bob walked out of the church after mass and, as was customary in the parish, shook the pastor's hand as he stood outside the doors greeting and chatting with his parishioners. "See you in a few days Father; I'm counting on you," Bob said softly as he smiled and shook the man's hand, then disappeared into the crowd heading for the bustling parking lot.

Bob climbed in his truck, fought his way out of the parking lot full of the hurried faithful and drove off to the mall to do some shopping. He needed some luggage and a few more things for his trip, not the least of which was some new clothes. He was looking forward to spending some of his new wealth on himself. He wasn't used to fine clothes nor was he planning on getting any. He was comfortable in jeans, a cotton-flannel shirt, and a pair of boots. That was really who he was and he had no intention of changing that now. He was, however, looking forward to some new ones of each of these. He also needed some new jackets and had a surprise or two planned for Ann. He didn't have time to learn a lot about jewelers or specialty stores but he had planned a stop at the fine jewelry store in town on his way back from the mall. It was open until six on Sunday and Bob didn't care too much for the crowded malls anyway. So, he figured he had plenty of time to get all his shopping done today. He considered asking Betty to come along but he didn't want to get her involved too much just yet. Better to let it appear that he was just catching up with an old work acquaintance for now.

He pulled into the parking lot, parked his truck, and walked into the already bustling two-level shopping mall. He found one of the outdoor clothing catalog stores and bought five new pairs of jeans, four blue and one black. Half a dozen long sleeved shirts and half a dozen short sleeved ones, and a couple of pullover sweaters. He knew it would be cooler in Indiana than it was here and he intended to be back and forth a few times in the near future. He paid cash for the clothes and lugged the bags down the mall to the western wear store. He told the clerk he wanted to try on some boots and needed a few pair. Obviously, this young lady worked on commission because she greeted him immediately when she saw all the bags he was carrying. She was elated to hear he wanted a few pair and explained everything they had from exotic skins for dress to the tough bull hides just for kicking around in. Bob looked around for a few minutes but knew exactly what he wanted. He was excited about this portion of his shopping because he was about to purchase some things he had wanted for a very long time. He asked the young lady to bring out a pair of gray and a pair of cognac colored full quill ostrich-skin boots in his size. He also wanted the same colors in elephant ear. They were the toughest material boots were made of he believed. He had seen the sales manager there some years earlier scrape the tip of his knife along the length of the skin and not even scratch it. That little demonstration had made an impression on him and the skin was just as soft and comfortable as it was tough. The clerk emerged with six boxes, two in half sizes because the tougher elephant skin usually took a half size larger than one normally wears because of the manufacturing process.

"These boots are hand-crafted and they will last a long time. You'll have to re-sole them two or three times before you wear out the top if you take good care of them," she volunteered. "You have to try each pair on both feet, Sir. Boots have to fit just so or they won't be comfortable. You need to make sure they are just right, especially when they cost this much." Bob tried on each pair and got a perfect fit after considerable deliberation from the young lady. He was very impressed by how much she knew about boots and the manufacturing process. Commission on a sale or not, she knew her stuff and was extremely helpful. She even left him a few times to help out the other salesperson who was obviously much less experienced and knowledgeable than she was. Bob thought it was refreshing to see she was a team player, willing to take time to help the lesser skilled person working with her, especially in light of working on a big sale herself. She apologized several times for having to leave Bob unattended but never blamed or demeaned her coworker for her lack of experience or knowledge.

She even showed him what to look for on each boot to make sure they were constructed properly. Bob looked over each of the boots to make sure they weren't defective and each one looked great. He smiled as he examined the gray ostrich skin boots beneath the new pair of blue jeans he was wearing. Just because he liked jeans and boots was no reason not to look good and feel good in them. He looked up and asked, "Can I wear them out?"

The young lady smiled and said in a friendly tone, "After you pay for them and I take the electronic anti-theft tag off of them, you can."

"Good, I'll take them," Bob smiled at her. She beamed at the sale and picked up the box, gently placing his old boots in the place of the ostrich skin beauties. She began walking toward the register and grabbed him some boot cream to condition the exotic skin when Bob spoke again, "I meant I'd take all of them...all four pair. Not just the one's I am wearing." Bob had a slightly correcting edge in his voice just to get a reaction from the young lady. He was certain this was going to be her biggest sale and he wanted her to remember it and him, too. He would shop here again, and he wanted the same kind of service the next time he came. The look on her face was shear surprise, and she smiled.

"Well, that will be even better yet. You won't be disappointed with any of them, I promise you that. If you have any trouble with any of them, just bring them back and I'll get you squared away," she offered dutifully. She carried the boxes to the front of the store and grabbed gray and cognac boot creams from the rack and put them in the boxes. "That ought to hold you for a while. You really need to make sure you take care of those skins and they will last you twice as many years than if you don't. Do you know how to use that stuff?" she asked. Bob nodded affirmatively, and she proceeded to ring up the sale. "Total is three thousand, one hundred and eight dollars." She looked nervously at him, expecting him to decide to put something back on the shelf. She got the facial reaction she expected and cringed a bit when Bob spoke.

"Will you round it down to thirty-one hundred even? You won't have to make nearly as much change. Do you take cash?" Bob smiled at her.

"Yes, we take cash. And I can make it thirty-one hundred, that will be just fine Sir. I suppose anyone who buys four pair of boots from me can get a two dollar a pair discount," she smiled at him as he counted out the bills.

"Can I tell you something?" Bob asked her. She nodded at his comment which wasn't really phrased as a question. "I was impressed with your knowledge and your ability to work with people. You're a talented salesperson. I especially liked how you helped out your co-worker without ever demeaning her inferior knowledge to either her or me.

That was very professional and I know it's not easy to do when you are working on a sale yourself. I just thought I'd tell you that I was impressed. A little positive feedback...in case you ever think nobody notices stuff like that anymore, you should know they really still do."

"Thank you," she beamed. "It is nice of you to notice and even nicer of you to take the time to say it. I really appreciate that. If you don't mind, I'd like to give you my card. In case you need anything else, just ask for me and I'll see if I can get it for you. You're going to need new boots one of these days...maybe for your girlfriend or someone else." She was half suggesting and half inquiring. Bob was flattered by her flirtation but decided not to let this discussion go anywhere beyond boots.

"That would be great. Maybe I'll bring my fiancée by when I come back through town."

She smiled half thankful and half disappointed at his reply, "Super, hope to see you again Sir, and thanks again. It was a real pleasure helping you." She handed Bob his boxes. Tied neatly together, they stacked two feet tall. He was heavily laden now with boxes and bags. It was time to go unload some of this stuff. He walked out to his truck, trying to look inconspicuous beneath all the packages. After that encounter with the attractive young saleswoman, Bob was in the right frame of mind to go engagement ring shopping so off he drove to the jewelers. He was a little hungry, so a quick burger from the drive through would hold him over while he shopped for the ring he would give Ann the next time they were together. He entered the jewelry store with no idea what to expect or what Ann would like. He was glad to see a woman working behind the counter who, he thought, was going to make his task a lot simpler. She greeted him with a smile and asked how she could help him today.

"I need an engagement ring and, frankly, I don't know what to get her," Bob replied honestly, hopeful the woman would sympathize with his plight and lend her expert opinion on the matter.

"Have you decided on a style, stone, size, shape, or price range," she inquired.

"No, no, no, no, and no," Bob smiled, hoping his humor would help but not surprised that it did not. "How about showing me diamond rings that I can add a wedding band to. That is a good start. I'm not worried about price, yet." Bob tried to narrow the search options.

The lady looked at him over her glasses with her eyebrows raised. Bob could see this wasn't going to be nearly as easy or enjoyable as his boot buying experience. He followed her over to a glass counter filled with engagement rings. He looked down at the glitter of precious stones and metals. He decided to let the prices substitute for his lack of knowledge. The most expensive ones must be the best ones he reasoned. "Look, I could really use your help, here, and I am not just here to look. So, if you could find it in your heart to help out a guy who is about to make the most important purchase of his life, I'd really appreciate it." Bob could see the thin layer of ice melt from the lady's face as she smiled and shook her head back and forth.

"I am sorry," she smiled at him, "it has been a really rough day and the other salesperson didn't show up today. I apologize, really. Now what do you think she will like, a solitaire or a marquis? Sorry, circle or pear shaped?"

"Round, I think. The regular round kind. I think she will like that the best," Bob smiled. Now they were getting somewhere he wanted to go. "Gold and round; that is the style." She pulled out a tray of quarter to half carat solitaires and laid it on the counter for Bob to get a better look at some of the rings. "You got bigger ones? Like about the width of her finger I think?"

"Sir, that would be about four carats, the largest I have in the store is two and three quarters and it is very expensive. That would be a huge engagement ring," she warned him.

"Good then, let me see that one," Bob instructed. She looked with an air of disbelief at him, wondering if he was there to buy, look, waste her time, or rip her off. She laid down a pad with three rings on it. There were no prices on any of them but they were exquisite. Bob looked at all three as the clerk explained the value of a diamond is based on clarity, color, carat weight. Bob held up the nicest of the three rings to the light. It reflected the light through the clear stone in an amazing blaze of color. He smiled as he held it and it spoke to him, somehow, letting him know this was the one for Ann. There could be no other; his task was all but done. The ring was gorgeous, but it was also very expensive. "I'll take this one. Can you put it in a box and wrap it for me?" Bob asked politely.

"This ring is forty-two thousand and eighty-dollars, Sir," she said with an air of superiority that Bob didn't appreciate. It had been a fun day up until now and Bob thought about going somewhere else for a brief moment. Then it hit him. That little voice telling him not to sweat the small stuff. The lady just told him she was having a bad day so he took a deep breath and let it out slowly.

"If I pay you cash, can we just make it a flat forty-two thousand?" Bob asked, returning the bit of attitude in his question. "You do take cash don't you. I am not writing you a check for this. I hate all that electronic stuff. Whatever happened to the good old days?" Bob asked. The look on her face was priceless as Bob began to count out bills from his pocket. He had just bought Ann a beautiful engagement ring for forty-two grand and he couldn't wait to give it to her. He left the store glad to get out of there but satisfied that he got a great ring for a fair price. He would remember the look on the clerk's face for quite some time he mused to himself. He drove home, stopping to pick up some Chinese carry out to eat in front of the television when he got home. He was tired of shopping and the earlier burger only served to make him even more hungry. He had gotten everything he set out to get today except the luggage and he felt good about his accomplishments. He unloaded his stuff into the spare room of his house and sat down to eat his dinner in front of the television. Ten minutes after he finished eating, he fell asleep in his chair. He had always believed that shopping until you dropped was an old wives' tale. He played it back again for himself in the morning and suddenly realized that shopping was almost as tiring as work. They were both physically challenging but right now he couldn't tell which one was easier.

He decided to try to call Zach and find out how much longer it would be before Ann could leave the underground facility. It took a series of connections, transfers, and authorization codes to get through the labyrinth of security measure for a call in but it was worth the wait. Finally, Bob heard Zach's voice on the other end of the line, "Zach here, who's this?"

"Bob Mcleod, I'm calling to..." Bob began but was immediately cut short.

"I know why you are calling. You're impatient; that's why you are calling. I trust the outside is being very good to you Professor; we are all doing quite well here. Well, I will dispense with the pleasantries, Bob, because I know you really only care about how Ann is doing. I won't keep you because I don't have much time myself. I am arranging her departure this morning. Your ears must have been burning because I was just talking about you. She will fly into Indianapolis this evening. If you tell me you will meet her, I won't have to arrange for transportation from the airport to wherever she is going from there. How about it, Sport? Want to surprise her and do me a favor at the same time? I figure you owe me that much, right?" He finally took a breath and Bob jumped into the conversation.

"Yeah, I'll get her at the airport...no problem...what time? I can't get there until evening, I have to fly myself and get a rental car," Bob asked.

"I'll have her arrive at nine fifteen on a government charter flight. Meet her at the baggage claim area before nine thirty. Usually there is no way to tell how these places get passengers into the terminal since the plane isn't big enough to use the large jetways. The tail number will be N8755, just ask them where it is coming in and they should tell you. Don't let her down, Bob. I won't tell her you're meeting her. We'll let that be our little surprise, okay?" Zach concluded.

"Fine, I'll be there. Anything else?" Bob asked.

"That's it. Once she is safely in your arms at the airport, I will have all our phone numbers and access codes changed so there will be no way for either of you to contact me. Rest assured, if we need to get in touch with either of you, that won't be a problem. Any questions for me?" Zach asked.

"No, that is it. Thanks Zach. I probably owe you a night on the town. If you ever get out of that place, look us up and I'll make good on it. I promise. Take care of yourself." Bob never knew quite how to take the guy but he always kept his word and that was what really mattered. Even if he didn't agree with a decision, he carried it out. There was something to be said for loyalty and Bob didn't want Zach upset with him if he didn't need to be. There was something about him that felt evil.

"I'll remember. Have a nice life, Bob." The line went dead and that was that. Bob hung up the phone and then it struck him. He would see Ann tonight if all went according to plan. This was great! He called and arranged for a ticket on a flight to Indianapolis that left in two hours, a limousine, and a one week's stay in an executive suite at the nicest hotel in the city. He showered, packed his old luggage with new clothes, and loaded his truck. He called Miloc and asked him if he would look after Buck for another week or so and he eagerly agreed. Bob drove to the airport, parked his truck and proceeded to the gate to check his luggage and pick up his ticket. He thought how nice it was to be able to just pick up and go whenever, wherever he pleased. He only had about thirty thousand dollars in cash with him and another hundred thousand packed into a boot in his suitcase. He realized that was a fairly loose way to handle that much money but he didn't have time to make other arrangements and he would need the money up there. He was not about to leave too big an electronic trail by using checks and credit cards right now. He would have time for all that when it didn't matter who knew *where, when, or how* he spent his money. Right now, it mattered, and he wasn't going to make it easy on those tracking his actions. Sure, he reasoned they could track the serial numbers on the bills he was using, but that was thin and time consuming. Just what he wanted. He strode up the counter, paid for his ticket and checked his bags. He had half an hour before the plane boarded so he went to one of the bars and grabbed a beer. This would be the first time he ever flew first class and he was looking forward to seeing what the big deal was. As the waitress brought him a beer, he saw Miloc walking slowly through the terminal. He looked like he was looking for someone and Bob thought that someone was him. He stood up and waved through the glass as Miloc looked his way.

The agent smiled and headed into the bar, plopping down beside Bob he said, "Man, when you go, you go, huh?"

"You looking for me, or just hanging around the airport hoping to spot dangerous fugitives from justice just passing through your neck of the woods?" Bob chided the agent as he sipped his beer and waved for the waitress to bring another for his friend.

"No, man, I can't, I'm working. But thanks. You still have time to drink another one anyway. I came here to ask you a favor. Well, kind of to offer a favor maybe...I don't know. Look, Bob, I know you haven't been around much lately and, well, you haven't had Buck too long either. Well, I'm just wondering if you wouldn't mind if I adopted the guy. Before you answer, let me plead my case. You're getting married soon and you'll be on the road doing whatever rich married people with no kids do. We kind of bonded over the past two months. I don't really have anyone, and, well, I kind of like being around the dog. We get along well and only argue over bones once in a while. I wanted to ask you before you left. I could take him and all his dog stuff to my house and he could stay there. You could come visit him whenever you want. I'll even feed you beers when you do come by. What do you say?" Miloc asked as he batted his eyes and made a sad face for added affect.

"You're serious, aren't you? You really want him that bad...came all this way?" Bob remarked. Agent Miloc nodded as Bob laughed. "Okay, I owe you. I figure you'll treat him right and give him a good home and that is what all dogs should have. Okay Miloc, you can take him if you promise to take good care of him. You better have this beer anyway. You're gonna need it to recover from that unprecedented display of heart and emotion."

"Don't mind if I do. Thanks Bob. And thanks for letting me take the dog. It—well, he—means a lot to me for some reason. I appreciate it." Agent Miloc smiled as if the world was a brighter place now. Bob was glad he could do something to bring some joy to the man's life. It must be tough he thought to himself, battling bad guys and walking through the negative side of society twenty-four hours a day. They sat and chatted until the boarding call came for Bob's flight. "Good luck man, I hope she says yes. Get her to agree early before she really gets to know you or figures out what she is in for. Check in on us once in a while and I'll keep my eyes open downtown. If I don't know how to get a hold of you, I won't be able to help you if it ever comes down to that."

"Thanks, I will. Take good care of the dog." They shook hands and Bob walked up to the line for boarding the flight. He turned but Miloc was already gone, faded into the crowd of people in the terminal area. Bob found his seat in the first-class cabin and sat down next to a man in dark suit, obviously well to do and headed for some kind of meeting. They greeted each other and the man went immediately to work reviewing his notes and portfolio. Bob smiled as the flight attendant took their drink orders. A ginger ale for the suit, and a double bourbon over ice for the man in the ostrich skin boots and jeans. There was an obvious difference between the two on the outside but Bob wondered just how different they were on the inside. The aircraft taxied and shortly thereafter they were airborne. Bob leaned back and tried to relax while thinking about Ann. The ring in his pocket made him too fidgety. He looked out the window, read a few magazines, and stared at the back of the seat as time in the sky crawled by slowly.

"You look worried about something if you don't mind me saying so," the man seated next to him said matter-of-factly.

"Really? Is it that obvious?" Bob asked genuinely surprised. "Actually I am. I am giving my fiancée her engagement ring tonight and it has really got me nervous. We already agreed to marry but this is pretty scary for me."

"Well, I think everyone who has been married has been through that, a few folks more than once. Just make sure when you do it, whatever you do, that you are sincere. That's the secret, believe me I know," the man offered.

"You done this a few times have you then?" Bob asked.

"No Sir, just once. That is why I know it works," the man smiled and resumed his reading. Bob smiled, too. Maybe they weren't that very different inside after all, he thought.

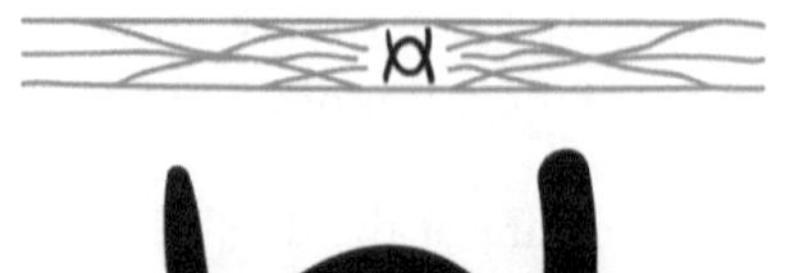

CHAPTER ELEVEN

FREEDOM

The airplane landed and taxied to the gate. Bob filed off and skeptically looked for a man holding a sign with his name on it. He was pleasantly surprised when he saw one in the crowded terminal. He found him and checked the time again; he had an hour and a half until Ann's plane was supposed to arrive. They walked toward the baggage claim area and waited for the bags to be unloaded from the plane and placed on the revolving luggage carousels. After exchanging a few pleasantries with the young limousine driver, Bob saw his bag spilling down the chute onto the moving black mat of the carousel. When it came past, he grabbed it and placed it on the floor beside the driver. That's it, just the one. He checked with the driver to see how long it would take to get to the hotel and back from the airport. It was about half an hour each away if traffic cooperated, which it usually did here.

Bob decided not to risk going to check in, make a few preparations in the room, and then get back for her arrival. If he missed her here, there was no telling how long it would take for them to link up. He instructed the driver to load the bag and to be back here at the baggage claim area in an hour. Bob left to find out the status of Ann's flight. After fifteen minutes of blank stares and searching, Bob found himself at the charter flights desk and learned that Ann's airplane was due in early. Fifteen minutes at the gate to his left.

Bob found a comfortable chair and sat down to wait. There were a surprisingly large number of people there for charter flights he thought, but he paid little attention to them. He kept an unobstructed view of the door that arriving passengers came through as they entered the terminal from the flight line.

His mind was wandering a bit when suddenly there she was. Ann walked with purpose, looking up for a sign to direct her where she intended to go. Bob smiled a pleased grin. He figured she was looking for her luggage or a bathroom. He waited until she walked past and then he fell into step about ten feet behind her. She went directly into the lady's room. Bob smiled and thought to himself, another forecast verified. He positioned himself across the hall from the restroom exit door where he knew she would see him if she had her head up and her wits about her. When she exited, she saw him. Her face beamed as she ran across the hall to greet him with a hug and a long kiss. "I missed you; I missed you so much," she began to cry. "How did you know?" Bob smiled and returned the look he saw on her face.

"I just knew. I missed you, too. If you care to accompany me, I have a car waiting for us. Dinner reservations and a suite that I hope you will find to your liking," Bob grinned, as he had a few surprises for her, too.

"It is so great to be free of that place. You have no idea, well maybe a little, but it was scary not having my freedom down there. Everything is controlled but it's not. Still, you're not free to go anywhere. You can't just get up and do something because you feel like it. I feel free now and I will never, ever, take my freedom for granted again. You look great! Look at you, new clothes and everything. Eventually you'll need to do something with that hair though," she laughed as she mussed it up with her free hand.

"There you go, that's much better. I think I like it like that." Bob tried to put it back in place with his free hand but wasn't too successful.

As they walked into the baggage claim area, he saw the driver standing there waiting for them. He was still holding the sign in case Bob didn't recognize the only young man standing there in a black suit and hat with Limousine Service embroidered into the front. They collected Ann's bags...four of them in all.

"These are just my clothes. My books, personal works, and computers have to go through security and classification verification. Then they will ship them to me. I expect that will take months. So, I won't hold my breath on ever seeing them again. If I play my cards right, I won't miss them anyway." She smiled an alluring smile at Bob that nearly melted him dead away. This weekend looked like it was shaping up to be much less nerve racking than his insecurities had led him to believe.

When they got Ann's bags loaded into the limousine, Bob instructed the driver to take them to the hotel. As he pulled out into traffic, Bob lifted a bottle of champagne for Ann to inspect. "Champagne my dear?" he offered in a bad accent. "Of course," she replied in the same brogue. Bob poured two glasses and toasted his lovely fiancée. "To us...together." They each drained their glass and placed them in the holder next to the bottle. He leaned over held her close and they kissed.

They were glad to have the roomy limousine to enjoy the ride to the hotel and, before either of them was ready to be, they'd arrived. They checked in, tipped the driver, and went up to their room. It was a luxurious suite, with a hot tub and a view of the city from the top floor. It wasn't all that impressive a skyline but it was a wonderful view that seemed to go on forever. The bell hop placed their luggage and left with way too large a tip and instructions not to bother making up the room until they called. Bob and Ann held each other in a long hug which led into a long kiss. They fell on to the large bed, which led to a long night.

The following morning Bob awoke to the sound of Ann's voice ordering a room service breakfast for both of them. She spoke to him when she noticed him stirring, "I am going to take a quick shower. I'll be out before breakfast gets here. I'd kind of like to have breakfast with you in the hot tub. Think about it and let me know," she said, and disappeared into the bathroom with a daring smile on her face.

By midafternoon they decided to do a little shopping around the hotel. Ann didn't want to call her father and tell him she was coming home; she wanted to surprise him. She had two surprises for him and she wanted to present both of them in person and at the same time. She needed a couple of days with Bob just to herself, just to be safe, just to be sure, just to be together. They had a wonderful time piddling around the shops, acting like teenagers again, enjoying their freedom and getting to know each other better with each new conversation.

Ann bought several things she didn't have with her but wanted for the remainder of their weekend, including a bottle of her favorite perfume. They dumped their shopping bags in the room and enjoyed a long kiss. "Come on it's time to go to dinner. I want to eat at that barbecue place we saw a couple of blocks from here. You told me barbequed baby back ribs are one of your favorites, right? Let's go there for dinner. We're dressed for it and it smelled great. I'm starved; aren't you hungry?" Bob asked her nervously.

"I'd rather stay here, and eat in the hot tub again," she said wickedly and smiled at him as she put her arms around his neck.

"Come on Ann, be a sport. Let's go to dinner. We can have our desert in the hot tub, I promise. Desert will be just as enjoyable as dinner. Humor me, will you?" Bob asked her.

"Okay, but only because I love you and I am thinking of you and your outdated masculine need to be in control. Well, that and I am hungry, too. The more I think about a slab of ribs the hungrier I get. Besides, a wet dessert sounds even better than a wet dinner. Let's go my hungry man," she grinned and walked out the door knowing he would be right behind her.

He had been waiting for the right moment all day to give her the ring that was tearing a wound in the part of his leg beneath the watch pocket of his jeans. Dinner would be just the right setting to present it to her.

They walked to the restaurant and laughed the whole way, holding hands and just being in love. When they had eaten all the ribs they could and were working on the last of their beer, Bob got a serious, painful look on his face. "Are you all right?" Ann asked him concerned.

"Yes, I'm great," Bob sighed as he pulled the ring from his pocket, relieving the pressure the large diamond had been keeping on his now chafed leg. He held the ring under the table and instructed Ann to close her eyes. He wanted to ask her a question and he wanted her to concentrate on the answer. She willingly complied.

"Ann, will you marry me?" he asked plainly and loudly. She kept her eyes closed and replied, "Yes Bob, I will marry you. I want to marry you and be your wife."

He was slipping the ring over the end of her finger when she opened her eyes, and she held still for him to complete his task. "Oh, my goodness, Bob. It is gorgeous; it's beautiful. I don't know what to say," she choked out the words.

"You've already said it," he replied. "I need another beer, how about you?" he asked, and got only a nod in reply. They held each other's hands through the rest of their dinner and beer. They returned to the hotel, picking up a quart of Ann's favorite ice cream along the way. Bob was determined that he was going to keep his dessert promise, one way or another. The next morning Ann was ready to take Bob on a drive over to her father's machine shop. This was the place she grew up really and now she was back again. This time she had her fiancé with her and she was worried about what her father would think. She decided the best way to do this was the way she knew best, directly.

They drove up to the shop and parked in the lot where her dad had killed her assailant several years ago, starting the chain of events in her life that brought her and Bob together. She had thanked *Uncle* Gary time and time again in her prayers for what he did for her that night and now she believed she knew the reason why he had given his life that night. It was not only to keep her safe, but to toughen her by her trials and make her happy by bringing her and Bob together through a long string of events that led them to that underground facility at the same time.

She pointed out to Bob the spot where they struggled and Gary was shot, and the spot where her dad had exacted justice for their assailant's crimes. They walked in the door and, with a bottle of Wild Turkey in one hand raised above her head, she yelled at the top of her lungs, "Where's the old coot that runs this joint and how come nobody's working?" Men stopped in their tracks, looking up to see who was making such a ruckus in the office area.

Her father was behind a desk on the telephone and immediately came out to see who was disrupting the morning calm in his shop. He was a barrel-chested hulk of a man with hands as big as dinner plates. He looked strong and weathered from years of working with the metal that he turned into useful items for industry. He looked like the kind of man you didn't want angry at you...like the kind of man you wanted on your side when things got tough.

He roared in a deep voice, "Who the hell is that? What do you think you're doing barging in here raving like that?" He rounded the corner to see the disrupting force in his shop was his daughter. "Ann? Ann, come here you sweet thing you!" he cried as they ran to each other and nearly squeezed the life from each other. The men in the shop were starting to notice the frenzy now and word was spreading quickly that Annie was back. She was hugging each man that came into the office and she knew every one of them. This was her family and Bob liked what he saw. Hard working men who cared about their work, their families, and their shared values. There was now the entire group of eight men in the office with Bob seeming to fade into the background. It was where he wanted to be right now. After all, this was her homecoming. There would be time for introductions soon enough. Ann held up the bottle and got everyone's attention.

"Here's to the best machine shop and the best machinists in the country," she exclaimed and took a drink from the bottle and passed it to her father.

"Here's to the best daughter in the world! Welcome home Annie!" he yelled, then took a drink and passed the bottle to the line of waiting *uncles*. They cheered and began to pass the bottle among them to celebrate the return of their little girl. Ann took her father's hand and led him over to where Bob was standing. She stood before him and held his hand too, making sure the engagement ring was clearly visible to her father.

"Daddy, I'd like you to meet Bob Mcleod. He is my friend and he is my fiancé. We are going to be married, Daddy. A lot has happened since I left and I can't wait to tell you all about everything," she blurted out.

"It's a pleasure to meet you, Sir. Ann has told me a great deal about you. I'm looking forward to learning more firsthand. I know this is a quite a surprise—a lot happening at once—but let me assure you I love your daughter. I believe I love her as much as you do and I would like your blessing on our marriage," Bob asked.

"Well, I doubt seriously that you could ever love her as much as I do mister." He looked Bob up and down, then stared at his daughter, then back at Bob for what seemed like hours before he spoke, "My daughter had a good head on her shoulders when she left...could have married a dozen men but never even considered any of them seriously for one reason or another. I guess, if she picked you, it must be there is something special about you that I'm not seeing yet. Unless that place messed up her head—and we'll know that soon enough—you stick around awhile and we'll see about that blessing later. Right now, we've got some celebrating to do because my little girl is home. Today is not the day to be asking me if you can take her away from me again, son. You ask me that later...after I know you a bit? I'm damned glad you brought her home to me, though, and it is my pleasure to meet you, Bob. You're welcome here as long as she'll have you."

He reached out his hand and shook Bob's with a vice-like grip that Bob was unable to hold as hard as he tried. "Good grip, son. At least you're not afraid of trying. My name is Steve and you can call me Steve. Not mister and sure as hell not dad, well, not yet anyway. Here, have a drink, you look like you could use one." He passed Bob the nearly empty bottle as it made its way back to Ann's dad. "Well men, I'd like to introduce you to Bob Mcleod. He is Annie's fiancé. She says they are getting married so now we have two things to celebrate."

Cheers went up for Ann and the men struggled to get a look and meet the man their Annie had deemed worthy of her affection, indeed, her love. "Shut your stuff down. The rest of this day is for welcoming Annie home. We are going to have a party and it starts as soon as the last man is squared away. So get to it and get it done!" The three went into Steve's office to finish off the bottle and open up one he had on his bookshelf for just such an occasion. "It's time this came down off the shelf. It sat up there for the past two years watching me lose my hair and my mind worrying about you. I am glad that is over; I missed you." Her father broke down and cried for a moment on her shoulder in a long hug.

It had been harder on him than it had been on her to be gone Bob realized...like she was doing his time for crimes he had committed. The guilt in his eyes was plain but the love in hers told the simple fact that she would have done it a hundred times for him. There was a bond between them Bob hoped he would someday share in but he knew today would not be that day. This was theirs to revel in and he would hang with them, but he wasn't about to try and push his way into something so special. This was something he was going to have to earn and, from the looks of it, it would take some doing. They all went down to their local watering hole and drank, ate, talked and played darts.

Bob learned a lot about Ann from her shop uncles...each of them more than willing to share their favorite stories about her. Ann was on cloud nine all night. She was with the men she loved, her family, and sharing them with the new man she loved, Bob. The men slowly drifted out to their homes, families, and other commitments. After several hours of drinking and eating, in that order, Ann, Bob and Steve found themselves the only remaining members of their group.

"Bob, what do you intend to do after you two are married? Where you gonna live and what are you going to do— I mean work wise—since you said you're between jobs now?" Steve asked him with parental concern clearly visible in his eyes.

"We've decided that we'd like to live in the area here. We'll get a place, settle here...maybe forever, if it suits us well enough. I know Ann would like to be close to you all again and I'd like her, well us, to be able to do that. Family is important; I know. Mine's been gone for years now and we never were that close when they were here. I regret that. You don't often get a second chance at things so I'd like to stick close...to family I mean." Bob replied truthfully. But Steve was still suspicious of his daughter's fiancé's motives and was playing the protective father. He sensed that close to family and unemployed might also be interpreted as Bob wanting to stay close to a meal ticket while Ann was looking for a job, or maybe he already had some kind of trouble., or maybe he was hinting for a job at the machine shop. Steve pressed for more information as he sized Bob up.

"What are you going to buy a place with, or eat, and how you going to take care of stuff you need if you're not working? You got some money saved up for all that, do you?" Steve asked somewhat accusingly.

"Dad! What kind of questions are these? What are you getting at?" Ann defended Bob with a smile, knowing he had been taking it easy on him all day, so far.

"They are fair questions. The man comes here with you today and you announce the two of you are getting married. Neither of you are working. You don't know where you're going to live, work, or pee next. I think it's a fair question to ask, how the man intends to take care of my daughter before I even consider giving my blessing to this wedding you're planning," Steve demanded.

"He's right, Ann. I don't know yet what I'll be doing in the future. I have made some career changes this past year and I have some maneuvering to do before I decide," Bob began to explain but was interrupted.

"That sounds like a lot of mumbo jumbo for a lazy man who can't keep a job or who isn't mature enough to stand up and finish what he started when he finds out he doesn't like it very much. That's a bad kind of man to marry. Is that the kind of man you are Bob, really?" Steve was pushing for the truth, and he thought he was getting somewhere closer to it with this line of questioning.

"No, Sir, that is not the kind of man I am. I stick with what I start and I don't start it unless I am committed to finishing it. That is in fact why I am between careers right now. I need to finish something I started but my job doing that has recently ended," Bob defended himself. Ann was looking a bit perturbed as the testosterone continued to elevate on both sides of the table but she knew this was between them and she needed to keep quiet for now.

"I'd love to hear that story sometime," Steve began.

"I promise you will hear about it, Steve, but now is not the time," Bob interrupted.

"Did you save any money from this old job of yours that you can live on or are you going to need Ann's money or my money to get you going again?" His tone was venomous and it was all Ann could do to hold her tongue.

"I put some money away, yes Sir. And no, I won't need your money or Ann's money from her contract. You don't need to worry about that," Bob replied evenly.

"I do worry about that," Steve fired back. "How much is some put away? How long can you last on that if you can't find work right away? Things aren't cheap up here and work is hard to come by, especially scientist kind of work. How long before you burn through your savings Bob?" Steve pressed him.

"I doubt I'll burn through my savings any time soon, Steve," Bob shot back before he thought long enough about his answer.

"That is optimism talking unless you're independently wealthy. What if you don't find a job any time soon is my question. Okay, then tell me how much have you squirreled away and I'll tell you how long it will last you two up here?" Steve demanded.

"Several billion dollars. I have a lot of money squirreled away Steve. It's all legal and I earned it working for the government. We'll be okay financially if I don't find work for quite a while," Bob assured him. Both Ann and Steve stared at him. Ann had never asked him about his finances because she had just over two hundred thousand dollars saved from her contract and she wanted to know Bob and Ann as people before practical matters such as a budget came into play. She thought he had some money, too, but had no idea it was anywhere near this much. They sat silently for a moment and Steve was the first to speak.

"You said billions. Several billion dollars? Is that what you meant to say Bob or are you just backing me off?" Steve asked with a serious tone.

"That's right Steve, several billion dollars. I am not after your daughter's money, or a job in your shop, or your money, or anything else except a long life with your daughter and your acceptance of those things. Money gets in the way of relationships and everything else...just the same whether you have too much of it or not enough. I never brought it up with Ann and I apologize for the way it came out tonight. I love your daughter and I want her to be happy.

"That happiness is not about money. It is about her relationships with you and me. There are two men in her life now and I have no intention of pushing for her to pick one over the other. I hope you don't intend that for her either. I don't think you do. I want to be part of your family, and I know that will take time. I know I will have to earn it, not buy it. I am willing to work hard at that. I have worked hard all my life but never for something so worthwhile," Bob concluded by taking Ann's hand.

"Well, I'll agree with that," Steve smiled. "One day you'll understand this when you're a father. You may not now but someday you'll understand it." He smiled as he drained his glass. "You really have that much money? Billions, I can't even imagine how much that really is."

"Yeah, it's a lot of money and I have a lot I need to do with it. That is my new career you see. I haven't been rich for all that very long. Truthfully, my net worth is right at five billion dollars, billion with a *B*. I don't even understand how much that really is myself," Bob smiled.

"Well then, I guess you got enough squirreled away so you won't have to find yourself a job right away then, okay. I am glad we got that settled. You think you might even have enough to buy us another round?" Steve conceded.

"My pleasure, I think I can use a double after that session," Bob smiled and waved to the waitress to bring another round. Ann still sat there staring at Bob in disbelief. She had no idea he had that kind of money. She thought she was being noble and honest getting to know him without discussing money only to find out he was doing the same but, on a scale much greater than her own. That made her feel good, though. He had the same concern and took the same course of action she had chosen. That pleased her immensely. And finding out she was marrying a man so wealthy didn't hurt her morale either.

They finished at the bar and walked Steve home and visited for another hour, talking about Ann's days growing up in the house near the shop. Money never came up again in their discussion that night. It got late and Ann announced it was time for them to go, but they were staying just up town and would be back tomorrow to visit and go out to dinner. Steve's disapproving glare was noted as the cab she called pulled up to take them back to the hotel.

She explained that they couldn't stay there, and asked her father to relax. They would be fine. "It's not you being fine I'm worried about. It's you not being married yet but staying together like you are that bothers me. That's another thing you'll both realize when you're parents. Just remember, what you're putting me through right now when your kids do the same thing to you. You'll have it coming; it will be payback time." They agreed to disagree on their staying together in a hotel and off they went for some much-needed rest. It was a long, eventful, and emotional day. Everyone was ready for a good night's sleep and they each got one.

Bob and Ann spent the next few days with her father, catching up on the happenings of the time she was away and getting to know his plans for the future. They spent time in the shop visiting individually with each of the men who worked there, getting updates on their families and sharing their own wedding plans. It was three days of relationship building and the two learned more about each other with every conversation. The more they learned, the more they were convinced they were the right ones for each other.

Bob was relatively certain that he had spotted at least one of the men who were following him but he wasn't sure how many there were. He would be surprised if they only had one man on him but he also realized it is much easier to blend in when everyone around you is a stranger. It didn't really matter, though. He wasn't trying to conceal his relationship with Ann because they already knew about it. He was in fact trying to convince them that he wasn't up to anything. It was just him getting on with his life.

Bob asked Steve if he could design and build a vault. A room sized steel structure, too large and heavy to move without construction equipment. It needed to be climate controlled with multiple locking mechanisms. It was to contain large quantities of cash, gold, and diamonds. Bob needed his own bank vault where he could store a portion of his new wealth outside the banking system. If they froze his assets, he wanted to be able to continue to operate and exist without intervention. He needed it quick though, and Steve reluctantly agreed to stop his current work to begin construction on the vault.

It would take a week to construct the most rudimentary vault, and Steve wasn't comfortable with the design for securing the door but Bob spurred him on, "I need it in four days and I would like to keep it here for the time being. I know that is a lot to ask but, if anything ever happens to me, I know you will take care of Ann like you have your whole life, and you'll have enough money on hand for all of you to live however you choose." Steve agreed to build a smaller scale version for Bob, about the size of a large walk-in freezer. He had a spot in his office that he could break up the floor then dig out, putting the vault in the ground for added security and making it easier to conceal. This would also serve as a pseudo climate control to eliminate that portion of the task for expediency. A small crew of men worked on it around the clock until it was completely built installed, and checked. Steve and Bob set the combinations on the two locks. They weren't written down, and they weren't to be shared. They had been there a little over a week now visiting and working.

Bob asked Steve to accompany him on some errands in the morning while Ann watched over things and visited at the shop. They set off in a rental truck and Bob explained his intentions as they headed off to the bank. They drove around on the interstate for nearly an hour, racking up miles on the rental Bob knew could eventually be traced back to him if anyone checked, which he was relatively certain they might. He went into the bank and, after a series of quick, formal meetings with bank officials and much cross checking and paperwork, they were ready to go. Bob had made initial arrangements only yesterday but that was just about all the notice he was comfortable giving anyone.

Reluctantly, by that afternoon, the largest bank in the region had acquired the seventy-five million dollars in cash and gold that Bob had requested. They loaded it into the rental truck as Bob and Steve looked on nervously. The bank officials were professional in every way but this was not that common a transaction for an institution of this size. They were, however, appalled at the lack of security to accompany such a large amount of cash as it was being loaded into the rental truck. Bob assured them it would be fine, "The best place to hide a car is in a parking lot, right? This is no different, we will just deliver this like it was a bedroom suite and nobody will pay us any mind," Bob assured the bank officer. "After all, it is my money. If I lose it, then that's my problem, right?"

They drove the truck to the shop and unloaded their cargo into the newly completed vault. They had done the calculations beforehand to ensure it would all fit. When they were finished, they set out to return the truck. On the way back from the rental company Bob stopped and got five cases of cold beer and a pile of ribs and fixings from the local Bar-B-Q and headed back to the shop. They all shared dinner and beers now that their project was complete. Each man in the shop received a thousand-dollar bonus from Bob for getting the vault done on schedule. Steve approved it and would welcome any such offerings to help take care of his shop family.

They had grown to accept Bob over the past week and he was glad for that. It wasn't hard to like Bob Mcleod once he let you get to know him. Steve was immensely nervous about sitting literally on top of seventy-five million dollars although he knew it was safe as long as nobody knew about it. It was however a risk and he agreed to it for only as long as Bob needed a place until he could make other arrangements. For his part, Steve would accept no money for the vault. He said he'd just keep and use it after Bob got all his crap out of it. Money worried Steve. Too much of it or too little, it didn't matter. He agreed with Bob on this point.

It was time to head back. Ann was going with Bob to visit his home now. It would be the first time and he wanted her to meet Betty and Miloc, see the University, drive the trapline, and, most importantly, get together with Father Gannon. They left the next morning after a swing by the shop and lots of hugs and kisses from the uncles. Steve's task from Ann was to start looking around for a large tract of wooded land convenient to the shop but not in the city. They wanted to build a house and a small lake on at least eighty acres of land with both woods and pasture. They wanted to look for a place to settle down in the local area. Ann gave that chore to Steve because she knew how much he loved the outdoors and, besides, he needed something to do for her while she was gone. Nervous fathers get to be dangerous and, if he had something to keep him really busy while they were gone, he couldn't get as nervous or so she reasoned.

They flew in, picked up Bob's truck from the airport parking lot and were back at his house before they knew it. Everything in the refrigerator had gone bad, so they walked down to the grocery store and picked up a few essentials for a quiet, romantic dinner for two on their first night in his house. It was revealing to Ann to see how Bob lived...what he prioritized in his life before all the events of the last several months had changed it forever. It was a nice night and she etched it into her mind. She was making a memory and she wanted it to be a good one.

The next day they met Betty for lunch and had a wonderful visit. She and Ann hit it off very well and Betty assured her that she was getting a wonderful man and should consider herself very lucky. She also told Bob he had made a wise choice not to let Ann get away because she was definitely a special lady. They each knew she was right and, after Betty assured them that Durbin was just his usual self and there were no problems, they parted ways.

Bob and Ann walked all over the University grounds. Bob explained where he went and what he did as both an undergraduate and a graduate student. Bob wisely avoided Durbin today. He didn't want anything to disturb his time with Ann nor did he need any undue attention to his activities right now. He called Father Gannon from a pay phone in the student center where he and Ann were getting a soft drink. He agreed to block all day for Bob and Ann tomorrow. The four of them were going to drive out along the trapline and see some of the beautiful places Bob used to collect the weather data. Bob, Ann, Father Gannon, and Doc Auster's second Thor's Hammer.

They could talk along the way and it would be easy to detect anyone following them. They needed to test the device to ensure it worked properly before they could continue with any plan. Father Gannon seemed nervous on the telephone. He was glad to hear from Bob. It was obvious that he was worried about something they couldn't really talk about over the phone. They arranged for a pre-marriage counseling session and that was that.

Bob made a mental note to watch the news tonight. He hadn't done that since he left to meet Ann's family; there was just too much to do. You only get one chance to make a first impression and Bob wanted to make sure his was a good one. He believed correctly that he succeeded in doing that with Steve but it was time to get his head back into the game he thought.

There was just as much at stake here as there was up there. They finished their sodas and then continued their walk across the campus and through the sites of the town. They found themselves back at the house late in the afternoon and Bob was ready for a nap. "All that fresh air made me tired," he conceded.

"I bet that's not all that made you tired," Ann smiled and raised her eyebrows at him reminding him of just how little sleep they had gotten the night before. "I am going to take the truck down to the grocery store and stock up on all the stuff I didn't want to carry back yesterday. I'm going to make us a home cooked meal that I know you will love."

"You can cook, too?" Bob smarted off to her. "Do you mind if I invite a friend? I want you to meet Special Agent Miloc and I don't know when I'll be able to get a hold of him. If he's free tonight, would that be okay? It's always hit and miss with those guys."

"Sure, I want to meet him. I'll see you in a while; enjoy your nap." She waved and darted out the front door. Bob plopped on the couch and turned on the news channel just in time to catch the top of the hour headlines. He did not like what he was hearing. The announcer was explaining the devastation caused by the extensive rains and resultant flooding in the agricultural region of central India. The rain had persisted for three days at a considerable rate and the video showed vast expanses of water covering the fields of young crops. There would be no surviving the deluge and no hope for replanting in time for a secondary harvest. The rains had come just two weeks before a US and India trade summit focusing on Indian markets' increasing appetite for US technological and agricultural products. He went on to explain how this natural disaster, though unfortunate for Indian farmers and those counting on the harvest, would significantly improve the US position during the scheduled summit.

The grain surplus now in from a record growing year in the United States would likely be insufficient to replace the crops lost to this flooding. But the Indian loss would provide a wholesale outlet for the record grain harvest, eliminating a surplus and driving up worldwide demand for US grains at the same time the supply was near peak. Ideal conditions for the

US farmer but devastating to Indian economic growth. They stood now at the mercy of the US trade envoy, if the majority of the Indian crops were lost, and it certainly appeared that would be the case. Bob couldn't believe his ears. *It looked like these guys were wasting no time putting his technology to use,* he thought to himself. And this was likely just the beginning Bob realized.

While he had no proof, he knew it was the US government using Thor's Hammer to leverage economic and political pressure on the nation whose growth and burgeoning capabilities were a looming threat. Bob could tell and he was correct. He knew they would have had to really spin up fast to pull this off but he also knew that Zach could set something like this up just as a weekend project. There was no telling what he would be able to do if he had time and resources to really plot something out. Bob was appalled and, indeed, ashamed that his machines were being used to starve a nation, force them to buy goods from the US, making commodities speculators and the farmers a lot richer at the risk of a starving Indian population. It was time to get his plan on the road before things got any worse. Then he realized how very little difference there was between this and his pumpkin futures endeavor just a short time ago and he was ashamed. True his plan didn't run the risk of starving masses of people but he had ruined their work and hurt them financially. He made another mental note to repair whatever financial or other damage he had done to them a hundred-fold if he could but, right now, he had a much larger, much broader project he had to complete first.

Bob called Miloc and left a message on his machine even though he figured the agent was not likely to check his messages any time soon. Bob sat and watched for a while and the longer he sat there the more frustrated he got. When Ann came in, he asked her to sit down. They needed to talk about their meeting with Father Gannon tomorrow. The time for action was now and they would have to move fast before more innocent people were hurt for the benefit of a few. The President wasn't living up to his word and Bob wasn't going to let him get away with it. Bob would keep his word, technically yes, but he was about to jump back into this business with both feet.

CHAPTER TWELVE

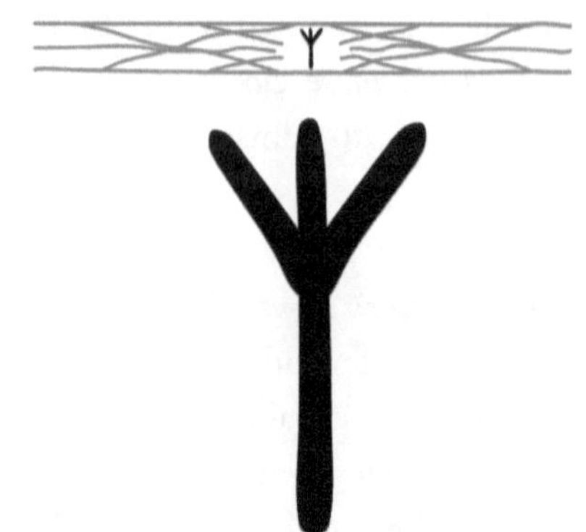

MORE WORK TO DO

The next morning, they set out early to pick up Father Gannon and his cargo. After brief introductions they were back on the road by six a.m. heading for the southernmost trap in the line. Bob explained that this one was the most remote, as well as, the furthest one from the military installation. They were going to need some privacy for this and he didn't want to take any more chances than necessary. It would take several hours to reach the remote area but Bob knew the route well. It would be easy to spot a tail if they were being followed.

He half expected to be, figuring news of his seventy-five-million-dollar withdrawal may have sparked some suspicion, but hoping bureaucratic complacency had already gripped the process of watching him. They settled in for the lengthy drive and Father Gannon began to ask Ann some questions to get to know her a bit. The discussion quickly led to the engagement ring on her finger. "I noticed it before we got in the truck; it is quite exquisite," the priest said admiringly.

"Thanks, Father. I do like it a lot. Bob is so great; I don't know how he stayed single for so long. Nobody in this town like handsome, talented, gentlemen anymore?" Ann smiled.

"Well, I don't know about that but I do know that everything happens for a reason, even if we don't understand it at the time. Perhaps we never will understand why something happens, but God does. It may not be ours to ever understand or it may take many years for his revelation before we do understand it. Perhaps you are why Bob has stayed single for so long Ann. It just took a while for the right conditions to bring you both together. It took a while for all this to happen. We all need each other to pull this off I suppose," Father concluded and was followed by a long silence as everyone contemplated what he had just said.

There was a lot to think about really. They were about to try something nobody else had ever done before and they were about to *take on the world* in a manner of speaking. They would need each other. That was for sure, but they all wondered along the way what they had done to bring them to this point and, though they didn't understand it now, they believed the words that it was all happening for a reason. They just hoped one day they could see what that reason was.

The rest of the drive was filled with conversation designed for each person to learn more about the other. Each was comfortable talking about themselves and listening to the pasts of the others. They were forming a team and building trust between themselves, a trust they knew they would need. By the time they got to the area Bob had known as the trap, he was certain they were not being followed. They pulled off the highway onto a dirt road and drove for three miles back into the woods to a small clearing near a creek. There at the center of the clearing in the forest stood a white meteorological shelter that housed a series of instruments and data recorders. They pulled in and stopped at the tree line, got out and began to stretch.

Bob walked over to the shelter and disconnected the data feed cable from the recorder. He wanted to be able to read the instruments but didn't want the weather at this site to be recorded. There was to be no record of this morning's test of Thor's Hammer number two. Bob walked back to the truck and dug around until he found the roll of toilet paper he had packed. He pitched it to Ann, "Pick a tree darling, any tree.

We'll be gentlemen about it, I promise." Bob teased, "It was long trip so please get comfortable. We're going to be here a while so remember which one you used. Father, I believe our stalls are over here." They each took care of business and then got to work.

They tested the device for three parameters and all three failed. The disappointment was visible in each of their faces. Ann asked if she could examine the device. She placed it on a blanket she had laid on the tailgate of the truck and listened to the sounds around her with her eyes closed. She ran her hands along the outside of the device with her eyes still closed and said, "You have to get to know it, make it a part of you to really understand how it all works together. You have to let it know you care about it if you want it to be good to you...to do what you ask of it. All metals are that way, you have to be gentle but firm when you work with them. It is a secret most folks don't know."

Bob and the priest watched her with curiosity, hope, and a trace of skepticism. Ann retrieved a small tool bag from the truck and removed the cover from the device. She poked and probed and touched the machine, searching it with her eyes and her hands, looking for the imperfection she knew had to be there. She had memorized everything about the original device while she was working on it at the underground facility. She knew it well. She knew it like the machine it was and found one of the components disconnected, apparently on purpose, because the coupler was in place, intact, and deliberately placed back into its position but not tightened down.

"It seems our friend Doc put a safety precaution on this one in case anybody got too curious. It will only take me a few minutes to get it back the way it should be; then it should work fine," Ann beamed confidently. "Maybe this was my reason for being, just to fix this one little problem? All those years of work and learning...just for this moment. Helping fix this so we can do what we need to do? It's possible, in fact, it would be enough if a lifetime boiled down to something as simple but important as this. That sounds so corny but, if it's really that simple, it would be all the better." She smiled, replaced the cover on the device, secured it, and handed it back to Bob. "Okay weatherman, give it another whirl and no more unscheduled pit stops. We didn't bring a big enough crew for much more of this."

"I think you are all the crew we need, Ann," Bob smiled as he took the device from her. "At least you are all the crew I need for anything. I know that sounds corny, too, but I love you and I want to remind you of that every day."

"If you two love birds don't mind getting back to work here, I'd appreciate it. I don't want to be gone any longer than need be, and well, no offense but all that was just too *lovey-dovey* cute for me. Change the weather, Weatherman so we can get gone," Father Gannon added, more in truth than in jest. Bob took the device and dialed in a ten-degree temperature drop for two minutes, a significant task for the small device. Sure enough, this time the command resulted in the desired atmospheric change. Ann was in awe at the phenomena. Confidently skeptical from the beginning, all her doubts vanished in a single moment as she felt the sudden chill on her skin in the bright sunlight. Father Gannon was equally impressed, as he had never seen the device used, but was cautiously optimistic, since Doc had only demonstrated its capability indirectly on several occasions.

The two sat on the back of the truck as Father Gannon walked around the clearing with the device trying one recipe after another for wind directions and speeds, calling out the changes as he entered them, and responding to the applause when the elements cooperated. He entered a small rain shower to be certain the device was functioning through its full range and sat down on the truck with his partners to await the final show. The small clouds began to appear almost instantly on the clear day and one began to build above the rest as they watched from below.

"It is beautiful," Ann remarked as the cloud built higher into the atmosphere. They could literally watch the towering cumulus grow against the blue sky above the green treetops. "I wasn't sure how I'd react really. I thought I'd be scared of this—seeing it really work—but it's beautiful.

Are you sure they are using it against India? That is so incredible, it is hard to believe," she continued looking up at the cloud. "How could someone take something so wonderful and use it for such a horrible thing?" she continued.

"That, my dear, is a question that has been around since the beginning of time," Father Gannon commented. "If you think about it for a moment, you could ask that question of every good thing ever given to mankind, including free will. Man is the only one of God's creatures with a free will and how could anyone take something so wonderful and use it for such horrible things as many people choose to do to each other every day? Mankind, it seems, can be self-destructive and, as long as, there are people, we will have that question to apply to many things...including this."

"I understand, and I think you're right Father. Did they teach you that in the seminary or did you just pick that up out here today?" Ann kidded the priest.

"Yes, to both. Maybe that is why I am on this earth...for this...today. Maybe it is just as simple as that, to teach you that one lesson. If it were just that simple, it would be cool and it would be enough," he smiled at her as the first raindrops began to fall from the shower overhead. They sat on the truck, undaunted by the brief shower. Bob watched them soaking up the experience of changing the weather for the first time and it reminded him not to take it for granted.

He was focused on doing a test but realized that he needed to stop and appreciate the magnitude of what they were doing each and every time he did it. This power was his as a gift and it was only temporary. He would see to that. He needed to make sure that, even after all his tests and demos, he did not underestimate it or take its beauty for granted. It would only take a moment and he could be gone too, just like Doc. Bob reminded himself to try to never take anything of natural beauty for granted—life, the trees, water, and *especially*, Ann.

They conducted a few small heating tests and, confident the device was performing properly, claimed victory for the day and loaded up the truck to head back. The snacks they packed were gone by now and Bob suggested a fast-food drive-through on the way back. He didn't want to stop at the local haunts for fear someone might recognize him or place them there later. Being one of many vehicles through a chain restaurant drive through along the interstate was a lot safer, even if they had surveillance cameras. They were pretty hungry by now and reminded themselves that a low profile was still best. They could make up for it when their mission was over. The drive back was uneventful and they discussed in detail the actions required for the next phase of their plan. As they pulled up to the church to drop Father Gannon off, he remarked, "Do you really think this will work, Bob?"

"It has to Father. I'm counting on you and the big guy upstairs both to come through for me. I'll call you like we talked about. In the meantime, take care of yourself and this thing, too. Find a safe place for it because, when we need it, we will need it quick. Don't argue about the money, either. Take all of it. You may need it for plane fare to who knows where and all that other stuff you might need but don't know about yet. If there is any left over, use it for the church stuff you need. It's only fifty thousand. Now get going and I'll call you when the time is right okay? One more session and we should be ready," Bob instructed.

"Okay. Well, I'll do my best. But I'm warning you, I am not a very patient man. Try not to test my virtues very long, okay? Thanks for a great day. I will always remember it no matter what happens. God bless you both." Father Gannon waved the sign of the cross over the truck and turned up the walk to the rectory carrying the bag with Thor's Hammer and fifty thousand dollars in cash. Not your average day's work for a priest but Father Gannon was not your average priest.

Bob and Ann drove back to the house and flopped onto the couch, both tired from the traveling. It had always amazed Bob how much traveling wore him down. Even after all the times he ran the trapline, it seemed like at the end of every run he was more tired than the days he wasn't spending time on the road. Ann volunteered to cook some dinner and

Bob turned on the news so they could catch up on events. With the Indian and American summit less than two weeks away, Bob knew he didn't have much time to get everything done. He was concerned as he watched the news story which was updated every fifteen minutes and marveled at how convenient it was to get up-to-date intelligence on the activities he was interested in watching.

Bob was concerned about Father Gannon. It was entirely possible that he could get into big trouble with the Church hierarchy for not making them aware of this capability and seeking their counsel on what to do about it. Bob knew all bureaucracies were slow to action and they wouldn't have that much time. He regretted that but told the priest, if he didn't help, there would be no church involvement or opportunity to influence his actions.

Bob would understand Father Gannon's unwillingness to help,but instead he chose to be an influence on the action rather than an uninvolved spectator. That took courage on the priest's part and Bob admired that. He and Ann ate a quiet dinner and then went off to bed, tired from the day but looking forward to the next one. A quick breakfast and once again they were in the truck headed for the rectory to pick up Father Gannon. Bob had deliberately left the recorder on the weather sensors disconnected yesterday, figuring it would take the new guy at least a few days to detect a problem with the data, even if he examined it quickly and thoroughly.

When they arrived at the rectory to pick up Father Gannon this morning, he was waiting for them on the porch of the rectory. He walked down the path to the street carrying the same bag as yesterday and a box of doughnuts. He handed them to Ann and climbed into the truck, greeting them as he did.

"Good morning. I thought doughnuts would be nice for the drive today. Hope you like chocolate because that is all that is in there," he smiled his charming smile at them as Ann took the box, opened it, and passed a doughnut over to him.

"Is there any other kind worth eating?" Ann replied and passed one over to Bob as he pulled away from the curb and headed for the highway. "Bob says we'll go north this time and use one of the sites up there today. Are you ready for more training, Father?"

"I'm ready. I never imagined that one day I would be the man controlling the weather. I memorized the recipes like you asked me last night. They really aren't that complicated if you think of them as such. Leave it to Doc to come up with such an efficient and effective way to simplify something so complex. It was truly genius on his part. There are so many things I wish I knew about him but don't."

Father Gannon continued, "He was a good man, but so private. I now understand why but what a sacrifice that had to have been on his part to bear this burden alone for as long as he did. He had to have been bursting at the seams to tell someone in his field about his success. He had to have been a stronger man than I because I know I've been troubled by this knowledge every day that I have possessed it. I am glad you came to me. It freed me of that burden and lightened my load. I am ready to get on with finishing this one way or another. I do, of course, have a preferred outcome," he chuckled as he took another bite from his doughnut.

"I know what you mean, Father. It is nice to have a team on this instead of working alone. I did that for too long, both on this and the rest of my life as well." Bob's comments were none too subtle for Ann but he squeezed her hand to be sure and she leaned over and kissed him on the cheek. "I guess I am one lucky man. Well, actually, I know I am."

"You sure are. Now quit all this mushy stuff. I still don't understand why we don't all three go together and just do this. It is obvious, even though we can't prove it, that the President is not keeping his word. Isn't that enough all by itself to void your contract?" Ann asked.

"I don't think so. There is too much enforcement of the letter of the law instead of the intent of the law. No, this is something we have to be very careful about. The contract says specifically that I get a five billion-dollar, tax free, lump sum payment for the weather modification technology and four Thor's Hammer devices. I am not to work on this technology in any way, ever again without the personal permission of the President of the United States. It doesn't say anything about Father Gannon's device and, as long as, I am not working on the technology, which I am not, a good lawyer should be able to win this in court."

"All I have done is help Father Gannon understand the dangers of the device he has in his possession and plead with him not to use it. What he does with his property is his decision. Even though it is a technicality, I didn't know this device existed when I made my contract and the President got the four devices he paid me for. I need to keep my word and I will. But he has broken a promise to me, even if he had good reasons—which I doubt—he broke a promise. I will not stoop to that level but I need to play by his rules. What we need is to get him into a position where he has no other choice except to give me his personal permission."

"Then we win both ways. We get to keep all the money, enough to do a whole lot of good for a whole lot of people, and we get the technology fielded so it can help everyone. It is the only way I can see. We have to get him in a position where he comes out looking okay but cannot deny us what he promised. I have to keep my word to make that happen. Otherwise, all of this will have been for nothing," Bob looked worried.

He knew there were risks and he needed some good luck, but he was confident they could do this, and do it in time to prevent a humanitarian disaster in India. They may be looming on the horizon as a potential threat both economically and militarily but that was no reason to inflict such hardship onto scores of people. This was the right thing to do and Bob Mcleod knew it was something he had to do, if he was ever to find peace and purpose in his life.

"I do understand. I guess I just wish there was a simpler way to go about this. It's like you told us the first time you described how this thing worked to our group. It is simple; it is just not easy," Ann conceded. "I hope this plan works. If he did give the go ahead for using the devices in

India—which we think he did—how do you think he pulled it off? Military, CIA, who would he get to do that for him, especially so quickly?"

"Zach. Probably with some military help. Someone to get him in, around, and out without being compromised. They won't be as worried about Zach as they are losing the equipment or getting caught using it on foreign soil. Technically, it would be an offensive act of war, I think. Zach has a direct line to the President somehow and he certainly has the capability and temperament for something like this. I'm sure of it. I've seen it in action and in his eyes; it's him." Bob's words so surprised Ann that she was speechless for a moment.

"Do you really think that? I know he was eccentric, but so malicious? That means lots of what we did there was intended to be developed and used like that. I understand that sometimes stuff happens and people misapply technologies but this means some of the things developed there were specifically for some kind of use against enemies of the country? Like an advanced weapons lab without the title but with a good cover story fed to all the people working there?" Ann was reeling.

"Yes, pretty much, that's it. Most folks stay there and, if you do leave, you are not allowed contact with those inside again. Security, all that stuff generates the proper environment and feeds the illusion. Lots of good comes out of there to be sure and that is a tremendous economic incentive. Some of the stuff has enormous military potential but not in the traditional sense. Power is gained and lost and these technologies—just like advanced fighter aircraft—are instruments to keep or gain power. The technologies, although unconventional, are instruments of power just like an Army or a Navy. You guys just don't get issued weapons to fight; you come up with new weapons or new untraditional ways to fight.

"You have to remember, though, it is like a gun. It's not the tool that does the killing; it is the person using it who is the guilty party. You guys—well, actually, all of us—developed things that can be used by good people for good things. But bad people can use them for bad things, too. No different than a tree. Make a house from it or a wooden club to beat someone to death.

The people behind the bad are responsible for it, not the people who make the instrument; it's the people who use them who need fixing.

"It's still makes what they are doing to us wrong. They are lying about the applications of our technological advances and inventions. While we were there trying to help people, they are using our stuff to hurt others, if necessary, and to help enrich and empower themselves. I understand how this makes you feel about your technology and I understand now why you—no, why *we*—need to do this," Ann said.

"Well, though I am sure all of that is true, it is really much simpler than that. We need to do this because it is the right thing to do," Father Gannon offered. They had been traveling now for some time and Bob turned off the main road heading into the woods on a wide dirt road. Another ten minutes down that road he pulled onto an overgrown tractor path that led back to a clearing along a dry riverbed. They stopped, and everyone got out and stretched, walking around to loosen up after the drive. Father Gannon was eager to get started and put his training to the next test. Bob instructed him on some of the finer points of starting and stopping the phenomena and explained some of the functions in more detail. Father recited some of the recipes for Bob and explained back to him the exact keystrokes he would use under various conditions. A few more dry runs, some additional coaching and clarifications, and Bob was satisfied the priest had the knowledge to do whatever would be asked of him to pull off his part of the plan.

Bob instructed Father Gannon to begin the first of the practice runs, the dress rehearsals for what they hoped he would have the opportunity to do again in the very near future. The session continued through the morning and all the tests were accurate and successful. Father Gannon was delighted in his ability to operate the devices and even more excited about the fact that he was once again personally modifying the weather with this device. He found it gratifying to be helping his old friend and his new friends and he hoped to be helping a lot of people around the world that he didn't know. Satisfied with the outcome and the performances of both

Father Gannon and the device, Bob decided they should wrap up and depart the area. "Are you comfortable with everything now Father?"

"Yes, I can do this," he replied. "But I am not comfortable with it. It scares me to death, actually, but I know I can operate the device and do the things I will need to do. That should be enough. I think we should head back, too. Those doughnuts aren't holding in there very well. I think they need some company. Changing the weather sure makes me hungry. Let's grab some lunch on the way back."

They packed up their gear and were on the road a few minutes later, training and rehearsals complete. It felt good but it put them one step closer to beginning their operation and that feeling left them all uneasy. The drive back was uneventful and they dropped Father Gannon off in the early afternoon. They agreed to depart early the following morning. It took a bit of doing to get another priest to cover his parish duties for a week but Father Gannon was a very persuasive man. "Don't be late, I don't want to be sitting around all morning waiting for you. Besides, I am anxious to get to New York. I've never been there and the earlier we start, the earlier we finish the drive. I wish we could fly but I understand why we can't. See you in the morning." He waved and headed up the walk with his bag.

"Goodbye. See you bright and early," Ann yelled as they pulled away and headed home. "Do you think he'll be able to do this?" Ann asked Bob.

"Yes, he'll do fine. He's got it together; he'll do just fine. Besides, he's got an inside advantage and you can bet he's already praying hard for all the help he can get," Bob smiled at her. She was truly a beautiful woman and a beautiful person. He was glad that his prayers were answered when she came into his life. They pulled into the driveway and noticed the gray car parked down the street. Bob recognized that car but noticed it was empty. He and Ann walked to the front door and nearly jumped out of their skin as Miloc stepped off the porch directly into their path. He was equally startled and it took a few seconds for everyone's nerves to settle again.

CHAPTER THIRTEEN

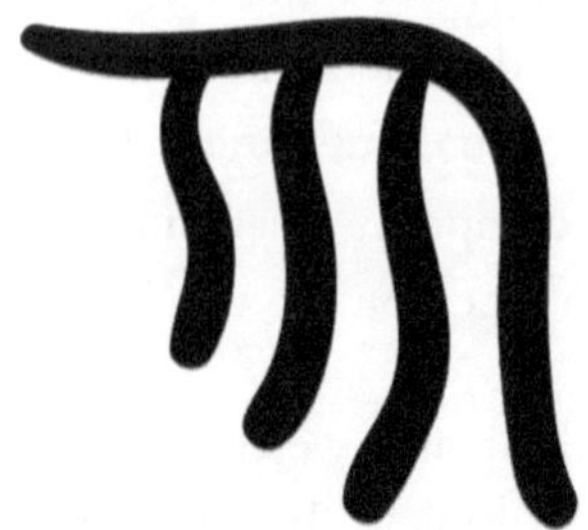

NEW YORK, NEW WORK, NEW WORLD

I t's about time you showed up; dinner was two days ago. It's all gone now but how about staying for lunch instead?" Bob invited the startled agent.

"Now, I thought I was hard to get a hold of. I been trying to link up with you for two days, where you been?" he asked in retaliation to the comment. "Before you answer that, yes, I'd love to stay for lunch."

"Sightseeing and trying to decide what to do with ourselves for the rest of our lives," Bob offered. "Trying to show Ann all the things she wanted to learn about me. I can't have her believing I'm a great guy without any actual proof from my past, now, can I? I even think she kind of likes this town of ours."

They moved the conversation right along because, although Bob believed he could trust Miloc, he couldn't reveal any of their plans to him. It would be too risky to tell anyone but especially discussing it with a federal agent. Bob would not consider putting his friend in a position where he had to choose between a new friendship and his career. He knew Miloc was professional through and through and, while what they were planning was perfectly legal, it was more of a case of not being explicitly illegal because there was never a reason to make a law about it before. They enjoyed the nice lunch Ann prepared and then he was on his way.

Bob and Ann packed their stuff and completed their preparations for an early departure.

"That's that," Bob announced. "All ready. What do you want to do now?"

"I think we should get lots of rest. Leaving at four is earlier than I am used to. Let's go to bed," she replied.

"It's not even dark yet. Isn't it a little early to go to sleep? We don't need to get up for nine more hours," Bob protested.

"Who said anything about going to sleep?" Ann smiled and turned down the hall heading for the bedroom. She shot a glance over her shoulder just in time to see the look on Bob's face and was pleased to see he had abandoned his protest and was closing the gap between them.

The alarm clock sounded and they both popped up almost immediately. They'd had quite an evening, going to bed early and skipping dinner. Both famished, they grabbed a good breakfast, showered and were on their way to pick up Father Gannon in no time. They arrived right on time, packed up his gear and were on the road headed for the interstate.

"What? No doughnuts this morning, Father?" Ann teased him. She was in a particularly good mood this morning he thought but didn't really want to consider why.

"Not yet. I figured by the time we need to make our first pit stop we might be able to find one. Even bakers don't get up this early I don't think," he remarked to her in a pleasant voice, especially for so early in the morning. The traffic was light and they shared some small talk along the way, finally stopping for a break, some gas, coffee and a few doughnuts.

When they were back on the road, they reviewed their plan once again. By the time they were through, their heads ached and they were ready for more gas, a real break, and a meal. They intended to drive straight though to New York, alternating drivers and sleeping along the way. They hated the idea of driving all the way but it was just too risky to fly. They would leave an electronic travel trail but more importantly checking the device in the baggage would be irresponsible and risky. Carrying it on was out of the question...no way to explain it to security. Mail, carrier, or delivery service were out of the question, as well, so driving was the only logical way to get it there.

Keeping the team together was also important Bob believed. Driving together would build on that teamwork and they could review the plan over and over again, so everyone got it right. They would not get a second chance at this, if they failed, and they all knew it. It was too important to take any undue risks. During the long drive to Manhattan, the three took turns driving, sleeping, and keeping each other awake. Much of the conversation between interactions of their plan reviews was about their pasts and what the world could be like in their future. They discussed the philosophical side of the impacts of their mission if it were completely successful.

They already knew to a letter the mechanical side of what each was to do when they got to New York. They had gone over it what seemed like a million times already. Once they got there and were rested, they would conduct a couple of dry runs to make sure the mechanics were physically possible and work out any logistical issues that may pop up. They had to conduct the rehearsals to make sure the real thing went perfectly. Bob knew there would be no second chance if they screwed it up. Finally, they wheeled into the hotel parking lot. It was the closest multi-story hotel along the East River near the United Nations headquarters. Bob went in to arrange accommodations for two weeks while Ann and Father Gannon stretched and gathered their senses.

Key to their plan was getting the United Nations Security Council (UNSC) and the Economic and Social Council (ECOSOC) together to deal with the new technology Father Gannon was about to deliver to them. The ECOSOC is one of the six principal agencies of the United Nations, composed of representatives from 54 countries. ECOSOC's early activities were directed at providing aid to war-ravaged countries in Europe and Asia. Today. The problems of many developing nations are its primary concern. The council still carries out studies on international economic, social, humanitarian, cultural, educational, and related matters and coordinates the activities of the UN's specialized agencies in these areas.

ECOSOC usually operates through its various standing committees, functional and regional commissions. How to control the weather in order to feed the world would likely fall into ECOSOC's job jar. Their organization was best suited to handle such issues from both regional and global perspectives, although they certainly never envisioned having such a mission thrust upon them. Doing that and ensuring cooperative safety for the world at large would require the Security Council's expertise and fell well within its charter. The two councils would likely soon find themselves lead partners in this endeavor for it to prove successful and keep it safe for everyone. There were certainly no guarantees but the best chance seemed to be starting this chain of events in ECOSOC's house and then involving the security council.

It had to be pitched as a social and humanitarian aid technology with security implications to keep the right focus within the United Nations and its members. At a minimum, publicity of the existence of such a technology would proliferate worldwide almost instantly, generating enormous pressure for both protection and application on a global scale. The United States could not do this alone, nor should they, and the United Nations could be the correct body to facilitate the application of this technology. It was also long overdue for some modicum of success on the world stage in order to restore its declining credibility. The UN needed a meaningful mission and some quick wins to overcome its ongoing record of mediocrity. An opportunity to do something new in the worldview was long overdue but about to land square in their laps courtesy of these three weary travelers.

Bob came out and explained to his partners, "I have two adjoining suites on the fourth floor." He handed Father Gannon a set of key cards. "I suggest we go in, unpack, grab a shower, and something to eat and then get some rest. We'll start fresh in the morning."

It was late afternoon and there was little they could accomplish today anyway. There was a lot to see for three people who had never been to New York before but they'd agreed earlier to play tourist some other time. There was work to do and distractions now could be disastrous. They went up to their rooms and unpacked. Father Gannon placed the device in the mini-fridge in his room and went on to get a shower then meet his companions for dinner in the hotel restaurant. Bob was still paying cash for everything and he doubted there was much of a chance that they had been followed or discovered there yet, although he was sure someone would be nervous about not knowing exactly where he was.

The three enjoyed a relaxing dinner and, feeling a little better, they were looking forward to a good night's sleep in the luxurious beds in their rooms. This was not a typical Midwest motel along the interstate and they expected to enjoy their accommodations. They agreed to meet at seven a.m. back in the restaurant for the first dry run and Father Gannon headed off to turn in and get some sleep. Ann and Bob decided to stay awhile and enjoy the view, another drink, and some quiet time together.

They talked about a wonderful place in the future where their children and grandchildren could all live happily. Where food and economic worries were not their primary concerns. They could focus on helping each other and working together on projects of greater relevance because the basic necessities of life were attainable for all. This new potentially Utopian view of what could happen concerned them both a great deal but they had discussed it a little bit before.

How many future Einsteins, Ghandis, Martin Luther Kings, and Mother Theresas had never made it past infancy because of malnutrition, famine, and diseases brought on by starvation? How many in the world died before they could see their children or grandchildren grow up because they starved themselves so their families could have a chance at survival. It was staggering to be sure. The number of people of all ages who die each year from starvation and its related maladies. The complexities of governing and monitoring countries with a technology capable of controlling the weather were mind boggling indeed. But, when compared to the life-preserving application of such a power to meet the fundamental need for food—of abolishing hunger as we know it—those complexities were indeed worthy of everyone's effort.

It was simple; it just wasn't easy as Bob liked to say. Knowing what to do was the simple part but figuring out how to do it in this case was not easy. It reminded them as they sat there sharing ideas with each other that few things in life that are worthwhile are easy, but most of them are quite simple. It was a lesson they hoped to teach their children someday. This was the second time the topic of children came up tonight.

Bob and Ann departed the restaurant and went up to the bar on the top floor looking out over the city to continue their conversation. They agreed to have only one drink and then turn in so they didn't complicate things by making an unexpected scene or being hung over in the morning. The conversation turned to parents and children and then shifted back to the grown-up versions they had become. Bob realized that much of the discussion was about a part of himself he never really identified with very much. He confessed that through the years he had always worked hard to get what he had and accomplish what he set out to do, trying not to hurt anyone along the way.

He helped others out when he could but, aside from taking on Hugh Durbin, he rarely went out of his way to help others he didn't know. He always had the knowledge to be good and he was but he never really recognized the desire to help others get to where they wanted to go, that is until recently. He realized that his desire to keep a simple, comfortable existence like Doc had was so he could spend time doing for others without having to worry too much about his own needs. In the simplest of terms, he would now be helping others do the same thing if they successfully transition this technology to agriculture and energy. People would no longer have to worry about having enough food, or heat or air conditioning. Food and shelter could be available for everyone who wanted it. Those were two of the most basic needs of all mankind.

Bob argued that would also give them more time to figure out new ways to hurt each other but Father Gannon argued for the good side of humankind. There would be a new spirit of giving, confidence in receiving and a basis to trust in each other. This could unite nations in common efforts to care for their disparate regions with common solutions, developing teamwork and new trusts where before there was fighting over the simplest of needs, for survival.

He claimed men fought mostly to ensure their survival, both physical and ideological. If their physical survival was commonly achievable and recognized as such, they could focus on their ideological commonalties instead of their differences. He knew there would be much work to do, and tough times for sure, but the hope was evident to all who bothered to look with their eyes open. This technology would make the world a better place, and the people would benefit more from having it than if they didn't. They all deserved the opportunity for self-government and freedom to choose how to apply this technology and they were going to get it.

Father Gannon was going to deliver it to them because Bob could not. Bob felt both bad and good about that and he was struggling with his failure to do it right the first time but pleased with his ability to see a way to make up for it. Now, he had to deliver for everyone's sake. He and Ann finished their drinks by toasting their new careers as philanthropists. They would see to it that the technology was available to provide for food and shelter for all but, for now, they also had a lot of money to spend on helping others learn to help themselves. Churches, schools, hospitals, research, all needed help and they would do what they could to organize an effort to have them all work together. It was getting late for them and they were pretty tired already, so they left and turned in for the night. The wakeup call rang almost as soon as their heads hit the pillow it seemed, but they were well rested and excited about taking on the new day.

They met Father Gannon in the restaurant for breakfast as planned and enjoyed the view while they ate. Small talk and pleasantries filled their discussion in the crowded restaurant and, once they had finished, they went to Father Gannon's room to review the day's plan. They would drive along the road running along East River near the UN Headquarters. Bob and Father Gannon would get out while Ann drove to the designated pickup point and found a place to park on the street where she could observe them. It seemed Ann would have the toughest assignment given the scarcity of parking spaces in the area and the size of the truck.

Father Gannon would walk to an open area along the grounds and sit on one of the concrete forms, waiting for a representative of the ECOSOC to contact him. Bob would watch from nearby and assist Father Gannon if things went wrong and they needed to make a quick getaway. Their route would be through the open area to a covered path that spilled out onto the one-way road where Ann would be moving to pick them up. They each had an unobstructed view of the others in the distance and the space was such that they thought they could egress and get away if the need arose. They walked their evacuation route and climbed into the truck and drove off.

"I think there is enough space to maneuver and see anyone coming who might intend to interfere," Father Gannon began.

"Me too," Bob agreed. "There aren't too many places to come in on us from but that also means there aren't too many routes out. I don't think there are any convenient places to come at us with vehicles either, at least not from the streets. It looks pretty good to me really, unless they just start shooting at us from the rooftops."

"You guys look like sitting ducks out there to me," Ann added. "There weren't too many people out there and I don't think you'll have enough of a crowd to fade into, if you have to get out quick and can't make it to the road. I had to drive a good way before the first cross street too so, if they cut off my street, we are going four wheeling across the grounds to get out. There are lots of options, if I have to do that, so I think it's okay on that end. It might even be fun!"

"Well, aside from the points made, anybody see any other problems?" Bob asked and waited while the others thought about the question. "I think, if we got some small radios, we could each have one and talk if we needed. Mostly for Ann to alert us if she sees anything from the road that we are too close in to notice. They will be faster and easier than texting, just another safety option, in case we need to talk or deviate from the plan, or the backup plan. They might come in handy and they are small; we can get them almost anywhere," Bob added.

"That is a good idea. I can't think of anything else. I'm ready to do this; waiting just isn't for me," Father Gannon added.

"Okay with me," Ann agreed. "Looks like tomorrow is the big day. Let's go pick up some new toys. But I want you to remember something, Father. I am not going to sit out in this truck or in my hotel room all day while you are up in that nice building. So, you get them going quickly so we can get in there and help you. A lot of people you don't know in India and elsewhere are counting on you."

"I will remember your warning, Ann. The last thing I want is to have you mad at me. I think it would be easier if I had to contend with all of India," he responded. "You just make sure you two keep ready and available for when I need you. If I have my way, it should only be a few hours after I am inside."

"We'll be ready for you, Father. I promise. And, believe me, doing is the easy part. It is the waiting around wondering what is happening that is the tough part. I learned that on the first go around of this thing," Bob assured him as they drove past the front of the building one last time to make sure they all knew the area as well as they could without drawing attention to themselves.

Picking up the radios, some batteries and a few other odds and ends, they proceeded back to the hotel. They assembled in Father Gannon's room once again and went over the tasks a few more times to make sure they each knew what to do. The toughest part was going to be convincing them he was not a crackpot and they really needed to meet him face-to-face. But they had a plan for that; they just hoped the device would work as well here in the northeast as it had in their mid-west rehearsals. They spent the rest of the day talking, watching TV and just relaxing.

Resting from the trip was what they called it but really it was just keeping a low profile until the next morning when they would get to work. They agreed to another vehicle reconnaissance that evening to make sure nothing had noticeably changed. So, after dinner, they drove around for about an hour. Randomly touring, but not getting too far away from the main roads near the hotel in the area. Satisfied that everything was in order, they returned to the hotel and back up to Father Gannon's room.

"Well, I am ready. But, if you two wouldn't mind terribly, I'd like to finish up this evening alone. I've got some serious praying to do and I really need to get my head on straight for tomorrow. I'm sure you two could use a little quiet time yourselves. What we are about to do tomorrow could change the world as we know it. Probably worth a little reflection as we are going in, don't you think?" Father Gannon reminded them even though he knew it was unnecessary.

"You're right Father. We'll see you in the morning. Seven thirty breakfast at the restaurant, sleep well." Ann rose and took Bob's hand tugging him up to follow her out.

"Good night, Father and thank you. We'll see you in the morning." Bob patted him on the shoulder as he and Ann walked past the man and out the door into the adjoining room, closing the door behind them. It occurred to Bob that he had asked a lot of this man. He appeared to be up for the task at hand but, nonetheless, it was a lot to ask of any man. All too often he thought, priests are thought to be more than just men no better or worse than the others around them. They are supposed to be there to guide the entire community in their times of need, to be strong when others are weak. They are looked to for leadership and strength in adversity, role models for our children and ourselves.

Most priests are all of this and more. Their faith is what makes them special in their calling from God. But they are mortal men with fears and failings of their own and, sometimes, we expect too much because others have been able to deliver before them. Father Gannon was just such a priest, always able to deliver whatever was needed at the right time in the right way. Bob had always seen him that way until this evening, when he saw a concerned man who happens to be a priest. He made a mental note that it would be important to remind himself of that in the future.

Ann walked to the window and opened the curtains and the pane to let in the evening air. It was brisk and it was refreshing on their faces as Bob walked over to her and put his arms around her waist, holding her from behind. "He can do this you know?" she said of Father Gannon.

"I know. I'm not as worried about him as I am about how the whole thing will turn out...about what will become of you and me if any of this goes wrong," Bob confessed to her. "I don't want to lose you now that I finally found you."

"You won't. Even if something bad does happen, which it will not, you'll always have me here, and here," she said as she turned and touched his heart and the side of his head. "In your heart and in your head, and I will always carry you in the same places. Every moment we are together I am making another memory that I can think about in the future. I am burning another mental image into my head that I can call upon whenever I need to see you, in whatever mood I want you to be in when you arrive. Every moment with you is one more to treasure. Tomorrow will be a long day for sure but, in the end, we'll be fine; you'll see. Now, how about making another memory with me?" she asked, as she walked away from the open window, leading him by the hand across the room to the bed.

Bob awoke to the cold chill of the air blowing through the still open window. It was late—or early—depending on your perspective. He stood at the open window looking out at the lights and remarked to himself how insignificant he had been only a few short months ago. He reminded himself that as one man he still was insignificant in the scheme of things. But today he was going to do his best to make a significant contribution to the world he lived in. That, he thought, was the right way to look at it.

He was insignificant but his contribution could be lasting. He was just the messenger and it was the message that was important. He closed the window and walked back over to the bed. He climbed back in and gently slid under the cover, making a point not to disturb her. He quickly fell back to sleep. He was okay with the coming day and at peace with himself. It felt good.

The phone rang, their wake-up call announcing the day at six thirty. Bob rolled over and found Ann was already in the shower. He staggered into the bathroom and began to gather his wits about him. "Did you sleep okay?" she asked him. He admired how quickly she woke up in the morning; coffee or no coffee she was perky and he liked that about her.

"Slept good…You?" he managed to grumble back as he rubbed the sleep from his eyes. He stepped into the shower as she stepped out and kissed him on the way.

"Great. I think today is going to be a great day for it. The forecast is still calling for cool and clear all morning. I guess Father has it going on. It must be nice being well connected and having things come in the way you need them too. See what a little faith and good will can do?" Bob agreed and got into the shower as Ann dried her hair. Fifteen minutes later they were both in front of the TV sipping coffee and flipping back and forth between the weather and news channels trying to get the extended forecast and an update on the situation in India.

It all came together and they headed down to breakfast. Father Gannon was already seated and waiting. "Good morning. Looks like the weather will be great this morning, at least for a while," he greeted them with a grin. It looked like he was beginning to enjoy this already. They shared a large breakfast and talked about what they had seen on the news earlier that morning. The rains had begun to taper off in India, but it was too little, too late to save their young crops. It appeared doubtful that the ground would dry up soon enough to replant and, even less likely, that any re-plantings could produce a substantial yield unless they had perfect growing conditions and an unusually long growing season.

The news predicted there would be a significant increase in demand for both stored reserves and this year's grain crops to compensate for the tremendous loss. Prices were rising with the expected increased demand and decreasing supply. Speculators were buying up grain futures at a feverish pace all week. It looked like India would be in for an expensive winter season this year, and it would cost them a sizable chunk of their GNP to supplement the population without their usual homegrown agricultural offsets.

They reasoned that Zach was probably still there but laying low. He would need to ensure there were no unexpected aftereffects from using the devices over such a large area. It was also a great opportunity to collect performance data to be analyzed and used later. They reasoned that such a record rainfall event would probably have another significant, but less severe, sister storm not too far behind it. They expected Zach would wait three or four days for a little bit of damage assessment and recovery efforts to get underway and then bring in another significant rainfall event to make sure the area remained heavily saturated and completely beyond recovery for the season.

It would also serve to demoralize the people of the region, resigning themselves to a tough, expensive year ahead and preparing them to pay the high price of such a catastrophic event. Physical and economic recovery would be slow and the slower it was the better it was from the view of United States farmers, investors, and military analysts. The more money spent on this, the less they had for economic and military growth both within and outside their borders.

The three departed the restaurant and returned to their rooms. They made their final preparations and met in Father Gannon's room. "Well, let's say a prayer we do this right and then let's go," he said looking at the two of them. "Dear Lord, guide us and protect us as we go about this task. Show us the way. Do not let us falter and keep all the bad guys away from us until we're done. You have given us a gift to share with the world. While we don't fully understand your plan, we know it is your desire for good things to come of this. Help us move along that path. Amen," he concluded and looked up to the door.

He checked to make sure he had his cell phone in his pocket, a charger, and the small radio they had gotten yesterday. "Let's go before I change my mind." He led the way down to the truck with the Thor's Hammer securely under his arm, in the original bag Doc Auster had delivered it in, what seemed like a lifetime ago. It was time.

They drove the short distance to the drop off point and Father Gannon and Bob both got out of the truck. A kiss for luck from Ann and they were on their way, walking to an open area near the river. Father Gannon entered a recipe and the specifications into the device and set it down on the ground. Bob was looking over his shoulder to ensure the proper entries were made. Then he walked off to his designated observation point.

Father Gannon had taken out his cell phone and dialed a series of numbers. After several minutes of waiting, he had gotten through to one of the ECOSOC division chiefs who spearheads the committee on international economic affairs. "Good morning," Father Gannon began. "My name is Father Gannon. I am a Catholic priest and I know you are very busy but I need a few moments of your time. You see I have a problem that I believe you can help me with and it has worldwide economic ramifications. In fact, it is a solution to world hunger. I know by now you are thinking you have a crackpot on the line with you, but I assure you I am not. Do you have a couple of minutes to talk to me, please?"

The voice on the other end agreed to indulge the priest for just a few minutes and Father Gannon proceeded, "Thank you, this is very important. You see I have a device that allows me to control the weather. I know that sounds crazy, but it is true. And if you'll bear with me, you'll see it work in just a few minutes. Did you see this morning's forecast Sir?"

"Yes, I did. It was mostly clear and cool. Nothing memorable really," the voice sounded impatient now.

"Right, but in a little while you will see outside your building a very rare weather event that could only happen if I am telling the truth...if I am able to control the weather. You will see a thunder snowstorm. I am sitting outside your building on the grounds between the river and your main entrance. You can already see the cloud forming to your south if you look out the window.

In about fifteen minutes you will hear thunder and see lightning but, instead of rain, it will be a heavy snow shower. It will only last about fifteen minutes and then it will dissipate. I know this because I am the one who will make it happen. I really need to talk to you and the ECOSOC because I would like to give you this technology to feed the hungry around the world and for other humanitarian and economic benefits for mankind." Father Gannon had gotten his main points in and was thankful the man had not hung up on him already.

"Well, that is quite an interesting problem you have Father. You say you want to give us this technology? If it exists, it is surely worth a fortune. Why would you just give it away?" he challenged in a comforting tone.

"It is too dangerous to sell and, besides, the United States government already has the technology. I think you can use it to alleviate some of the emerging crisis in India. I assure you, Sir, this is weighty stuff and, as you will see, the potential for its use in your ECOSOC mission is essentially limitless. That is why I contacted you. It will surely garner security council concerns but it is a humanitarian and economic tool not intended to be used as a weapon. I will wait out here for you to come and talk to me about my terms and, if you agree to them, I will give it to you.

"I hope you understand that this technology can change the world. It can certainly change the weather, whatever you want to affect, on a scale of several hundred miles at a time. If it were mounted on satellites, it could probably provide regional, hemispheric, or even global control of the weather. I want the UN to control the application and proliferation of this technology. It cannot be left to a single individual or country and, right now, the US is the only country who has it. That simply won't do," Father Gannon paused to check his tone and tenor.

"Well, I must say you do have my curiosity piqued. How did you come to possess this technology, Father?" the voice requested.

"One of my parishioners developed it and gave it to me for safe keeping. He was killed in an accident a few months ago. I want his name and his work to be recognized and used for the good he intended. I know this sounds like a wild story but that is why I am doing the thundersnow for you this morning...so you'll take me seriously. This is dangerous and valuable technology; it must be handled and applied judiciously. The UN is the only organization with such a charter and maybe enough influence and credibility to do it with equity and deliberation."

Father checked his watch and checked the sky. Seven minutes on the phone line now, and the clouds were beginning to build very rapidly against the cobalt blue background. "Can you see the clouds building? Are you near a window that you can see them from? All I ask is that you watch and you will see that I am for real. I need you to get the right people together to work this today, right now. I will wait here until you come get me and remember I am a priest. I am not dangerous but I am intent on convincing you to take me, and this technology, very seriously. It is, obviously, a time sensitive matter I have dropped in your lap this morning. I apologize for disrupting your day but it will be well worth your while before it is all said and done. Do you have any more questions of me?" Father asked.

"In fact, I do Father. You mentioned India. What did you mean about helping alleviate the crisis in India?" he asked.

"You could use the technology to warm the region, to dry it out quickly enough to replant a large portion of the agricultural regions and extend the growing season long enough to get a late harvest. Mostly wheat and grain but it would be quite a relief over buying and importing everything outright. But you don't have any time to lose, if you hope to pull that off. You will need the help of the United States and their devices to cover a large enough region," Father Gannon offered.

"You said that before, Father. You mean the United States already possesses this technology?" the voice asked, accusingly. "Did you give it to them too?"

"No, they recently acquired the technology for a large sum of money from another source but they are the only ones who will ever have it unless I can convince you to accept the technology from me today. I am offering you the same technology free of charge and I will provide you the device I am using today, as well. I must operate it for you, however, at least initially, then I can turn it over to you once the proper training and agreements have been reached," Father concluded. It had been ten minutes now and the sky was beginning to churn, vertically climbing clouds casting ominous shadows near the UN building.

"And you would do that just so we could do good around the world, feed the poor and needy...all that kind of good-for-mankind activity that we are intended to promote here?" the man asked.

"That's right. What is your name, Sir, if you don't mind my asking?" Father Gannon inquired.

"I am Kevin Armstrong. I am one of the regional directors here Father. I must also tell you I can see out the window here and I see some pretty dark clouds building to the south. You have my attention," he added.

"Good, because it is about to start snowing and I don't particularly want to sit out here and get hit by lightning while I freeze my tail off in a snowstorm that shouldn't be here. Would you mind coming down now so we can talk while we watch this marvelous display of man-induced natural splendor?" Father Gannon pressed.

"I think I can do that, Father, but I must ask you if you will mind if I am accompanied by some of our security personnel. This will be for both our sakes of course; I would hate for anything to happen to either of us. If this turns out to be exactly what you say, then we will need some tight security. If you do turn out to be the crackpot you claim you are not, then at least I will have an armed escort and a fighting chance," he explained over the open line.

"Sure, that seems prudent. I will be waiting. Can you see me from your window? I am waving right now," Father asked him.

"Yes, I can see you waving. I will be there in about five minutes; will you wait right there for me, right where you are now, okay?" Kevin asked.

"Okay. I'll see you in a few minutes," Father Gannon agreed and sighed in relief as the line went dead. He ended the call on his cell phone and reached into his pocket and keyed the mike on the radio. "I'm on my way. I talked to one of the ECOSOC division chiefs and he is on his way out to meet me. He is bringing security so be ready in case it goes bad. He sounded okay, though. I think I'll be okay with this guy. His name is Kevin Armstrong. He'll be out in less than five minutes so look alive out there. Did you hear me?"

"I copied," Bob replied.

"I got it too," Ann chimed in. "Good luck Father...do good."

The first snowflakes began to drift down, slowly swirling to the ground in the turbulent wind the shower was pushing toward the earth. The intensity quickly increased and the sky continued to darken all around them as the storm grew more intense in a very short time. Father Gannon began to shield his face from the whistling wind and increasing snow. He watched as eight men emerged from the front entrance of the building. They were all dressed in suits and fanned out to cover each possible avenue of approach that Father Gannon could use to access the front of the building. Three vehicles took up positions blocking off the road access to the front of the building. Father saw a lot of activity beginning around the side of the building as well. He heard Ann's call on the radio reveal they had blocked her access to the egress route.

They were taking this very seriously, he thought, and fear began to build inside him. He told himself to remain calm and just let them come to him. The device sat ten feet from him and he thought that was a safe enough distance for them to see it was not connected to him by any wire or trigger switch. He heard Bob's voice over the radio remind him to stay cool. This was all normal security procedures they expected and he was still nearby. Several minutes passed and the snow increased and five more men emerged from the front of the building. Three were walking in a triangle around the other two. It was a three-man security detail and two men worthy of their protection.

As they cleared the road and began across the now snow-covered grass, they heard the first crack of thunder from above. Twenty-one minutes Father Gannon noted...pretty good timing he thought to himself as the men approached him. He raised his hands into the air to show that he was unarmed and stood facing the approaching men with his coat open and flapping in the wind. The lead man approached the priest with a hand on his weapon which was visible but holstered, while the other two trained their weapons on Father Gannon covering their partner. He searched the priest and pronounced him clean. The two men being escorted approached Father Gannon in the blowing snow. "It is a pleasure to meet you, Father. I am Kevin Armstrong and this is my boss, Mr. Dau. This is quite a show you have put on for us. I must say I am as impressed as I am intrigued. Shall we go in and talk?"

"It is my pleasure gentlemen. I must bring the device with me, but I assure you it is already finished with its work for the day. It is quite safe as long as nobody messes with it," Father assured them.

"That will be okay but we must place it in a bomb bin for security. That is simply not negotiable, Father," Mr. Dau insisted.

"Certainly, I understand. I can assure you I have no intentions of hurting myself, or anyone else. I will follow you to the door," Father pointed to the building.

"I'd prefer we load it into the bomb bin first and ride to a security entrance and proceed that way if it is all the same to you. We are extremely security conscious here, as you might have anticipated," Mr. Dau continued as he waved the vehicle in across the lawn. Father Gannon bent and picked up the Thor's Hammer and walked it over to the vehicle, placing it into the bomb bin almost as soon as it was opened. The man in the rear sealed the container and motioned to the men to search the priest again for weapons or a remote triggering device. The cell phone and the radio brought immediate questions.

"I understand the cell phone was how you got to me but why the radio Father? Who else are you talking to?" Kevin Armstrong asked.

"Two of my parishioners are waiting for a call from me to report how I am faring and to make sure I get back okay. You needn't worry about them unless something happens to me," Father informed them.

"Fair enough, Father, I guess this took a little bit of thinking through before you just waltzed out here and hung it out for everyone to see, huh? That took a lot of guts as far as I am concerned and I am Australian, so my gauge is already a bit slanted some say. Shall we proceed on in then, Mr. Dau?" he asked.

"Let's. Please inform your colleagues that your electronic devices will not work inside the building. You may call them from a land-line indoors, if you wish. I will provide you my direct number where you can be reached in a few minutes," Mr. Dau suggested. Father Gannon repeated the instructions and phone number into the radio and climbed into the truck. They drove into the security perimeter and then were searched again, badged and escorted through the series of metal detectors and security staging areas. The bomb bin was on wheels and was rolled along behind them by two of the guards. Half an hour later they found themselves in Mr. Dau's office. The snow had tapered off to a small flurry and the clouds had lost their menacing dark color as the shower began to lose its intensity and fall apart. He offered Father a glass of water and poured one for himself and Kevin.

"Once again, Father, I apologize for the inconvenience but security is a very important part of our mission here. Now, what exactly can you do with this technology of yours?" Mr. Dau asked. Father Gannon explained in detail the capability to control every aspect of the weather from temperature, wind, precipitation type and on down the list. Intensity, type, duration and area and range of coverage just as Bob had explained to him and they rehearsed over and over. He was on his A-game, but it felt good getting this over with.

Father explained the virtually limitless capability to modify the weather in any location around the world for virtually any duration. He further explained to them that the President of the United States had purchased the technology and four devices from another man whom he could not identify to them. He explained that only the President himself could order the release of the expertise they needed to both understand and use the technology for its intended purpose.

"I can only do a couple of things with this device. The expert who knows the rest is the man the President bought the technology from. You see, I only possess it because a prototype device was left with me by the inventor. I don't have any information about its operation or the theory behind what makes it work. That is what you need to make it worth your while, unless you have a lot of use for thunder snow showers. Having said that, it is important that you understand that the President does not know my device exists or that I have brought it to you.

"I suggest you let me show you the other two things I can do with it to assure you that it is indeed capable of modifying the weather upon demand. That done, you should announce that you possess the technology and pressure the United States into a cooperative effort with the UN to develop and apply it as negotiated by treaty or something. Otherwise, you may find yourself in a security battle with the United States over concerns for the proliferation of this technology for offensive applications. I fear that may already be happening and we don't want another cold war on our hands, literally...pun intended," Father Gannon concluded with a grin.

"You sound as if you don't think the President intends to share this technology, nor use it for its intended purpose. Is that why you are here Father?" Mr. Dau asked.

"That's about right," Father concurred.

"Do you perhaps know what the United States intends to do with this technology? Have they already used it perhaps, that you are aware?" Mr. Dau continued.

"I don't have any way of knowing that, Sir. I do know that, if they wanted to use it, they certainly could. Whether they have or not I don't know but, if they used it, they could go unchecked as long as nobody else knows about or possesses the technology. That would not be right. That is why I brought you the technology. So you can expose, proliferate and control its application for the good of all. Feed, shelter, and protect everyone by providing them the technology free of charge. If everyone has it, then it can no longer be used as a weapon against those who don't. You remove the threat by removing the comparative advantage and that is your job here at the UN, if you chose to accept the technology, I have brought you. If not, I'll take it and be on my way. What do you say gentlemen?" Father Gannon asked.

"Do you think they used this over in India, Father? Is that what you were referring to and why you came to see us today? Do you know if the US is already using this technology as a weapon?" Mr. Dau persisted.

"No Sir, I do not know that and I did not say that. That is not why I am here but it is certainly a possibility for you to ponder. From what I understand, the devices, if used together, could have easily produced the recent rain events in India. Just think of the implications if the US were using the technology as a weapon.

Every natural disaster from now on could be blamed on them if they were the only ones who possessed the technology. They could threaten every nation—every person—with economic and physical destruction by whatever environmental phenomena they chose. That would be most unsatisfactory no matter which single nation possessed it Mr. Dau. That said, I have no proof the US has done anything with it in India. Anyone and everyone could also blame the US for every natural condition that produced some harm, which would make my country perpetually guilty until proven innocent, a presumed bad actor around the world. We can't have that either," Father Gannon offered.

"As Kevin said before, we are grateful for your courage Father. There is no way to wash our hands of this task or look the other way. Of course, we must act on what you have brought to us. Let us figure out how to go about doing what needs to be done." Mr. Dau smiled for the first time since he met Father Gannon. He picked up the phone and called another director and asked him to arrange an emergency meeting of all the directors and key staff, including the Secretary General, at the earliest possible time today. The subject was classified but both critical and urgent.

Once he finished that call, he put in a call to the Secretary General himself to arrange a personal meeting as soon as possible. "He said, if it is that important come up and see him immediately. Shall we Father?" Mr. Dau motioned for him to follow. The men and the device made their way through the building and up the elevator, ending up in the anteroom outside the Secretary General's office. They had not even taken a seat when the aide waived them into the office, commenting that he was ready for them.

Father Gannon shook the Secretary General's hand as Mr. Dau introduced the priest. After nearly half an hour of discussion, Father Gannon had explained everything he knew, and could tell, about the device and the circumstances concerning Thor's Hammer. He then asked if he could contact his friends, so they didn't worry about him. He needed to assure them he was okay.

He called Ann's cell phone and informed her all was well. Bob was with her, both waiting anxiously in the truck at the designated pick-up point. Father Gannon told them to be on their way and he would contact them once he was finished here. Mr. Dau assured him they would see that he would get a safe ride to his destination whenever he chose to leave. They concluded their brief conversation and the men decided to take a break for some coffee and light snacks. Father welcomed the sight of the few doughnuts on the tray of bagels and reached for one with a still-shaking hand.

Bob and Ann were pleased and hugged each other before they drove off toward the hotel. Father Gannon had used the pre-arranged words that meant all is truly okay. He did not use the duress signal words, so they knew he was in no immediate danger and believed he was going to complete his mission. They would go back to the hotel and wait for the next check-in call hoping they would get the same positive message in two hours.

Father Gannon removed the device from the bomb bin as some very anxious security men hovered all around him. They were all a bit nervous as Father Gannon explained some of what he knew about the device. He changed the temperature in the room to Mr. Dau's specification and duration. Father then increased the atmospheric pressure inside the office enough to make everyone's ears pop but not blow out any of the glass in the windows. He admitted that was the first time he had actually done either one of those indoors and was a bit nervous working inside a multi-story building. He had made his point earlier with the thunder snow and now these little tricks to provide them confidence in his otherwise wild tale. They didn't feel the need to go outside to see more and his comments made it very clear that Mr. Dau was well established in the Secretary General's inner circle of trust. There was never a question when he spoke about what was fact or opinion. The man clearly trusted Mr. Dau.

"We will meet in fifteen minutes in the main conference room. We will only allow directors; no deputies or strap-hangers in this meeting. We have some critical issues and we must be candid if we are to be successful. We do not want this in the press until we have decided exactly how to proceed. Do you agree, Sir?" Mr. Dau asked, and the Secretary General simply nodded his concurrence.

"Please see to it, Mr. Dau. I would like a few minutes to chat privately with Father Gannon please. We will be in directly; see you all in a few minutes." The Secretary waved them all out, insisting that Father Gannon and the device stay in the office alone with him. When they were gone, he continued, "Father I want your opinion even if you don't have any proof. I know, as man of God, you will answer truthfully or you will not answer me at all. May I ask your opinion?"

"Yes, most certainly, Sir. I brought this burden upon you uninvited, so I will share with you whatever I can. My opinion is mine alone to offer, and I will share that with you," Father agreed.

"Do you think the President is capable of using those devices to cause the flooding in India?" he asked.

"He controls this new technology and it is certainly capable of causing that damage. So, yes, he is capable of using them for that," Father opined.

"And do you think he did? In your opinion, do you think he ordered it?" the Secretary General asked.

"Yes. Even though I have never met the man I think he likely ordered it, but I have no way of knowing if that is true," Father Gannon said, as he felt the blood leaving his face.

"Do you think the President of the United States will allow us to foil his plans, if your opinion is correct? Then how do we do this without accusing him or destroying the credibility of either the US or the UN, Father? Surely you considered this before you came here today?" he persisted.

"Yes, Sir. You hold a press conference to let the world know that, as of today, you possess the technology. You also announce that you intend to hold a summit of world leaders to discuss the application of this newly verified technology. I believe he will contact you immediately. Read him this statement and ask him for his help. He should recognize that he has only one practical way to proceed and that is where we want him to go. He will have to help you or he will be ruined. I believe he has no intention of letting this ruin him when it could do quite the opposite," Father Gannon offered as he handed the Secretary General a folded piece of paper from his wallet and waited as the man read the short paragraph aloud.

"The United States gives Robert Mcleod a five-billion-dollar, tax free, lump sum payment for his weather modification technology and four Thor's Hammer devices. He is not to work on this technology in any way, ever again without the personal permission of the President of the United States. That would be your friend then, this Robert Mcleod?" Father smiled but shrugged his shoulders. "I see. You cannot tell me, and I must tell the President that I have gotten all my information from you Father Gannon,

including the device that your friend, Doctor Auster, left in your safe keeping? And that is all true, yes?"

"You are correct Mr. Secretary. I presume you have seen the President's signature enough times to know this is genuine. That is why I brought you the original. It is very valuable, though, and I must insist on having it back before I leave the room. I have a copy here for you to keep so that you can read it verbatim to the President, if and when the time comes." Father Gannon handed him the paper in exchange for the original which he placed back into his coat pocket.

"I think I would very much like to meet this Robert Mcleod but I also suppose that will have to wait until I speak with the President to secure his services before that happens?" he asked.

"I believe you are correct, Sir. I would bet that, knowing his fortune was secured, the issue of being compensated by the UN for his services would likely never come up. I gotta think a man with five billion dollars might work for the UN on his favorite project out of benevolence, just for the satisfaction of helping see it applied for the good for which it was intended to provide. Of course, if he were broke, with his expertise being invaluable, he may feel obliged to charge an extremely high fee of his employer to secure his unique services and sole expertise. But that would just be my opinion, of course, if I *were* to offer my opinion on such a matter," Father smiled.

"I understand that opinion very well Father. In that scenario, everyone could claim a win. The President keeps his credibility and wades into the unfolding events from the sidelines as a benevolent lead partner. We get to field the technology out to the world and Mr. Mcleod sees his dream come true and keeps his fortune in the process. This sounds simple but may not be so easy," the Secretary General stated as he rose from his seat.

"Those are exactly the words I would have chosen myself. But it is certainly doable." The Secretary General smiled and nodded in agreement. He led Father Gannon through the private entrance into the conference room where the group had already assembled. All rose to their feet when the two men entered and all sat once the two were seated at the head of the table.

Kevin Armstrong went into the office and retrieved the device, placing it on the large conference table, while the Secretary was making his formal opening remarks to the closed session that was now officially underway.

"Ladies and gentlemen, now that you know the ground rules, I would like to introduce Father Gannon. He has brought us a remarkable gift and, with it, a remarkable story. I assure you it is true and I will give the floor to him to tell it to you. But first, know that our job is the *how* of this story. Father Gannon has brought us the *what*, we must now decide the how. We already know the *who* and the *when*, for it is us and it is right now. We must determine how this story will end and how history will record it. Father, please share your story with the rest of the room. The floor is now yours."

He concluded and sat back confidently in his chair. Father Gannon told the now-familiar story once again to all in the room. He started by taking credit for the storm that morning and, amid some bewilderment and whispering, he continued until all was told, except for the part about the President's involvement. That was for the Secretary General only and they both knew what had to be done with that.

The goal now was to get the staff of the United Nations to come to the same conclusion without that critical piece of information. It was relatively simple once the Secretary General outlined his proposed course of action and put it to them for a vote. It was unanimously approved and they set to work immediately to put the plan into action. There was much to do, but the group set to their tasks in an impressive display of teamwork. Father Gannon made a quick call to the hotel and passed a brief update that all was going well but he had to go.

CHAPTER FOURTEEN

THE UNITED NATIONS

I t was just past midnight when Father Gannon knocked on the door, waking Ann who had fallen asleep earlier. Bob was watching the news, intently waiting for the breaking headlines that had not come. He jumped to the door and opened it for the priest, who quickly entered and closed the door behind him. "I think we did it!" Father Gannon squealed as he threw his arms around Bob in a big Irish bear hug. "I think we are going to get it just right," he said.

Ann came in wrapped neatly in a robe and ready to hear the news, wiping the sleep of her nap from her eyes. "Tell us all about it, please, don't keep us waiting. We've been doing that all day," she scolded the man. Father Gannon proceeded to explain the events of the day, sparing no detail of his adventure. When he told them of his private meeting with the Secretary General, Bob perked up and asked what he planned to do next.

"You're skipping ahead, Bob," the priest protested.

"Father, you better tell me the deal or you may see how this all pans out from the Emergency room. Now get to it will you?" Bob said, only half joking.

"All right you don't have to be a bully. Tomorrow, I put on my best priest clothes and go with the limousine at 0630 to the UN building where I will link up with the Secretary General, himself. We will then proceed to a press conference at some hotel that he will have his staff set up for 0730, and he will announce the technology to the world. He wants to introduce me, explain the technology, its potential applications, and then request an immediate summit with the world leaders to discuss its possible use, suggesting some relief effort in India for a starter. It will be then that he will request the US help spearhead the effort with its leading scientists."

"When the President calls him, he will request you be brought in to assist in the project. If the President resists, the Secretary said he appreciated the option to use the copy of the letter I left with him but he hoped he would not need it. He was pretty certain any remaining resistance would be token at best and will also try to ensure you will be able to keep your fortune, if you agree to work with him on fielding this technology. You would likely be asked to volunteer your scientific expertise on the project and see to it that nothing gets screwed up. It looks like he is going to do just what we had hoped for," Father concluded.

"That is, if the President does exactly what we expect him to do. He has shown us that he can be predictable; I just hope this tiger keeps his stripes and remains predictable a little while longer," Ann added Bob's thoughts before he could verbalize them himself. They talked a while longer about what and how to do things tomorrow but all agreed it was much too soon to declare victory and celebrate. There were still an inordinate number of things that could go wrong and screw this thing right into the dirt. They needed to stick with the course of action they began today so they agreed to sleep on it and meet at 0530 for breakfast and some additional discussion on how to proceed tomorrow if it went as planned...or otherwise.

Father bade them goodnight with another hug and was on his way. You could tell by looking at the man he was pleased with himself and the progress made thus far. It was clear to him that he had delivered the goods *and then some* today and, when one member of the team looks good, everyone looks good. He also knew he had a lot more praying to do if he was going to pull the rest of this off. They each went off to bed to get a few hours of much needed sleep.

Very quickly they found themselves back in the restaurant at 0530 ordering coffee and large breakfasts to hold them for what promised to be a long day. The short night's sleep had done nothing to dampen Father Gannon's positive mood from the previous night. He was excited about getting things underway this morning because this would be his first ride in a limousine. "I suspect, once the news breaks, they will carry it often enough that it will get to the President fairly quickly. I am concerned about whether we will have had enough reaction time to mount a good plan within the UN by the time he calls. After all, the man just spent five billion dollars on this technology and will be losing his advantage almost as soon as he got it," Father Gannon commented.

"You're right. I know in my gut he must have ordered it used in India. I worry about where Zach is more than anything else. Once the word is out, he will pop back up and the President will likely offer him as a subject matter expert to the UN. I don't know yet if we want him close where we can watch him or far away where we can keep him out of what we are doing," Bob added another worry to the fracas. "I don't think we want him in a position where he can undermine or discredit our efforts in the early stages. If he can sabotage an entire region's agricultural livelihood, he can surely find a way to discredit us. Well, I think I just answered my own question."

"You guys are just worrying yourselves about everything. Now, stop it. You both know people. You know how they think and how they react and, so far, you have been pretty good forecasters. It is just too late to change your minds now. Focus on the positive...on what we can do to keep this plan on track or make it better. Let's not second guess ourselves now; it's too late for that. The train has left the station so get on board fellas," Ann scolded them both. "Now, I think Bob and I should stay in our hotel during this press conference. In fact, until the President or the Secretary General calls us, don't you? I think we should stay put until we are invited to the game...so we don't, inadvertently, screw it up."

"I think she's right," Father Gannon agreed with Ann's attempt to keep Bob at a safe distance for now. "You need to be here, ready to go, when you get the call. If you're seen in person or, especially, just panned by a

TV camera somewhere, you risk losing your whole fortune. Right now, they can't get anything out of me that would risk the money. Everything that could do that was told to me in confession. I can't reveal it, not ever. What we have done since then is my work and he can't hold that against you unless he finds you in the middle of it, somehow, and can prove you did something you shouldn't have. Seeing you on video at or near the UN right now will motivate him to do just that. You sit tight and wait for someone to ask you to the dance. Trust me, someone will call. It may not be for a few days but good things come to those who wait. It is now your time to wait. Sometimes the best action is inaction. This would be one of those times, Bob. Have I said this enough different ways yet for you to get it?"

"I'll keep him here, even if I have to tie him up. Well, that's not exactly what I meant, but let's not go there. Sorry, Father," Ann blushed as she responded to a cracked smile and mischievous look from Bob. "What I mean is, don't worry about Bob. I'll see to it that we sit tight and wait. Besides he is going to promise you that he will, and a good man never breaks a promise. Especially one he makes to a priest. Right dear?"

"Okay, I'll sit out until I get the call. But do your best to make it sooner rather than later, will you please, Father?" Bob gave in to their demands.

"I will but I better get going. The car should be here soon. I hope it's a white one not a black one," Father Gannon smiled at them as he rose from the table. "By the way Bob, promise. You haven't promised, yet. Let's not push your luck this late in the game okay."

"I promise I'll sit tight, Father. I know you're both right but it goes against my need to participate. I'll stay put until called in, I *promise!*" Bob added emphasis for effect.

"Thanks. That is why we are doing this as a team. The whole team is more effective than the sum of its parts. There is no "I" in team. All that kind of stuff. You've already made the big play. Let's just make the last few steps of the run into the end zone, shall we? We are almost there.

Then we turn over the ball and field the defense. We need to be ready to hold them so get your head on the right part of the game now coach."

Father Gannon's tone changed, and Bob knew he was right. There was still a lot to do but it had to be reactive to what came today. Bob needed to be watching the news and staying sharp to keep the long view of how to proceed based upon events as they unfolded. Father Gannon smiled as he turned and walked toward the door. "Put my breakfast on his bill," he smiled at the waiter who had served them breakfast again this morning.

The limousine was waiting at the hotel entrance and the driver was standing in the lobby waiting. Father was glad to have his hands free to touch the beautiful car's polished white paint as he climbed inside. "White is my lucky color," he said to the driver, who only smiled in return and closed the door behind the priest. Father Gannon was surprised to see Kevin Armstrong seated inside the limousine reviewing a stack of papers. "Good morning, Kevin, I am surprised to see you already this morning."

"Forgive me, Father. Good morning; please sit down," Kevin replied.

"Is this going to be a confession?" Father asked jokingly, "because, if it's not, then there is nothing to forgive yet. How are you this morning?"

"Tired as hell. Sorry. I mean I'm okay, but I was up all night working on the Secretary's press release and answers to questions we can expect the news people to ask him. I want you to look them over and make sure they are accurate. We don't want to find ourselves in a pickle on this one, Padré. Got to be sharp and accurate when you turn everyone's world upside down, eh?" Kevin looked beat and Father noticed he was still wearing the same suit he had on yesterday. So, he cut the man the slack he needed. It was going to be a long day for Kevin and they both knew it.

"Sure, what do you have for me?" Father agreed as the limousine pulled out and they were on their way to pick up the Secretary and a large security detail to protect both the group and the device they were to transport to the news conference site at one of the downtown hotels.

The media center was kept available for the convenience of the big press players so it was easy to get if you had a breaking story. Father began to read over the words Kevin had given to him. He smiled with pleasure as he reviewed the short speech the Secretary General would deliver. "Whoever wrote this has a great future in homilies. It is direct, short, and delivers the message loud and clear. Good thinking. Was it you Kevin?"

"Thanks, yes, Father. That one is mine; I just hope the old man likes it. I scrapped about twenty before I got to that one so there's lots of options in the recycle bin if that one doesn't suit him. Mind taking a look at the questions and answers?" he asked. "I'm sure some of them aren't exactly right and I need your smarts on it pretty quick." As he handed Father Gannon another stack of papers, the car stopped at the side of the UN building at a spot discretely marked as private entrance. Almost immediately, the door opened and several men stepped out and escorted the Secretary General into the limo. Two security guards and the Secretary seated themselves inside and waited as the doors closed and several other security vehicles joined up to establish the small motorcade.

"Good morning, gentlemen," the Secretary General smiled to them both. "Are we ready to change the world this morning?"

"Good morning. Indeed, I am, Mr. Secretary but Kevin is feeling a bit spent, I think. The lad's been working his tail off through the wee hours of the night and just now finished what I believe is an extraordinary piece of work. Well done, son," Father added in his best Irish brogue as he handed the speech to the Secretary.

"Good morning, Sir, and I must thank Father Gannon for the pitch. It was a long night indeed, Sir, but I think we are just about ready. Father is reviewing the Q&A right now. I'll make any changes needed and then it will be ready for your review," Kevin added.

"Good. Just make sure that you are ready for anything out there, Father. I will handle the very basics, but I will pass any technical questions to you. Answer the simple ones the best you can but we will defer a lot of them for later. We don't want to look too evasive but we cannot afford to embarrass or discredit ourselves this early in the process."

"I don't expect the whole thing to take more than five to eight minutes. That way they can run the entire briefing over and over again all day. We want it short enough that we get all our comments in context every time with no excuses for not playing the entire session. I watched earlier and it is a pretty slow news day this morning. They will be chomping at the bit for something to sink their teeth into and this will be all they can chew," he smiled. "It should be about all we can stand for today, too."

Father Gannon was surprised at how well Kevin understood and captured both the letter and the intent of the capabilities of the technology he brought them yesterday. The questions were easy enough to think of but good answers such as these took a certain talent to phrase and it appeared Kevin had quite a knack for that. "They are all great. I am very impressed; wouldn't change a thing really," he complimented the man, and handed the papers to the Secretary who began reviewing them immediately. There was not much traffic this morning and they would be at the hotel in just a few minutes, a little ahead of schedule.

The Secretary smiled as he read the Q&A sheets and agreed that Kevin had done an excellent job, indeed, and he didn't mind telling him so. The limo circled several blocks away from the hotel for about five minutes giving the Secretary a bit more reading time and getting them closer to their announced arrival time.

After several radio calls the driver got the go ahead from the security detail inside the lead vehicle and pulled up to the front door of the magnificent hotel which so graciously allowed itself to be filmed for many news releases from the city. There was a myriad of photographers, videographers, and cameramen from every imaginable news agency. Both domestic and foreign correspondents were yelling questions to the occupants of the limo before the doors had even opened. Father Gannon had never experienced such a spectacle from this perspective before and it was unnerving. The car stopped in a secured cordoned off area and the security detail dismounted and took up their assigned positions before the three men were allowed to exit the limo.

"Get used to it. You will be seeing a lot of this for quite a while, whether we are successful or not. And please give my best to the Pope when you see him. I expect it will probably be sooner than later; I like that guy," the Secretary encouraged the visibly nervous priest staring out at the assembled media. "Take a deep breath and relax. They are just people, even though they sometimes forget to act that way and it is too late to back out now my friend. We have come too far. It would be rude to keep them waiting, Father; are you ready?" He nodded, the door opened, and a hail of white flashes and questions greeted them as they climbed out of the limousine. The Secretary smiled and waved to the media as the other two men followed close in behind him.

Kevin's last-ditch efforts to make himself presentable had worked well enough to earn him a trip inside so he could assist if either man needed rescuing during the Q&A portion of the press conference. The men moved directly into the briefing room area. The Secretary shook a few hands near the front by the podium to allow the photographers a chance to get into position. He was ready to begin and that was their cue to get set or miss out. He motioned for Father Gannon and Kevin to take seats right next to the head chair at the table adjacent to where he was standing and began to speak almost immediately.

"Ladies and gentlemen of the press, I thank you for indulging my request for a press conference on such short notice. My esteemed colleagues and the leaders of the great member nations of the United Nations organization, as well as, the leaders of all nations, large and small, that make up our world today...I must extend my sincerest apologies for the method in which I bring you this urgent dispatch. Technology is my ally today. The nearly instant global communications that bring you this news conference is but one great technology which I will celebrate today. We are here to announce a new technology that will impact all our lives even more than the advanced communications networks that will carry this story. Unfortunately, time is not our ally in applying this technology such that it can live up to its potential." He paused for effect, looking at Father Gannon long enough to ensure the cameras followed his gaze.

Bob and Ann smiled as they saw their friend's face covering the TV screen in their hotel room. "As you know many of our fellow men, women, and children living in India have suffered tremendous losses in the very recent past as a result of the catastrophic weather events there. Flooding and the loss of this year's crops promise tremendous hardship and a very long winter of suffering for the masses. Without some intervention or assistance, countless individuals and families will either starve or spend their life's savings trying not to. This would indeed be a human tragedy but it need not turn out that way. Technology can help us lessen the impact of even a tragedy of this magnitude but technology cannot do anything by itself. Technology needs people behind it to make it work for the good of mankind. People like Father Gannon who I have with me today."

"Yesterday, Father Gannon brought us all a new technology to improve our lives and eliminate much of the suffering that saddens our world in times like these. With people like Father Gannon standing for, and defending the fundamental precepts the United Nations organization was founded on, we can accomplish great things in our world by combining existing and new technologies. That is just what he enabled us to do, and why we are here speaking to you all today. Father Gannon has given us the ability to change the weather upon demand. He has provided us with a device that allows the selecting, controlling, and timing of all naturally occurring meteorological phenomena. Many of us in the local area experienced it first-hand just yesterday. The freakish thunder snow shower on what was otherwise a clear day was Father Gannon's way of getting our attention so we would take him seriously. We did. After a few more demonstrations he has proven to us this technology exists, is viable, and can be applied on a larger scale."

The crowd was frenzied with questions, flashes, and yelling in many languages. The Secretary raised his hands gesturing to the group to regain its composure so he could continue. "I know you have a lot of questions and we will get to some of them right away. Father Gannon came into possessing this technology from a parishioner who was killed a short time ago in a tragic auto mishap. The generous priest has donated this invention to the UN in that individual's name, Doctor James Auster. Father Gannon has explained to me that he knows how to operate the device to perform several tasks but he is not very fluent in the theory which backs the physical device used to modify the weather. We are convinced that this technology holds great promise for all mankind. Father Gannon brought it to us at this moment in hopes that we can apply the technology in time to reduce the suffering in India by warming portions of the region to speed the drying process from the recent flooding. This will extend the growing season a few weeks in order to get a crop in before winter.

"Failing that, it is conceivable in that time period to lessen the severity of the oncoming winter to decrease or prevent any loss of life due to the agricultural product shortage or extreme cold. That will take the cooperation of many technologically advanced nations, as well as, the establishment and chartering of a new council within the UN to develop international policies on how to apply this fledgling technology. Naturally, the member nations will be heavily involved in determining the magnitude of the efforts undertaken for the judicious, fair, and deliberate use of such a technology and must be debated and agreed upon. The political, economic, and social ramifications of such a capability are enormous and must be considered with the greatest care and deliberation.

"I am proposing that, as news of this technology propagates throughout the world today via our advanced electronic social networks, media and personal phone calls between key national leaders around the world, we undertake the application of this technology with two goals. First, a short-term goal of helping relieve the tremendous current burdens in India and other countries, if possible, as a result of the tragic loss of their agricultural base so as not to erode our global grain supply. This is using the technology in the spirit in which it was presented to us by Father Gannon, on behalf of the late Doctor Auster.

"The second goal is longer-term, designed to ensure the fair, judicious, moral, and ethical application of this technology for all generations to come. All men, women and children should benefit from this gift. The potential to end world hunger as we know it now exists. The potential to address ongoing climate concerns and provide shelter for our global population is now real. The magnitude of these advantages must be weighed heavily because they affect all humankind. They must bring us together, working as a team for the common good and not be used to drive us apart through competition and partisanship. This technology is only as valuable and good as the people behind it. I am convinced that the world is made up of people like Father Gannon, the good people of our world who are not in it for personal gain but for the good of everyone to make our world a better place if they can. He could have made a tremendous amount of money selling this technology but, instead, he has given it to all in the world to enjoy, for free, to use for freedom.

"We will be hearing a lot more about this in the days, weeks, and even years to come. Your children will read about this in their history books and you will tell them you were here when it happened. But remember, this only works for us if we let it. Only if we work together. But it can also work against us, if we let it. I implore you all as citizens and leaders to view this technology in its most positive applications and help us quickly and efficiently move out to meet the two goals I have just mentioned. We can and should embark on an immediate effort to meet them at the soonest possible time. Thank you very much. I will take a few short questions now."

The reporters sat there silently for a moment, basically stunned at the news they had just heard. All the frenzied discussion earlier had quieted for a moment as the Secretary finished his comments much quicker than they would have liked. The quiet didn't last long. The first words opened a floodgate of simultaneous questions. The Secretary General really liked it when they all asked different questions at the same time because he could hear them and select the one he wished to answer from the many being shouted at him. He chose a simple one first.

"Yes, the question was *Does anyone else currently possess this technology, or is it exclusively under the UN's control?* To my knowledge, as Father Gannon explained to me earlier, the late Doctor Auster only left him one of the devices. That is the device Father Gannon has delivered to us and he hasn't shared this technology with any other organization because of the potential damage it could cause if it were misapplied. He brought it to us at the UN for the reasons I mentioned earlier." Father Gannon nodded in agreement at the Secretary General's answer and the roar of questions came again. Bob smiled at Ann, who was sitting beside him on the couch. So far everything they had said was true, and it was going well.

"The question was *Why not bring the device to the Catholic Church, let the Pope take the lead instead of the UN?* Simply put, Father Gannon was carrying out the wishes of Doctor Auster. The Church will have a significant say in the application of the technology but the UN must be the body to facilitate its application across many nations, cultures and religions." The Secretary smiled and looked up, trying to pick out another easy question from the many faces in the crowded media center.

"You asked two good questions, so I'll give you both of them. *With only one device, how large an area can it cover and how difficult will it be to build more?* We don't know for sure how large an area one device can affect but Doctor Auster's notes indicate several hundred square miles at one time. The device appears to be very complex but it should be easy enough to reproduce from the design charts and notes Doctor Auster left with Father Gannon. The right team of experts with a diverse mix of technical backgrounds and experience should have no problem reverse engineering, testing and building as many as are needed. Of course, initially at least, we will want to strictly control the number and use of any devices for what I hope are obvious reasons. We don't want anybody to try to use this technology with malicious intent.

"We have seen, as recently in India, what harm nature can do in her own right. We certainly must concern ourselves with the security issues surrounding the capability to control the weather. We cannot afford to allow rogue states or outlaws access to this technology so they can use it to inflict pain or suffering on their enemies in the near term. We must all work together to ensure that does not happen in the immediate future. The objective is for this technology to eventually be available everywhere on demand. So proliferated that there is no relative advantage to changing someone else's weather because they could just as easily change it back. That would take most of the sting out of having it; relative advantage would be virtually nil. That is the near term goal. I expect we will be there easily inside the year, with the right help."

They were all surprised by that answer, especially Bob Mcleod. He shot a glance at Ann and rolled his eyes, "If that is true, it is going to be a much busier year than even I expected. It might just be firing for effect, though. I bet the President comes out of his chair when he hears that one. That must be why he said it," Bob smiled. He was beginning to really like this Secretary General guy.

"Father Gannon, would you like to respond to this one? The question was *What can you tell us about Doctor Auster, the inventor?*" The Secretary General waved an invitation for Father Gannon to join him at the podium.

"Doc was a simple, generous man. That is what we called him, Doctor Jim Auster. We called him Doc. He worked on this project in his spare time and built the thing. Before he could decide how best to present this gift to us all, he was killed in an accident. He was run over by a young man who had too much to drink at a party and made the bad decision to drive himself home. Doc never saw the car. He did see the potential in being able to control the weather and we talked about it several weeks before he passed away. He left the device with me and donated all his estate, modest as it was, to the church."

"That is how I came to possess his notes. It took me awhile to understand them and decide the best way to bring Doc's gift to the world...to you all. I must admit I had to think a lot about how to convince someone as important as the man at my left that I wasn't just some crackpot...that he needed to believe my story and take me seriously. So, the storm yesterday was the best way I could come up with to get his attention.

It worked, and here we are," Father smiled, the relief of the unknown now lifted from his shoulders as he knew he could answer the questions.

"Last question, please. As I am sure you can imagine we have a tremendous amount of work to do in a very short time. I can assure you, though, as we get more details and information becomes available, we will share them with you at the earliest possible time. You will be seeing a lot of us in the next few days, I am sure. Okay, yes...question was, *Do we really think we can get something together in time to help the Indian people through their hardship, the scope of that disaster is substantial?* I believe we can and, with the right help right away, I know we can. But not if we stand around here talking about it all day. Thank you all very much for your time. We will be providing you updates and, as we get new information, we will share it with you. Thank you and thanks to Father Gannon and Doc Auster for providing us the reason we are all brought together this morning."

The Secretary General stepped back two steps and over one. He then began to clap his hands together and the rest of the room followed his lead. Father Gannon stood there for a moment and then waved to the applauding media and followed the Secretary General and a now-enlarged security team directly out to the waiting limousine. It was pulling away from the hotel before Father Gannon really gathered his thoughts.

"That went well I think," Father blurted out, "an exceptional speech Sir. Remind me after all this settles down to invite you to give a homily or two in my church. On second thought, I'll get you an invite to someone else's church. I don't think I am near that good and probably don't need to remind my parishioners."

"You did fine and you're right, Father, it went very well. I think we came in under seven minutes, though, not by much. I bet our phones will be ringing off the hook before we can get back. I am particularly anxious to talk to the President of the United States. I hope he calls soon." The man smiled, feeling comfortable in his position. He had a good hand already and he hadn't even gotten to play his trump cards yet.

The limo cruised quickly back to the UN building and, before Father knew it, he was sitting in the Secretary General's office staring at the news over a cup of coffee and a plate full of his favorite doughnuts, watching what most other people were seeing for the first time. They sat and watched as the entire speech aired just as it was recorded a short time earlier. The phones in the outer office were ringing like crazy and, as soon as, one director hung up they were handed another line. Father Gannon watched as each call was recorded into an electronic log for later review.

He was glad to see that only the most senior and powerful people in the organization were handling the incoming calls. It was clear that the Secretary General understood the magnitude of the problem Father Gannon had brought to him. He also noticed the Secretary General was not taking any of the calls himself. Then it occurred to the priest that he was waiting for one call...and one call only. The place was frenzied with activity but there seemed to be an order to the chaos. People knew their jobs and were doing them in a careful hurry. They were proceeding quickly into an area that was uncharted for all of them. Their ability and professionalism were impressive.

It was about fifteen minutes after the first airing on cable news when they all ran the entire news conference again. A few minutes later, the phone rang in the Secretary General's office. He picked it up on the third ring. He motioned for Father Gannon to close the office door and then put the call on the speaker phone so they could both hear the words from the other end. He held his finger up to his lips, so Father Gannon understood he was to remain silent.

"The President of the United States is holding for the Secretary General, shall I put him through Sir?" the voice from the other end requested with some urgency.

"Certainly," he replied and smiled a fat-cat grin at Father Gannon. The line made a series of clicks and buzzes while it was being encrypted and then was crystal clear as the President's voice boomed in from the other end.

"It would appear you have been very busy this morning. I just saw the news. Do you really have a weather modification device, Mr. Secretary?" He came right to the point.

"Yes, Mr. President I do. And I fully intend to do everything I laid out this morning at the news conference. I hope I can count on participation from your government and your professional communities, scientists, economists, lawyers and the like?" His statement carried the tone and inflections of a question and he paused, waiting for a reply.

"You bet you can count on my participation but let's cut the crap. How did you get it? Who gave it to you and who else has it?" the President demanded.

"Just like you saw this morning...Father Gannon brought it to us and he got it from Doctor Auster some months ago. The only other person that may possibly have this—to my knowledge—is you, Sir." The words rolled off his tongue with innocence but the sting could be heard across the line as the shot found its mark and gained the desired reaction. Father Gannon found himself holding his breath, finding it difficult to continue his conscious effort to breath quietly and deliberately so as not to betray his presence in the room.

"What makes you think I have it?" The President asked in an accusing tone. "I have never met your Father Gannon or your Doctor Auster."

"No Sir, I don't believe you have. But you see, I think you recognize the good Doctor's name. He is the one who left one of his two devices for your friend, Professor Mcleod. You see the Professor didn't know that Father Gannon possessed one of two prototype devices. Father Gannon was equally unaware of Professor Mcleod's knowledge of Doc Auster's invention. The good Father's device may be a bit cruder than the ones Mcleod made but, nonetheless, it works just fine. Should I continue Mr. President?" the Secretary asked.

"I am listening." Stern tone and restraint clearly carried the words across the speaker phone. The Secretary winked at Father Gannon. He was cool and seemed to be enjoying this far too much. Father Gannon was sweating like a fiend and his shirt began to show the heavy perspiration as he wiped his forehead with a napkin.

"So then, when Father Gannon approached Professor Mcleod for assistance, he told him he could not help. He was under contract not to work on this technology and the only person who could provide him permission to assist the priest was the President of the United States himself. Well, naturally, Father Gannon found that hard to believe and chastised the man for not aiding in this noble effort that Doctor Auster had embarked upon. The Professor showed his priest a contract which appears to be genuine and bears both your signatures. So, naturally, Father Gannon no longer sought Professor Mcleod's assistance on the technology. He wouldn't think of jeopardizing the terms of his contract with you. After all, five billion dollars is a lot of money to risk losing."

"That is when Father Gannon came to me. He knew it was the right thing to do and he was right. He donated his device and the technology behind it to the UN. I suppose one could argue about who has what legal rights in this case, the priest or the professor, but I think they both have the same right to dispose of their property as they see fit. There is no patent on the device. So, it seems, for now, it should be free to duplicate under common statutes. The UN got ours for free and the US got theirs for five billion dollars," he paused and waited.

"That is quite a tale you have there, Mr. Secretary. Let's just suppose we do have this technology and we did get if from this Professor Mcleod you mentioned. What does that have to do with your effort?" the President chased along the hypothetical trail.

"Well, Mr. President, I would like Professor Mcleod to work on this project for the UN. He is, I believe, the subject matter expert on the technical side and I am told his fiancée is quite an expert on the physical construction of the devices. I would consider it a personal favor from you, Sir, to allow Professor Mcleod and his fiancée to join my team in developing and fielding this technology. I would also consider it a matter of principal and honor that he be allowed to do so with no threat to his person or his fortune, regardless of how it was acquired," the Secretary argued and waited for a reply.

"I want to make sure I understand this. You want me to let Mcleod help you on this project, keep the five billion dollars I supposedly paid him to stay out of it and walk away from any obligation he may or may not have signed up to?" the President nearly laughed at the suggestion.

"No, not exactly, Sir. Professor Mcleod can help with technology transition and development for the UN effort only. No commercial gain...no production of commercial systems for sale...no unilateral proliferation of technology... and no cowboying of this technology by any one nation. He will help the UN apply and proliferate this technology just like I said this morning. He won't get anything except what the UN as a body authorizes and that will probably only be a small salary and whatever probably large sums of money he can make for personal appearances on the speaking circuit. The technology is free and gets out to everyone in a controlled, deliberate manner. But, rest assured, Sir, it will be made available to everyone and it will be done very soon. There will be no point in weaponizing this and I intend to keep that promise," he paused to check his emotionalism and keep sharp.

"I paid Mcleod to help you, then, and I get nothing for my five billion dollars? That hardly seems fair as a matter of principle and honor now does it Mr. Secretary?" the President offered, waiting for some incentive to continue the discussion.

"Mr. President, I am surprised that you do not put a higher value on the advantage to US participation in this UN effort. Providing top of the field experts to help us operationalize this technology in the shortest of time could not have been done without you. In fact, I believe you may soon be able to take credit for having quickly done some of the work you have done already. We would like to benefit from the work you have already done on this and you can call it an additional contribution over and above Professor Mcleod's participation.

"Your labs have already done much of the work and you would save us a great deal of time if that were shared with us quickly. You and your experts will have been instrumental in fixing much of the damage to India's agricultural base...an extremely positive effort and benevolent gesture going into your economic summit in a few weeks. That would paint you and your country in the most positive of lights and that is prestige and press coverage money cannot buy. Consider it return on your five-billion-dollar investment," the Secretary General offered.

"If I want that kind of prestige you mean. If I don't give you Mcleod, and I don't give you any of our advances or devices it slows you down to a crawl. You'll have to spin up from scratch. You will not get it done in time to help India for this season anyway, and your credibility plummets fast. I hold out, and don't play at all, maybe I can convince everyone you can't handle the task and the US should take the lead. Then I have it all."

"I am willing to take the lead on operationalizing this technology for you and Mcleod works for me to do it. Hell, I'll even pay him more than you will to do it. What do you say? Is that option still open under the terms you laid out this morning? US led, UN effort to control the weather and the weather modification technology proliferation. Just like nukes, chemical and biological weapons stuff. We are the experts. We can defend against them and, if someone gets out of line, we have the military might to bring them back into the fold where they belong. I like that a lot better, Mr. Secretary General," the President offered. Father Gannon was white as a sheet at the prospect. This was not what he had signed up for and he knew Bob would not like this deal at all.

"No, I don't like that scenario. I think we'll just stick with a UN effort with Professor Mcleod working for the UN and some vital technical assistance from the US. Do we agree then Mr. President?" the Secretary summarily dismissed the President's veiled threats and counter proposal.

"I'm not sure you understood me correctly, I believe..." The President was interrupted in mid-sentence by the Secretary General who now had an edge in his voice and made it perfectly clear this was no longer a negotiation.

"Look, Mr. President, I have given you my terms. They are fair and, as of now, they are non-negotiable. A UN-led effort, Mcleod on the staff, he picks the crew from your experts, and you look great helping us offset the damage you caused in India. Are we in agreement now? We have much work to do." There was a long pause at the end of the Secretary's words, and the President spoke a carefully worded response with indignation.

"If you are referring to the flooding in India, I did not cause that," he defended.

"I believe you were not there to do the dirty work. But I assure you I can paint that picture so clearly that it will take your lawyers forever to prove you didn't do it. You had cause and motive and means. The odds of that freak of nature storm happening by itself while you secretly possessed the technical means to create it for your own gain are truly unbelievable and circumstantial evidence alone will roll worldwide opinion in the direction of your guilt whether it is true or not.

"That secret you can keep between you, and God and whomever else was involved. But all it will take is one more press conference and one piece of paper with a good story behind it to generate a scandal of monumental magnitude. You know as well as I do that it is *feasible*, at least, and easy to portray as *likely* being true. Now, the only question left is about Professor Mcleod and your technical staff assistance. I want everyone to come out a winner on this effort, Mr. President, including you. Are we in agreement then?" he offered one more time.

"I believe I can find your terms acceptable Mr. Secretary General. Professor Mcleod can lead your effort under the terms you outlined only. Have him request who and what he wishes us to contribute to your effort and submit it to Mr. Henry. We will do our best to support your effort, as well as, your timeline. You have my word on that. We will try to help in every possible way to assist the two goals you've outlined today.

"But, and I mean, Sir, *hear me clear on this...you will never, ever even suggest that the United States or its government, especially its President, had anything to do with that tragedy in India.* So help me, I did not order that technology to be used in such a way and any suggestion from you or anyone else that I did will result in direct action from me, personally. I take great offense to your suggestion, your tactic and your opinion that I would even be capable of such a crime. That boils down to an accusation of premeditated murder plain and simple.

"I am not a murderer, Mr. Secretary General, but you are correct. You could paint me up as one and I would lose to the mass doubt whether I had anything to do with it or not. I assure you, Sir. *I did not.* Now then, I don't know what kind of shenanigans went on between Professor Mcleod and Father Gannon during their meetings before they left for New York together, but I am sure you already have a prepared explanation for those conspirator's actions as well. Probably in the confessional—vow of silence—since he is a priest or something like that.

"If you don't have one, you better get one quick. It's probably true, though, since the Pope claims he doesn't know anything about Father Gannon or his technology and new relationship with the UN. Although you should be getting a call from the Pontiff in short order. I believe we need to work closely together on this to protect the economic, social, and political order of things as we proliferate this technology in the most advantageous and expedient manner for all involved. I suppose it is true that the US stands to lose much of its global competitive advantage by this technology proliferating but there is also much for us to gain by it. Not the least of which should be a near term reduction on welfare and social program expenditures.

"That alone might be enough to keep my party in power even after my Presidency is over. Every cloud has a silver lining; every challenge creates its own opportunity. I appreciate you taking my call so promptly Mr. Secretary General. Please let Mr. Henry know what you need and. if I can do anything else to assist, please call me. I expect we will have an emergency session of the UN council sometime today, where I can announce our full support and you may even have some specifics worked out by then?" the President concluded.

"That is correct, Sir, we will be shooting for 5pm tonight, and I expect, because it is our first meeting on the topic, it may go quite late into the night," the Secretary General agreed. "Thank you, Mr. President, for your support in this matter. It was of the utmost concern to me before our discussion. I am very pleased to have your word and cooperation on this most important, historic endeavor. And feel free to use that quote in your press release this afternoon, Sir. Shall I pass your regards to Professor Mcleod or will Mr. Henry or yourself be contacting him directly to tell him of the news?"

"You can tell him yourself. I'd be surprised if he isn't sitting in the office there with you and Father Gannon. No, wait...I'll go you one further, just to show you I am a good sport. I'll announce that I have promised the nation's leading professional in weather modification technology to your team during my press conference. Just let me have that little piece of fun, if he is not in the room. Then he'll know he has my permission and that he'll have to answer a lot of questions. He deserves at least that much grief for all I am paying him to do for you," the President added.

"Done, Sir. I am confident he is watching the news intently this morning and I assure you he is not here in the room, nor even in the building for that matter. But I do believe you are correct; I think he may be in New York. Father Gannon will likely know how to contact him but I will ensure that he is not informed by us until after your press conference. Good day Sir." The Secretary General hung up the phone and smiled at Father Gannon, "I believe we got what we went after didn't we Father?"

"I will need a few minutes to recover from that. In fact, I may never recover from that call. I am quite impressed at how you handled that, Sir. That was masterful statesmanship," Father Gannon complimented the man seated in front of him.

"Father that wasn't statesmanship that was brawling about the future of our world. And, if he keeps his word, we will get this technology out of the barn in a positive manner. I will admit, though, I was a little worried there for a while," he grinned.

"I guess he saw a taped version of the first release, made some calls and gathered more information and then called you after the second release to make it appear reactionary?" Father Gannon asked.

"Probably, he had time to get to the Pope and his folks to check on you and Mcleod. So, either that or he was just bluffing," the Secretary offered. Father Gannon had not even considered that option but, either way, he would probably have an opportunity to discuss this with the Church hierarchy for some time to come. He had always hoped to meet the Pope but under more cordial and less contentious conditions.

"I don't know what to think about India now, though. He was most convincing that he had nothing to do with ordering that disaster. I don't think it was the words he chose to use or legal technicalities in his statement like presidents tend to be good at doing. I wish I could have seen his face because I believed his words that he had nothing to do with murdering those people, and those were his words not yours. What do you think?" Father Gannon asked.

"I don't know about that one. It makes good sense that he did it but he may not have known about it. I know he is capable of a lot of things but I don't know whether he is capable of cold-blooded murder especially on such a large scale. I *want* to doubt it to be honest. That doesn't mean someone within his inner circles didn't see an opportunity and take it for the President in an attempt to gain position or approval. He did make a point to defend himself and the government, so, I think a rogue inside order is just as likely as the President ordering it himself. We will probably never know for sure, though. That subject, as far as I am concerned, is closed until the President of the United States himself brings it up again. Is that crystal clear, Father? You are never to discuss that part of the conversation with anyone, not ever," the Secretary made his point to Father Gannon...all too well.

"Yes, it is. May I impose upon you for a favor?" Father Gannon asked, and continued when the Secretary nodded. "I know you promised the President you would let him see for himself but I also promised I would let Bob know the minute I knew anything. Could I call him and just tell him to keep watching the news but to get his stuff together...that I have a job lined up for him?"

"If you do it from here and I can listen. I am a man of my word, Father. I believe in the trust-but-verify approach to everything. I can support that call and I do owe you a favor or two for flicking this bugger onto my forehead yesterday," he conceded. The phone rang in the hotel room and Bob picked it up before the first ring was complete.

"Bob, this is Father Gannon. I only have a few minutes so listen up. Everything is aces." That was their code for all is well; no problems this morning. It would be a different code this afternoon, so Bob knew all was truly okay and this was not a call made under duress. "Keep watching the news, but I think I have a job lined up for you here in New York. You better give Betty a call and have her bring your stuff up as soon as she can. I gotta go. Give my best to Ann and Betty and don't wait up for me tonight. I think I am going to be working late."

"Okay, Father. Will do. You looked great up there this morning. I've been watching it over and over. Everyone has picked it up and it has caused quite a stir." Bob was cut off before he could ask any questions.

"I have to go now, goodbye," Father Gannon interrupted him and hung up the phone. "That should do it, then. Thank you, Sir. I believe you have kept your word to the President."

"Who is Betty?" He asked.

"Professor Mcleod's private secretary. She has some of the documentation he will need in order to do the work you need him to do. I thought the sooner she gets up here with the papers the better for all of us. I think Bob needs to get to her before she sees all this on the news and gets too nervous. He'll need the paperwork she will bring to expedite his work," Father Gannon replied.

"Speaking of work, we have a lot of work to do ourselves. I suggest we get started on what we intend to tell the group at our meeting this afternoon. We will need to give them some more details and specifics now that they have had a few hours to formulate some questions. Let's work on some more answers for the next level of detail, shall we? We can meet with the directors in about an hour to discuss who has called and what they have been told so far. You will get to do a lot more talking this afternoon. They need to get to know the man who brought them this technology, and you are the best one to talk about yourself and Doc Auster. Gotta keep Mcleod out of it for now. He gets to keep a back seat...probably for quite some time. He will go in the books as the implementation subject matter expert but you and Doctor Auster will go into the history books as the men who brought the technology to the world. I am afraid Bob won't get that credit even though he probably deserves much of it. Do you think he can handle that?" the Secretary General asked.

"I know he can handle that. There is no need to worry about Bob. He is committed to doing the right thing. He doesn't really care about doing things right. He will be glad to hear that Doc will get credit for the work he completed before his death. That always worried Bob. Now he'll have one less worry. Bob can take care of himself and then some. Let's get to work, shall we?" The two began to get down to the business of what to say and how to say it for their next press conference just prior to the emergency meeting of the UN general assembly.

Bob hung up the phone at the hotel and looked at Ann with a smile. "That was Father Gannon, as I'm sure you could tell. He said we needed to keep watching the news but I should call Betty. He thinks he has a job for me here in New York. I guess that is a good thing. He gave me the all-clear code but he didn't have time to talk. I guess we'll get more information through the news than we will through him today. I suppose they are going to be very busy just as we expected. He said not to wait up for him tonight; he was going to be working late."

"Well, I guess that means things are going just as planned. That should scare us all, I didn't know you were such a good forecaster. I guess we could just sit around here in the hotel all day watching TV or we could maybe find something to do to pass the time between news conferences; what do you think?" Ann flashed him a coy grin that he immediately recognized as an invitation that he was very willing to accept...just not this very minute. He walked over and kissed her a long, passionate kiss. Then he walked across the room to the phone.

"I need to call Betty first but that shouldn't take too long. I promise," he smiled at her and began dialing the phone at her office where he knew she should be this time of day.

"University department of Meteorology; this is Betty; may I help you?" she said in her usual perky tone.

"Betty, hi. This is Bob Mcleod and I need your help today," he began.

"Okay, what can I do for you, Sir?" she replied more formally than she should have.

"Is the Dean there where he can hear you?" Bob asked.

"Why, yes Sir, that is correct," she replied.

"Okay then just listen. I need you to get the first flight you can to New York. I need you to bring the six boxes of stuff we marked as *first to go*. I'll need you for two weeks. Can you make it happen by yourself or do you need some help? This is important, Betty. I really need you out here," he begged.

"I'll take care of it. Thanks for calling. Do you have a number where I can reach you?" she added and jotted down the number in her address book. She hung up the phone and reached into her purse and pulled out the small tape recorder and put it in her pocket. She then walked into Dean Durbin's office. "Excuse me Sir, but I need a word with you."

"What is it, Betty?" Dean Durbin grumbled. "I have a lot to do getting ready for the board meeting."

"I need two weeks off beginning right now, Sir. I apologize for the short notice but I really need to take care of an urgent family matter," she stretched the truth a bit but she did consider Bob the closest thing she had to a family now.

"I am sorry, that is not possible. The soonest you could leave is next week. Do the leave request and I'll approve it for then. I need you for this board meeting; you know that. It is our department's turn to host and I am chairing the meeting for the first time. This is very important for me Betty. I am sorry but next week is the best I can do," he waved her off and resumed his work but she stood fast.

"Sir, perhaps you misunderstood me. I need two weeks beginning today, with or without your permission. I need to tend to some urgent family business that cannot wait. I would prefer to do it with your permission, Dean Durbin," Betty protested.

"Well, you most certainly will not have my permission. I have told you next week and that is final. Be glad to get that before I change my mind. Now, I know you have a lot of work to do, so you may get back to it," he persisted. Betty pressed the "play" button on the recorder and set it down on his desk. He looked perplexed as the hiss slowly changed to words in his own voice.

"I am taking leave Dean and I will do so *with* your permission. Oh, by the way, that is only a copy. I have a few more scattered about. I'll see you in two weeks," she said and turned on her heel and returned to her desk to gather her things. The tape played and Hugh Durbin heard the conversation he and Bob Mcleod had earlier and knew it could really hurt him if it were to get into the wrong hands.

He walked out to Betty's desk and said in a calm, venomous voice, "This is blackmail, and it is illegal."

"What you said on that tape is illegal, Dean Durbin. You'd lose your job, your reputation and, possibly, even go to jail. All I am doing is taking leave; there is nothing illegal about that. I do apologize for the short notice, though. It only just came up a few moments ago. I will be in New York if you need me but I am sure you will make do just fine. I'll see you in two weeks; hope your meeting goes well," she added as she rose from her desk, walked past him and headed for the parking lot. She drove home with a grin on her face the entire way.

Betty decided she could use a vacation and now seemed like an excellent time to take one. She mentally went over her task list: flight reservation including excess baggage...get some of the money Bob left her...arrange for a cab and on she went. She hadn't seen the news today and the radio was off in her car so she could concentrate on her list. It was a good thing she hadn't seen the news yet; it made the President's press conference even sweeter than he could have known when she did see it.

Bob had returned his attention to Ann but the news broadcast was interrupted for a live report from the White House, the President was about to address the press corps about the Secretary General's earlier announcement. Bob and Ann watched as the President strode in confidently, taking the podium and addressing the cameras more than the group of reporters. He began by confirming the capability to modify the weather did exist and validating the Secretary General's claims to be able to control virtually every aspect of the weather. He could not disclose the details but he, too, had seen a demonstration of the technology and was convinced the Secretary General had a sound plan in place to deal with the impressive technology.

He pledged full US support in all aspects of the UN effort, financial, economic, social, political, technical, and academic expertise. All would be granted to ensure the UN could meet its goals and its timeline. The President wanted to make every effort to meet the UN goal and help those in India and he would assure the Indian government of every possible assistance during their summit. This indeed was great news and great timing for all. There was much they could do together to address the crisis.

He went on to say, "I want every American, and every member of our UN team to know I will do whatever is in my power to assist the

Secretary General and I urge all of our member nations, and any other nation wishing to contribute to our efforts, to do so in the spirit of cooperation and good will. I am appointing my premier subject matter expert, Professor Bob Mcleod, to head up the US effort to assist the UN. Professor Mcleod's expertise will be invaluable to the UN effort and I wholeheartedly agreed to the Secretary General's personal request for Professor Mcleod to lead the US technical consultants on the project. He will have my full support on this effort." The President went on to say other things but Bob wasn't hearing any of the political mumbo jumbo that filled the air in the room. He swung his glance to Ann and they both yelled in excitement.

"That was so *cool*; I think I am speechless," Ann said. "Just wait, our kids and grandchildren will watch that and beam with pride just like I am now. We did it; you did it. Congratulations! It looks like you have three new jobs now. UN guy, philanthropist guy, and my guy," she said as she wrapped her arms around him and fell onto the bed.

Betty was watching a rerun of the President's speech in the airport terminal gate area as she waited to board her flight to New York. She was shocked to hear the words but proud of Bob and the part she now expected to play in his new role. She thought she may not even go back to the University, if Bob needed her to help him on this. This was monumental and she knew she would work forever on this if he asked her. Technically, he already had. She was grateful for the opportunity Bob had given her...for throwing life back into her existence that had somehow come to be more of a routine than a life. She boarded the aircraft with a sense of purpose and adventure. She was heading to New York with a very positive attitude and some *historically* important boxes of documents in her checked baggage.

Hugh Durbin answered the phone himself; it was the University Chancellor on the other end. "Did we actually fire Bob Mcleod a few weeks ago or is he still an employee of the University?" he asked.

"Sir, Professor Mcleod, I am glad to say, is no longer an employee of this institution. He was in fact removed—fired if you will—personally by me several weeks ago for numerous violations and breach of terms. You also approved that action yourself, Sir," he replied proudly.

"Yes, I know. I was just hoping you hadn't processed the paperwork yet," he responded.

"Oh, no Sir. I processed that the day you signed it. No need having that kind of cancerous employee festering a minute longer in our institution than was absolutely necessary," he gloated.

"Pity. Have you seen the news today, Durbin? I am assuming you haven't, so perhaps you should turn it on and see this for yourself." The chancellor hung up the phone.

Dean Durbin turned on the TV in his office just in time to catch a recap of the day's events, including the part where the President of the United States named Bob Mcleod as his personal expert being assigned to the UN for their new weather modification effort. He first thought there must be some mistake, maybe someone else with the same name, but when they flashed a picture of him on the screen all doubt was removed.

This was not right, Hugh Durbin thought to himself. He was missing out on the biggest event in the history of weather and he would probably lose his job over it. He vowed to himself to get to the bottom of this somehow. For now, though, it looked like he had a new topic for his board of directors meeting and he was not looking forward to that at all.

EPILOGUE

Zach sat in the simple, small house trying to keep himself busy with notes and planning his discussion with the President. He was anxious to get back to the United States and see if he could get himself a better deal than he currently had at the underground facility. After all, Bob Mcleod got five billion dollars from the President for doing almost nothing but he would surely be impressed by this little bit of initiative Zach demonstrated on his behalf in India. Zach was certain the President would make an even bigger deal with him. If not, he would simply claim the President ordered the eco-terrorist attack. That part was simple but keeping a low profile in a small village in India was no small task for the obviously American middle-aged scientist. The most difficult thing for him to do was the waiting.

He adjusted the small, portable satellite dish to improve the signal and finally found an English-speaking news station. He was incensed to see Bob Mcleod's picture on the small television as the President, his boss, announced Bob would lead the team fielding the new weather modification technology announced this morning. "Well, well, it appears I have two fish to fry now. That will make it all the more interesting. Let's see if those two can survive the political firestorm I might just create for them. I guess no deal from the President for me, then. Apparently, he has chosen his partner. The UN has no idea what they are in for or who they are up against now. I guess I'll just have to see to it that I am the man in charge. I have the technology, I have the financial resources and I have the information on both of them. I know their strengths which I can avoid but, more importantly, I know their weaknesses and I can exploit those. There are more than a few groups and governments out there who will gladly help me topple the mighty US if I need any help. I never liked that man anyway. I was starting to warm up to the idea of Mcleod and Ann together. "What a pity they ended up on the wrong side of this one," Zach spoke to himself as he picked up one of the modified Thor's Hammers from the table and rubbed it gently. "Seems we have more to do my friend; our plans have changed."

Symbology

	Thunderstorm, discovery
	Wet Fog
	Lightning
	Heat, visibility reduced by smoke
	Disruption, confession, loss, change
	Growth, beginnings, liberation
	Fusion
	Decompose
	Reduction of gold to powder through heat
	Dawn, break-through, awareness
	Mirage
	Protection, shield, sanctuary
	Zodiacal light
	Heavy thunderstorm with snow.
	Magic, mystery, feminine.
	Love, success, peace, fellowship
	Revelation, knowledge, creativity, inspiration

Note to my Readers

Thor's Apprentice is a story about Bob Mcleod's inadvertent discovery of Dr. Auster's mature weather modification technology, a device he dubbed Thor's Hammer in reference to the god of thunder. Thoughtful consideration about the good and bad that could occur when weather modification becomes a viable technology is encouraged. While it may seem fantastic, it is not a matter of *if* this happens, but rather *when* and *how* it will happen on scale. By treaty, the United States does not conduct weather modification experimentation but there are a lot of countries who have done so for decades and continue to do so. Given the potential weaponization of such a capability, particularly in the hands of a determined adversary, perhaps this is a position that should be reconsidered. Cloud seeding for rain, fog dispersion, artificial snow at resorts are all real and successful examples of localized weather modification that have been used for decades. Why would we think these limited successes are boundaries not to be exceeded?

Thor's Journeymen will be the continuation of this story, where we see what successes and challenges Professor Mcleod encounters as he continues his work beyond simply daylighting this new technology to the world. Much still remains to be done.